A BRIDGE TO *Love*

Keep building bridges!

Nancy Herkness

Nancy
HERKNESS

Red Car Press

A BRIDGE TO LOVE
by Nancy Herkness

ISBN-13:978-1466437975
ISBN-10:1466437979

Cover design © 2011 Nancy Herkness
Cover design by StoryWonk

For information, contact Nancy Herkness at
nancy@nancyherkness.com

Published by Red Car Press
PO Box 124, Glen Ridge, NJ 07028

Also by Nancy Herkness:

Music of the Night
Shower of Stars

To Jeff,
who believes in the extraordinary

"Even memory is not necessary for love. There is a land of the living and a land of the dead and the bridge is love, the only survival, the only meaning."

—Thornton Wilder, *The Bridge of San Luis Rey*

One

IF CLIFTON WALKER called her a "gal" one more time, Kate Chilton was going to pour her ice cold beer over his patronizing blond head.

"What does a gal like you want with an engineering degree from M.I.T.?"

Kate gritted her teeth and kept her beer under control. So Cliff hadn't been staring at her chest for the usual reasons. He had been reading her name tag. And since this was a college alumni picnic, her friend Georgia had printed not only Kate's name but her alma mater on it.

She decided that it was time to end this particular conversation.

She smiled sweetly and said, "Well, before I got married, I did structural work on some skyscrapers in New York City. I had to calculate stress loads and determine how to best distribute them over the materials available to us at the time. And of course, there were multiple agencies in the city whose regulations I had to take into consideration. You would not believe the amount of paperwork involved, especially since we always needed zoning variances—"

"Excuse me," Cliff said, his expression glazed over with boredom. "I see an old friend by the bar."

"Nice meeting you," Kate said cheerfully to his back.

Moving to the edge of the crowd, she walked up the steps of an elevated terrace to look for Georgia and wished that she had never let her friend talk her into coming. She took another sip of beer. The familiar longing for David swept over her with painful intensity. She closed her eyes to ride it out. Her husband had died more than a year ago, and most of the time she functioned just fine. Then a situation like this reminded her that she used to be part of a couple, and she felt as if half of her soul were missing.

When she opened her eyes again, she found herself looking straight through the throng at a man's forearm. A solid curve of muscle drew her gaze down to the plain gold watch shining against his tan wrist. Kate swallowed hard as her imagination conjured up a picture of that big square hand—now wrapped around a beer bottle—splayed across her bare skin.

"You always did have good taste. That's Randall Johnson you're staring at."

Kate jumped as Georgia's voice shattered her unwanted daydream.

"I wasn't staring," Kate said, quickly averting her gaze. She was shaken by the intensity of her physical reaction to a total stranger. "I was looking for you."

"Sure you were," Georgia said, rolling her eyes. "There's nothing wrong with admiring a good-looking man. It shows you're human." She glanced toward Randall Johnson and smiled. "I think that he's admiring you, too, lucky girl."

Kate flushed faintly as she deliberately turned her back on the subject of their conversation.

"Listen, can we get out of here now? If I have to talk to another Clifton Walker, I cannot be held responsible for my actions."

Georgia looked slightly guilty. "Sorry about that one. I'll make it up to you. I'll introduce you to Randall Johnson."

Kate shook her head emphatically. "No, thank you. I'll stay another half an hour if you swear to keep me away from Clifton Walker *and* Randall Johnson."

Randall Johnson had noticed Kate's attention. He stopped in midsentence to say, "Cliff, is my fly unzipped?" Clifton Walker did not look down.

"I'm sure it isn't."

"Good," he said with a slight smile and a Texas drawl. "Do you know who that is, standing beside Georgia Jenson?"

Clifton's lip curled. "We've met. Her name's Kate Chilton and she went to M.I.T. Let me warn you that asking her about her chosen field will unleash a torrent of deadly detail."

"She seems to admire my watch. I think I'll let her get a closer look."

Clifton did look down this time. "Why would she admire that piece of junk?" he said to thin air.

Randall Johnson was already strolling in Kate's direction.

She wasn't tall or blond, his usual preferences. He would have said that her smooth, chin-length hair was brown until the sun hit it and it glowed red. Auburn, he'd call it. When he had caught her staring at him, he'd noticed that she had fine features: a straight nose, elegant brows and Hepburn cheekbones. Her eyes were a silvery gray.

She reminded him of a duchess he had met in London on a business trip: she had the look of fine china reinforced by a backbone of steel.

"Hey, Randall, good to see you!" Kate heard one of Georgia's friends say. She shot a dagger glance at Georgia, who held up her hands in a silent protestation of innocence. She was forced to turn around as introductions were made. He nodded to her slightly and held out his hand as someone said, "This is Kate Chilton, an infiltrator from the Massachusetts Institute of Technology."

Kate shook hands, assuring herself that he couldn't have noticed her staring at him amid all the noise and commotion of the picnic. "Nice to meet you."

"A pleasure," he drawled with a quick flash of a smile.

He joined the general conversation, and Kate got a good look at him. He had strongly defined cheekbones and heavy black eyebrows. His hair was brushed back, and the slight silvering in it softened the harsh planes of his face. She guessed that he was five or six years older than her thirty-seven. He was dressed simply in a white, button-down shirt and faded blue jeans, yet he radiated power. His voice was a combination of dry, flat Texas twang and deep, dark velvet. She wondered what he did for a living. Georgia would know since she kept tabs on every eligible bachelor in the tristate area…

"It's a Timex."

For a moment, she didn't grasp the meaning of his comment. Then it hit her that he had, in fact, caught her staring and heat blazed up into her cheeks. She decided to brazen it out. "I'm sorry," she said with a smile. "You looked familiar and I was just trying to think where I might have met you."

Randall was smiling in anticipation of her discomfiture,

but at her comment his expression became decidedly cynical. Kate blushed even harder when she realized she had blurted out a classic pick-up line.

Randall's glance flicked down to her name tag. "We didn't meet at Princeton since you didn't go there. And I never took a road trip to M.I.T."

Kate was sure of that. From the look of him, he had probably headed straight for the southern women's colleges when he went hunting. Suddenly, she was tired of being polite. "Wait a minute," she said, pretending to search her memory. "Were you sitting in first class on the midnight flight to Paris last Tuesday?"

She had the satisfaction of seeing him frown in thought. "No, I was in Los Angeles."

"Oh," Kate said, doing her best imitation of a social butterfly. "Then we must have met at the after party at the Academy Awards."

Comprehension flashed across Randall's face. "Definitely not. I have nothing to say to a bunch of actors," he said without missing a beat.

"Did you run the Boston Marathon last year?" Kate asked.

"I skipped it to go cliff diving in Acapulco."

Kate was starting to enjoy herself. "We must have been on the same expedition climbing Mount Everest."

The corners of his lips twitched. "I hate being cold." He snapped his fingers. "You sat across the conference table from me at the Microsoft board meeting."

Kate gave an exaggerated shudder. "Only in my worst nightmares. I'm on the board at Apple."

"The last cabinet meeting at the White House?"

"You must be thinking of the Joint Chiefs of Staff."

"I have it." Randall looked up suddenly. "You were the

5

engineer on the last space shuttle flight I piloted."

Kate opened her mouth and then started to laugh. "I can't top that one."

Randall's dark eyes focused on her face, as a slow smile curved his lips. "Have dinner with me Friday," he said with the unmistakable confidence of a man who never hears the word no.

"What?"

"I'll pick you up at eight. Here's my card."

Kate stared at him, realizing with a shock that this man thought she was flirting with him. Even worse, he was right. Five minutes ago, she had been mourning David and now here she was, flirting with a total stranger. She was aghast at her own disloyalty.

With an air of deliberate insolence, she took his card and slid it into his breast pocket. "I appreciate the invitation, but no, thank you."

His smile never wavered. He took the rejected card out of his pocket and returned it to his wallet. "That's fine," he said. "It would have been an interesting dinner." He lifted his beer bottle in a salute and turned back into the group they had been ignoring.

Kate sucked in a deep breath and tried to quell the riot in her body. Even as her rational side was appalled at her own behavior, every nerve ending yearned toward the large, warm, male body standing not two feet away from her. She decided to blame it on a year of total celibacy.

She pulled Georgia aside and said in a low voice, "I think I've had enough of remembering college days. Can we go home?"

Once the car was in motion, Georgia pounced. "Okay, I want to know what Randall Johnson said word for word."

Kate sighed. "He said, 'It's a Timex.'"

"Yeah, right," Georgia said, as she turned onto the street.

"The conversation didn't go well. I was in a bad mood because of Clifton Walker, because I was missing David, and because I was embarrassed to be caught staring at a strange man."

"I'm sorry," Georgia said. "I thought this picnic might help distract you from the memories of David."

"When you're married for fourteen years, everything reminds you of each other."

Georgia reached over to squeeze Kate's hand.

"He asked me to have dinner with him," Kate said, looking out the window.

Georgia whooped. "You're having dinner with Randall Johnson! I knew dragging you along was a good idea!"

"I turned down his invitation."

Georgia practically hit the car in front of them. "You turned down dinner with Randall Johnson! Are you out of your mind?"

"Georgia, I don't date total strangers. In fact, I don't date, period."

Georgia banged her head on the steering wheel. "He's not a total stranger; he's the founder and CEO of RJ Enterprises! He buys companies like you and I buy shoes! He's gorgeous, unmarried and generally has a very tall blonde glued to his side. And he asked you out!"

Kate shrugged. "I guess there's a shortage of blondes in his life right now."

Georgia groaned as she pulled into Kate's driveway and stopped. "You are truly crazy."

Kate got out of the car, then leaned back in and faced Georgia. "Georgia, any man with that kind of money, power and blondes is way out of my league. He's probably got mirrors on his ceiling and cocaine on his night table and I would faint from shock if I saw either one."

"It would have been a hell of a date."

"More like a date from hell."

Randall Johnson accelerated up the highway's access ramp.

What kind of game had Kate Chilton been playing? First, she gave him a look he could feel across a crowded party. Then she blushed when he took her up on it. Just when he decided that she was too prim for him, she made wicked fun of the pretentious conversations that went on at Princeton alumni gatherings. He had been sure that she was flirting with him, but the next thing he knew, she had turned him down flat!

He was still amazed at her refusal; he couldn't remember the last time a woman had said no to him. She hadn't even looked pleased or suggested another time. Suddenly, he started to laugh out loud. "You are one conceited son of a bitch," he told himself. "Kate Chilton just didn't like you. Live with it."

Sparring with her had put him in the mood for female companionship. He punched a button on his car phone to call one of his usual dates, but disconnected before she answered.

Damn, he really wished that Kate Chilton had said yes.

Two

KATE WALKED INTO an uncharacteristically silent house to find a note in her oldest son's handwriting: "Gone to park to play soccer. Took Gretchen. Brigid will make sure we get home in time for dinner."

She smiled. Clay and Patrick felt that at ages twelve and ten they no longer needed a baby-sitter. However, they always had fun with Brigid. She checked her watch; they should be home soon.

She sat down and let the peace and quiet of her much-loved house wrap around her. She and David had bought it two months after they had gotten married. It was a Victorian, very dilapidated, and they had loved it on sight. She smiled at her memories of choosing wallpaper, curtains and furniture together. David had been as involved as she was. With his architect's spatial perception, he was a wizard at arranging furniture. She had been the one who got the tiles to line up and mitered the corners for the ceiling moldings. David's presence was so vivid in this house, their home, that the whole encounter with Randall Johnson began to fade into unreality.

The telephone interrupted her thoughts.

"Hello, Kate." It was Oliver Russell, one of David's two partners in his architectural firm. Actually, Oliver was far more than a business associate; he was a trusted friend. Since David's death, he had come by regularly on weekends to play soccer and chess with the boys. He often stayed for dinner, keeping her company in the lonely evening hours.

"Oliver! We missed seeing you this weekend. Georgia dragged me to a wretched Princeton alumni picnic..."

"Kate, I'd like to stop by the house tomorrow. I have some business to discuss."

"It sounds like bad news."

"No, not really. Just inevitable, I suppose. Would one o'clock suit you?" Oliver sounded more cheerful as he continued, "I'll come visit the boys next weekend. Tell Clay I have a new opening gambit for him. And, Kate, don't worry; everything will be fine."

Now she was worried, but she had no time to speculate. As she hung up the phone, she heard voices coming around the side of the house, so she simply pushed Oliver's visit to the back of her mind as she unlocked the door. The sight of her two handsome young sons always lifted her spirits.

Patrick spilled through the door first, his streaked blond hair dark with sweat. He allowed her a brief kiss and then pulled away, saying, "There was the coolest radio-controlled plane at the park!"

Clay followed, looking so tall and grown-up that Kate had to give him a hug. He bore it with a charming grin. "It's only been three hours since you saw us, Mom."

Kate laughed. "I know. But I just love hugging sweaty boys."

Clay ran his hand through his own thick blond hair in a gesture so like David's that Kate's heart lurched. Although both boys had her gray eyes, they looked more and more like David as they grew. "We sure are sweaty. A bunch of guys were there already so we got into a good scrimmage."

Brigid came in with their black Labrador, Gretchen, and closed the door behind her. "You should have seen your lads kicking that football. It was a joy to behold."

"Soccer ball," Patrick corrected.

"Och, I'm too old to be changin' my vocabulary to American," Brigid said.

"Kate, you get more gorgeous every time I see you."

Kate laughed. Since David had died, Oliver had been paying her ridiculous compliments to boost her spirits. His flattery sounded particularly absurd because he said it in the same calm, composed tone with which he asked you to pass the salt. She ushered him into the living room, where she had a tray of tea and sandwiches ready. He was early.

"Would you like some tea?" she asked, as they sat down.

"Thanks," he said, accepting the cup she poured him but then putting it down without tasting it. He leaned forward with his elbows resting on his knees. "I'm here because we need to talk about the future at C/R/G. David was terrific with the clients, you know, and brought in a lot of business for us. We're suffering without him."

He adjusted his horn-rimmed glasses and stared at his hands for a moment. Then he seemed to brace himself. "Ted and I feel that we have to bring in a new partner to fill that gap. A classmate of Ted's from Cornell is ready to leave Polshek and Partners, and he's a good man for the job. The problem is that we can't support four partnerships right now. He would have to buy out David's share of the company."

Kate froze. The company had been a part of her life since before Clay and Patrick were born. She had taken as much pride in its success as David had. Creating C/R/G had been his dream. To have to sell it... And the income from the partnership paid the household's basic living expenses. She had accepted a reduced share of the firm's profits after David died, but the amount she got, she counted on.

"How much would the new partner pay for David's share?" she managed to ask.

The figure Oliver named seemed horrifyingly small. He offered her several sheets of paper that explained his calculations. She took them, but couldn't focus on the numbers.

"I'll have to look at these later," she said, dropping them on the coffee table.

Oliver was watching her with concern. "Kate, I'm terribly sorry. We didn't arrive at these decisions without considerable debate." He jumped up, scraping his fingers through his dark blond hair. "Damn, I hate this. You should never go into business with people you care about."

Kate felt tears gathering in her eyes and willed them not to start down her cheeks. All she could do was nod; she didn't trust her voice.

He came over to sit beside her, and took her hands in his with a gentleness that threatened to undermine her control. "Take some time to think about this. Call me when you want to talk about anything at all. I'll go over the facts and figures with you whenever you're ready."

"I will," Kate said.

Oliver stood up to go. Before he left, he rested his hands lightly on her shoulders and said again, "Call me if you need *any*thing."

She dredged up a smile. "Thank you."

Kate closed the door behind him and then leaned back against it, feeling the solidity of the big oak door that she had lovingly stripped of its old dull varnish. She ran her hands along the grain, feeling the smooth, satiny surface. She probably wouldn't be able to keep this house. She would have to uproot the boys from Claremont and rent an apartment in a less costly area in a different town.

An unaccustomed flare of anger burned through her. David had reduced his life insurance policy and refused the mortgage insurance that their agent had recommended. She hadn't thought that it was a good decision, but she trusted his judgment. They had sunk every penny of their savings into the C/R/G partnership. Despite her reservations, she had agreed. Now Oliver said it was worth far less than what David had always led her to believe. And she and the boys were going to pay for it.

The thought of Clay and Patrick pushed Kate's brain back into gear. David had kept his own papers regarding the firm in a file cabinet in the attic. Maybe she could find something there that would increase the value of his share. At the very least, by taking some action she could stave off the panic threatening to swamp her.

She picked up the papers Oliver had given her and scanned them as she walked slowly up two flights of stairs to the attic. Fitting an old brass key into the file cabinet's lock, she pulled open the drawer and started looking through the various folders. All were labeled in David's beautiful architect's printing, but they weren't in any sort of order. She pulled out a handful and sat down on the floor to sort through them. She was skimming through some contracts when she spotted a folded handwritten letter

13

stapled crookedly between the pages. It had obviously gotten mixed in with the papers by mistake so she pulled it loose. Idly curious, she unfolded it and started to read.

> *Dearest David,*
>
> *You've just left and already I miss you so much that I can barely breathe. I thought that if I wrote to you, I could almost imagine that you had just stepped into the next room and that we were holding this conversation through the doorway. But of course, I won't hear your voice answering me or have the joy of knowing that you could walk back in at any moment and kiss the back of my neck as I sit here at my desk.*

Kate stopped. This had to be an old, old letter. She flipped it over but there was no date on it anywhere. It was signed "Sylvia." She desperately tried to remember if David had mentioned an old girlfriend with that name. Failing at that, she looked at the document it had been stapled into. The contract was less than two years old and was for a private home in Baltimore. Kate read the clients' names, neither of which was Sylvia.

She remembered David talking about that house. He had made a dozen or so trips to Baltimore to check on the project.

But he always made a point to meet with clients regularly. He said that he could catch problems before they became disasters that way. She returned to the letter.

> *And that's all that you would have to do—just*

kiss me once—and we would be back in my now-empty bed. But I have to stop thinking about that; my body aches for you.

I know that the house will soon be done. I will have to find you a new reason to come here: a skyscraper so enormous it will take decades to finish. I will make sure the contract requires you to supervise even the smallest detail so that you will be here every day. And every night, we can have dinner at my table and talk about everything in the world and not have to hurry to the bedroom in desperation.

She couldn't bear to read any more. She had to be misinterpreting something! This couldn't be to the David who was her husband, and it couldn't have been written just two years ago! She searched frantically through the rest of the file, looking for something, anything to explain the letter.

There were only more contracts from that same year, the year that he had died so suddenly of a heart attack, leaving her alone with two young boys to raise. She couldn't catch her breath.

In those first terrible days after David died, she had wondered how she could survive without him. She put up a brave front for Clay and Patrick, only to collapse in despair the minute she was alone. She found the strength to keep going in the love of her children and in the memory of the love that she and David had shared. In difficult moments, she even imagined that David was standing beside her, supporting her decisions.

She anchored her future on the foundation of a secure and happy past.

Now that, foundation lay shattered, blasted to pieces by a single sheet of paper.

David had not loved her.

Kate stared at the letter in her hands as she tried to reconcile the image of her golden, loving husband with this evidence of his other self. She felt so hollow that she was afraid her body would simply crumple inward. She forced herself to breathe as she kept staring at the letter. She sat there as the afternoon light faded. No coherent thoughts formed in her mind.

She felt only a swirling sense of cold, of being totally, utterly, completely alone.

Three

"MOM? MOM? WHERE are you?"

The vibration of a slammed door reached some recess of Kate's mind. Clay and Patrick. She frantically shoved the papers back into random file folders until only the letter was left lying alone. She jammed all the files back into the drawer as she heard the boys' calls moving closer.

She didn't want to touch the letter again, but she had to hide it until she could destroy it. The one certainty she had left was that she never wanted Clay and Patrick to know this about their father. She picked it up by one corner and carried it to a bookcase under the eaves. She folded it with her fingertips, and then closed it into the middle of a dusty copy of *On the Origin of Species*.

"Mom? Are you here?" Clay's voice had taken on a worried edge.

Kate tried to call down to reassure him. Her first attempt came out as a hoarse whisper, so she cleared her throat as she started toward the steps. Clay met her on the landing. "Mom, didn't you hear us? We've been looking *all over* for you."

Kate shook her head. "I'm sorry. I didn't realize what time it was," she managed to push through her throat.

"Are you okay? You sound kind of weird," Clay said, then shouted down the steps, "Pat, I found her. She's in the *attic*!"

He turned back to her with obvious concern on his young face. "Are you sick? You don't look normal."

Kate tried to remember how to look normal, but she felt so different that she couldn't summon up the appropriate expression. So she enveloped Clay in a hug and murmured in his ear, "I'm fine, just a bit distracted."

Patrick came pounding up the steps as Clay disentangled himself. "Hey, Mom. What are you doing up here? We kept yelling all over the house for you."

He came over and gave her his usual perfunctory peck on the cheek and suddenly Kate found "normal" again. Normal was what life had to be for Clay and Patrick. If she could throw herself in front of a bus for them, she certainly could pretend that she had never found one small piece of paper. That just happened to annihilate her.

She managed to fix dinner, clean up and check homework. But when bedtime came, she went straight to her bathroom, flipping on the switch that lighted the mirrors over the sinks. Kate braced her hands on her sink and stared at her reflection. She looked like the same person she had seen in the mirror that morning. Why didn't she appear crushed, or betrayed, or scared out of her wits? The woman staring back at her looked confident and serene and, yes, attractive. Attractive enough to prompt a connoisseur of women like Randall Johnson to invite her to dinner.

So why the hell had David slept with another woman? How had she failed so completely in their marriage? And how could she have been so *unaware* that she didn't have even the slightest *clue* about what was happening?

"God damn it, David! Why aren't you here to explain this to me? How can I understand if you aren't here to talk to me?"

She knew that she couldn't deal with this alone. She had to talk with *someone* or she would go in circles until she went insane. The only person she trusted was Georgia. She returned to her bedroom and called to ask her friend to come over after work the next day.

Mechanically, she got ready for bed and climbed between the sheets. She didn't bother to pick up a book from the bedside table or to click on the television news. She turned out the light and lay there, staring sightlessly upward in the darkness. She found some comfort in the occasional soft dream whimpers from the dog, who was stretched out as always on the rug beside the bed. But even Gretchen's faithful presence barely penetrated the swirling fog of failure and loneliness that engulfed her. Kate's brain spun like a kaleidoscope, shifting jagged images of David in bed with a strange woman around thoughts of selling the house against panic about paying college tuition. She sorted through her memory, reinterpreting scenes from her now ruined marriage, finding dissatisfaction where before there had seemed to be none.

She could manage neither tears nor sleep.

Somehow she smiled for Clay and Patrick the next day. They were stunned but grateful to be treated to Domino's Pizza for dinner. Clay eyed her a little worriedly but evidently decided not to look a gift horse in the mouth and so kept quiet. When Georgia breezed in after dinner and saw the pizza box, and the dirty dishes still scattered around the kitchen, she stopped dead and looked hard at

Kate. Going straight to the refrigerator, she opened a bottle of wine and poured two large glasses, one of which she thrust into Kate's hand. "Drink this now. We'll talk when the boys are in bed."

Kate put down the glass. "No, I don't really feel like wine, thanks."

Georgia put it back in her hand. "If you don't drink this, I'll pour brandy down your throat and you know what a hangover that will give you."

Kate took a sip of wine. "Thanks for coming, Georgia. I've been feeling so alone."

Georgia turned to Clay. "Why don't you and Patrick head upstairs and let your mom and me talk woman-to-woman?"

The boys agreed to her request with unusual promptness and pounded up the steps.

"All right, Kate, spill it," Georgia said once they were ensconced in the den with the doors firmly closed. "And feel free to cry on my shoulder. You look like you need to."

Kate blinked in surprise. She hadn't cried once since she read the letter. She couldn't summon up enough strength to cry. She hadn't really thought about how to tell Georgia the awful truth, so she just said flatly, "I found a letter from another woman to David. He was having an affair sometime in the year before he died."

"He was *what*? Jesus Christ, what a bastard! How could he do that to you? And he saved her letters?" Georgia was so angry she couldn't sit still; she got up and paced around the room.

"Letter," Kate corrected. "I only found one. And I don't think that he meant to save it. It was stapled into a contract."

Georgia came over to Kate's chair and knelt in front of

her, taking her hands. "I'm so sorry, Kate. To find out now when there's no way to change things... it's awful. What can I do to help?"

Suddenly the tears came.

"Tell me what I did wrong. Tell me why David needed to sleep with another woman. Tell me that my family's life wasn't built on a huge lie." Kate lifted her tear-streaked face. "Tell me how I could have been that *blind*!"

"You did not do anything wrong. You were a wonderful wife. My dates always envied David."

Kate shook her head and wrapped her arms around her own waist to hold in the sobs.

Georgia took Kate by the shoulders and shook her gently. "Stop blaming yourself. David is the creep here, remember? *You* didn't go off and sleep with another man."

"I never even *wanted* to. That's what I don't understand. What made him even think about it?" Reaching a decision Kate put down her wineglass and stood up. "I'll show you the letter and then we're going to burn it. I don't want Clay and Patrick to know about this. Ever."

She brought the letter down from its dusty hiding place and handed it to Georgia. She wanted Georgia's clear, legal mind to find the flaw in her reasoning, to tell her that she was wrong about David.

"Son of a bitch!" Georgia muttered as she finished reading. "She definitely wasn't a one-night stand."

"How could I not have known? I thought that we were so close, that we knew each other so well."

Georgia sat on the arm of Kate's chair. "I remember you saying that year that David was traveling constantly. You thought that the stress might have contributed to his heart attack. You probably didn't see him enough to be able to tell. Stop beating yourself up."

21

"Why did he do it, Georgia?"

Georgia moved back to her own chair and stared up at the ceiling for a minute. "All right, I'm going to give you my honest opinion of David. Promise you won't hate me."

Kate almost felt like laughing. "At this point, the worse it is, the more I'll like it."

Georgia looked relieved at this small flash of spirit and launched into her argument.

"When you and David met, you were both rising stars in your firms. You were a brilliant engineer, and David was a brilliant architect. You also happened to be poised, beautiful and great with people, the perfect up-and-coming architect's wife."

"Oh, please."

"David went after you with every weapon in his arsenal. Remember how flattered you were?"

"How could I not be? David could have had any woman he wanted; they were falling all over him. Evidently even after we were married."

"Stop it. But you've put your finger on something important. David was used to being the center of attention. He loved working with clients because they admired him and listened to him."

Georgia paused a moment, then continued, "David expected you to be the adoring and supportive wife, so he tried to eliminate anything that competed with him. He made you shut down your very successful consulting business the moment he could afford to."

Kate couldn't believe Georgia's implication. "*I* shut it down because I couldn't keep up with the work while I had small children."

"That's because David focused entirely on his own career and left you to bring up the children, run the house, entertain clients and draw plans for C/R/G. He forced you into a situation where you had to give up your profession for your family."

"And I've never regretted it." Then she remembered her financial difficulties and amended that, "Until now."

Georgia looked at her speculatively, but she was on a roll and didn't want to change the subject. She brought forth the clincher. "David could force you to dump the job but ultimately he couldn't compete with the children."

Kate felt completely dazed. Georgia was painting a picture of a manipulative self-centered man whom Kate didn't recognize as her husband. "David was crazy about the boys!"

"Of course he was. They were his sons. Men love having sons. But he missed the focus on him and on C/R/G. David leaned on you all through your marriage."

"We leaned on each other..." Kate faltered in her defense. Her nighttime agonies came back to support her friend's comments. She had asked Georgia to tell her why David had betrayed her, and Georgia was building a formidable case against him.

Georgia ignored Kate's comment. "I think he found this woman who stroked his ego with her undivided attention, and he indulged himself in an affair with her."

Kate could not refute Georgia's logic, so she changed the subject. "We're getting rid of this right now," she said, taking the letter to the fireplace. She picked up a long fireplace match from the mantel and lit three corners of the letter, letting it fall on the grate as it flamed. She torched every remaining fragment until only a pile of ash was left. She looked up at Georgia. "We are the only two people who will ever know about this letter."

Georgia crossed her heart with one finger. "My

discretion is absolute. Now, what are you going to *do* about this?"

"What do you mean do about it?" Kate asked, stirring the ashes around with a poker.

"You can't just burn the letter and forget about it. You have to do something to help you get over David's betrayal."

Kate looked at Georgia and realized that she was serious. "What would you suggest? Painting a scarlet *A* on David's gravestone?"

"You could find Sylvia and throw rotten eggs at her house. Or slash all the tires on that old Porsche that David was always working on."

That reminded Kate of her other problem. "I need that Porsche in mint condition. I'm selling it."

"I thought that you were keeping it for the boys when they got old enough to drive."

Kate slumped into her chair and let her head fall back on its cushion. New tears welled up and she angrily wiped them away with the back of her hand. "I forgot to mention my other problem. Oliver and Ted want to sell David's share of C/R/G to a new guy, which means that I have no income."

"Can't you invest the proceeds and live on the interest?"

"Not if I want to keep the house."

Georgia looked murderous. "If David were standing here now, I would give that bastard a piece of my mind."

"I thought that his share was worth more than Oliver says it is."

"Do you trust Oliver?"

"Completely. He would never cheat me." Kate took a sip of her wine before the irony of her statement struck her. "Of course, that's what I thought about David, too." Kate felt anger rip through her. Because of her husband's betrayal, she was even questioning Oliver's integrity.

"I have plenty of money, Kate. You can have as much as you want."

Kate's tears spilled over again. First Oliver and now Georgia offered her their help. She had no right to feel so miserably alone when she had such good friends. She reached for Georgia's hand and gave it a quick squeeze. "You don't know how much I appreciate your offer."

"But you're not going to take me up on it."

Kate shook her head. "I have to come up with a long-term solution."

"You're so damned independent."

"And you're such a clinging vine," Kate laughed. She raised her glass in a mock salute. "Here's to independent women!"

"And to hell with lying, cheating men!" Georgia said, raising her glass in return.

She woke up angry the next morning. It was better than the awful despair of the night before. However, she found herself snapping at Clay and Patrick over nothing. When Gretchen upset her water bowl, Kate swatted her instead of just cleaning it up as she normally would have done. All three recipients of her wrath looked stunned. Kate realized Georgia was right: she had to do something to vent this rolling boil of anger before it scalded everyone around her. But how exactly was she supposed to hit back at David when he was no longer there?

As she was putting the wine bottle in the recycling bin after the boys left for school, the image of Randall Johnson's large hand wrapped around a bottle of beer flashed across her mind. Was that what David had felt when he saw Sylvia, that shock of attraction? But she had said *no* to Randall Johnson. David had said *yes*.

So why the hell had she rejected Randall Johnson's invitation? That was easy; she still thought of herself as David's wife. Even though he obviously hadn't felt hindered by the fact that he was her husband. Well, the next man who asked her out was going to get an enthusiastic acceptance.

"And when exactly do I expect to get asked on a date again?" Kate said to Gretchen, who lifted her head and looked quizzical. "Randall Johnson was my one and only chance."

Looking at Gretchen's sympathetic face, Kate had a moment of clarity, her first since discovering the letter. She knew exactly how she would hit back. Since David had slept with another woman, she was going to sleep with another man. It wouldn't be quite "an eye for an eye," since she was no longer married, but the symmetry pleased her engineer's mind. She figured she could only do it once; she couldn't imagine facing a man she had gone to bed with on a first date with any self-respect the morning after.

Randall Johnson would be the perfect candidate; he was a stranger and a womanizer. And he was very, very attractive.

She picked up and put down the telephone half a dozen times. Finally, she called information for the number of RJ Enterprises in New York City.

"The worst that can happen is that he'll say no. And he'll think that I'm incredibly pushy. Not to mention indecisive," she said aloud to Gretchen, as she held the receiver in her hand for the umpteenth time. "But since I'll never see him again, what difference does it make?" The last thought gave her the courage she needed to dial the number. She asked for Randall Johnson and was amazed to be put through to his assistant immediately.

"Hello, my name is Kate Chilton. I wondered if I might speak with Mr. Johnson," Kate mustered after a moment's hesitation.

"He's in a meeting right now. May I take a message?"

Did she want to leave a message? If she didn't, she would never have the nerve to call again. "Um, yes, please. Would you tell him that I called and this is my number." Kate rattled off her telephone number.

"And what company are you with?"

"I'm not. I mean, it's a personal call."

"Thank you, Ms. Chilton. I'll give him the message as soon as he's out of the meeting."

"It's not urgent," Kate said, hoping that the message would somehow get lost at the bottom of the pile. "Thanks very much."

Of course, the telephone rang almost continuously after that. Each time Kate mentally braced herself for a conversation with Randall Johnson. Each time it was a telemarketer or a mother arranging a ride. She had finally forced herself to sit down with Oliver's sheets of numbers on David's share of C/R/G and was engrossed in deciphering the figures when the phone rang again. Kate picked it up without taking her eyes off the papers. "Hello."

"Kate Chilton. I have a message here from you."

Kate bolted out of her chair and banged her knee on the desk. Randall Johnson's voice in her ear sent a shock to her nerve endings. She wasn't sure if it was caused by fear or excitement. He sounded much more businesslike now, his Texas twang brisker and more clipped.

"Thank you so much for calling back so promptly." She

tried desperately to remember her speech. "We met at the Princeton picnic on Sunday."

"I remember."

Thank goodness for that. Now for the really hard part. Kate took a deep breath. "I wondered if your invitation for dinner on Friday was still open? I realized that I was hasty and even rude in refusing so quickly and I apologize. I hope that you would still like to continue our conversation." She knew that she was babbling so she stopped.

There was silence. She sat down and dropped her head onto one hand in mute humiliation.

"I'll pick you up at eight."

"Really?" Kate said before she could stop herself.

Kate could hear the amusement in his voice when he said, "Really. Just tell me where you live."

Kate gave him her address and directions. He repeated them back to her, said, "I'll see you Friday," and hung up.

Kate looked at the telephone receiver in her hand. "Yes, but how *much* of me will you see Friday?"

After he hung up, he swiveled his desk chair to stare out at the Statue of Liberty standing tall over the harbor.

Randall was sure that Kate hadn't enjoyed that phone call. So what had driven her to make it? There was some powerful motivation there, that much was clear to him. And it had to be more than his sex appeal. She had resisted that pretty successfully before. By rights, he should have told her to forget it, but curiosity had gotten the better of him. He chuckled when he recalled her incredulous "really?"

Randall got up and went into the next office, which belonged to RJ Enterprises' executive vice-president, Tom Rogan. They had met in Columbia University's night-and-weekend business school program. When Randall could afford an employee besides himself at RJ Enterprises, Tom had been the first person he hired. It had been a gamble for Tom to join such a new venture, and sometimes it had been a roller-coaster ride, but Randall had made sure that Tom never regretted it. RJ Enterprises had made them both wealthy beyond even Randall's dreams... and he had some big dreams. He dropped into the chair in front of Tom's desk and waited for him to get off the telephone.

Tom grinned at him. "It's always bad news when *you* come to *my* office."

"And this is no exception. I need you to take over for me at the Lexcon meeting on Friday."

"I thought you wanted to tell them where to go yourself," Tom said.

"Something's come up unexpectedly. I have to get out of here by seven."

"No problem." Tom clicked a few keys on his computer to put the meeting on his schedule. "Is this unexpected event tall, blond and female?"

"Is it any of your business?" Randall said without heat.

Tom leaned back in his chair. "It is when you ruin my Friday night for it."

"I know blackmail when I hear it. I'll let you know on Monday if it was worth ruining your Friday night."

"Thanks a lot."

"Anytime," Randall said with a sudden smile as he got up to leave. "I owe you one."

"You know you do," Tom mock-groused. "And all I want is just one—of your blondes, I mean."

"Be careful what you wish for."

Four

RANDALL JOHNSON WAS in a bad mood. His afternoon meeting had run late, and the Lexcon people had shown up early. They caught him in the hall outside the conference room and bent his ear for twenty minutes before he handed them over to Tom. When he finally got back to his office, he picked up the telephone to cancel dinner with Kate Chilton. Then he punched the speed dial for the company helicopter instead.

"Hey, Janine. Can you come pick me up at the office? I'm late as hell and I don't feel like fighting traffic tonight."

"Sure, boss. Where to?"

"Back to home base. And I need a ride."

"The Jeep is here."

Randall dialed Kate's number next.

She sounded distracted. He heard a dog barking and voices in the background.

"Kate. This is Randall Johnson. I'll be about a half an hour late. I apologize."

"I appreciate the phone call. Thank you for letting me know." Her voice sounded more focused now. "Traffic can be terrible on Friday nights."

He had no intention of telling her that he was flying to New Jersey. He was, however, eavesdropping on the conversation going on behind her. He heard something about "some *rich* guy" and "Mom hasn't been on a date since before we were *born*" and "she doesn't know what to wear." He was smiling as he said, "Sounds like you could use a little extra time."

"Oh no, it's just an average dinner at the Chilton house: total chaos." She answered cheerfully, but he could hear her shushing the speakers.

"I'll be there as soon as possible."

"Don't rush. I mean, drive carefully."

Kate put down the phone and shot the boys a look. "If Randall Johnson overheard what you said—"

"What?" they protested together.

"We were being quiet!" Clay said.

"We didn't say anything bad," Patrick mumbled, looking at his plate.

Kate rolled her eyes in mock exasperation. "Eat your dinners. I have to go get dressed."

Halfway up the stairs she decided she could use a glass of wine to fortify herself for the coming evening. "False courage," she muttered under her breath as she returned to the kitchen and filled her glass to the top.

Upstairs, she gulped down half, and then pulled out the two outfits she was debating between. The suit was tasteful and conservative; the dress was, well, provocative. She hung the suit back up. If she was going to act like a tart, she was going to dress like a tart. And that, Kate decided, included the underwear. If she got to the point where she was taking her dress off – which now she wasn't at all sure she would – she wanted to keep Randall Johnson in the

31

right mood. She scrabbled around on the top shelf of her closet until she found the box she had stashed there ages ago.

Brushing the dust off the yellowed cardboard, Kate flipped open the box and pulled out a wispy beige lace teddy, a bridal shower gift that she had worn once or twice for David. With it came stockings to hook onto the garters dangling from the frilled leg openings. Kate put it all on, wrestling with the old-fashioned fasteners. Miraculously, it still fit. She took a deliberately brief glance in the mirror as she walked over to put the dress on. "Frederick's of Hollywood, here I come."

As she zipped up, Kate walked back to the mirror and stopped in shock. She had forgotten how dramatic the dress was. The dark green brought out the red highlights in her hair. The soft fabric fit tightly around her shoulders and arms, and crossed low over her breasts, drawing attention to the expanse of neck and chest left bare. It draped subtly around her waist and hips, hinting at rather than clinging to those curves.

However, its hem stopped well above her knees and Kate twisted and turned to make sure that the tops of her stockings didn't show. She slipped on a pair of high-heeled pumps – also unearthed from the back of the closet – and immediately longed for her running shoes. She felt as though she were balancing on stilts. "You're out of practice, my girl," she admonished herself as she fastened on a pair of gold earrings.

But when she surveyed the full effect in the mirror, she felt a surge of pure feminine power. The soccer mom was gone and in her place stood a seductress. The dress whispered against the hidden lace as she moved. The waving ends of her hair tickled the tops of her almost bare shoulders. Even the wretched high heels put a seductive sway in her walk. "So there, David," Kate said, polishing off the rest of the wine.

A tottery journey down the stairs brought her mood down a notch, but the speechless stares Clay and Patrick gave her confirmed her transformation. Brigid had let herself in while Kate was upstairs.

"Save us and bless us! You look like a fashion model, to be sure," the baby-sitter exclaimed in her Irish brogue.

Kate laughed. "As long as I don't break my ankle." She had poured herself another glass of wine and was sipping it more slowly. Since she hadn't eaten dinner yet, the first glass was already giving her a delicious sense of recklessness.

The doorbell rang.

Kate reminded herself to walk slowly. When she reached the front door, she realized that Clay, Patrick, Brigid and Gretchen had all come with her. She could feel a slightly hysterical giggle rising up in her throat as she imagined Randall Johnson's view of Kate and Company. She quelled it with a deep breath and pulled open the big oak door.

In his dark business suit, Randall Johnson looked much larger than she remembered. The porch light threw sharp shadows across the planes of his unsmiling face. Kate's buoyant mood evaporated as she acknowledged the full extent of her miscalculation. She had involved a powerful and unknown quantity in her already complicated life.

Then Randall's eyes swept down her and he smiled in a way that said he had gotten the intended message. "Hello, Kate," he said. "I'm glad you reconsidered seeing me this evening."

The black velvet drawl was back and Kate swallowed

hard. "So am I," she lied as she stepped aside to let him in. He raised his eyebrows as he got the full impact of the welcoming committee, but he handled all the introductions with aplomb, even bending down to scratch Gretchen's ears. Kate was hugely relieved when both boys remembered to shake hands. She reached for her jacket but Randall picked it up first and held it for her. She slipped her arms through the sleeves and then jumped when his fingers brushed against her neck as he flicked her hair out from under the collar.

"I don't bite," he said softly in her ear.

Kate smiled dubiously as she laid her hand on the arm he offered her. "I feel a little awkward."

"You look stunning."

"Thank you," Kate said with real gratitude and a return of confidence. She suddenly realized that her hand was resting on the very forearm that had attracted her attention in the first place. She couldn't resist sliding her hand over the fine wool to feel the muscle underneath. She knew that Randall felt her near caress because he brought her closer to his side.

After she bade the boys good night, Kate squared her shoulders and walked bravely out of the shelter of her home. As she navigated down the steps, she gave a small snort of disgust at her precariousness. Randall looked down with a raised eyebrow, and Kate explained, "I hate high heels."

"Feel free to take them off anytime." His tone implied that she could take off more than her shoes. Kate shivered with nervous anticipation; he was much better at this than she was.

"I hope you don't mind if we stop at my house," Randall continued in a brisker tone. "I want to change cars."

"Of course not, I'd love to see your home." Georgia had told her that Randall Johnson lived in a magnificent post-modem mansion on a hilltop estate, the highest hill in Claremont. As an engineer and the widow of an architect – Kate grimaced mentally – she was fascinated by large man-made structures.

Randall ushered her into a Jeep, and they chatted on the drive to his house, but Kate realized she was barely listening to anything that either one of them said. She was too busy debating whether or not she had the nerve to carry out her plan. Was seducing a strange man really the best way to make herself feel better? Just how far was she prepared to go to strike back at a husband who wasn't even here to know about it?

The Jeep's headlights swept around a curve and through a metal gate that was still swinging open as they passed. Kate got the impression of trees arching over a cobblestone driveway as they roared through the darkness for what seemed like miles. Then the headlights flashed over a massive metal-sheathed door and around a completely private courtyard. They finally came to a stop. Randall turned to Kate and said, "Welcome to Eagle's Nest."

The stone and steel structure seemed to glow in its frame of trees. Kate was speechless in her admiration. As Randall came around to open her door, she refocused her attention, concentrating on keeping her knees together and her skirt down as she swung her legs out. She was about to grab the door frame to steady her descent when Randall offered his hand. Kate hesitated a fraction of a second before accepting. As he slid his other hand up to brace her elbow, his eyes glinted with mockery, "Having second thoughts, Kate?"

"No, I just wanted to make sure that my feet were firmly planted on the ground."

Randall laughed and Kate changed the subject. "Your house is magnificent. May I ask who designed it?"

"Your husband was an architect, wasn't he?"

Kate nodded, startled that he knew about David at all.

"Then you'll probably know the firm: Pei Cobb Freed and Partners. But the architect didn't work there long. His name is Frank Peltier. He's on his own now, out West somewhere."

"Actually, I've met him," Kate said. "He's a very interesting man. And obviously extremely talented." She gestured toward the house as they walked in.

Randall closed the front door behind them. "This was the last house he built before he left New York. I've never been sure whether to consider that a compliment, or a comment on my deficiencies as a client."

"Surely a compliment," Kate said, taking in the staircase that seemed to rise through the air unsupported, and the walls paneled in geometric patterns of different woods. "This house must have given him the confidence to strike out on his own."

"Thank you," Randall said, with a courtly little bow. Kate was taken off guard by his self-deprecation. Then the wicked glint was back in his eyes as he said, "Would you like to take your shoes off now? If you want a tour of the house, you might be more comfortable without the heels."

Kate looked at the highly polished oak floor and decided that dignity would have to take a backseat to personal safety. She started to lean down to push one pump off her heel, when Randall once again offered her his hand. "I seem to require an unusual amount of hand-holding tonight," she said with a smile.

"That's why short skirts and high heels were invented."

"By men, of course."

"Of course."

He took the shoes from her hand and tossed them onto the hall table. Kate winced as the heels skidded on the inlaid wood. "Would you like to see the house first or have a drink?"

"See the house," Kate answered, thinking that she had had enough wine for the moment.

"A true architect's soul mate," Randall said, taking her elbow and turning her toward the library.

Kate began by admiring the rooms and their furnishings, but soon she was more conscious of Randall Johnson's touch than of her surroundings. His hand moved from her elbow to the small of her back where she could swear he deliberately rubbed the fabric of her dress lightly against her. In the next room, she felt his hand slide up to the vee of skin left bare by the dress's low back and Kate had to stifle a gasp at the sensation of his warm skin against hers. When he called her attention to a chandelier by running his hand up the back of her neck and threading his fingers into her hair to tilt her head back, Kate gave up and closed her eyes.

He stopped talking, so she opened them. Randall was very close and looking down at her with that intensity she had felt at their first meeting. She dropped her gaze to his mouth in a blatant invitation and was shocked when he said, "I'm being a bad host. Let me get you something to drink," and shifted his hand back to her elbow.

He steered her toward the rear of the house. Kate wondered why he hadn't kissed her. She knew perfectly well that she was being seduced by a master of the art, but why had he stopped?

37

"What's your poison?" Randall's voice jolted her out of her thoughts. He was standing in front of a wood and brass bar with his hands poised over an array of bottles and glasses.

"Red wine would be lovely," Kate responded. She looked around the room, admiring the stone fireplace, the leather sofas and chairs that looked as though you would sink into them and never get up again and the panoramic view that stretched all the way to Manhattan. This was obviously the room where Frank Peltier had meant the house's inhabitant to spend most of his time.

"Frank let me pick the furniture for this room," Randall said, as he poured two glasses of wine from a decanter. "So you don't have to worry about scratching the tables."

Kate laughed. "I have a great respect for varnished wood. I've done a lot of wood-stripping in my own house."

The wineglasses were engulfed by Randall's hands as he carried them to where Kate stood. He held hers a minute before handing it to her. "It's better slightly warmed," he commented.

Touching his glass lightly to hers, he held her gaze over the rim of the glass as he drank. Kate sipped the full red wine. *He really is very good at building tension*, she decided. Based on their first meeting, she realized she had been expecting a more direct approach.

"Come and enjoy some fresh air," he said, swinging open a door onto the stone patio behind the house.

"I'll have to get my shoes," Kate said, starting toward the hallway with a wobble and realizing that she needed to get some food in her stomach soon or she would never be able to walk in those heels.

"No need. Frank Peltier was a disciple of Frank Lloyd Wright."

"He put radiant heat under the outdoor patio?" she asked in amazement.

"He wanted to make sure that it got the maximum use."

Kate tentatively stepped out onto the patio and then sighed with pleasure. The stones were slightly rough under her stocking feet but they were the temperature of bathwater. "Why don't you take *your* shoes off?" she suggested.

Randall looked down at his wing tips and then back up at Kate with a smile that was gone almost before she caught it. "Why not?" he said, untying his shoes and dropping them by the door. She watched in fascination as he stood stock still, his gaze focused on his sock-clad feet.

"It feels good," he announced, taking another drink of wine.

"You've never walked out here in bare feet?" Kate asked incredulously.

"Despite Frank's best intentions, I don't spend much time out here."

"I see."

Kate padded over to the waist-height wall along the edge of the patio, enjoying every warm step of the way. The view of Manhattan was beautiful. She and David had often admired it from both an architect's and an engineer's perspective.

She shook her head at the memory. The small movement made her sway, and she looked down at her wineglass to discover that it was almost empty. She decided to leave it that way; she would need to keep her wits about her if she was going to deal effectively with Randall Johnson. That reminded her of her mission, and she tried to think of a seductive comment to move things along. She put the wineglass down, tilted her head back and squinted at the distant lights, racking her brain for a suggestive line.

Then Randall's arm slid around her waist from behind. Evidently, he didn't need any verbal suggestions to get things rolling.

He moved closer to her back, and Kate felt him along the length of her body as the wool of his jacket rubbed against her bare shoulder blades, and the cuffs of his slacks brushed her ankles. She went very still. Instantly, Randall did the same. Somehow Kate knew that he would stop now if she moved away. Her muscles tensed.

Then the words of the horrible letter echoed through her brain: *We would be back in my now-empty bed... my body aches for you...*

She relaxed, leaned back against Randall's warm, strong body, and reveled in the feel of him. He kissed her on the side of her neck, and when she felt his hand splay across her stomach, bringing her even more tightly against him, she lost all coherent thought.

She reached up and back to weave her fingers into his hair as he moved his mouth down to her shoulder. His other arm came around her and he ran his palm gently up and over her breast. When she arched into his exploring hand, his fingers found her nipple through the thin fabric of her dress. She gasped as his touch sent a streak of sensation between her legs.

Feeling him harden against her made her brave. She turned in his grasp and brought his head down to hers with a confidence that astonished her. Winding her arms around his neck, she traced the outline of those stern, masculine lips with her tongue.

Randall groaned but let her continue her exploration, moving his hands downward to pull her even closer. Kate felt his thigh push against the vee of her legs, and she moaned herself. Then his lips were hard and open on hers and his tongue was inside her mouth. His hands cupped her buttocks and she felt herself being lifted onto the stone wall behind her. The cold stone made her gasp in exquisite surprise as it gritted against her bare thighs. She realized that her skirt had slid up as he lifted her, and she spread her thighs as he brushed his fingers between them.

"God, Kate," she heard him say and opened her eyes to see him gazing down at her legs. He ran his finger slowly down one garter and then traced the top of her stocking around to her inner thigh. As his finger moved upward, Kate's eyes closed again and her head fell back against his supporting arm. When he pushed under the teddy's lace crotch and gently touched her most sensitive spot, Kate clutched his shoulders and pressed into his hand. He moved the thin strip of lace aside and she could feel how wet she was as he slipped his finger inside her. She arched into him more strongly, reveling in the motion and heat of his hand against her. But she wanted more than his hand inside her. She reached for his belt buckle and was surprised when Randall released her for a moment to turn away.

She heard the rip of foil and he was back between her legs, entering her at first slowly and then as Kate moved with him, stroking fast and hard into her. He skimmed one hand down between her legs and Kate exploded into orgasm, embracing him with her spasms. She felt him withdraw and slide once more deep into her, then felt the pumping of his own climax against her, as he groaned in wordless pleasure.

Kate allowed her head to fall forward onto his shoulder as she savored the aftershocks of their joining. Her legs were locked around his waist and her muscles were trembling in fatigue but she didn't want to let go. She felt a tremor run through his arm and realized that he was holding her firmly away from the far edge of the wall. When she glanced sideways she saw that both wineglasses had smashed onto the rocks and tree roots below. She felt foolish tears pricking at her eyelids at his protectiveness.

Randall shifted slightly and brought one hand up to smooth her hair. Kate started to lift her head to look at him and then realized that she had no idea what to say. Now she understood why you were supposed to have dinner before you had sex with a man: you would have something to talk about after orgasm. She shivered as Randall kissed her softly behind her ear and then gently set her down on her feet. He turned away to strip off the condom and then came back to put his arms around her again. "You are an incredibly sexy woman."

"Th-thank you," Kate stammered and, unbelievably, blushed. "I think you may have gotten the wrong idea about me."

She felt Randall's arms tense but he looked down at her with a slight smile and drawled, "You're not going to tell me that you didn't want to do that as much as I did."

"Probably more," Kate said.

Randall threw his head back and gave a shout of laughter. "I love an honest woman."

Kate braced her hands against his chest and stared at his tie. "What I mean is that I don't generally, um..." Kate couldn't decide what to call what they had just done. "Have sex" seemed too vulgar, whereas she could hardly claim to have "made love" to a man whom she had known for all of forty minutes. "I don't generally do that," she tried again, "with someone I've just met."

Randall's smile disappeared, along with his velvet drawl. "And you think I do?"

"Well, yes," Kate was surprised into saying.

Randall withdrew the protection of his arms. "Thank you for that very flattering evaluation of my character," he said, stepping back. "I was about to apologize for my unseemly haste, but I see you had low expectations."

"No, no, I don't mean it that way. I just assumed that being who you are, you probably have lots of opportunities and that you might take advantage of them...."

She was met by cool silence.

"...occasionally..." Kate knew that she was going from bad to worse.

She was starting to feel chilly and wrapped her arms around herself. Randall handed her his jacket with a sardonic glance. She slipped it over her shoulders and felt guilty for enjoying the body heat that lingered inside.

Now she wasn't sure what to say to him at all. Her inner muscles were still rippling with a satisfaction that she found shocking but comforting. *I can still have great sex*, she thought with some smugness.

"Thank you," she said again, more firmly, as she pulled her scattered thoughts together. "That was... great."

Randall's lips twitched.

Briskly, in her best social voice, she said, "I think that dinner would be an anticlimax." Then blushed as she caught her unintentional double entendre. "So perhaps you would be so kind as to take me home now," she finished sheepishly.

Randall's mouth no longer held an amused curve. He leaned his hip against a stone-topped table, crossed his ankles and folded his arms across his chest.

"What's the catch?"

"The catch?" Kate repeated.

"Why are you here? What do you want now?"

"Actually, I just want to go home."

Randall looked down at the ground and then back at Kate with a raised eyebrow. "So I don't even have to buy you dinner?"

She shook her head and shivered again. An absurd idea flitted across her mind. Rich, powerful Randall Johnson was feeling used by average, ordinary Kate Chilton.

As she began to walk toward the door, Randall moved with the sudden spring of a tiger and blocked her path. He took her by the shoulders and dropped his head to kiss her so swiftly that Kate couldn't dodge him. With a slow and inexorable pressure, he forced her head back so their bodies were locked together from thigh to chest. In some distant corner of her mind, a small voice was urging her to stop but when Randall slid his knee between hers, the voice became a whimper as Kate melted against her tempter.

Randall lifted his head and smiled gloatingly at his conquest. "I'll consider this dessert," he said, bending down to slide his arm behind her knees.

When he picked her up, Kate expected him to take her to the stone table and deposit her there, but instead he kicked open the door and carried her to the bedroom, dropping her across the bed and following her down. He pinned her hands over her head with one arm and slid his other hand down between her legs.

She moaned when his finger flicked against her as he un-snapped the crotch of the teddy, and she cried out with satisfaction as he slid his finger against the damp folds of her skin and then inside her over and over again. She struggled to free her arms so that she could reciprocate but he wouldn't loosen his grip. Kate understood the message. He was controlling this encounter. She didn't care.

He released her arms to unbutton his shirt and throw it

off. Then he unzipped the bodice of her dress part way and pulled it down around her elbows. Kate ached to run her hands over the dark hair of Randall's chest, but once again he had trapped her arms. He practically drove her mad as he played with her already aroused nipples. She completely lost control when he lowered his chest onto her bare breasts and lightly brushed back and forth across them. Kate arched up to meet him and he teased her by lifting himself up just beyond her reach. The muscles in those marvelous arms were bunched in effort but still he wouldn't relent. Finally, Kate opened her eyes to see him looking down at her, sweat shining on his forehead and the anger in his eyes replaced by pure desire. "Are you ready, Kate?"

"Oh, yes!"

He pulled away to fit on a condom and then lowered himself between her legs and thrust into her in one fluid motion. Kate again arched up against him and he stopped. She tried to move her hips but his weight was pinning her to the bed. He was still punishing her so she fought back. She tightened her inner muscles around him as hard as she could.

He made a sound between a groan and a laugh and began moving again. Kate came in a convulsion of sensation and sound. Then Randall drove into her and shouted his own completion. He collapsed facedown beside her with his arm flung across her breasts. He turned his head just enough to look at her. "Where did you learn that trick?"

Kate smiled as she considered telling him that it was a pregnancy exercise, then decided against it. "In a brothel in Paris," she said.

Randall gave a bark of laughter. "I'm going to have to find that brothel."

Kate turned her head on the bed to look at him. "Well, you wouldn't let me move anything else."

The slight smile on his lips vanished and his flat Texas twang sounded sharp and hard. "I'm not a nice man, Kate. You don't want to mess with me."

She looked away from his steady gaze and found herself admiring the curve of his biceps. She ran her hand up his arm, enjoying the feel of skin over muscle.

"You're very... touchable," she said, exploring back down his arm to his wrist.

She felt the bed shaking and realized that he was laughing silently. "I've been called a lot of things, but this is a first for *touchable*. Don't spread it around."

Kate laughed, too. It struck her that she was lying beside a virtual stranger, her dress bunched around her waist, and she was enjoying it. One-night stands were quite liberating. Of course, she gave Randall Johnson credit for being an above-average partner.

His stomach growled loudly. Kate giggled and then gave a little gasp of pleasure as Randall rolled onto his back, caressing her breasts as he pulled his arm away.

"Lady, I need food if you want to continue this depravity. I make a mean burrito."

Kate sighed with regret. She wanted to stay lost in this sexual haze but reality was seeping into her reluctant brain; she knew that she had to leave. There must be some ancient taboo about accepting food from a man you had no intention of ever seeing again.

Randall picked up his shirt from the floor and pulled it on. He started to button it when Kate said, "No, wait."

He raised an eyebrow in question. "I just want to do one thing," she explained as she got up and pulled her dress up and down enough to cover the bare minimum. She walked over to him and pushed open his shirt. "You wouldn't let me do this earlier," she said as she ran her hands over the springy hair on his chest and abdomen. As she brushed over his nipples, he groaned.

"We'll never make it to the kitchen if you keep that up."

Kate ran her hands once more down his ribs and stepped back, feeling bereft.

Randall opened his eyes. "Forget the kitchen," he said with a wicked grin.

Kate laughed but turned around and offered him her open zipper. He fastened her up so quickly and competently that she couldn't help contemplating how much practice he must have had. She adjusted her skirt and then braced herself as she said, "I'd love to stay for dinner but I have to coach a soccer game tomorrow morning. I need to get some sleep."

It amazed Kate how quickly Randall Johnson could go from sexy to scary. When he focused those eyes on you, you knew you should run. Randall buttoned his shirt without looking away from her. She fidgeted uncomfortably but stood her ground.

"You're very good at that, aren't you?"

He raised his eyebrows again. "At what?"

"Intimidating someone without saying a word."

He tucked his shirt in, still watching her. "Silence is a powerful weapon."

He was dressing with an almost insolent deliberation so Kate turned and stalked out of the room. She gathered up her purse and jacket and headed for the hall. She heard Randall go out onto the patio to retrieve the jacket he had pushed off her shoulders earlier.

She was balancing against the hall table, pulling on her second shoe when he appeared beside her with a jingle of car keys. He held her jacket for her again, and Kate was astounded by the fact that the slightest touch of this man's hand made her entire body vibrate.

Randall still hadn't said a word as he ushered her to a sleek Jaguar, and Kate felt her temper rising. Once he had settled into the driver's seat, she said, "You know, it's customary to at least attempt to make polite conversation."

"Okay. You're great in bed."

Kate gasped, and then started to laugh. "If that's how you make polite conversation, you must move in unusual social circles."

The corner of Randall's mouth curved slightly.

Kate decided to drop it as he put the car in motion. She took another quick look sideways and found his profile so distant and unapproachable that she too fixed her gaze on the road. He seemed to have forgotten her presence entirely.

Randall was ticked off. He had been looking for entertainment tonight, but he had gotten more than he bargained for. He had had no expectation of making love to Kate. He had been toying with her, seeing how far she would let him go before he got his face slapped, either literally or verbally. He hadn't anticipated her melting into him or her sexy underwear or his own explosive reaction to all of the above. Hell, he was getting aroused again just thinking about it.

In many ways, he mused, *it could be considered the perfect date: great sex and good-bye. No dinner, no small talk, no strings.* But instead of being grateful, he felt mad as hell. He was choking on the undeniable fact that Kate Chilton had set out to seduce him and had succeeded.

During the silent ride, Kate was trying to formulate a farewell that would be cool, sophisticated and final. Her plan had succeeded. She felt her lips curl in a satisfied smile. It was worth it, and now she had a good reason never to attend a Princeton alumni party again.

Randall turned into her driveway and stopped the car. Leaning back against his door, he sat watching her in silence. The shadows emphasized the dark glint of his eyes and threw his cheekbones into sharp relief. Before Kate could say anything, he was out of the car and opening her door. She let him help her up the steps, then turned to say good-bye.

"Randall, I want to thank you..."

"All the ladies do," he said, taking hold of her chin.

"But..."

"Shhhh," he said as he bent down to lightly brush her lips with his. Then he deepened the kiss. Kate kissed him right back.

He lifted his head to say, "I'll call you."

And then he was heading back down the front steps.

Panic drove Kate to rudeness. "No, don't," she said loudly. "This won't happen again –"

"I think it will, darlin'." He kept walking as he drawled over his shoulder, "I'm not a one-night stand."

Five

"It's SEVEN A.M. on a beautiful September morning. The current temperature is fifty-two degrees, going up to..." Kate punched off the radio alarm. The scrapes on the backs of her legs hurt where the sheet brushed them. "Rock burns instead of rug burns. What was I thinking?" she groaned.

Her stomach was queasy from too much wine, and it got worse as images from the night before pounded through her brain. She had felt satisfaction in carrying out her plan, not to mention a certain physical afterglow, when she had crawled into bed last night. Now, in the cold light of morning, she winced at the memory of her outrageous behavior. Her only comfort was that nobody knew about it except Randall Johnson. And she had no intention of ever looking him in the eye again.

"That's one more thing to chalk up to your account, David," Kate muttered to the ceiling. "I let you drag me down to your level. But it won't happen again."

With that resolution, she threw off the covers. She dressed, hauled two sleepy young men out of dreamland

and got them all to their soccer game on time. For two blessed hours, she concentrated on penalty kicks, player rotations and post-game Dunkin' Donuts. When they got home, Kate herded them into the den for a serious family conference.

Clay and Patrick glanced at each other silently, and then sat down in the two armchairs across from the couch. Kate dropped onto the sofa and gave them a straight look.

"You know that your dad was a partner in C/R/G."

The two boys nodded.

"Well, he made the business very successful and to keep that up, Oliver and Ted need to get a new partner to take his place. That means that the new partner will buy Dad's share in the business from us."

Clay clearly felt that he needed to help his mother get through this discussion. "So we won't get a share of the profits anymore?"

Kate nodded. "That's right. So we're going to have to make some changes and I want to talk with you about them."

"Mom," Clay said. "We can get jobs."

"Yeah," Patrick chimed in. "When I'm sixteen, I'll work at McDonald's."

Kate's eyes blurred with tears. "You guys are wonderful, but I'm the one who's going to get a job."

She almost laughed at the skeptical expressions on their faces. "I was a structural engineer when I met Dad, you know. And I worked as a consulting engineer even after you were born, Clay."

"But that was a long time ago," Clay said. "Do you remember all that stuff?"

Kate sighed because she wasn't sure herself. But she said firmly, "Of course I do. And I loved building things.

Your dad and I worked on one skyscraper together. We showed it to you in New York City, remember?"

Clay looked at Patrick. "That was the day you wanted to go to the video arcade."

"And you wanted to go to the Museum of Natural History," Patrick said. "We went to see buildings instead."

"We also went to the Statue of Liberty," Kate pointed out.

"That was cool," Clay admitted.

"I miss going on adventures with Dad," Patrick said in a small voice.

"Me, too," Clay said.

"We all do," Kate said, her heart breaking for them—and herself. She brought the conversation back to the original topic. "The problem is that it probably will take me a while to get a good job, and right now I think we need some extra money to tide us over. I hate to do it but I think that we're going to have to sell the Porsche."

Patrick opened his mouth but Clay stopped him with a warning glance. "It's okay, Mom, we understand," he said. "Mr. Hennessey might be interested. And he'd take good care of it."

"I'll call him first," Kate promised. Their neighbor, Tim Hennessey, had sometimes worked on the car with David and the boys before they took it out for its once-a-week drive.

"And if he doesn't want it, maybe your boyfriend, Mr. Johnson, would buy it. He's rich," Patrick said helpfully.

Kate choked, and then quickly recovered enough to say, "I don't think I'll offer it to Mr. Johnson. He's got several cars already."

She patted the sofa on both sides of her. "That's enough serious stuff. How about a hug for Mom?" The boys rolled their eyes and dragged their feet, but they stayed beside her on the couch for a long time.

Monday morning found Kate on the telephone to every former business associate and client she could unearth from her old Rolodex. She had concluded that with some creative scrimping and saving she could get by with a part-time job. That way she could still spend time with Clay and Patrick. She had also braced herself to beg rides for the boys, since she wouldn't be able to drive them around if she was at work. She hated to impose on her friends, but she realized she was going to have to sacrifice her pride along with the Porsche. The responses to her business calls were discouraging, so she welcomed the interruption when Georgia called at lunchtime.

"Kate, are you mad at me?"

Kate was taken by surprise. "No. Why?"

"Because you didn't tell me that you had a date with Randall Johnson on Friday night. How could you keep that from your best friend? I'm hurt, I'm insulted, I'm dying of curiosity."

Kate groaned. "Who told you that?"

"Patrick. On Sunday when you were out jogging with Gretchen."

"He didn't tell me that you called!"

"Does that surprise you? But don't try to change the subject. You've been holding out on me and I'm going to get to the bottom of this. What happened?"

Kate sighed. Georgia wasn't a lawyer for nothing; she never let up on a witness. In this case, however, Kate had no intention of telling her what had really happened. She hated to lie – and she wasn't very good at it – but she let her genuine embarrassment show in her voice as she made up her story. "Well, I kept stewing over what you had said about David and finally I just called Randall Johnson at his office and asked him if his dinner invitation was still open."

"You must have been furious. The Kate Chilton I knew would never call a man. You go, girl!"

"It wasn't such a great idea. He took me out to dinner but I think he was bored." Kate hoped that downplaying the date would keep Georgia from asking questions she couldn't think of an answer for.

"Why do you think that?"

"He didn't want to talk about his work and he wasn't much interested in Clay and Patrick's extracurricular activities, so we sort of ran out of subjects to discuss," Kate ad-libbed.

Georgia sounded suspicious. "Where did he take you?"

Kate came up with the name of an expensive New York restaurant she and David had gone to once and prayed that it was still in business.

"Very nice," Georgia approved. "What did you eat?"

Now Kate knew that Georgia was trying to trip her up. "Georgia!"

"All right. Listen, I don't know what happened between you and Randall Johnson, but I do know that you've never in your life bored a man at dinner. You realize that if you married him, you'd never have to worry about money."

"That's not funny."

"It's true."

Kate was silent a moment, then stated with quiet vehemence, "I will not depend on a man ever again."

"It was just a passing thought. I don't really see him as husband material anyway. Many women have tried and failed to get a wedding ring out of him. Although I do know one lady who got a very nice diamond bracelet,"

Georgia said in a musing tone. "You could always pawn it. Sorry, there goes my other line. I'll talk to you later."

When Clay and Patrick came home from school, they requested permission to go on a mysterious errand. Since they promised to stay together and remain in the neighborhood, Kate let them go. She was starting to fix dinner when they came in the back door looking very pleased with themselves.

"Mom, we have an important announcement," Patrick said.

Kate stopped chopping carrots. They looked so handsome standing shoulder to shoulder that she had to smile. The brothers exchanged a silent look and then Clay took over.

"We have a job," he said, breaking into a proud grin.

Kate came around the counter to stand in front of them. "You do? That's wonderful! What kind of job?"

"We're walking dogs," Clay said.

"Four dogs," Patrick grinned. "Max, Jonesy, Sherri and Thunder. Every weekday after school."

Clay said seriously, "We'll make enough money to buy lunch at school and have some left over. We thought that it would help."

Kate gathered them into a hug. "I'm so proud of you two. It will help a lot. You are the greatest children a mother could have."

Clay realized that his mother was crying and said, "Mom, we wanted to cheer you up!"

Kate smiled through the blur. "You have cheered me up more than you can possibly imagine." She stood up and grabbed a Kleenex. "This calls for a celebration! We'll have ice cream sundaes for dessert."

"Cool," Clay said as he hauled his backpack up the stairs to start his homework.

"Yeah," Patrick agreed, following his brother. "Too bad we still have to do homework." He looked hopefully at Kate. She gave him a fond smile but waved him upstairs. "Oh, well," he sighed.

Kate stood in the kitchen, her tears flowing freely, as she let the torrent of maternal pride sweep through her. She felt a small surge of her old confidence; she couldn't have been a total failure if she had raised Clay and Patrick.

The three of them would be just fine.

Tom Rogan walked past Randall's administrative assistant, Gail Anderson, on his way to the CEO's office. "Tread carefully," she said, glancing up from her computer screen. "He's touchy this morning."

Tom tried to hand off the sheaf of papers he was carrying. "Then you take these into him. I prefer not to get my head bitten off so early in the week."

Gail laughed and waved him past. "Just don't tell him anything he doesn't want to hear and you'll be fine."

"My *job* is to tell him things he doesn't want to hear." Tom braced his shoulders and with an air of martyrdom that made Gail laugh again, walked into Randall Johnson's office.

His boss was reading and deleting E-mails at a dizzying pace. He glanced up quickly and then went back to his task. "You don't look happy, Tom."

Tom sat down and stretched his long legs out in front of him. Despite his banter with Gail, he was completely at ease.

"I'm not happy because you're not going to be happy," he said, leaning forward and pushing some of his papers across Randall's desk. "It's the Mason deal. Gill Gillespie and his Texas lawyers are at it again. They object to clauses 22c and 29f this time."

"Now how the *hell* am I supposed to remember what clauses 22c and 29f are?" Randall said irritably as he swiveled to face Tom.

"They're circled in red," Tom said neutrally, as he pointed to the contract.

Randall quickly skimmed the offending sentences. "That's it? Fine, take them out. Then tell those sons of bitches that I'm coming down *personally* on" – he checked his computer screen –"October twenty-third to sign the deal. If they haven't signed off on the contract by then, the whole thing's off."

Tom jotted the date down. "Why are we wasting our time on Mason Bank? If you want to buy a bank I can find half a dozen with better balance sheets. And less annoying lawyers."

Randall's smile disappeared. "It reminds me of my youth."

"Don't tell me that you're getting sentimental all of a sudden."

"Have I made a bad deal yet?"

"No," Tom admitted. "But this one isn't making sense to me."

"Just get it done," Randall said, as he turned back to his computer.

Tom recognized his cue to leave but he felt like probing Randall's mood. "How was your date on Friday?"

Randall ignored him.

"That bad?" Tom said in a saccharinely sympathetic tone. "Well, I'll leave you to brood over your lack of success with the lady."

"There's nothing to brood over. If anything, I was too successful."

Tom sat forward in his chair. "How can you be too successful?"

"We never made it to dinner."

"Incredible," Tom said, shaking his head in admiration. "You seduced her in the back of your car?"

"Why am I having this discussion with you?"

"Because this is as close as you get to a locker room bragging session, and we all need to brag about our sex life occasionally."

"If you have some more business to discuss, go ahead. Otherwise, this meeting is over."

Tom got up to go. "First, a sentimental attachment to a two-bit regional bank. Next, complaints about a woman who's too willing. I'm starting to worry about you; you must be getting soft."

There was nothing soft about Randall's expression, however, and Tom decided that retreat would be wise. As he passed Gail's desk, he bent down and whispered, "I wouldn't go in there for at least a half an hour."

By Friday, Kate's fragile optimism was fraying around the edges. No one had a part-time job for a civil engineer or even a draftsman, and she was getting desperate.

She had come to regard the ring of the telephone with the same enthusiasm as she would the rattle of a diamondback. She couldn't ignore it in case it was a job offer. But each time she picked up the receiver she braced herself to either be turned down by another engineering firm or, even worse, to hear Randall Johnson's drawl on the line. He had said he would call, and she was quite sure that he didn't make idle threats. Just thinking of her evening with him made her blush with shame. However, sometimes as she lay in bed on the edge of falling asleep, memories of the physical pleasures drifted through her mind.

She enjoyed those memories more than she wanted to admit.

That afternoon Clay and Patrick presented Kate with their first week's pay. Together, the three of them cleaned out a cookie jar, labeled it *Dog Dough* and stashed their earnings in it. They all agreed that whatever they hadn't spent at the end of the following week would be divided equally between the boys.

"I'm going to save up to buy a CAD-CAM program for the computer," Clay announced.

"I have one already," Kate said.

"Mom, that one's obsolete."

Kate winced. She had used that program for her consulting business. She hoped that Clay's comment didn't apply to her qualifications as well.

Patrick thought for a minute. "Can I put it in my savings account?" he asked.

"Well, sure," said Kate. "But isn't there something you'd like to buy with it? You've earned it, you know."

Patrick shook his head firmly. "I like to earn interest best," he said.

Kate rolled her eyes. "A budding J. P. Morgan."

"I'd rather be Bill Gates."

Kate laughed. "You'll be even richer than Bill Gates if you start saving your money at this age."

"Isn't Mr. Johnson rich, too? Clay says he owns a whole bunch of companies."

Kate looked at Clay, who shrugged. "I looked him up on the Internet. He owns an airline, an oil company and a bunch of other stuff."

"And a helicopter," Patrick added. "It showed a picture of him getting in it. Mom, it's a Bell JetRanger!"

"I imagine that it belongs to the company," Kate said in an attempt to quell his enthusiasm.

"Well, he owns the company, so he owns the helicopter, too," Patrick said with unassailable logic. "Maybe he'll give you a ride in it."

Kate shuddered; she hated to fly in anything. "I hope not. And you don't need to do any more research on Mr. Johnson. I won't be seeing him again."

Clay looked torn between sympathy and relief. "Bad date?" he asked.

"Just boring," Kate said. "Now what about a movie?"

Oliver had promised to come on Sunday for soccer practice and dinner. He arrived with a bouquet of flowers and a new soccer ball. Kate watched him rumple her sons' hair and listen to their loud and simultaneous descriptions of dog walking, winning Saturday's soccer game and acing tests in school. She thought what a heartwarming picture the three of them made: the tall, quiet man with two energetic boys orbiting around him.

Oliver looked up to catch her watching, and his slow smile lit up his face. Kate smiled back. He handed her the flowers with a small bow. "Congratulations on your unde-feated record in soccer," he said, giving her a kiss on the cheek.

"Thanks. I'm beginning to feel like a real coach. That *Soccer for Dummies* book really works."

The whole group moved into the kitchen where Kate filled her sons' water bottles and put her flowers in a vase before heading out to the backyard. Although Oliver and her sons could run rings around Kate, they always insisted that she participate in their Sunday afternoon scrimmages. When Kate pointed out that coaches were paid to supervise, all three males would look sad and beg her to even up the sides. Usually she agreed to play goalie since it required the least amount of ball-handling skill.

As the sunlight slanted lower across the yard, Kate decided that she had put in her time and she needed to start dinner. "This is the last shot on goal," she called. Oliver neatly passed to Patrick who gave the ball a hard kick to the corner of the goal. Kate threw herself at the ball and caught it just before it went by her.

"Way to go, Mom. Great hands!" Clay cheered.

Oliver gave her a male jock slap on the rear and said, "Great save."

Kate smacked his rear right back and said, "Thanks. You can play awhile longer."

She walked into the kitchen chuckling and heard the telephone ringing. Without thinking, she picked up the receiver. "Hello," she said as she opened the refrigerator door to get out the hamburger meat.

"Hello, Kate. This is Randall." As if that voice could belong to anyone else.

Kate straightened up abruptly and let the refrigerator door swing closed. She took a deep breath. "Hello, Randall. How are you?"

"Well, I'm standing here on my heated terrace with my shoes off, but I'm not having as much fun as the last time I did that. I was hoping you would come up here and join me."

Kate closed her eyes. She had a vision of Randall dressed as he was at the Princeton picnic, in blue jeans and a white shirt, but barefoot. She was suddenly overwhelmed with a longing to feel the warm skin and muscle under the

61

shirt and jeans. "No, no, I can't," Kate said, horrified at the obvious regret in her voice.

"Can't or won't?"

"Both."

"I understand. You have kids. So we'll have dinner on Saturday. I'll pick you up at seven."

"No, Randall. I'm not..."

Kate realized that she was talking to a dead telephone line. He had hung up.

"What an arrogant –" she said, slamming the phone onto its cradle. Then she sagged against the wall. She had intended to be polite but very firm in her refusal and instead she had sounded like a wimp. Randall Johnson was pushing her buttons and he knew it. She resolved to call him back, give him a piece of her mind and tell him never to call her again.

She'd do it on Monday.

Six

DINNER WAS OVER, and the boys had disappeared upstairs. Oliver and Kate had carried their wine out onto the porch to listen to the crickets and watch the moon. Kate remembered evenings when this scene had included David. Not long ago, the recollection would have made her smile through a haze of tears. Now she wanted to scream at David for ruining even her memories.

Kate dropped onto one end of the wicker porch swing as Oliver seated himself two feet away on the other end. She tucked her legs up under her, giving Oliver the job of keeping the swing going.

"I didn't know that you had decided to start dating," Oliver began. "Patrick told me that you went out to dinner last weekend. With a man who owns a helicopter."

Kate laughed without much humor. "That wasn't a date; it was a mistake."

"I'm not surprised. Randall Johnson isn't exactly in your league."

"Excuse me?" Kate said in a slightly frosty tone.

Oliver smiled as he said apologetically, "I didn't mean it that way. I meant that he has a certain reputation, which wouldn't appeal to you."

"What reputation is that?"

Oliver shrugged. "He's a womanizer. Here today, gone tomorrow. He attracts starlets and fashion models."

"All blond, according to Georgia," Kate added.

"Exactly. The very rich live by a different set of moral standards than you and I do."

Kate couldn't repress a bitter laugh. "Don't be so sure about that."

Oliver raised an eyebrow in silent inquiry.

Regretting her outburst, Kate stared into her wineglass for a moment. "It's not worth discussing."

Oliver looked as though he had more to say but he obligingly changed the subject. "The boys tell me they're walking dogs to make money."

"Yes. It was all their own idea, and I'm about to burst with pride."

"They also said you sold the Porsche."

"It's hard to keep a secret with the two town criers in residence," Kate said lightly.

Oliver reached over and took Kate's free hand. "Kate, are you in that much financial trouble? I don't want you to struggle. Let me help."

Kate let out a shaky breath as she gave Oliver's hand an affectionate squeeze. "I'm just trying to plan for the future. This old house is expensive to maintain, the boys' expenses are going to keep going up, I have to save for college tuition... the list goes on and on. The bottom line is that I have to go back to work."

"Clay and Patrick are still pretty young, Kate. You don't want them to be latchkey kids, do you?"

Kate pulled her hand away. Oliver was making her feel guilty so she snapped at him, "No, I don't, but sometimes one doesn't have a choice, does one? David didn't make any provision for his death, so I'm left to cope with the consequences."

"You seem angry with David." Oliver sounded shocked.

Yes, she was but she wasn't about to tell Oliver why.

"No, no. Just upset and a bit overwhelmed. I didn't expect to be in this position and I wasn't prepared for it," Kate said, sagging back into her corner. She mustered a weak smile. "I'm sorry. I don't want to leave Clay and Patrick alone either."

"I have no business commenting on your decisions," Oliver said with an apologetic touch on her hand.

"Sure you do. You're my friend and that's what friends do."

Oliver was silent for a while. His long legs were stretched out and crossed at the ankles, his knees folding and unfolding with the swing's motion. Kate couldn't help comparing his short straight nose and classic features to Randall Johnson's strong profile and slashing cheekbones. Kate shook her head to banish the image. Oliver was a very attractive man with clear blue eyes and a slow smile. He was considerate, caring – the exact opposite of Randall Johnson. He was also slightly dull.

Kate sighed and Oliver spoke at the same moment. "Have you considered marrying again?"

"You and Georgia!" Kate said in exasperation. "This is not the Dark Ages, you know. Women don't solve all their problems by getting married. Besides, I'm sure that my hypothetical husband would be just delighted to know that I married him so I didn't have to get a job."

65

Oliver laughed. "I'm not suggesting that you marry someone you don't care about in other ways."

Kate sighed again.

"I have to do some rebuilding first," she said.

"Rebuilding?"

"Of my soul, of my confidence, of something inside," she groped for the proper phrasing. "It's hard to explain."

Of course, she couldn't explain the real reason for the devastation of her sense of self.

Then it suddenly struck her. Oliver might have known about Sylvia. She winced just thinking of the woman's name. She looked at Oliver with new intent. He had been David's closest friend. Would David have told him about an affair?

Kate was pondering how she could find out, subtly, whether her husband had confessed his adultery when Oliver spoke again.

"You loved David very much, didn't you?"

"What?" Kate was startled by the question's odd relation to her own thoughts. "Yes, I did," she said truthfully. "But that's the past and I have to go forward now."

"I'm glad to hear you say that."

"I know. I'm supposed to be out of the mourning period after all this time."

"Not just because of that."

"Then why?" Kate asked, sipping her wine and looking at Oliver curiously.

He hesitated and then smiled at her. "Because it's hard to compete with a memory."

For a split second, Kate thought that Oliver meant that *he* was competing with David's memory. Then she realized she was reading too much into his comment.

She changed the subject. "I'm ready to sign the partnership sale papers whenever they're ready. I've been over the numbers and I can't make them come out any higher, no matter what I do."

"Don't you think I tried that already?" Oliver asked angrily.

"I was joking," Kate said, taken aback at his vehemence.

"I'm sorry. I just feel so terrible about this...."

"David would want us to do what's best for C/R/G," Kate said quickly.

After they had sat in silence for a while longer, she took his empty wineglass, carried it into the kitchen and began tidying up so that he could go upstairs to say good night to the boys. She was disconcerted when he came back into the room and drew her into his arms, holding her lightly against him. "Kate, think about what I said earlier. And remember to ask me if you need anything at all."

"Thank you. I will." Kate put a little distance between them. "Good night, Oliver. I'll talk to you when the papers are ready."

As she watched him pull out of the driveway, she was still considering the best way to approach him about David's affair.

Monday morning she braced herself and dialed Randall's work number. She got the same lovely female voice, which informed her that Mr. Johnson was out of the office for the day. Kate heaved a sigh of relief, and then said, "Please let him know that Kate Chilton will not be able to keep her engagement with him Saturday night."

"Ms. Chilton, I'm so glad that you called," his administrative assistant spoke as though to a long lost friend. "Mr.

Johnson asked me to give you his private telephone number."

"He did?" Kate squeaked, automatically picking up a pen and scribbling it down. "Thanks, but you'll give him my message, won't you?"

"Of course, Ms. Chilton. Good-bye."

Kate stood looking at the square of paper with the private number on it as though it contained hieroglyphics. She had to give him full marks for this maneuver. It was the most subtle but profound kind of flattery. And she wasn't immune to it. She stashed the paper in her cutlery drawer.

Resolutely putting Randall Johnson out of her mind, Kate immersed herself in the plans and design proposals of her former life. She was relieved at how quickly her brain started to follow the old paths. If only someone would hire her! She was actually looking forward to analyzing structural stresses and load-bearing points again. She even pulled out the set of blueprints of the George Washington Bridge that David had given her for her birthday years ago. Kate loved bridges and the GWB was her favorite. She traced its soaring piers and curving cables with familiar affection and admiration. She could still think like an engineer.

Clay and Patrick came home to find their mother engrossed by the computer. "What are you designing, Mom?" Clay wanted to know, looking over her shoulder.

"A new tunnel under the Hudson River," Kate said, as she clicked away with the mouse. "I'm tired of sitting in traffic when I go into New York City."

"Cool." The two boys settled down on either side of her, asking questions and offering suggestions. They would have worked right through dinner if Patrick's stomach hadn't rumbled. Kate wondered why she had never shared this part of her life with her sons before.

She was loading the dishwasher with dinner plates when Clay suddenly called her from the family room. "Mom, Mr. Johnson's company is on the news. His storage tanks are burning."

Kate dashed in to see a dramatic aerial view of flames shooting up against the night sky. The television screen was captioned *TexOil storage tanks, Elizabeth, NJ*. The camera cut to a reporter standing in front of an array of fire trucks. "Eyewitnesses say that the tanks seemed to literally explode into flames about a half an hour ago. Fire-fighting equipment is on the scene but a spokesperson states that all they can do is try to keep the nearby tanks from catching fire as well."

There was the unmistakable racket of a helicopter over-whelming the reporter's commentary. He stopped to watch it land behind the fire trucks and the view shifted back to the aerial shot.

"Do you think that was Mr. Johnson's helicopter?" Patrick asked without taking his eyes off the television.

Before Kate could answer, the screen shifted back to the reporter. "The helicopter you saw landing belongs to RJ Enterprises, the corporation which owns TexOil. It has been confirmed that CEO Randall Johnson was on board. Sources say that employees working in the control center of the storage facility are still unaccounted for. Although the fire does not threaten that area, there is a danger of smoke inhalation. Firefighters are mounting a rescue expedition."

Suddenly, Kate spotted him. "There he is, in the dark suit, talking with the fireman and another man in a suit. See him? By the ladder truck?"

"How many men did you get out of the control room?" Randall barked at the fire chief.

"Two. That's all that were in there."

"There should be four. Tom, was one of the two they found the foreman?" Randall asked, turning to Tom Rogan, who had arrived on the scene first.

"I don't know. They took them straight to the hospital."

"Damn! The other two must have gone for the manual shut-off valves behind Tank C." Randall turned back to the fire chief. "Give me a coat and five of your strongest men."

The fire chief didn't like taking orders, especially from a civilian. "You can't go in there."

"The hell I can't. Those are my people and my oil tanks." Randall grabbed a fireman's coat off the nearest fire truck and shrugged into it. "I know where the valves are and you don't. Get your men or I'm going in alone."

The chief cursed but called out several names. "Mr. CEO thinks he knows where the missing men are. Take care of him."

Randall addressed the firefighters, yelling over the noise of the blaze, "We're heading behind Tank C over there. We're going to close the valves feeding all the tanks and bring back my men. Let's go."

"Mom, I think that Mr. Johnson's going after the missing guys!" Patrick exclaimed in disbelief.

"The firemen are trained to rescue people. He should let them do their job," Kate said tartly. *What was he thinking? Those oil tanks could explode at any minute!*

"He'll be okay. He knows what he's doing," Clay said in a clear attempt to comfort her.

Kate gave him a strained smile and then exclaimed "Oh, for Pete's sake!" as the news program cut to a different story.

She looked at the clock and said, "Time to do your reading. Go upstairs. I'll call you if the oil tanks come back on."

Clay and Patrick grumbled and dragged their feet as they trudged upstairs.

Kate was amazed by the weight of her concern for Randall Johnson. She had wanted to scream at him to stop as he dashed into the flames. Evidently physical intimacy, even with a virtual stranger, created ties she hadn't been aware of.

Kate called the boys when the news was back to the aerial view of the fire. All three Chiltons were glued to the television as the camera cut back to the reporter standing on the ground. "Just moments ago, a team of firefighters returned from a rescue expedition carrying the two missing employees. The unconscious men were whisked away in the RJ Enterprises helicopter, presumably to a nearby hospital. Sources report that the tank feeds have been closed and that the fires will soon be under control. Right now it's still a spectacular sight as these flames leap hundreds of feet into the sky."

Kate had stopped listening as she searched the group of rescuers milling around behind the reporter. She watched two of them sit down on the side step of a fire truck with their elbows resting on their knees and their heads dropped forward. A medical worker rushed up to them but one lifted his head and waved him off. Kate let out her breath. "That's Mr. Johnson sitting on the fire truck," she said to the boys.

"He looks tired," Patrick said.

"I'm sure he's not used to rescuing people from burning oil tanks. It probably takes a lot out of you. Now upstairs and to bed."

Once they were settled, she pulled open the cutlery drawer.

The paper with Randall Johnson's private number on it lay just where she had put it earlier.

"Damn! How can I not call a man who just risked his life on television? He won't be there now so... so I won't have to talk to him. I'll just leave a polite message. That's the decent thing to do," she rationalized out loud, as she picked up the paper and punched the number into her telephone. She heard two rings and then the Texas drawl: "I can't take your call now. Leave a message after the beep." It was so typical of him not to identify himself on his answering service.

The phone beep sounded. "Hello, Randall. It's Kate Chilton. I saw your oil tanks burning on television. I just wanted to make sure that you were all right after your dash into the flames. I hope that everything is under control now. Good night."

The telephone rang. Kate propped herself up on her elbows and peered at the illuminated numbers on her clock: 3:45 A.M. Still half asleep, she picked up the receiver quickly before it could wake the boys. "Hello," she rasped, wondering if this was a wrong number or a crank call.

"Thanks for the message, Kate."

Her eyes flew open as she recognized Randall Johnson's voice. In the darkness, it seemed as though it was coming from the pillow beside her, and she found herself suddenly aware of every place where the sheets touched her skin. She clicked on the bedside lamp. "Are you all right? I saw you sitting on the fire engine, looking totally exhausted."

"I'm exhausted, I'm filthy and I smell like burning

petroleum, but I'm fine."

Kate could hear the fatigue in his voice. "You sound hoarse."

"I breathed in more smoke than I should have, but all I really need is a shower and some sleep. Will you come scrub my back for me? I'm too tired to do it myself."

Kate chuckled. "Now I know you're fine." Then she said seriously, "I'm so sorry about the damage. Is your loss very severe?"

His voice changed. "We'll do an assessment tomorrow but the facility is insured. I'm more interested in what caused the fire."

"I assume that it was an accident?"

"It takes a hell of an accident for two tanks to burst into flames at the same time."

"So you think that someone set the fires?" Kate was appalled.

She could almost hear Randall's shrug. "We'll find out tomorrow."

Kate felt that she had to mention the rescue effort, no matter how unnecessarily dangerous she thought that it had been. "Randall, the boys and I saw you go with the firefighters to rescue your men. That was pretty impressive. Are the men all right?"

"They're in the hospital now but the doctors say that they'll be okay. All I did was show the firemen where to find them."

"Well, it looked as though you were running straight into the flames. You scared the heck out of us."

A low chuckle rumbled through the telephone and vibrated against Kate's ear. "You sound more annoyed than impressed."

Kate suppressed the impulse to tell him how stupid she

thought he was to endanger his life and get in the way of professional firefighters. Instead she softened her tone and said, "You should go take that shower now and get some sleep. It sounds like you have a lot to do tomorrow."

"You're right. I appreciate the late night conversation. I needed to unwind. Oh, and I got your other message. Good night."

He hung up, leaving Kate literally open-mouthed as she began to explain why she had cancelled their date.

Pressing her lips back together, Kate dropped the phone onto the cradle.

She turned off the light and slid down onto her pillow. Every nerve ending in her body had started to hum the moment she had heard his voice. It wasn't really fair; he had awakened her from a sound sleep and all her defenses were down.

Randall Johnson's head fell back against the couch as he closed his eyes. He let his cell phone drop onto the cushion beside him. When he had heard Kate's slightly stiff but concerned voice among the messages waiting for him, he had felt a moment's ignoble triumph that she had used his private phone number, even after her attempt to ditch their date. Then the need to actually talk to her had hit him with the force of a sledgehammer. He knew that he had no business calling her in the middle of the night, but he had found himself dialing her number anyway. Her seductively sleepy voice distracted him from worries about arson and insurance claims and drew a response from his body that he thought would be impossible in his exhausted state.

He fell asleep while imagining what he would do with Kate Chilton in the giant Jacuzzi in his bathroom.

And he was smiling.

Seven

KATE PACED UP and down the sidelines of the soccer field. She couldn't figure out what they were doing wrong: the Claremont Comets were scoring fine, but the Oak Grove Asteroids were running rings around her defense.

"You look like a lady with a problem."

Kate froze. How could *Randall Johnson* be at her children's Saturday soccer game?

But here he was, all six-feet-plus of him, with his hands in the pockets of a black leather jacket he wore open over a black polo shirt and a pair of faded blue jeans. Certain parts of Kate's body began to tingle with the unwelcome memory of those hands.

"What on earth are you doing here?" she hissed.

Randall's quizzical smile widened into a grin.

"Hello, Kate," he drawled, all velvet and seduction. "I'm watching some fine soccer players. I could help you

75

out with your defense. Why don't we make it a wager: your team wins the game and you have dinner with me tonight. You lose and I eat alone."

Kate recalled that Georgia's summary of Randall Johnson's assets had included: "He was some kind of a soccer star at Princeton." She debated as she watched the Asteroids drive down the field again. When Patrick had to dive headfirst across the net to stop the shot on goal, she turned to Randall, held out her hand, and said, "It's a deal."

He gave her a firm but brief handshake. "How long until the halftime break?"

Kate checked her watch. "About two minutes."

"Okay. I'll talk to your players then," he said and focused his attention entirely on the game. Kate saw his eyes narrow as he scanned back and forth across the players, and she couldn't help smiling. He was bringing all the force of his brilliant business mind to bear on the problem of a boys' soccer game, of all things.

The referee whistled halftime and the Comets walked dispiritedly off the field to grab their water bottles and orange slices. Kate saw her sons look at Randall and then at each other, but she didn't have time to offer an explanation. She gathered her team around her and said, "Guys, this is Mr. Johnson. He was a soccer player at Princeton University, and he's going to give us some suggestions on defense."

Kate watched Randall squat down in front of her players. In three quick sentences he explained what the opposing team was doing. As he outlined a strategy to combat their opponents, Kate could see the light of comprehension dawning on all her boys' faces.

The whistle blew again and Kate sent her team out with words of encouragement and a renewed sense of hope. Sure enough, after a couple of minutes, her boys were stopping Oak Grove cold. She turned to Randall with a smile of genuine gratitude. "Thank you so much. You explained the strategy so clearly that I feel like an idiot for not figuring it out myself."

"You're not an idiot. It's a very unusual offense—and much too complicated for kids this age. You can see how easy it is to derail it, though," he said, gesturing to the field. "Their coach is obviously counting on playing against inexperienced coaches."

"Well, he certainly wasn't counting on having you around," Kate said. "Neither was I, obviously. I'm sorry for being rude."

"No apology necessary. I like a strong reaction. It means that you're paying attention."

"I wouldn't think you'd have to worry about that much," Kate said and smiled warmly again, before she turned back to the game. "Way to go, Ricky!" she yelled as the Comets scored a goal.

Randall couldn't take his eyes off Kate for a moment. That smile of hers... it had been warm and open, without wariness or calculation, and he felt like she had punched him in the gut. He briefly wondered if he needed to rethink his plans for the evening. Then a quick survey of Kate's snug blue jeans put his mind back on track. There was no need to make this complicated. He indulged himself by imagining snaking his hands up under her "coach" sweatshirt and feeling her nipples harden under the lace of her bra as he brushed his thumbs over them. He was mentally running his hands back down and under her jeans to cup those smooth curves when Kate yelled, "Subs, ref!" and turned to him.

77

His expression must have revealed the direction of his thoughts. He saw Kate's eyes widen.

"I was going to ask for your advice, but I don't think that you've been concentrating on the game," she said dryly.

Randall chuckled, "Just keep up the good work."

Kate forced herself to focus on rotating her players. Having Randall's leather-and-denim-clad body only an arm's length away was disturbing enough, but turning around to find him looking at her with focused lust was enough to drive her right over the edge. She had already noticed the curious glances and whispered comments among the soccer moms and dads standing on the sidelines.

She looked at Randall again. He lifted one eyebrow at her and turned to watch the game. Kate caught the smug smile on his lips. "We haven't won yet," she muttered under her breath.

The Comets tied up the game, and it was almost over. Kate put all her energy into cheering the boys on, and when the final whistle blew, the Comets were victorious by a goal. She went out to supervise the team handshake. Her boys gave a cheer for Oak Grove and waited a decent interval before erupting into exuberant leaps and high fives to celebrate their unexpected win. As they filed off the field, Kate saw Clay and Patrick head toward Randall.

Clay offered his hand and said, "Thanks for your help, Mr. Johnson."

Randall shook it and responded, "Nice work at midfield, young man."

Patrick came next and the rest of the team followed suit. Kate decided that he'd been paying more attention than she gave him credit for because he had an appropriate comment for each boy.

"Who's your new assistant coach?" Denise Costanza, a long-time friend and the mother of Clay's best buddy, Robert, asked in Kate's ear.

Kate sighed. "Randall Johnson. I'll introduce you."

"You sure will. If I wasn't a happily married woman, I'd be doing my best to cut you out right now."

"He's just an acquaintance."

"Honey, I saw him looking at you and he's got more than acquaintance intentions, even if you don't. If I were you, I'd take him up on them."

Kate made a rude noise to cover her blush, and then steered Denise over to Randall. She found herself introducing several more parents who thanked Randall for the victory. To add to her discomfort, one father greeted him without introduction, referring to some business dealings that they had had. Now she was positive that the gossip would fly. Randall walked with the team to the parking lot.

"Would you like to join us at Marzullo's for pizza?" Kate asked stiffly.

"I would, but I've got a conference call coming in this afternoon."

"On a Saturday?"

"Yes."

"Well... thank you again for wresting victory from the jaws of defeat. The boys and I really appreciate it." She mentally heaved a sigh of relief that he couldn't join them.

Randall leaned down to whisper by her ear, "I'm counting on your appreciation lasting until tonight. I always collect on wagers." He straightened and said in a normal tone, "I'll pick you up at seven."

His whisper had sent tiny ripples of sensation brushing across the surface of her skin. She frantically racked her brain to find some valid reason to back out of their agreement. He forestalled her by taking her chin in his hand and locking his gaze on hers. "I'm sure you're a woman of your word."

"You're a calculating, manipulative..." Kate sputtered to a stop.

"Son of a bitch?" Randall offered with a laugh. He flicked her cheek with his finger and walked away. As he opened the door of his car, he called, "See you tonight."

Kate stood with her hands on her hips as he roared off in his black Jeep. *Insufferable! ... Obnoxious! ...* Her thoughts were racing.

"Toad!" she spit out.

The Comets were the first team in the league to beat Oak Grove, and the team lunch was a jubilant affair. The boys verbally replayed the entire second half of the game over and over again. Randall Johnson's name came up repeatedly in the rehash. Kate managed to avoid discussing him with the other parents by keeping busy serving pizza and refilling Cokes. However, when she got home, she told the boys and Brigid that she needed to take a nap and fled to her room.

She fell backward onto her bed and flung her arm over her eyes. It was only human to be flattered that Randall Johnson had tracked down her sons' soccer game. She had to admit that. And she was impressed at how clearly he had explained the defense strategy to all of them. But he had made it clear that his motives were of the basest kind. And she wasn't at all sure that hers were much better. Why had she agreed to his ridiculous wager? Reluctantly, she got up and started to rifle through her closet.

Since she had no idea where he was taking her, she

settled on classics: a short black skirt and a salt-and-pepper tweed blazer over a moss green turtleneck. She laid the outfit on the bed and then stepped back and faced the final question: she knew his intentions for the evening. What were hers?

She went to her dresser to pull out the lace teddy and some black stockings to attach to the garters.

She was dressed when the doorbell rang.

"I'll get it, Mom," the boys called in unison, racing to the front hall.

Kate followed at a more sedate pace. Clay and Patrick were bombarding Randall with questions about his soccer career at Princeton. She stood back and gave him an appreciative once-over, admiring the understated quality of his charcoal slacks and silver-gray shirt under a black blazer that she suspected was cashmere. The muted colors were the perfect foil for his strong features and she was sure he was aware of it.

As she moved forward to say hello, she knew he was comparing her rather conservative attire with last week's ensemble. She gave him a cool look.

"Hello, Randall. Sorry about the cross-examination," she said, draping her arms lightly around Clay and Patrick's shoulders. She gave them a quick hug and dropped a kiss on the tops of their heads. "I'll see you two in the morning."

Patrick spoke up. "We still want you to show us how to nutmeg."

"*Nutmeg*?" Kate asked.

"You kick the ball between the defender's legs and pick it up behind him," Randall explained.

"Interesting name for it."

"Sometimes you kick too high."

"Those are two nice boys you have," Randall said, closing the front door for her.

Kate glowed at the compliment to her children. "Thank you. They seem to be turning out all right."

"It must be hard to be a single parent, particularly a mother of boys."

Amazed that he gave any thought at all to raising children, Kate hesitated a moment before answering honestly, "It is. I always worry about them needing a role model and having someone to talk with who can empathize rather than just sympathize. Fortunately, I have some good friends who are willing to help out."

"Well, you're doing a fine job."

Randall opened the door of the Jaguar that crouched gleaming in her driveway. Kate settled into the soft leather seat with a sigh of contentment, then ran an admiring fingertip over the burled wood of the dashboard. As he pulled out of the driveway, she took a deep breath and said, "I've been wondering how you knew about the soccer game."

He kept his eyes on the road. "Patrick told me."

Kate waited for more and when she realized that he was done, prodded him with, "When? Where?"

"On Friday. On the telephone."

"I keep telling him to write down messages if he's going to answer the phone!"

"I didn't leave a message."

"Oh." Kate wasn't through yet. "And why did you come to the game?"

Randall didn't answer immediately. He glanced sideways at her and poured the drawl on thick, "I'll let you figure that out, pretty lady." He reached one hand across the space between them and laced his fingers into her hair. The warm pad of his thumb circled slowly around the whorls of Kate's ear, exploring and declaring his intent as clearly as if he had spoken.

Torn between the desire to jerk away and the desire to lean into his hand, Kate sat stiffly even as her breathing quickened. Randall dropped his hand to navigate a sharp turn, and Kate's wandering attention focused on the fact that they were sweeping up the twisting road to Eagle's Nest. Her pulse jumped but she kept her voice calm. "I forgot to ask where we're having dinner."

"At my house. Don't worry, my housekeeper cooks like Julia Child."

Randall stopped the car in the enclosed courtyard and slid out of the driver's seat. Opening her door, he offered his hand and, as his fingers closed around hers, she felt the contact through her whole being. He pulled her upright and closed the door behind her.

"I've been waiting all day for this," he said and, before she could react, he pinned her back against the car and brought his mouth down on hers. In some distant corner of her mind, sanity and decency protested, but she too had been waiting for this, and Randall's lips felt like solid velvet against hers. When he worked his thumbs between their bodies to circle her breasts, the sensation streaked from her nipples directly down between her legs so fast that she couldn't stop herself from arching into him.

His hands shifted lower and came up under her skirt. As his warm palms slid up the backs of her thighs above the stockings to touch bare skin, he lifted his head to murmur, "Thank you," then continued his exploration upward, slipping his fingers under the lace teddy to cup her buttocks. Kate gasped against his mouth.

She frantically unbuttoned his shirt, pushing it farther open as each button came loose. Tracing the lines of muscle on his shoulders, she gave into the urge to taste him and put her lips against the triangle at the base of his throat, touching just the tip of her tongue to his skin. She inhaled his clean, male fragrance and felt, rather than heard, him groan with pleasure.

Then Kate stopped thinking about anything other than Randall's fingers coming between her thighs from behind and finding the most sensitive spot on her body, stroking it, gliding against it and up inside her. Kate felt her muscles begin to flood and tighten when Randall suddenly withdrew his hands. Ignoring her whimper of protest, he swept her up in his arms and carried her around to the front of the car.

She was briefly aware of warm metal beneath her and then Randall was between her thighs and inside her. He stretched her arms up over her head and held her wrists against the hood as he began to move against her, withdrawing almost completely before he drove himself back in. Kate found the bumper with her heels and opened herself to him fully, catching his rhythm with her own hips. Her climax hit so hard that only Randall's weight kept her from arching right off the car. The clench of her muscles triggered his orgasm and then they collapsed back on the Jaguar's sloping front.

Randall levered himself up onto his forearms to look down at Kate. "I think we've come up with a brilliant new ad campaign for Jaguar," he said, still breathing hard.

"Depends on whether you're on the top or the bottom."

Randall shifted and reversed their positions so that Kate found herself lying on top of him. "I'm willing to try it this way, too," he said.

"You couldn't possibly..."

"Not immediately."

Kate let her head drop onto his chest, enjoying the feel

of his arms loosely crossed over her back and his hard thigh cradled between her legs. She sighed with sheer physical well-being.

Randall's arms tightened around her and she lay there with his heart beating in one ear and the sounds of crickets and wind-rustled leaves in the other. Her eyelids drifted closed.

"Are you asleep?" Randall's voice, a mixture of amusement and incredulity, rumbled in her ear.

"Of course not," Kate said, dragging her consciousness back from the edge of oblivion. "I'm just very, very relaxed."

"Well, as much as I like this pose, a Jaguar's hood leaves something to be desired as a mattress."

Kate laughed and pushed herself to a standing position. Randall gave her a light kiss on the neck as he helped her straighten her clothes. "You just fulfilled a long-time fantasy of mine."

"You've been drooling over too many auto parts calendars."

Randall roared with laughter. "What do you know about auto parts calendars?"

"I've bought my share of alternators," Kate said, grateful to turn the subject away from what they had just done.

Randall put his arm around her shoulders and steered her up to and through the front door. "So you fix cars, as well as coach soccer?"

"No, I just got sent out for spare parts. David and the boys worked on the car."

Randall's arm dropped from her shoulders to the small of her back. "This way."

Kate preceded him into the big den with the view of

Manhattan.

"Let's see what Rosa cooked for us," he said.

"Is your housekeeper still here?" Kate asked in dismay.

"No, I gave her the night off. And I'll erase the videotape in the security camera."

Kate was horrified until she saw the evil glint in Randall's eye. "Wretched man."

"Actually, I think that I'll keep the videotape for a lonely night."

"There is no videotape," Kate said with more certainty than she felt.

Randall held up both hands at shoulder height in a gesture of humoring her, then said, "Wait here," and disappeared through another door.

She spotted the table set for two, positioned to take full advantage of the view. She smiled wryly at the vase of yellow roses. For Texas, she supposed.

A bottle of Merlot was open and breathing on the table. She decided that good manners would have to take a backseat to need. She filled the two glasses and took a gulp of hers as she stared out the window at the lights of New York City.

Her body was still tingling with the aftereffects of making love on the Jaguar. She envisioned sitting at this small table, locked into his dark gaze, listening to that Texas drawl and knowing what he felt like inside her. The tingling became a hum of longing. She should get out of here. Now.

Footsteps made her turn around. Randall was carrying a large tray, loaded with dishes. He slid it onto a serving table.

"We have duck cassoulet tonight, one of Rosa's specialties," he said as he lifted a lid and a most delicious aroma wafted past Kate's nostrils. "She says that it suffers less than most dishes from being left in the warming pan for hours."

Kate ignored her Pavlovian response to the smell of food.

"I'm sure that it's wonderful but I really think that it would be better if I went home now. I'm sorry to be an ungrateful guest," she added as Randall's eyebrows became straight, angry lines across his forehead.

He dropped the lid back on the plate with a clatter. "What is the problem with you, Kate? We have an incredible time on the hood of my car, and then when I try to be a gentleman and give you dinner, you turn and run."

The problem was that she didn't want him to be a gentleman. He was supposed to be an instrument of revenge, not a living, breathing human being.

She crossed her arms and looked at the fireplace, trying to formulate a plausible lie to get out of his house without further damage.

"Oh, no," Randall said, shaking his head as he came toward her. "I can see the wheels turning in that pretty head of yours. I don't want an excuse. I want you to look me in the eye and tell me the truth. Why do you want to leave now? In fact, go right back to the beginning and tell me why you called me in the first place."

By this time, Randall was so close that Kate was looking straight at his chest. She could feel his breath stirring her hair, but she refused to look up at his face. They stood like that for a moment as Kate's mind raced in circles. Then Randall put his hand under her chin and slowly exerted pressure upward.

"I said to look me in the eye and tell me the truth," he repeated. Kate reluctantly raised her eyes to meet his cold stare.

She didn't like being bullied and suddenly she was just as angry as he was.

"Truth is vastly overrated," she said, lifting her chin out of his grasp and turning her shoulder on him as she moved away.

Then she faced him squarely. "This particular truth is not flattering to either one of us."

"I can handle it."

Kate shrugged. As humiliating as it was to her, telling Randall why she had called him would undoubtedly cure him of any desire to spend more time in her company. Kate felt a momentary regret that he would have such a bad opinion of her forever. *Well, that can't be helped.*

"Shortly after I met you, I discovered that my husband had been having an affair prior to his death. I felt the need to retaliate in some way and you were my retaliation."

There was dead silence. Then, incredibly, the corners of Randall Johnson's mouth twitched upward. He started to chuckle and then he laughed outright. And kept on laughing.

"What is so funny?"

"I didn't think that anyone could surprise me anymore, but you've gone and done it."

He dropped onto the couch behind him, wiping his eyes. Then he stretched out his legs and put his arms behind his head. "So you were using me as payback. Too bad your husband's not around to know that."

Kate flinched. "Yes, well, I wasn't thinking clearly at the time."

"Is revenge sweet, Kate?"

"No, it was a terrible idea, and I'm not proud of it. But now you know the truth. We can shake hands and go our separate ways." Kate wished she felt happier at that prospect.

"I think you owe me."

"*What?* No. No more debts," Kate said. "I've paid the last one off."

"You don't need to rush away, Kate. We can work this out to both our advantage," he said, his drawl thick and slow. "I'll be happy to pick you up, bring you here, and... enjoy your company anytime you feel the need for revenge."

"I told you that you wouldn't like the truth."

"I'm willing to work with it."

"I thought that all men fantasized about enjoying a woman's company with no strings attached."

"We do."

"Well, that's what you got. So why are you angry?"

Randall gave a bark of laughter. "Sheer perversity, I guess."

Kate was on a roll and she wasn't ready to let it go at that. "No, that's not it. It's because *I* decided that *I* didn't want any ties to you. *You* didn't get to control the situation."

Randall's expression had been darkening throughout her speech. "I don't know where you get your ideas about me, lady, but they're way off base." He rubbed the back of his neck in a gesture of exasperation.

Kate crossed her arms and made a pretense of waiting patiently. Secretly, she was relieved that he hadn't exploded. Her temper rarely got the better of her, and when it did she was always terrified of the consequences. Fortunately, Randall's anger appeared to have fizzled into mere annoyance.

"Oh hell," he growled. "I'll take you home."

Kate flashed him a false smile and started toward the front door. In two strides, he was by her side with his hand resting at the small of her back. When she glanced sideways, though, she found that he was looking straight ahead. He helped her into the car and slid in himself in silence. As he put the car in gear and swept around the courtyard, Kate said in a tone of polite interest, "How's the investigation of the oil tank fire going?"

Randall looked at her and shook his head. "Incredible. We go straight from true confessions to small talk."

"There's no reason we can't be civilized about this."

"I'm just a country boy from Texas. I don't know how civilized people carry on."

Kate snorted.

Randall capitulated. "We caught the man. He's a former employee with a grudge against the crew foreman."

"So he'll go to jail?"

"No, he'll go for treatment. He's an alcoholic and he'd been on a bender when he set the fire."

"That's very humane of you."

Randall glanced over at her. "Don't feel that you have to revise your opinion of me. It should have been caught when he worked for TexOil. We pay for any substance abuse treatment. It was our mistake; somehow he slipped through the cracks."

"You sound more like a social worker than a capitalist."

Randall shrugged. "Obviously, unstable employees – and former employees – are bad for the company. And this man has a wife and children who deserve a break. My mother was an alcoholic, so I know what it can do to a family."

Kate was astonished by the personal revelation. She voiced a realization without thinking. "You know, I've never thought that you were a terrible person, or I couldn't have done what I did."

"Much obliged."

Kate flushed and kept quiet.

"What happened to being civilized? I was enjoying our conversation," Randall prodded.

"It's your turn to think of a topic."

"Hmm, what can we easily chat about?" Randall mused. "I know. What was your favorite locale: the terrace wall, my bed, or the Jaguar?"

Kate looked out her window and ignored him.

"You have to think about it?" he filled in for her. "Well, I know that mine was the Jaguar. There's nothing like a hot woman on the hood of a hot car."

Kate couldn't suppress a snicker. "You sound like an advertisement for a bad pornographic movie. You could call it 'Body Shop Babes.'" Her snicker turned into rib-wrenching laughter.

"I do my best to shock and provoke you and you laugh at me," Randall complained.

"I'm sorry," Kate gasped as she wiped her eyes. "I seem to be beyond shock these days." She lightly touched his arm. "You know, Randall, I really do want to thank you."

"All the women I make love to do."

"No, seriously. You've made me feel better, and I'm grateful."

"I'm not sure that I can return the compliment."

"I wish that we could have met under different circumstances," Kate said, looking down at her hands. "We might have liked each other."

Randall's lack of agreement was made plain by his silence. Kate noticed with relief that they were nearing her house. After the Jaguar glided to a stop in her driveway, she waited for Randall to come around and open her door. They walked up her front steps side by side without speaking. Kate pulled her key out of her pocketbook and said with a rueful smile, "It's been very interesting knowing you."

"Interesting is one way to describe it," he said. Then he slid his arms around her and pulled her firmly up against him. Kate involuntarily looked up and saw his eyes gleaming in the porch light just before he lowered his head to kiss her. Kate allowed herself to lean into him this one last time and by the time he was done, she almost hoped that he would suggest a visit to the backseat of the Jaguar. He knew it, too; he held her in one arm and, with an insolent smile, ran his other hand slowly and deliberately across her breast and down her hip. Kate shuddered as his fingers brushed along her inner thigh. Then suddenly, he released her.

"Sweet dreams, Coach," he said over his shoulder as he walked down the steps.

Eight

AS SOON AS she had worked the kinks out of her back the next morning, Kate stomped into the kitchen and pulled the scrap of paper with Randall's number on it out of the knife drawer. She found a particularly repulsive rotten banana peel in the kitchen garbage and shoved the paper firmly under it. Washing her hands, she felt a gray mist of depression swirl around her. She stared blankly out the window over the kitchen sink as the water poured unnoticed over her thoroughly rinsed fingers.

"Hey, Mom. Can we have French toast for breakfast?" Clay asked as he came down the back stairs into the kitchen.

Kate jumped, then turned off the water and smiled at her son. She wasn't meant for mountaintops and Jaguars. She was meant to fix French toast on Sunday mornings for the two most wonderful boys in the world. "Sure. Pour yourself a big glass of orange juice and one order of French toast will be up in a minute."

"Did you see the message I wrote down about Oliver coming today?" Clay said, pointing to the piece of paper on the counter.

Kate groaned inwardly. She had seen it last night and couldn't believe her bad luck that Oliver had called while she was out with Randall. "Yes. Thanks for writing it down."

"Unlike some people we know," Clay said, as he rolled his eyes upward toward Patrick's room. "Oliver couldn't believe that we beat Oak Grove! I told him about Mr. Johnson helping with the defense."

Kate groaned out loud this time.

"What's wrong? Was that a secret?"

"No, no. I was thinking about something I forgot to do," Kate lied shamelessly.

Clay hesitated. "Mom, did you know that Mr. Johnson was coming to our game?"

"No, he surprised me. But evidently your brother had some knowledge of it."

Clay snorted in brotherly disgust. "Patrick is a moron."

Kate let the insult slide, glad that her redirection of the conversation had worked. Clay did not mention Randall Johnson again.

Oliver arrived at two with steaks, a bottle of wine and sports magazines for the boys. After soccer and dinner, he joined her again on the porch swing. Kate tried to avoid the lecture she expected on Randall Johnson by bringing up business. "When do you think the partnership papers will be ready for me to sign?"

Oliver grimaced. "Who knows? Once you get lawyers involved, everything gets slower and more complicated."

Kate laughed. "I'll tell Georgia you said so."

"She'll sue me for slander," he said smiling. Then he blew out a breath. "Our lawyer drew up the papers – which he claims are very straightforward. But then Paul

Desmond's lawyer wanted to look at them. And of course he wants to change some clauses. It'll probably go back and forth another half a dozen times before the lawyers feel that they've collected enough billable hours for the whole thing."

"Paul Desmond is the new partner?"

"Yes. You'll have to come and meet him, Kate. He's bringing a very extensive client list with him. He'll be good for C/R/G."

They chatted for a while about the firm's future and then Oliver said abruptly, "I thought you weren't dating Randall Johnson."

"I'm not," Kate said, bracing herself.

"The boys seem to think you are. Clay told me that you were having dinner with him last night when I called. And that he came to their soccer game yesterday."

Kate looked down into her wineglass. "Yes, well, both of those things are true. But his appearance at the soccer game was a total surprise to me. And I won't be having dinner with him again."

"You said that last week."

Kate winced. "I did, didn't I? This time I mean it."

Oliver brought the swing's gentle rocking to a sudden halt. "Kate, you need to consider your position as the single mother of two young boys. When people see you with a man like Randall Johnson, they'll start to think the wrong thing. And the boys may hear about it. I know you well enough to know that you aren't that sort of woman, but other people might not."

For some reason, Kate felt obliged to defend Randall. "He's not as black as he's painted."

"He won't marry you. A man like that is interested in only one thing, and once he gets it, he'll forget your name."

Kate rolled her eyes at how wrong Oliver was. His persistence on the subject was beginning to irritate her. "I saw Randall Johnson twice—or three times, if you count the soccer game, which I don't. I don't have any expectations of him, and I don't plan to see him again. Now could we talk about something else?"

Oliver stood up and paced across the porch, leaving the swing vibrating under Kate. "I don't think you realize how people like Randall Johnson live. They don't care who they hurt in the process of pursuing their own gratification."

"Yes, well, at least he's not hurting a wife," Kate said bitterly as she took a gulp of wine.

Oliver must have caught the edge in her voice because he swung around to look at her closely. "What do you mean?"

Kate shrugged. "Just that he's had the sense not to get married since he wants to fool around." She looked Oliver straight in the eye. "Some men aren't that honest."

"What are you getting at?"

Using her anger to give her courage, Kate took the plunge. "What do you know about David and Sylvia?" She practically choked on the name. She waited, wondering if he really knew, and if he would try to protect David.

Oliver turned away and stared out over the yard. "You knew about Sylvia?"

Oliver knew.

"Not knew, know. I found out the hard way. Right after you came here to talk about taking on a new partner, I discovered a letter that she wrote to David. It wasn't a pleasant experience to learn that my deceased husband had been committing adultery shortly before his death."

Oliver glanced briefly at her, then looked away again. "No, I imagine that it wasn't." He suddenly came back to sit beside her on the swing, saying, "I'm so sorry you had to find out about it. But David had ended the relationship before he died. You must believe me about that."

"How long had he been sleeping with her? And who was she?"

Oliver's concerned expression vanished. "I don't think that you need to know the sordid details. David made a terrible mistake, but he realized it and stopped."

"I would hardly call knowing who my husband's mistress was and how long she had been his mistress *details*," Kate said. Softening her voice, she tried a different approach.

"You're my friend, Oliver. I need to know these things to help myself deal with this horrible blow to my whole concept of my married life. And you're the only person who can help me because the person I would normally ask is dead."

Oliver drummed his fingers on the swing's arm. "Why do you want to hear about David's infidelity? It can only hurt you."

"I'm already hurt to the very bottom of my soul," Kate said quietly. "And I can't start healing until I know what happened and why it happened."

"Christ, I don't know why it happened. I don't think that David knew why it happened."

"That's crap. David let it happen."

Oliver looked shocked. Then he changed tack.

"Now you know why I'm so disturbed by your involvement with Randall Johnson. I don't want to see you mixed up with another man who will not treat you well. You deserve better."

"I appreciate your concern. But you could demonstrate it more constructively by telling me what you know about

David's affair."

Oliver shook his head. "I'm sorry, Kate. I don't see what could be gained by bringing up old ghosts."

"Isn't that my decision to make?" Kate was furious at his patronizing assumption that he knew what was best for her.

Oliver shook his head again. "When you think about it calmly you'll be glad I didn't tell you."

Kate made a wordless sound of anger and frustration. She got up and walked across the porch, crossing her arms and leaning her hip on the railing.

"I got involved with Randall because I was angry with David." She paused for a moment and then took a deep breath. "In fact, I went to bed with Randall because I was angry with David. And he hasn't forgotten my name. Now would you like to tell me about Sylvia?"

Oliver's look of horrified disbelief would have been funny if Kate had been anywhere near a laughing mood. He said quietly, "How could you demean yourself that way?"

Kate felt a flush spreading up her neck to her face, but her sense of shame evaporated when Oliver stood up and strode over to her. His gray eyes had grown dark and his face was set in harsh lines. Putting his hands on the railing on either side of her hips, he leaned in close to her. "I love you, Kate. You're everything that I admire in a woman. But I wanted you to have time to mourn David. So, like a decent human being, I kept my feelings bottled up inside." Oliver pushed back and paced across the porch. "Now I find out that you've jumped into bed with a man who has nothing to recommend him but a pile of new money. It turns my stomach to think about it!"

Kate slumped against the railing and dragged in a shaky breath. "I had no idea..." Her voice quavered slightly. "I don't know quite what to say."

In two strides Oliver was again in front of her. Kate jumped when he brought his hands up but he just took her gently by the shoulders. "Say that you'll look at me as more than a friend. I never understood how David could be unfaithful to you. I told him what a fool he was, and I tried to protect you from knowing about his affair. When he died, I'm ashamed to say that once I got over the blow of losing my best friend, I was almost happy because now I had a clear chance with you."

Kate closed her eyes to block out the face that suddenly seemed like a stranger's. She felt her precariously balanced world tilting on its axis and struggled to stay calm. Steady, quiet Oliver had nurtured a hidden passion for her? He had helped David hide his affair from her? And he was upset by her fling with Randall Johnson?

She opened her eyes fast when she felt his lips touch hers gently, then insistently. Holding very still, she pressed her lips together and willed him to stop. But Oliver took his time exploring the curves of her mouth. When he finally drew back, he showed no sign of apology or embarrassment.

To forestall any further intimacy, Kate hurried into speech. "I need to think about this. I'm very fond of you but I need some time to consider you in this other way." She tried to smile. "It might be a good idea for you to go home now."

"Of course," Oliver said, as his hands slid down her arms. He grasped her hands in his and squeezed them gently. "I'll call you tomorrow. We'll go out for dinner and talk."

"That sounds fine," she said to placate him. She walked with him to the kitchen and put the counter between them as she said good night. Oliver hesitated a moment, then lifted his hand in farewell and let himself out the back door. Kate collapsed into a chair and, resting her elbows on the counter, rubbed her hands across her mouth.

"Hey, Mom, did Oliver leave already?" Clay asked as he came down the steps. "I wanted to show him something on the Internet."

Kate lifted her head and said, "He was in a hurry and didn't have a chance to say good-bye."

"That's weird." Clay looked at her curiously. "Are you okay?"

"Yes. Just a little tired."

Kate wrapped her arms around his waist and hugged him tight.

Clay gave her a quick squeeze back. Then she let him go because she knew that at his age being hugged by his mother – even in private – embarrassed him. "Why don't you show me whatever it is on the Internet?" she suggested.

"Sure." Clay launched into an explanation as she followed him up the stairs, leaving her problems with Oliver firmly behind in the kitchen.

Once the boys were in bed, Kate poured herself a glass of wine, closed the door to the family room and dialed Georgia's telephone number.

"Hey, Kate. How are you?"

"Crazed. Off balance. Thrown for a loop."

"Whoa, girl. You didn't find another letter to David from some other woman?"

Kate snorted. "I wish. This has to do with the living. You're not going to believe this but Oliver Russell just told me that he loves me."

"I wondered when he would get around to that. He

hangs around your family way too much for a normal single man."

"He was David's friend," Kate insisted. "He likes all of us."

"I think that he likes the whole idea of your family; you all are so picture perfect."

"You make us sound like the Brady Bunch."

"If the shoe fits..."

"Why didn't you warn me?" Kate collapsed in her chair. "I feel like I'm at some weird costume party. Now it's midnight and everybody is ripping off their masks and the faces underneath are scarier than the masks. You'll probably turn out to be the twin sister who was separated from me at birth."

"Wasn't that in the last episode of *Days of Our Lives*?"

"Great, my life's become a soap opera. You know the worst part of all this? I don't trust my own judgment anymore. I'm afraid to do anything, to decide anything because I've been so completely wrong about my life."

"Don't let other people's betrayals change the way you think. It's not a bad thing to assume the best about the people you love."

Kate choked on a laugh. "Even when I assume the worst about someone, I'm wrong."

"What do you mean?"

Kate realized that she had gotten herself tangled up in the web of her own lies. Kate explained the soccer game bet and glossed over the rest of the evening.

Georgia whistled. "It looks like Johnson is in hot pursuit. I'm jealous but I have to warn you about this one: you're playing with fire."

Kate sighed. She knew it all too well. "It's just an ego problem. I'm supposed to fall at his feet instead of refusing his invitations."

"Listen, this is way too complicated to discuss on the telephone. The soonest I can get over there is Wednesday night. We'll have a nice long talk. Do you think that you can fend off your two lovers until then?"

Nine

THE BOYS WERE at school. The weekend's laundry was on the heavy-duty cycle in the washing machine. Kate poured another cup of coffee, pulled on a light jacket and walked out onto the porch with Gretchen at her heels. The cheerful sunlight streaming through the brilliantly colored leaves that framed her porch made the scene with Oliver the previous night seem like an insubstantial nightmare.

Kate sipped her coffee and reached down to pat the dog. "So where do I stand now, Gretchen? I don't have a job. I'm running out of money. My husband was unfaithful. I'm keeping secrets from my best friend, and Oliver has turned into Mr. Hyde. My attempt at a one-night stand was a disaster. All I need now is to find out that Clay and Patrick are drug dealers."

She sank down on the porch floor, wrapped her arms around Gretchen's warm, furry neck and sobbed into her shoulder. "I built my life so carefully. Why is it all falling apart?" The dog sat patiently as Kate cried.

At last, she ran out of tears. Gretchen nosed her face in mute concern, and she took a deep breath.

"You're right, Gretch. If my life has fallen to pieces, it's up to me to rebuild it. Only this time, with myself as the foundation."

She pushed herself up from the wooden planks, dusted off her jeans and went back to the kitchen to dump out her cold coffee. As she was rinsing the cup, the telephone rang.

"Kate? This is Susan Chen from Adler Associates Engineering. I used to work with Phil Gabelli."

"Of course, Susan. What a pleasure to hear from you!"

Kate had worked for Phil Gabelli herself for two years and had sent him her resume in the hope that he might have a position for her. He had been unable to hire her, but had promised to see if he could find someone else who might be able to. Kate sent a silent prayer of thanks his way as Susan continued.

"Phil forwarded your resume to me with a strong recommendation. Right now, we need a creative solution for a particular project, and we need it quickly."

"Oh?" Kate made her interest clear.

Susan laughed. "It's a bridge on a heavily used commuter highway in Connecticut. The bridge isn't such a problem, but the design has to include a viable rerouting of traffic while it's under construction. Someone has to go up and scout the location, then come back with suggestions. It's a demanding project, but the firm would like to get in with the Connecticut highway people; they've got a lot more work coming up."

"It sounds like a full-time position," Kate said.

"If we get the job, it is. More than full-time."

Kate hesitated. A full-time job. Maybe she should consult Clay and Patrick first? It would be a big change for them. But this sounded so wonderful...

"Susan, I'm very intrigued. Could I come in and talk

with you about it?"

"How about tomorrow at lunchtime? That's the only time I'm free, believe it or not."

"I'll be there."

Kate hung up and blew out a breath. To build a bridge! Her all-time hero was Othmar Ammann, the designer of the George Washington Bridge. She danced a little jig around the kitchen table. Then she stopped dead. What did she know about traffic flow? How out-of-date were her design skills? And there was the prospect of leaving Clay and Patrick alone for the hours after school. How would she cook them dinner and supervise their homework?

"What am I thinking? I can't do this..."

Gretchen's tail thumped on the floor.

"You have confidence in me?" Kate asked her.

Gretchen's tail thumped harder.

"You're right. We'll cross each bridge as we come to it – or in this case – we'll build each bridge as we come to it."

Kate waited until the boys tossed down their backpacks and rummaged through the refrigerator for snacks. Then she said, "I've had a job offer."

"That's terrific, Mom!" Patrick said around a mouthful of bagel and cream cheese. "What are you going to build?"

"Hopefully, a bridge."

Clay chimed in. "That's perfect! You've always wanted to build a bridge."

Kate was warmed by their enthusiasm. "It sounds very interesting, but there's a big problem with this job. It's full-time and then some, if I get it."

Clay and Patrick were quiet for a minute. Then Patrick said hopefully, "So we'll be having more pizza for dinner?"

"Probably," Kate said.

"Cool!"

"You'll get tired of it," Kate warned. Patrick looked unconvinced but left it at that. Kate took a deep breath. She had debated how frank she should be with her children. But she realized that they were growing up. They should be able to participate in the decision fully informed.

"Here's the bottom line. I've worked out some numbers, and if I work full-time, and we don't have Brigid come in the afternoon, we can continue to live here about the same way we do now. If I can find a part-time job, we might or might not be able to stay here, but we would definitely have to spend less money on everything. And if I don't find any job, we will have to move to a smaller house, possibly just to rent. And we'll have to make some serious choices about spending money."

Kate paused a moment to let them absorb what she had said. "I don't know what the right answer is. We all need to think about it. However, I have to point out that part-time engineering jobs seem to be few and far between, so that option may not be a real one."

Clay said with complete conviction, "I think that you should go for the full-time job, Mom. You can trust me to be responsible for myself and Patrick in the afternoon."

The boys looked at each other for a long moment and then Patrick gave a slight nod. Clay continued, "We want to stay here and we want you to build a bridge."

"I know that I can trust both of you." Kate surreptitiously touched the wooden cabinet twice with her knuckles. "I just want to be sure that you two are happy and comfortable."

"I promise to start my homework as soon as I get back from dog-walking," Patrick said.

"And learn to write down phone messages," Clay

added.

Patrick socked Clay in the arm. In his new role of mature elder brother, Clay rolled his eyes but refrained from retaliating.

"You guys are the greatest," Kate said, walking between them to give them both a quick squeeze around the shoulders. "I'm meeting with Susan Chen tomorrow to talk about the job. That gives you another twenty-four hours to think about this. It's not too late to change your minds."

"We're too old for Brigid to watch us anymore, anyway," Clay said, then added firmly, "Mom, we can handle it."

"I'm sure you can. I'm just not sure that *I* can," Kate said.

The next afternoon she came home with a map and a job offer, both of which she contemplated with numerous misgivings.

Susan was willing to hire her on the strength of Phil Gabelli's verbal recommendation, even though Kate hadn't worked with him in over fourteen years. Kate wasn't sure Susan trusted Phil *that* much. Her instincts during the interview told her that the job was such a long shot that Adler Associates didn't really expect to win the contract.

Clay and Patrick burst in the door. "Did you get the job?" they asked almost simultaneously.

"Yes, if the firm gets the contract," Kate said.

"Way to go, Mom!"

"Yahoo!"

They both gave her high fives and then Clay surprised her by hugging her. "Don't worry about us. You concentrate on the bridge."

Kate hugged him back. "Thanks, buddy. Tomorrow I

go up to inspect the site. So tonight while you're doing your homework, I'll be doing mine."

Kate stood by the highway inhaling exhaust fumes and shielding her eyes from dirt thrown by cars whizzing past her. She had already driven every possible alternate route and eliminated each one. Her shoulders sagging, she walked down the hill to the old bridge to look at the site from a different angle.

Now she really understood why this project was not popular. The bridge was in a valley cut by the river. Houses lined the riverbank right up to the right-of-way. Three lanes of traffic streamed steadily across the bridge in each direction. There was no room to build the new bridge beside the old one. There was no viable detour. Because of its location, using prefabricated components was going to be hard because there was no place to store them. They would have to be trucked in as they were needed. So much for speedy construction.

Stymied, she suddenly recalled the words of her first engineering professor: "Ladies and gentlemen, we are doing engineering, not oil painting. *Think in three dimensions!*"

Kate looked at the bridge again, and saw the new bridge over it. It would be longer and therefore more expensive, but traffic could continue to use the old bridge until the last possible moment! She could also justify the expense by pointing out that flooding would not be a problem if the new bridge were higher!

She felt a rush of exhilaration.

Flipping to a clean page on her drafting pad, she began to sketch the site and her ideas. She scrambled up and down the riverbank, noting where the new pylons would go, listing survey points, and estimating distances. She bit her lip in frustration when she checked her watch: she needed to get home to take Clay and Patrick to a chess tournament. As she trudged back to her car, she realized that this was just the beginning of the tug-of-war between home and work.

And it was only going to get worse.

Bringing an unconventional design in on your first day at the office was risky, and Kate packed her briefcase the next morning with some trepidation. Of course, Susan Chen was looking for an unusual solution, but still...

Kate had to stop a moment to compose herself before walking into Susan's office.

When she finished, Susan was silent for a long moment.

"I wish I had thought of this," she finally said. "We were spinning our wheels looking for detours or space to put up temporary reroutes, and the space was there all along, right *over* our eyes." Susan gathered up the copies of Kate's drawings and stood up. "Phil told me you would deliver."

Kate sighed in relief and felt a small glow of pride. "I have a lot more work to do, obviously, but I'm glad that you like the concept."

"I'm going to run it by Bruce Adler right now, but I'm sure that he'll green light it. In the meantime, make yourself comfortable here. If you want to take a look at our design program, feel free to use my computer."

Within a half an hour, Susan was back. "Bruce says to go forward with the drawings and specs. He'll meet with us in two days to review the plans. Let me show you your new desk!"

She led Kate to a cubicle that held a computer, a

calculator, a drafting table, flat files for blueprints and drawers filled with angles, scales and T squares. Kate hung up her coat, made a mental note to bring in some family photos and was soon immersed in the nuts and bolts of designing a Connecticut state highway bridge. Time flew by and she had to race out of the office to catch her train.

Kate had grabbed take-out Chinese food on her way home from the station in honor of Georgia's visit. Clay and Patrick were delighted but Georgia made a face. "This is what I always eat," she complained. "I forgot that you're a working woman now, so I won't get any more home-cooked meals here."

"Are you trying to make me feel guiltier than I already do?"

Georgia sighed dramatically. "No, I just miss that scrumptious French onion soup and your fabulous beef stroganoff."

"I haven't made beef stroganoff in years. No one liked it."

"Well, there is the Chocolate Orgasm Cake."

Kate laughed. "You wouldn't eat that because it was too fattening."

"So, how's the job going?" Georgia asked, as they all dug into fried dumplings and moo shu chicken.

"Great!" Kate said and described her design and her cubicle for everyone's benefit.

"And how are you guys doing without Mom?" Georgia asked Clay and Patrick.

"No problem at all," Clay said breezily.

"We can handle it," Patrick affirmed. "We're already paying for our own lunches by walking dogs. It's fun except for Mrs. Handley's German shepherd. He doesn't like to be on a leash."

"Maybe you should find a different dog to walk," Georgia suggested.

"No, Mrs. Handley pays the most," Patrick said. "Because she knows that he's a pain."

"We don't need money so much that you two have to walk a difficult dog," Kate said, between bites.

"Mom, it's cool," Clay said with a glare at Patrick.

Kate let the subject drop.

After the boys retreated upstairs to do homework, Kate and Georgia settled in the living room. "Maybe I'm telling them too much about our financial situation," Kate worried. "I don't want them to feel pressure to take jobs just because they pay well."

"Kate, they are incredibly well-grounded children. And they know that if they have a real problem, they can tell you. Let them deal with it themselves," Georgia said. "I think they like their new responsibilities."

"Now you're trying to make me feel better."

"No, I mean it. Let them stretch themselves a bit. They're ready for it."

"I hope you're right."

"I'm a lawyer so I'm always right, until proven wrong. But let's talk about your other problems. Have you heard from Oliver?"

"Sort of. I've gotten two phone messages from him. Fortunately, I was working so I didn't have to talk with him. But I'll have to call him back soon."

"Is there any chance that you might reciprocate his feelings?"

"No," Kate said flatly. "It makes me sad, because I've lost a good friend and I need all the friends I can find right now. But I can't count on him anymore."

"You can count on me," Georgia said.

"That thought keeps me sane," Kate said, saluting her friend with her wineglass.

"Speaking of men and friendship, I thought this might entertain you," Georgia said, getting up to pull two sheets of folded paper out of her suit jacket pocket.

Kate flipped open the papers to a color photograph of Randall Johnson looking straight at the camera. She had to stifle a gasp. "Where did you get this?" she asked, glancing at Georgia to get away from those demanding eyes.

"By a little illicit use of a database we have for doing background checks on people we might be dealing with in court."

The photo was followed by a list of Randall's business holdings. "The man owns everything except the Brooklyn Bridge," Kate said scanning down the page. "And that might be part of Johnson Real Estate, Limited."

"He's impressive," Georgia agreed. "But check out the biographical information on the second page. Not that there's much of it."

Kate switched pages.

Born: Mason County, Texas.

Father: Deputy Sheriff, deceased. Shot and killed during gas station robbery while off-duty, age 44.

Mother: Assistant store manager, deceased. Known alcoholic, chain smoker. Died of lung cancer, age 46.

Siblings: Five.

Without looking up, Kate said, "Sounds like he had a

rough family life. He told me that his mother was an alcoholic, and he knew what it could do to a family."

Education: B.A., Princeton University, economics. Full scholarship with work/study. Completed degree in six years. M.B.A., Columbia University.

"I guess he has to be smart to be a CEO," Kate muttered. "Wonder why it took him six years to finish Princeton."

Marital status: Single.

Sexual orientation: Heterosexual.

"Someone researches people's *sexual* orientation?"
Georgia shrugged. "Knowledge is power."
"Well, I could have saved you the trouble," Kate said without thinking, as she skimmed through categories such as drug use, psychiatric treatment, gambling and gun licenses, all of which stated unequivocally *none*.
Noticing her friend's uncharacteristic silence, Kate lowered the papers. Georgia was watching her over the rim of her wineglass.
"What?" Kate said.
"You told me that your date with Randall Johnson was boring. You also said that you didn't get along. But he told you about his mother, and now you're willing to vouch for his sexual preference. Something doesn't fit here."
Kate groaned and tossed the papers on the coffee table. Slumping in her chair, she locked her eyes on the ceiling light fixture as she confessed, "I didn't just have dinner with Randall Johnson. In fact, I didn't have dinner at all.

We, um, were intimate."

Silence reigned again for several long seconds and then Georgia recovered her powers of speech. "You had *sex* with *Randall Johnson*?"

Kate winced at Georgia's phrasing, but she nodded.

"Two Saturdays ago?"

Kate nodded again.

Georgia stood up and walked over to look down at Kate's face. Evidently, she saw something there that made her ask, "And last Saturday?"

"Yes," Kate said, finally looking at her friend. "I'm not proud of what I did, but I wasn't thinking clearly. It's history."

Georgia stared at the fireplace. "Kate, I wouldn't ordinarily begrudge you some well-deserved fun, but messing around with Randall Johnson just isn't a good idea."

"I know, I know."

"He's very sexy, and brilliant in business, but he isn't interested in relationships..." She picked up the database printout and ripped it into pieces. "This is my fault! I should never have introduced you."

Kate was touched and amused by Georgia's sudden fit of protectiveness. "I'm a grown-up. I knew what I was doing."

Shaking her head, Georgia said, "Not with this man. Did you read that bio? He came from worse than nothing and built an empire. You don't do that by being a nice guy."

"Don't *worry*. I'm done with Randall Johnson."

Ten

THE COMETS WERE running "give-and-go's" when Kate spotted Oliver's tall figure sauntering across the soccer field. She turned her back on him and started the team on a complicated drill. Despite her body language, Oliver walked right up to her and kissed her on the temple.

"Hello, gorgeous."

"Oliver's here!" Patrick shouted and raced over to punch him on the arm before returning to the drill. Clay raised a hand and said, "Hey."

Oliver nodded back.

The referee blew the starting whistle.

Oliver kept his gaze on the game as he said, "I tried to call you to apologize for Sunday."

"This isn't really a good place to talk."

"I can't apologize to your answering machine."

"I'm sorry," Kate said uncomfortably. "I've been so busy with work. I've got an engineering job in the city now. I'm still adjusting to the new schedule –"

"I found that out from Patrick."

Oliver sounded both hurt and annoyed.

"It came up very suddenly – way to go, Robert!" she yelled as the ball flew past the opponent's goalie. Deciding to face the inevitable sooner rather than later, she said, "Why don't you come over to the house after I take the team for pizza? We have things to talk about."

Oliver's eyebrows rose. "I don't rate an invitation to the pizza party?"

"Of course you're invited. I just know your opinion of Marzullo's pizza."

"If the Comets win today, I'll choke down two slices."

The Comets won 2-1. As the parents and boys milled around collecting water bottles and sweatshirts, Denise Costanza followed Kate to the far side of the field to gather up flags and cones. "I see that Oliver is staking out his territory now," Denise said as she bent down to pick up a red marker.

"What do you mean?" Kate took the cone from her and added it to the stack.

"I don't think it's a coincidence that the week after Randall Johnson comes to a soccer game, Oliver suddenly shows up. He hasn't been here in months. Not only that, but he hovered over you the whole time." She handed Kate two more cones.

Kate yanked a flag out of the ground with unusual force. "Did it really look that way?"

Denise relented slightly. "It wasn't that bad. I imagine that most people figured he was here as the proverbial family friend."

"You didn't."

"Yes, but I'm particularly observant." Realizing that Kate was genuinely distressed, Denise stopped picking up cones. "It's been over a year since David died. You're allowed to start dating again."

Kate sighed. "I don't want to start dating again. And I hate being pushed."

As Denise started to apologize, Kate said, "Oh, I don't mean by *you*, I mean by Oliver and Randall."

"Well, it ought to be real interesting when they both show up at the same soccer game," Denise replied. Seeing Kate's expression, she added, "Don't worry, I'll run interference for you. Just assign me Randall."

Kate forced a smile and grabbed another cone.

"Kate, I'm very sorry for the way I behaved last Sunday."

This was the conversation she didn't want to have. She had lingered with the team over pizza as long as she could. Now they were home on the porch, the boys were upstairs, and she had no choice but to hear Oliver out.

She started to say something politely soothing, but Oliver raised his hand to stop her.

"My only defense is that I was shocked and disappointed. I had hoped that when you began to think of another relationship, you would think of me." He produced a rueful smile.

"It was my fault," Kate said. "I was *trying* to shock you. I just didn't get quite the reaction I expected."

Oliver winced. "I reconsidered your questions about Sylvia. I'll answer them if you still want to know about her."

Kate was stunned into silence. She supposed that this was a peace offering – or a bribe – if one were cynical. Suddenly, she wasn't sure that she did want to know... Maybe it was better to keep the images vague and fuzzy.

Oliver noticed her hesitation. "I can't tell you all that

117

much. But you have a right to know what I know."

She couldn't go on being the only person in the dark about her husband's secret life. "Who was she? How did they meet?"

Oliver sighed and stared at the ceiling as he said, "Sylvia Dupont. She was the interior designer on the DePaolo house in Baltimore. She's one of those high society designers, very connected, doesn't need the money. The DePaolos insisted on hiring her. David wasn't happy about that since he'd never worked with her before and the house was an important commission."

"Evidently, she won him over. How long did it take him to go to bed with her?"

Oliver sat down on the swing and leaned his elbows on his knees, keeping his eyes on his hands. "I don't really know. David said that she went after him in a big way. I think that their affair lasted about six months."

Kate rocked back in her chair. *Six months.* Her husband had been making love to another woman for six months, and she had been totally unaware of it. He had been in Baltimore often during that time but when he came home, he had been as enthusiastic about their physical relationship as ever. Kate shivered as she wondered if David had come from Sylvia's bed to hers.

"He broke it off," Oliver continued. "I think that Sylvia tried to get him back for a while afterward."

"Where did they do it? In a hotel? At her house?"

"Christ, I don't know!" Then he softened his tone. "Why are you doing this?"

"Because I'm trying to understand why the man I loved and trusted betrayed me. And why I had no idea that he was betraying me. Did he do it for the thrill of leading a double life? Was Sylvia unbelievable in bed? What does she look like?" Kate asked, leaning forward.

"I've only met her once. She's pretty: blond, tall, slim, well-dressed. She looks like what she is."

"So she's spectacular."

Oliver came over to Kate's chair and knelt beside her. "Kate, stop. It's not worth it. David did a stupid thing, a terrible thing, but he loved you. I know that."

Kate felt tears welling up and she blinked furiously. "It's a strange kind of love that lets you cheat on your wife."

Suddenly she was sobbing as pain and confusion swept over her. Oliver drew her up from the chair and put his arms around her, cradling her against his chest. In some small corner of her mind, Kate knew that she shouldn't allow him to do this. But his comfort lessened the frightening sense of being alone. She cried until she was exhausted. The moment she started to straighten, Oliver let her go, digging in his pocket to find her a package of Kleenex. Kate accepted the package with a watery smile. "I've already used your shirt as a handkerchief."

Oliver pulled the wet fabric away from his chest. "Luckily, I wore the extra-absorbent one today."

"Excuse me for a minute. I'm going to go throw cold water on my face." Kate escaped to the bathroom.

"You're an idiot," she told her reflection as she turned on the taps. "Now Oliver has every right to think you were encouraging him." Kate washed her face and then blotted it with the towel. "Well, let's go see how much damage you've done."

When she emerged from the bathroom, Oliver was standing in the kitchen. "You probably want some time alone, but my shoulder is here for you to cry on anytime you need it."

"Thank you," she said as he opened the back door.

She couldn't see the satisfied smile that spread over Oliver's face as he drove away.

Randall Johnson slapped the folder he was reading shut. He couldn't keep his attention on the numbers parading across the pages. Swiveling his big leather chair around, he rifled through the pile of newspapers and business magazines stacked on his credenza without finding anything to interest him. He got out of the chair and went to the minibar hidden behind a mahogany panel. Grabbing a bottle of mineral water, he walked over to his wall of windows.

As soon as he let his mind wander, it instantly gravitated to Kate Chilton.

He remembered lowering her onto the hood of his car and pushing up her skirt so that he could see the thigh-high stockings she wore. Damn, he loved those stockings! He recalled the feel of her under him. Then he quickly cut off that train of thought as he felt himself growing hard and mentally doused himself in cold water by recalling her brittle tone as she told him she was using him for a bizarre form of revenge.

He felt his anger surge again. Why did this particular woman rile him so much? Even though he had denied it, he wasn't generally averse to good sex with no strings attached. In fact, more and more, he preferred it that way.

Randall tilted the water bottle to his lips and stared out the window. Maybe it *was* an ego problem: he *had* expected to control the encounter.

He shook his head.

No, he had had higher expectations of Kate, *that* was it. There was a fineness about her that attracted him. He wanted to fence with her verbally, not just sexually. He wanted to teach her boys to nutmeg. He wanted to... He scowled and knocked back the rest of the water just as Tom Rogan walked into his office.

"The Mason people are promising a final contract by Friday so your trip is on as scheduled," Tom said, seating himself on the couch.

Randall grunted an acknowledgment.

"Are you planning to stroll down Memory Lane while you're in Texas?" Tom asked.

"I'm planning to *repave* Memory Lane."

"So you're going in with guns blazing."

"Guns are more Gill's style than mine. Money is my weapon—and it's just as lethal."

"I didn't mean that literally," Tom said, looking worried.

Seeing papers dangling from his VP's fingers, Randall changed the subject. "Do you need me to sign those?"

Tom flipped the papers up and looked at them as though he had forgotten what they were. "These? No, but I thought that they might interest you on a deeply personal level."

"What the hell is that supposed to mean?" Randall said, as he yanked the papers from Tom's hand. The top sheet was a note on an engineering firm's letterhead. The bottom sheet was Kate's resume. He went back to the letter and started reading.

> *Dear Tom,*
>
> *I'm forwarding this resume to you because I highly recommend Kate Chilton as an engineer and as an employee. I'd hire her*

myself if I had a position worthy of her talents. I'm hoping that you might be able to find her a place somewhere in RJ Enterprises. Give me a call and we'll talk.

Regards, Phillip Gabelli

"When did you get this?" Randall barked.

"This morning."

"Have you called Phil Gabelli?"

"No, I thought that you might prefer to do it."

Randall scanned the resume, noting that Kate's credentials were quite impressive.

"She looks like she'd make a great addition to the company. Just think of how much more interesting meetings would be. You could use this couch or the conference table or..." Tom stopped abruptly as Randall's expression hardened.

"Kate Chilton is off-limits as of now," he said flatly.

Tom nodded. "Understood." He made a quick and silent exit.

A minute later, Randall returned to his desk and flipped through his computer Rolodex, sending a telephone number to the auto-dialer.

"Hello, is Frank Peltier there? It's Randall Johnson. Hey, Frank! How are things out in the back of nowhere?... Yeah, I'll come out and see your place – the next time my plane runs out of gas. Do you know a firm called C/R/G in New York? They lost a partner about a year ago and I'm curious about the business. What's the status of the partnership, how's their financial position, that sort of thing... Yeah, I might go into competition with you... Thanks, I appreciate your help and your discretion. And

Frank, the radiant heat under the back terrace was a real good idea."

He hesitated a minute, then clicked another number into the auto-dialer. "Phil Gabelli, please. This is Randall Johnson."

In the few moments he waited, Randall picked up the cordless receiver and walked to his customary spot in front of the window-wall.

"Phil. Randall Johnson here. Tom just showed me your letter about Kate Chilton so I thought that I'd give you a call... I'm too late?... Do you know where she's working? Maybe I'll steal her away," he said with a chuckle.

After a very informative conversation, Randall buzzed Gail.

"Would you set me up for a tennis game with Lidden Hartley? Right, the lieutenant governor of Connecticut. Tell him I want a rematch."

Eleven

KATE HAD HIT the perfect rhythm as she ran along Oakwood Avenue with Gretchen trotting beside her. It was a glorious autumn afternoon, warm in the sun but not humid. The soccer game was over, the boys were happily occupied at home and she was free for a few precious minutes. She had stripped down to her sports bra and running shorts when she had broken a sweat. Now she enjoyed the breeze created by her own motion and let her thoughts roam free.

For the first time in weeks, she felt hopeful. It was amazing what an income could do for one's spirits. She was even excited about the bridge itself. To the commuters on the highway, it was just a different sound beneath their wheels. To Kate, it was a series of puzzles to solve while considering mechanical, economic and aesthetic factors. Her bridge was going to be both practical and beautiful. Assuming that she got to build it. Their proposal was going in on Monday, but Adler still had to win the bid.

The boys were handling her more limited parenting time without any noticeable ill effects. Kate thought that she probably missed them more than they missed her. The *Dog Dough* jar was filling up; evidently, both Clay and Patrick had cut some junk food out of their lunch purchases to save more money. So her absence was even improving their eating habits. Kate's chest swelled with motherly pride as she considered how well her sons were responding to the change in their lives.

She was the one having trouble handling change. She knew that Oliver was waiting, and she had a sinking feeling that if she hadn't known Randall Johnson, in all senses of the word, she wouldn't be so sure about rejecting him. Was she an idiot to turn away a man who wanted to marry her and be a father to her children just because he seemed colorless when compared to a multimillionaire playboy? Kate preferred not to pursue that question because she was quite sure the answer wouldn't be flattering to her. At least Randall hadn't called or shown up at any soccer games. He must finally be so disgusted by her that he was staying away.

She should feel happier about that.

She picked up her pace and resolutely turned her mind to the relative merits of different paving materials. She was recalculating the amount of riprap needed to protect the bridge's piers from scouring when she had a strong feeling that she was being followed.

"Oh, hell!" she exclaimed as she spotted the dark green Jaguar cruising just behind her.

She stopped dead, pulling a surprised Gretchen to a sudden halt. Randall Johnson lifted a hand in greeting and then pulled up beside her.

"Randall. Are you taking the Saturday afternoon tour of Claremont?" she asked coolly, as she tried to ignore the tiny thrills vibrating through her body at the sight of him.

Randall reached across to push the passenger door open. "Hop in."

Kate shook her head. "No, thank you. I haven't finished

my run yet. And I have Gretchen with me."

"Gretchen's welcome to the backseat."

Kate could tell that he was getting annoyed. It was impossible to see his eyes behind the aviator sunglasses but she saw his left hand flex on the steering wheel. "I don't want her to scratch the leather. It was good to see you." Kate gently closed the door and started to walk away, feeling very pleased with herself for escaping so gracefully.

"Kate, you can either get in the car or I will put you in the car," came an exasperated growl from behind her. Kate stiffened and swung around to see Randall explode out of his side of the Jaguar and stalk around to open her door again. As she hesitated he started toward her.

"I'm coming," she said quickly.

Gretchen scrambled into the backseat and sat panting happily. "Traitor," Kate muttered as she slid into the front.

She glanced up. Randall was looking down at her with an appreciative leer and Kate yanked her T-shirt out from around her waist and pulled it on over her head. His smile widened as he sauntered around the car. She had to admit that he looked good in a deep red polo shirt and khaki slacks. But then, she had yet to see him looking bad.

Kate crossed her arms and stared straight ahead.

"You might want to lower your nose a little bit," Randall said. "You'll get a crick in your neck trying to look down it."

She couldn't stop the corner of her mouth from twitching but she kept her tone frosty. "Were you looking for me or did you just happen to be driving by?"

"I went by your house to invite you, Clay and Patrick to come swimming in the indoor pool at Eagle's Nest. Clay told me your usual route. I'll admit that I got distracted by the view for a few minutes."

"These old trees *are* beautiful, aren't they?"

Randall wouldn't let her get away with that. "What trees? I was watching that trickle of sweat running down your back and under those very snug shorts, and imagining where it went from there."

Kate made a noise that was a mixture of embarrassment, annoyance and laughter.

He swung the car into her driveway and turned off the engine. As he got out, he said, "Just bring your bathing suit. I've got plenty of towels."

Kate leapt out of the car. "I don't believe that I accepted your invitation."

"The boys will be mighty disappointed."

"You are absolutely *shameless*."

"Actually, the *Wall Street Journal* says that I'm a 'brilliant but ruthless negotiator.' No, that must have been *Forbes*. The *Journal* is never that complimentary."

"I'd call you underhanded and without any moral principles, myself."

"You're right! That's *exactly* what the *Journal* said."

Kate stalked into the house. "Clay! Patrick! Go get your bathing suits."

Clay and Patrick came bounding down the stairs. "Cool! You're letting us go!"

Kate turned around to glare at Randall. He was leaning back against the door with his arms crossed and the aviator glasses dangling from his fingertips. He shrugged.

"Only if you both can be ready in five minutes," Kate said through clenched teeth. Then, as the boys raced back up the steps, she added, "Because I might murder him first."

He chuckled and pushed himself away from the door to come over to where she was standing. He reached out and ran his fingers from her earlobe under her hair to the back of her neck. Kate stiffened, thinking that he was going to pull her toward him. Instead he lifted her hair up to cool her neck off.

"You've worked up a good sweat. If you want to shower here, I'll wait. Or you can shower at my place."

Ripples of delight were racing over Kate's scalp as Randall shifted his fingers in her hair. When he bent down and blew against her overheated neck, Kate's eyelids closed, her head fell back and a small moan escaped her as his breath seemed to feather over every inch of her body.

Through the haze of sensation, she heard whispering in her ear. "Do you know what I want to do right now, Kate?"

She didn't bother to answer. "I want to rip that T-shirt in half. Then I want to pull that bra down to your waist and slide it over your hips along with your shorts. When you're naked, I'm going to lick the sweat off your neck and between your breasts and down in your belly button. And I'll keep going lower..."

His voice was just as effective as his tongue would have been, and Kate's breath was coming in small gasps.

Footsteps sounded behind them. He released her head so suddenly that Kate almost lost her balance.

"Is there a diving board?" Patrick asked. "Is it an indoor pool?"

"Of course, it's indoors," Clay said with brotherly scorn. "It's too cold for grown-ups to swim outside."

Randall started to answer Patrick's questions, and Kate escaped up the stairs. She shut herself in her bedroom and stood with her head in her hands, shaking. Her body was coiled tight with unsatisfied arousal, and she had the appalling thought that Randall Johnson could have brought her to an orgasm right there in her living room with just his voice. She stripped off her clothes and turned the shower on cold. The shock cooled her body but did nothing to settle her mind.

She finished combing her wet hair in front of the mirror and then said to her reflection, "You are a widow. You are a mother. You are an engineer. You are not a hormonally overwrought teenager with no control over your urges."

She. comforted herself with the thought that Clay and Patrick would protect her from her baser impulses. Then her eyes widened in horrified realization. "Oh God, he'll be wearing a bathing suit. And so will I."

Kate pulled on her black one-piece suit in Randall's elegant dressing room and firmly tied the matching sarong around her hips. She wasn't taking the skirt off until the last possible moment before she dived into that spectacular pool. Kate squared her shoulders as she strode out to join the boys.

"Hey, Mom! The diving board is great!" Clay said. He executed a back dive with a one-and-a-half twist and cut the water with barely a splash.

"A very handsome dive." Randall's voice came from behind Kate and she turned to see him sitting in a chair wearing dark blue swim trunks. A white towel was draped around his neck.

"Thanks, Mr. Johnson," Clay said as he surfaced. Kate was still reeling from the impact of having Randall's chest, shoulders and forearms bared to her eyes. She refused to look any farther down his body and instead averted her gaze to the pool itself.

"Frank Peltier must have designed this, too," she said, admiring the sleek marble columns and tiled walls. Sunlight streamed in through French doors that looked out over the Manhattan skyline. Kate closed her eyes against the memory that brought forth.

"It's a modern version of a Roman bath. It was his favorite part of the house, probably because it cost the most. Architects love to mess with water."

"Or ignore it," Kate laughed. "There's that famous story about Frank Lloyd Wright's client complaining that the roof leaked over his place in the dining room. Wright supposedly told him to move his chair."

As Randall laughed, Kate walked over to sit beside him. She realized her mistake when she turned her head slightly and found his shoulder mere inches from her own. She shifted sideways in her chair and looked straight ahead.

"Your boys are good swimmers. Did you teach them?"

"No, David was the driving force behind that sport. He loved the water."

"Mom, come in. It's warm," Patrick called from the edge of the pool. "Mr. Johnson says that the water heats his terrace and then circulates into the pool."

Kate flushed. Randall chuckled evilly. Suddenly, he was out of his chair and walking toward the pool. "Come on in," he said to her over his shoulder. As soon as his toes hit the edge of the pool, he launched himself into a long racing dive. He swam to the opposite end, giving Kate a breathtaking view of the muscles in his back flexing and stretching as he moved effortlessly through the water.

"Show-off," she said under her breath. She stood up and untied her sarong and then did her own flat dive into the water. However, she stopped beside Clay and Patrick, using them as both shield and distraction. Randall stroked easily back to their little group.

"Hey, Mr. Johnson, can we play Marco Polo?" Patrick asked.

130

"Sure, if you tell me how."

Clay and Patrick looked at each other in mute astonishment. The magnificent Mr. Johnson didn't know how to play Marco Polo?

"There weren't a lot of swimming pools where Mr. Johnson grew up," Kate said.

"At least you didn't say *when* I grew up."

The boys explained the rules with great enthusiasm. Randall volunteered to be "it" first. He missed tagging Patrick by mere inches at least a half a dozen times, then switched his attention to Clay. After several near misses, Randall got him. Clay tagged Kate and Kate nabbed Patrick. Patrick ignored everyone but Randall and finally cornered him on the steps. "I got you!" he yelled in triumph, leaping into the air and pumping his fist.

Randall picked him up and held him high in the air. "And for that you shall be punished," he said, launching him toward the deep end. Patrick landed with an enormous splash and bobbed up saying, "Cool!" Randall submerged and then without warning came straight for Kate under water.

"Watch out, Mom!" Clay yelled. "He's it."

Kate frantically dodged and dove and twisted away from the big hands but she couldn't out-swim him. He caught her ankle and reeled her in toward him, sliding his other hand up her thigh, over her hip and around her waist to pull her back against him.

"Being *it* has its compensations," he said, and then pulled her underwater. Kate wasn't ready and swallowed a mouthful of pool water. She surfaced sputtering.

"Mom, he dunked you," Patrick said in amazement.

Kate pushed strands of wet hair out of her eyes and looked speculatively at Randall's shoulders and chest. Then

131

she turned away and said, "I'm going to start counting."

Randall chuckled. "A wise decision. Retaliation is not a viable option."

Retaliation was definitely an option but Kate knew better than to launch a frontal attack.

They played a few more rounds of Marco Polo, and then Randall got out a water basketball set. He was standing on the edge of the pool adjusting the height of the hoop when Kate came up quietly behind him. As an engineer, she understood balance and leverage. So first she applied pressure with her knee behind his kneecap which started a good forward motion. Then she kept his momentum going with a firm push in the small of the back. Quick, neat and effective, she thought with satisfaction as she watched him sail through the air and into the water.

Clay and Patrick watched open-mouthed and then waited in tense silence for Randall to surface. Kate stood a safe distance away from the edge of the pool with her arms crossed. All of them jumped when he rocketed up from the bottom, laughing.

"A surprise attack! I should have learned my lesson. Never drop your guard near a woman with revenge on her mind, boys."

He vaulted out of the pool in front of Kate, causing her to step back several paces even as she glared at him. "I will deal with you later," he said in a low voice, flicking water at her from his fingers. Then he spoke louder. "Is anyone hungry? I'll get Rosa to bring down some sandwiches." The boys cheered and he walked over to an intercom and spoke into it briefly.

Clay swam to the side of the pool and said in a low voice, "Mom, you've got guts. He's twice your size and you *nailed* him."

Kate smiled. It was something to see the look of awed respect in his eyes. His mom had *guts*.

Just then a door swung open and Rosa appeared with a rolling cart filled with food. Randall introduced them all to his housekeeper, and Rosa asked Clay and Patrick their ages, grades, favorite subjects and sports. As they set out the food, Kate tried to decide if Rosa knew anything about her trysts with Randall and then concluded that she had probably seen so many women come and go here that she no longer paid attention to any of them.

Randall brought drinks over from the poolside bar and they all dug into the feast with gusto. Kate was very pleased when Clay politely asked Randall about his work. Randall explained that RJ Enterprises made its money from buying under-performing companies and making them profitable. "Sometimes we sell them again and sometimes we keep them," he concluded.

"Have you ever bought a company that you couldn't fix?" Clay asked.

"A few." Randall was silent a moment and then leaned back in his chair. "One time, my partner Tom Rogan and I had an oil field offered to us. Well, we got all excited because we always wanted to be oil barons. We were pretty new to the game then. We decide to go see the field for ourselves so we buy some work boots and hard hats and drive to Oilton, Texas, to take a look.

"We tramp around, getting more and more wound up. There were more wells than we'd expected and the equipment was in great condition. So we go back to our motel and call the oil company's headquarters in Houston. After haggling awhile over the price, we agree to buy the field. Tom and I slap each other on the back over the great bargain we got. We go back to our office and read the

133

contracts they've sent us. Suddenly, Tom turns white and points to something in the paperwork. The oil field we'd just agreed to buy was in Oilton, *Oklahoma*."

"So you didn't buy it," Clay said.

Randall shook his head. "No, we bought it. Sight unseen. We were too embarrassed to admit that we'd gotten not just the wrong oil field but the wrong *state*." He leaned forward to rest his forearms on the table. "In my business, your reputation precedes you. So if you make a mistake, you swallow it, and hope that you don't choke. If you do well, you thank your lucky stars and alert the press."

"So did you turn the oil field around?"

"No, I sold it as fast as I could – at a loss."

"Wow," Patrick said, awed at the high finance being discussed. But he wanted to discuss another of Randall's assets. "You have a helicopter."

Randall smiled. "That just sort of came with another company I bought. I thought that it might be useful so I kept it."

Patrick and Clay bombarded him with questions about engines, range and air speed, most of which he could answer. Finally, Kate took pity on him and suggested that the boys go swimming again. But before they left the table, Randall said, "Maybe you boys would like to take a ride in the chopper."

Two sets of pleading eyes turned toward Kate. She shifted in her seat and said, "One of these days."

"Mom, it won't crash," Patrick said.

"I know but it's expensive to fly a helicopter and we don't want to impose on Mr. Johnson," Kate said.

"I'll discuss it with your mother," Randall said, waving them toward the pool before turning back to her. "I guarantee that the helicopter won't crash."

"No one can guarantee that. I'd just rather that we didn't go flying. I hate to fly."

"I'm sorry I suggested it."

"No, no. It was a very nice thing to offer." Kate suddenly realized that Randall had taken her wrist and was softly stroking her skin with his thumb. He looked startled when she gently pulled away from him and stood up.

"I think that we've trespassed on your hospitality long enough. Clay, Patrick! Let's get changed."

"Aw, Mom," Patrick started to complain but Clay elbowed him and he swam over to the steps.

"Aw, Kate," Randall said, mimicking Patrick's tone perfectly. "Don't run away."

"I'm not running away. I'm just not overstaying our welcome."

"You're still welcome," Randall said, tilting his head back to look up at her.

"Thank you but we have plans for this evening."

The two boys were watching in fascination. They weren't accustomed to seeing an adult persist in the face of their mother's refusal.

"Mom's fixing us a nutritious, well-balanced dinner to make up for all the take-out during the week," Patrick said earnestly.

Randall laughed and stood up, lifting an eyebrow at her expectantly. The silence lengthened. Finally Kate said through clenched teeth, "Would you like to join us for dinner?"

"There's nothing that I'd like better..."

"But you need to make some business calls, I'm sure," Kate finished for him as she started toward the dressing room.

"No, I'm free all evening. I was going to say that I owe

135

your sons a lesson in the venerable art of nutmegging. Go get changed, young men."

"Yeah!" Patrick said, racing toward the other dressing room with Clay not far behind him.

Kate gave Randall one freezing look over her shoulder but she never broke her stride as she walked away from him. Randall called after her, "You don't keep any arsenic in the spice drawer, do you?"

"I prefer strychnine. It's much more painful," she said before she closed the door.

As Kate changed in her private dressing room, she wondered what Randall and the boys were chatting about in the "Men's Locker Room." She found out when they erupted out of the front door. "Mr. Johnson asked us if we'd like to ride in his Ferrari," Clay said. "Would you mind, Mom?"

Kate rolled her eyes. After turning down a helicopter ride, her sons were now asking to be driven home in a ridiculously expensive sports car. She knew that she should be annoyed with Randall's manipulation of her children, but his bribery was so blatant and so outrageous that her sense of humor was getting the better of her moral principles.

"That's fine. Maybe tomorrow he'll get you a seat on the space shuttle."

Clay and Patrick looked at each other, eyes wide, but Randall threw back his head and let out a shout of laughter. "Your mother's on to me, guys." He grabbed Kate's hand and said, "Come with me and see the over-powered chariot."

After inspecting the spotless five-car garage and pronouncing the Jeep "cool," the boys carefully and respectfully climbed into the black Ferrari. Randall was still holding Kate's hand, the warmth of his skin against hers radiating a pleasant but disconcerting sense of comfort. He walked Kate back to her dusty minivan, and before opening her door, lifted the back of her hand to his lips. Kate was mesmerized by his dark gaze, and by the heat of his breath and the movement of his mouth against her skin as he said, "We could try out the ad campaign on the Ferrari."

Kate had to swallow twice before she could say, "I think that Jaguar could sue for copyright infringement."

"I have a whole stable of lawyers who can deal with that." Randall dropped her hand to swing open the van's door. "I'll follow you down. It'll keep my speed under control."

Pretending that she was completely unaffected by his provocative comments, Kate turned the key in the ignition as Randall walked toward the garage. Once he was a safe distance away, she laid her arms on the steering wheel and dropped her forehead onto them as she took deep breaths to slow down her racing heartbeat.

She had to admire his strategy. He made her feel safe by inviting her children along, and then when her guard was down he launched his attack. He had left her feeling as though his warm, male lips had touched more private parts of her body.

"I'd hate to be on the other side of the negotiating table from you," she said aloud as his sports car growled out of the garage.

Twelve

KATE SPENT HER solitary ride home mentally upgrading her menu and trying to remember how big a mess they had left in the house. As the boys spilled out of the Ferrari into their yard, Patrick said, "Mom, did you know that Mr. Johnson has a *transmitter* in all of his cars in case he gets *hijacked*? The police can track every turn his car makes!"

"Amazing!" Kate said, wondering despairingly what a man whose life was so valuable that the police would follow his car's every move would think of her modest home and dinner.

But Randall showed a tact she hadn't anticipated. He sent the boys off to find a soccer ball while he waited outside in the yard. "You go on inside while I make good on my promise."

A ball sailed toward him, and Kate admired his footwork as he controlled it and neatly sent it back to Clay. She gave him an approving smile and walked calmly in the back door.

Once inside, she became a whirling dervish of activity: slicing, dicing, sautéing and straightening up. Occasionally she couldn't resist glancing out into the backyard to see how the soccer players were getting along. Watching Randall dodging and weaving toward the goal was a guilty pleasure; he moved with a speed and grace surprising for his size. She wished that he had on shorts so that she could watch the muscles of his legs flexing.

By the time three sweaty, panting males spilled into the kitchen, Kate had the dinner and the house well in-hand. The dining room table was set for four with the good china and silver, the lamps in the living room glowed warmly and the delicious scent of roasting lamb wafted out of the oven.

"Something smells good," Randall said after swallowing his first gulp of beer.

"It's a nutritious, well-balanced meal," Kate said. "Liver, brussels sprouts, spinach cooked in cod liver oil and wheat germ muffins."

Clay and Patrick made gagging noises while Randall laughed. "You forgot the prune wine."

"So I did. I'll have to go get it out of the cellar."

"What is it really, Mom?" Patrick wanted to know.

"Lamb, green beans, carrots and croissants," Kate reassured him. "Finish your drinks and go wash."

"Don't I get a tour of *your* house?" Randall said as he washed his hands at the kitchen sink.

"The downstairs only. I can't vouch for the condition of the second floor," Kate said, picking up her glass of wine.

Randall followed Kate slowly through the living room, dining room, den and onto the big open porch. He looked carefully at her home because he always learned a lot from observing a person's home turf. The furniture looked comfortable but each piece had also been chosen for its proportion and line. Old, intricately patterned Oriental rugs covered the polished oak floors. The walls were decorated

139

with architectural drawings of structures both new and antique, interspersed with colorful abstract landscapes. Antique brass-trimmed wooden tools lay among framed family photos.

Randall wondered if the prints and tools were Kate's or David's and concluded that the convergence of their professional interests would make that question irrelevant; the collection would please both of them. He briefly wondered what it would be like to have a lover whose tastes meshed so perfectly with your own.

He scanned the family photographs until he found a picture of a handsome blond man with a younger Clay and Patrick. Clearly this was David. His sons looked like him, and the trio radiated familial affection. Randall studied the man who had chosen to risk screwing up this life for another woman. What had he been looking for that he couldn't find right here? Randall shook his head in disgusted bafflement.

He followed Kate into the next room, still lost in thought. He had always explained away his unmarried state by saying that he simply didn't have time for a wife or family. But there was also a deep reluctance on his part to make promises that he might regret yet feel obliged to honor. He felt no sympathy for a man who broke his vows and betrayed the trust of the woman – the very desirable woman – who was also the mother of his two young sons. Randall was suddenly angry on Kate's behalf.

"This completes the tour of the historic Chilton residence," Kate said as she led him onto the porch. "Although the name of its architect is lost in the mists of Victorian time, we like it."

"I like it, too. It feels like a home."

Kate laughed. "Between the soccer cleats and the dog

hair, it always looks well lived-in." She patted Gretchen who had followed them through the tour and was now sitting at her feet.

Randall was gazing out at the street where young bicyclists, middle-aged runners and mothers pushing strollers passed by at frequent intervals. Kate wondered what he had really been thinking as he walked through her home. Showing him her house had seemed almost more intimate than being sprawled half-naked across the hood of his car. She felt as though his eyes had missed nothing. When he had stopped in front of David's photograph and then shaken his head, she longed to know what was going on behind his unreadable expression. "Oh, there's the timer," she said, dashing back into the house.

Once dinner was on the table, Kate relaxed a bit and enjoyed watching Clay and Patrick with their new friend. Obviously, they had decided that Mr. Johnson was "okay," and while they were respectful, they felt no hesitation about peppering him with questions about his life, his past, his soccer skills and whatever else intrigued them. Randall was far more forthcoming than Kate would have expected; he had succumbed to the flattery of being the object of two boys' admiration.

"That's an awesome watch," Patrick said, admiring the stainless steel multidialed gadget on their guest's wrist. "Is it one of those diving watches?"

"It's a Timex," Kate couldn't resist saying.

"Your mother's making fun of me," Randall said, unclasping the watch and handing it to Patrick. "This one's a Tag Heuer. That dial measures depth. This one tells you how long until you run out of oxygen."

"Do you have a Rolex or two at home?" Kate asked sweetly.

Randall shook his head. "All I need is a watch that keeps good time. There are better ways to impress people."

"Like helicopters and Ferraris," Kate muttered under her breath.

"We've started a business," Patrick said proudly, as he gave the watch back to Randall. "Clay and I are professional dog walkers. We're earning enough money to pay for lunch at school and saving the rest."

"I admire your entrepreneurial spirit," Randall said as he leaned back contentedly with a wineglass cradled in his big hand.

"We wanted to help Mom out with the finances," Patrick continued and then stopped abruptly. Clay had kicked his ankle under the table and his mother was frowning at him. "And we're really good with animals," he finished after a pause.

Clay jumped in. "I wanted to buy a special CAD-CAM program and decided to earn it myself. It's more satisfying that way."

Randall raised an eyebrow at that. "Very true." But Kate had seen the sudden sharpening of his gaze when Patrick mentioned the family finances. When Patrick got started on a subject, he forgot all instructions about what was private information and what wasn't.

"You know, Clay, we've got a different program at work," Kate said to steer the conversation away from dog-walking. "I'll bring home the disk for you to take a look at." She saw Randall's attention shift as she mentioned work and was relieved when he continued to address Clay.

"Are you thinking about engineering as a career?" Randall asked.

Clay flushed slightly. "I'd really like to be a sculptor, like Alexander Calder. You know, make big metal sculptures for outdoors. The computer programs are good for designing those so they're stable."

Randall leaned forward. "That's an unusual ambition for a young man. Do you know how to weld already?"

"Yes, Dad taught me how. We used to work on an old car together."

"Do you have any sculptures to show me?"

Clay's face lit up. "They're not big but I've done a few. The one on the table in the living room is mine. And I have a couple of bigger ones in the garage." He looked at Kate.

She waved a hand in permission. "Go right ahead. I'll get dessert ready."

To Kate's surprise, Randall rose and gathered up his plate and silverware. "First, we clear the table." The boys followed suit, racing into the kitchen with their glasses balanced precariously on their plates.

"No, no, I'll take care of that," Kate said, standing up and trying to take his dirty dishes from him.

"You have a very unflattering opinion of my manners," Randall said in a low voice as he moved his plate decisively away from her grasp.

"It's not that. I just know that you're accustomed to having Rosa around..."

His brows lowered in irritation. "I clear the table when Rosa's around, too."

Kate just looked at him.

"Most of the time," he amended.

Kate folded her arms.

"Some of the time. Oh, just get out of my way and let me put the damn dishes in the sink," he said, shouldering her aside.

Kate's lips curved into a satisfied smile as she picked up her own dishes. Randall pointedly made several more trips between the table and the kitchen. Finally, Kate said, "You've clearly demonstrated that I've grossly misjudged you. Go look at Clay's sculptures. And thank you for showing an interest," she added softly. "He's quite passionate about his art and quite sensitive, too."

"I'm no critic but the sculpture I saw earlier in the living room looked very interesting."

Kate sighed in relief as he left the kitchen.

When he was in a room with her, her nerves never stopped thrumming. She needed a break from his presence, although even his voice drifting in from the living room made her edgy with awareness. She wished that Clay would hurry up and take him out to the garage.

She concentrated on putting out the dessert.

Of course, the first recipe that had come to mind when she was revamping her menu on the way home had been the Chocolate Orgasm Cake. She had laughed aloud and instantly eliminated it. Instead, they were having apple crumble – which was slightly nutritious – served warm from the oven with vanilla ice cream melting over it. That particular combination of hot and cold is pretty orgasmic itself, she reflected, but at least Patrick couldn't embarrass her by blurting out the name.

Soon enough her respite was over. Randall's shoulders filled the kitchen doorway as he sniffed appreciatively. "I've always said that there are two ways to a man's heart, and you're real good at both of them," he drawled in his thickest Texas accent.

"I see that you've abandoned your attempt at civilized manners."

"I'm just complimenting the lady of the house on her skill in the kitchen," he said and then lowered his voice as he came toward her, "and in the bedroom."

"Quiet! There are minors in the next room." Kate shoved the ice cream scoop into his hand to distract him. Without missing a beat, he slid it into his back trouser pocket, ran his hands up her arms to her shoulders and pulled her against him. "I like Clay's art a lot. He seems to have a real talent."

Kate's face lit up. "So does his art teacher. But it's an unusual talent for a young boy. It's a little hard to know how much to encourage him in it."

She suddenly realized that Randall had trapped her between the counter and his body and that his hands were roaming over her back. She braced her palms on his chest and said, "You are the most underhanded person I've ever met. Let go of me."

She might as well not have spoken. Randall leaned into her so that her body was locked against his from the knees up to the waist. He lowered his head and ran his lips up the side of her neck to her earlobe, which he nipped gently.

Kate barely controlled the instinctive urge to arch her body even closer against his. "Stop it right now," she whispered, as she pushed hard against his warm chest.

For a moment he didn't move even a centimeter. Then he stepped away, saying, "What else is for dessert?"

"I should send you home without dessert."

Randall laughed and pulled out the ice cream scoop. "Hand over the ice cream or I'll be forced to use this as a weapon."

Kate retreated to the freezer, yanked open the door and stiff-armed the carton of vanilla ice cream to him.

"You're beautiful when you're angry... and aroused," he said in a stage whisper.

She glared at him and turned on her heel to march into the dining room. His taunting chuckle ruined her exit.

145

When the boys had gone upstairs and Randall showed no sign of leaving, Kate picked up a sweater and reluctantly led him out to the porch. Now that the sun had gone down, it was getting chilly. If the temperature didn't bother him, she would allow him to finish his glass of wine and then make it clear that it was time for him to go.

She sat down in a wooden rocking chair. Randall lounged on the swing. He seemed lost in thought and Kate watched him over the rim of her wineglass, trying to analyze why he had such a strong impact on her.

He had an athletic build, with wide shoulders and muscles defined by exercise. She wondered how he found the time. He had an almost arrogant self-assurance that should be abrasive but instead seemed right. His face would never be labeled "handsome." David had been handsome. But Randall's dark straight brows, intense eyes and razor sharp cheekbones were so striking that he made "handsome" unnecessary. And he had already proven that just his voice could heat up her body.

Kate took a swallow of her wine and leaned her head back against the chair. Not only was she no closer to solving the mystery of their chemistry than before, but she also had made it worse. She now wanted to drape herself over that large male body stretched out so tantalizingly near her.

Randall's thoughts had taken a different direction. "Tell me about your childhood."

Kate choked on her wine in surprise. "There's nothing to tell. Didn't Tolstoy say that all happy families resemble each other? I grew up in a happy family with two older brothers. We were comfortable but not rich. I went to private school and got a scholarship to M.I.T. And that's about it."

"Where did you meet David?"

He was lucky that she was enjoying having his body close by or she would have told him that it was none of his business. "At work. We got assigned to the same skyscraper."

"Do you regret marrying him?"

Kate stiffened. "That's a very personal question."

"Yes, it is."

She was surprised into a laugh. "But you expect me to answer it."

"Why not?"

Kate thought about it. If she hadn't married David, she wouldn't have Clay and Patrick, so clearly she didn't regret that. Furthermore, she wouldn't have had a life that, until David's sudden death, had seemed blessed and guided by some good fairy.

She also wouldn't have suffered the anguish of having the man she loved die in the prime of his life. She wouldn't have had to struggle with the sometimes overwhelming responsibility of being a single parent. And she would not have had her very being shattered by the betrayal of the man to whom she had entrusted her life.

"I hate not knowing why he did it," Kate said finally.

"He was a fool."

"You can't know that. You never met him." Despite her words, Kate felt absurdly comforted by Randall's unequivocal statement.

"I've met you. I've met your children. He was a fool." Randall took a drink out of the wineglass he'd been balancing on the back of the swing. "I know you want to beat yourself up about your marriage failing, but sometimes men do stupid things without considering the consequences."

"Is that the opinion of an expert?"

Randall half-smiled. "I've done as many stupid things as the next man, but I respect my promises."

"That I believe."

He suddenly straightened up and leaned forward to put his wine down on the wicker table in front of the swing. Looking up at her from under his eyebrows, he said forcefully, "You should stop trying to figure out what you did wrong and put the blame on him where it belongs."

Kate was touched by his attempt to make her feel better and surprised at the perception behind his comments. She also desperately wanted to believe him.

Randall had evidently had enough of playing the comforter because he got up and strolled around the table to her chair. Bracing his arms on the armrests and rocking her chair backward, he leaned down until his mouth was inches from hers. "Why don't I call Rosa to come down and stay with the boys and we'll go back to my house. Have you ever made love in a pool? You lie back in the water and wrap your legs around my waist. It lasts a long, long time because there's no weight and no friction. Just heat." His voice had dropped and slowed. His lips were practically touching Kate's. She let her eyelids close and tilted her chin just slightly upward so that her lips brushed his. She felt him shudder just as a jolt streaked through her own body. Then he was gone, striding over to the table and downing the wine in one swallow.

"You are the most unpredictable woman."

Kate was pleased to have knocked him off balance. She smiled. "I thought that I was being very cooperative."

"Just enough to make me die of frustration. Would you have come back to my house?"

"No."

"Would you have let me make love to you in that rocking chair?"

"That would be difficult. Too much enthusiasm and we'd go right over backward."

"I'll sit in the rocking chair. You can lower yourself slowly onto my lap."

All sensation centered itself between her legs as Kate visualized sliding slowly down onto Randall as he sat in the rocking chair.

"If you don't stop looking like that, I'm not going to give you any choice," he growled. "I have to get home."

"To make some calls?" Kate asked sweetly.

"To take a cold shower."

This time Kate got to laugh at him as he walked back into her house. She sauntered in after him, feeling very satisfied with her tactics. She knew that she was playing with fire but she felt safe in her own house with her children there. Despite Randall's pretensions to lechery, Kate was sure that he had never for a moment considered seducing her with Clay and Patrick in the house. A pleasant sense of power surged through her. She had called his bluff.

She arrived in the kitchen to find her guest saying good night to her sons. "Your mother's going to walk me to my car," he concluded as he took the glass out of her grasp and put his hand in the small of her back to move her toward the back door. Kate gave him two points for the maneuver but she didn't see what it would gain him. After all, she didn't have a private courtyard to park in.

But Randall hadn't spent an hour in her backyard without noticing the landscape. Kate found herself propelled into a pitch-black corner created by an odd angle in the join between the house and the garage.

"You're going to go to bed just as frustrated as I am,"

149

Randall said as he backed her against the wall and slid his knee between hers to hold her there. Kate gasped involuntarily as his leg pressed against the juncture of her thighs. "That's what I want to hear," he said.

He held her face between his hands and Kate braced herself for an assault on her mouth. Instead he lightly ran his lips along her eyebrows, over her eyelids, to her temples and finally to her ear which he simply breathed into. Kate's skin prickled deliciously, and she shivered against him. "Good girl," he murmured.

Two could play this game, and Kate suspected that she had a slight advantage. She slid her hands slowly up his chest until she found his warm skin through the open collar of his polo shirt. She wrapped her hands around the back of his neck and pulled him toward her so that she could kiss his throat. His muscles jumped quite satisfactorily when her lips touched his skin so Kate decided to see what happened when she tasted him with her tongue.

Randall's groan was all that she had hoped for. He was so hard against her pelvis that it would have been painful if Kate hadn't felt so pleased with his reaction. She laughed softly and then regretted it when Randall ripped her shirt-tails out of the waistband of her slacks and slid his hands under the fabric to unhook her bra.

"Stop it," she hissed, trying to lower her arms to push him away. But he had angled his arms under hers and he was far stronger than she was. He cupped her breasts and circled his thumbs over her nipples, turning Kate's furious whisper into a long moan. She wouldn't have imagined that there was any space to move but somehow as Randall's fingers played over her sensitive skin, Kate's hips rocked against his without any conscious thought on her part.

Now Randall laughed, although Kate detected a certain

ragged edge in the sound. "If you're going to engage the enemy, you have to be prepared to accept the consequences," he said and then slid his hands down to the belt buckle at her waist.

"Randall, no!" Kate dug her fingernails hard into his shoulders and did her best to keep her buckle out of his grasp. Since his leg was still firmly braced between hers, her evasive action created considerable friction.

Suddenly, his hands were clamped on her hips. "Hold still, damn it, unless you want to finish this right here and now."

"That seemed to be your intention."

He chuckled and let go of her. "I was trying to be helpful."

Kate wanted to slide bonelessly down to the ground. Instead, she locked her knees and drew in a shaky breath.

Before she could think of anything to say, Randall spoke again. "I've been playing this game a lot longer than you have, Kate. Remember that. Thanks for the nutritious, well-balanced dinner." He started to walk out the gate, then half-turned. "You should tuck your shirt back in before you go inside." He melted into the shadows before Kate could open her mouth.

She listened for the slam of his car door and the soft roar of the Ferrari's engine before she re-hooked her bra and loosened her belt to push her shirt back where it belonged.

She walked to the back steps and sat down. She reminded herself that he had said he was just playing with her. She recalled that he had told her he wasn't a nice man. Right now, she didn't care.

Until she walked in the door and saw the look that Clay and Patrick exchanged.

"Mr. Johnson's really cool," Patrick said, cautiously.

"I'm glad you liked him."

"It must be great to have your own indoor swimming pool," he continued. "He says that he swims every day, even if he gets home at midnight. Are you and Mr. Johnson dating, Mom?"

"What? No. I don't think so," Kate said. Her sons had clearly been discussing the relationship between Randall and herself.

Patrick's face fell as he accepted her answer. Clay, however, looked skeptical. Kate thought of trying "we're just friends" but it was so far from the truth that she couldn't get her tongue around it. Instead, she said, "I think that we're trying to decide if we want to date."

That cheered Patrick up. Clay remained silent, and Kate wondered what he was thinking. She didn't ask him because it was not a discussion she was prepared to have until she had straightened out her own thoughts.

As she shooed the boys upstairs to get ready for bed, she told herself, *Just keep in mind that he's playing cat-and-mouse with you and you're the mouse.*

Randall drove the Ferrari home at an entirely illegal speed. He was irritated for several reasons. He had an erection that was going to require an ice pack to get rid of, and it was too late to invite any of his usual female companions out for dinner and a release of tension. Randall couldn't think of one that he really wanted to go to bed with anyway.

Next, much as it bothered him to admit it, he had enjoyed his young hosts. Clay's sculptures were impressive. Patrick was a natural at soccer. They were smart boys. He had liked telling them about his business.

Then there was the revelation of his hostess. In her own surroundings, Kate's veneer of self-containment melted considerably. Randall had noticed the way she brushed her fingers through Patrick's hair or lightly squeezed Clay's shoulder. She had scratched Gretchen's ears anytime the dog came near her. The first sip of the quite respectable wine had made her close her eyes in overt pleasure. *This* was the woman who had seduced him on his own terrace. Randall swore as that thought brought on another physical reaction.

He turned his thoughts in a less incendiary direction. Based on Patrick's artless conversation and the circulation of Kate's resume, he concluded that she was having financial problems. Randall considered how easy it would be to solve them: he had so much money he could write a check and never miss it. However, he couldn't just hand Kate money. She wouldn't take it.

He was inventing and discarding less direct ways of getting money into her hands. He had passed out enough diamond bracelets and earrings in the past that a Tiffany's salesperson sent him personal letters. Of course he had never done it with the intention of improving his lovers' economic status. In fact, he had never given a moment's reflection to their economic status...

He banished that train of thought as he downshifted to roar up the curves to his mountaintop. Usually, when he was pissed off, he would work it out in the swimming pool, but right now that reminded him of Kate looking like some silent screen goddess in her black bathing suit. She undoubtedly thought that she was dressed conservatively, but she had way too many curves to look anything but sexy when she was wearing wet spandex.

That brought to mind his verbal fantasy about making

153

love to her in the pool.

"Oh, hell," he said in disgust as his erection pushed harder against his trousers. He shoved down the accelerator and forced himself to concentrate on driving.

He could hear his private line ringing when he walked into the house. He picked it up with the thought that it might be Kate.

"And where have you been?" Tom Rogan's voice asked.

"Is another oil tank on fire?" Randall barked.

"No."

"Then why are you calling me?"

"I wanted to find out if we're planning to invest in a chain of day care centers. Rosa said that you had been doing some research with children this afternoon."

"I didn't know you and Rosa were in the habit of discussing my guests."

"Rosa was so thrilled to have children in the house that she told me all about them. I was so astonished I listened. She also told me that you left in the Ferrari, a car I happen to know you hate."

"If you're trying to impress two preadolescent boys, a Ferrari is second only to a helicopter."

"So will it be helicopter rides next?"

"No, their mother doesn't approve of recreational flying."

"Too bad. I'd like to see Janine's face when you showed up with two small boys in tow," Tom said with a chuckle.

"I'm glad that I can provide you with your evening's entertainment."

"I'm just trying to figure out what's going on here."

"I've found the point of greatest vulnerability, and I'm exploiting it," Randall said, quoting one of their favorite lines from business school.

"I see. This is strictly business then. My next question would be: is this a merger or an acquisition?"

Randall's voice was as cold as steel when he said, "I don't do mergers."

"Just checking," Tom said agreeably and changed the subject.

But when he hung up, he shook his head. "Next you'll be coaching their Little League team."

Thirteen

THE CHILTON FAMILY slept late that Sunday morning. When the telephone rang, Kate had to clear her throat before she could manage a husky, "Hello?"

"Did I wake you? I'm sorry," Oliver's voice slid smoothly through the receiver.

Kate sat up in bed. "No problem."

"How did the soccer game go yesterday?"

"We tied. But we're still in first place in the league by the skin of our teeth."

"That's great. If you're going to be home this afternoon, I thought I would stop by and say hello."

"You're not going to join us for dinner?" Kate asked, secretly relieved. She'd had enough of amorous dinner guests.

"No, I have to finish a design for a meeting tomorrow. By the way, the final contract for the partnership buyout is supposed to be ready tomorrow as well. I'll try to make the signing process as quick and simple as I can. I know this is painful for you."

Kate took a deep breath. "Would you fax a copy to

Georgia? I realized that I should probably have a lawyer look at it, and Georgia kindly agreed to."

"Of course," Oliver said. "I want you to feel completely comfortable with the contract."

Kate could tell that he was annoyed. "I trust *you*, Oliver. It's the lawyers I worry about."

Oliver's chuckle sounded forced. "I'll be there at about three."

As Kate walked down the hall to see if Clay and Patrick were still asleep, she tried to figure out a subtle way to keep them from discussing Randall Johnson while Oliver was visiting. She didn't want to add fuel to that particular fire.

She found Clay reading in bed. "Good morning. What are you reading?"

"The next *Redwall* book," Clay said, flipping it over to show her the cover.

Kate glanced at the illustration and then shifted her gaze to Clay's face as he started reading again. The angle of his jaw and the sweep of hair across his forehead reminded her so much of David that her heart twisted in her chest. She brushed his hair with her fingertips. "You're a good-looking guy."

Clay gave her a quick, embarrassed smile and went back to his book. Kate stood up. "It's waffle time."

Patrick bounced into the room. "Is Oliver coming over today? I want to nutmeg him."

Kate stifled a groan. "Guys, I want to ask you a grown-up favor. Oliver doesn't really like Mr. Johnson..."

"I didn't know he knew Mr. Johnson," Clay said.

"They've met through business." It was a necessary white lie. "It might be better if you didn't mention that we spent yesterday afternoon with Mr. Johnson. It might upset Oliver. He worries about all of us."

"Why would Oliver worry about us swimming in Mr. Johnson's pool?" Patrick asked.

"He's not worried about *us*, he's worried about *Mom*," Clay said.

Her older son was far too smart for comfort. She acknowledged his statement with a nod.

"Oliver has his own reasons for believing that Mr. Johnson would not make a good friend. I don't agree with him but I don't want to hurt Oliver's feelings by letting him know that."

Patrick looked less puzzled. "Does that mean I can't show Oliver how to nutmeg?"

Kate gave his shoulder a quick squeeze. "You can show him as long as you don't mention that Mr. Johnson taught you how to do it." Kate hated dragging her children into adult deceptions.

They were just rolling their bicycles into the garage after a brisk ride around town when Oliver pulled up. He got out of his car carrying a cookie tin and a square box tied with a gold ribbon. The tin he presented to the boys. "Yeah, Gimmee Jimmy's Cookies!" Clay and Patrick cheered, ripping open the seal and stuffing chocolate chip cookies in their mouths.

"You might offer your mother one first, you barbarians," Oliver said, taking the tin away from Clay and holding it out for Kate.

"Thanks," she said, taking a cookie. "Their Gimmee Jimmy's addiction wreaks havoc with their manners. Would you like some milk to go with your cookies?" Kate led the way into the house wondering what was in Oliver's other box. Thank goodness it looked too big for a ring.

Once the milk and cookies had been devoured, the boys

went outside to warm up for soccer. Kate subtly put the kitchen island between herself and Oliver, but he walked around it. "I'd like you to come as my guest to the Beaux Arts Ball," he said.

The Beaux Arts Ball was the architectural social event of the year. Proceeds went to charity, but the real purpose of the event was for the stars of the architectural world to see and be seen. The attire was black tie, and everyone was supposed to wear a mask, which they or a member of their firm had created. The competition was fierce, and many of the masks were truly works of art. David had insisted that they attend each year.

She had no desire to go with Oliver.

"That's a lovely invitation but I can't create a mask worthy of the occasion –"

"I anticipated that objection." Smiling, he handed her the box. "The theme this year is 'Man's Best Friend.' I don't want you to think that I meant some subtle insult."

Kate untied the ribbon and lifted off the lid. Inside was a papier-mâché mask.

"It's Gretchen!" Kate gasped. "Only a *lot* fancier."

Oliver had perfectly captured Gretchen's doggy grin. However, the mask glittered with glass jewels and beads. As Kate examined it closely, she saw that the details of Gretchen's fur had been painted on in gold. It was exquisite.

"Oliver, this should be in a museum! It's too beautiful to wear."

He looked pleased. "We have to uphold the honor of C/R/G."

When she considered all the time and effort put into the mask – her mask – she couldn't bring herself to refuse.

"I'll be proud to go to the ball with you and wear this

mask to uphold the honor of C/R/G," she said, bringing it up to her face. "How do I look as Gretchen?"

"Lovely and mysterious."

"Woof!" Kate said, laughing, as she lowered the mask.

"Now you look stunningly beautiful," Oliver said. He reached out to smooth her hair where the mask had caught on it and then let his hand trail over her shoulder and down her arm.

She braced herself to keep from flinching away. When Oliver looked at her this way, he became a stranger. She was afraid that he was interpreting her acceptance in every wrong way.

"I suspect that I look better as a dog," she said lightly, stepping away from him to put the mask back in the box. "What breed is your mask?"

"A yellow Labrador, to complement Gretchen."

Kate considered suggesting that a wolf in sheep's clothing would be more appropriate, but that was the sort of thing she would only say to Randall.

"I thought that the gold satin gown you wore to the awards dinner four years ago would work well with the mask."

Kate was taken aback by his attention to her wardrobe. "You have a good memory. I hope I can dig it out of the attic."

"That's great. Shall we play soccer?"

Kate walked through the door he was holding for her wondering what in the world she had let herself in for.

Georgia called her at work on Monday to tell her that the contract was fine. "It's a standard buy-out of a partnership. As your lawyer, the one thing that I would advise you to do is to have the numbers audited. I checked with a couple of sources who said that they seemed low for an established and apparently successful architectural partnership."

Kate made a sound of disagreement and Georgia continued. "However, as your friend, I know that you won't do that for fear of hurting Oliver and Ted's feelings. Which is why you should never do business with friends or make friends of your business colleagues."

"I'm very open-minded about that. I even have friends who are lawyers."

"You may have *former* friends who are lawyers."

Kate laughed. "I really appreciate you doing this *pro bono*, although I wish you'd let me pay you."

"You can't afford me."

Kate smiled as she put down the telephone receiver. Georgia was truly the best. She loved it when Georgia pretended her nasty New York lawyer persona was real.

Susan Chen appeared in the opening to Kate's cubicle.

"I hear that the bridge proposal is on its way to the Connecticut Department of Transportation. Getting our name in front of the Commissioner for serious consideration is a real coup. We couldn't have done that without you."

Kate glowed as the pleasure of Susan's praise flowed through her.

"Since we probably won't hear anything for a few weeks, I have a couple of smaller jobs that I thought that you might be interested in," Susan continued.

Kate had been unsure about whether Adler would keep her on during the waiting period. After all, she was technically a consultant hired to do one specific project. She smiled in relief. "Let me at them."

As she tried to make sense of a set of old blueprints, Kate's intercom beeped. "Ted Gershon on line three." Kate let the blueprints curl back up with a snap.

"Hello, Ted." Kate had never been as friendly with Ted as she had with Oliver, but she had always liked the third partner in the firm. "I got the okay from my lawyer so I'm ready to sign the contract."

They agreed on a time and talked a bit longer about the firm and the new partner. Kate put down the receiver and stared straight ahead, testing this new feeling of calm at the prospect of selling her share in the company that David had worked so hard to build. It felt right to put C/R/G in the past. She was ready to let it go without regret.

She had found a newer set of blueprints for the same building and was comparing the two when her phone buzzed again with Ted Gershon on line two.

"We're postponing the contract signing because another bidder has come in." Ted's voice vibrated with controlled excitement. "A big California architectural firm called Tower Design wants to establish a presence here on the East Coast, and they want to buy into C/R/G to do it. They've made a very generous offer."

"How does it work? Will Paul Desmond still be buying in also?"

"We're just in preliminary discussions, but they seem to be agreeable to that. Kate, I'm so pleased about this for your sake. I know that it will change your tax arrangements, but even with that you'll be able to take far more money out of the firm this way."

Kate was puzzled by his comment about her "tax arrangements" but she let it go in the general flow of good news. They talked about the numbers for a while and then she asked, "Had you contacted this firm before? How did they know about C/R/G?"

Ted sounded like he was floating. "They came to us out of the blue. They knew our reputation, and they knew about

162

David's death, so they thought that we might be looking for a new partner. You know how gossipy architects can be."

"Don't I, though. Oliver must be thrilled."

"I haven't even told him yet. He's tied up with a client, so I decided to call you first."

Kate hung up the phone and tried to absorb her good fortune. Ted had warned her that it was far from a "done deal," but he sounded very optimistic.

She did some quick calculations. If she put away half of the money, the boys' college tuition would be completely taken care of. She could keep the rest as a safety cushion and just use the income. With that and her paycheck, she and the boys could live comfortably. Kate put her head down on her desk for a moment and heaved a long sigh of relief. She felt as though a lead weight had been lifted from her shoulders.

"Please let the deal go through," she whispered as she crossed her fingers.

She had decided not to mention the new offer to Clay and Patrick, so when Oliver called she shut herself in her bedroom. "I can't believe the good news," she said.

Oliver sounded substantially less enthusiastic than Ted had. "We need to do a lot more research on Tower Design. I don't know how much control we'll have to give up."

"Oh." Kate's high spirits sank. "Ted seemed very pleased. And even *I've* heard good things about Tower."

"The offer is financially very advantageous to us. In fact, it's so good that I'm suspicious."

"You certainly don't want to rush into any kind of a business deal if it might be detrimental to the firm. But it would be awfully nice to have that money in my bank account."

"I know, Kate." Oliver sounded contrite. "For your sake, I want it to go through without a hitch. But I don't want you to hope for too much."

"Don't worry. I've learned from hard experience to expect the worst."

"I'd like to change that," Oliver said quietly.

"I was just being dramatic," Kate laughed lightly.

Oliver clearly wanted to say more but he dropped the subject, and they finished with nothing more than a friendly good-bye.

Kate's next caller was even more problematic. When she picked up the phone, she was still mulling over Clay's math problem of the week.

"Hello, darlin'. How'd you sleep Saturday night?"

It annoyed Kate that Randall assumed that she would know who he was without identifying himself on the phone. Not only that, but his question transported her directly back to a certain dark corner of her yard. "Like a baby," Kate said, ignoring the sudden heat that the memory evoked. "And you?"

"My dreams were X-rated, and you starred in every one of them."

"I don't want to hear any more."

"Don't worry. I plan to sell the ideas to a pornographic movie producer, so I'm keeping them confidential. Until I get you up here alone."

It was getting harder and harder to pretend that her body wasn't both tightening and relaxing at every stroke of his voice. Kate closed her eyes to concentrate on sounding cool, calm and collected.

"I was in a good mood before you called. Try not to ruin it."

"Really? Maybe I'll come visit. I'd like to be there for

your good mood."

"Now *that* would definitely ruin my day."

Randall snorted out a laugh. "Any particular reason that you're feeling good?"

"Well, we submitted our bridge proposal to the Connecticut D.O.T. yesterday, so I'm riding a wave of accomplishment." Kate hesitated a second and discovered that she wanted to share the rest of her good news with him. "And C/R/G may be getting a nice infusion of capital soon."

"Congratulations on both, and good luck with the bridge bid. When do you hear if you've gotten the job?"

"They're in a big hurry to get construction going, so I would guess in two to three weeks, but it could be longer."

"How about the C/R/G deal? Should I be investing here?"

Kate could hear the smile in his voice. "Only if you've run out of airlines to buy. I haven't heard any details yet. You probably know better than I do how long these things take."

"Johnson's Law states that the length of time from opening negotiations to closing a deal is directly proportional to the number of lawyers involved."

Kate laughed. "One of my best friends is a lawyer."

"Georgia Jenson. I believe she introduced us."

Kate was astonished that he remembered such a detail.

"We'll credit the legal profession with one good deed."

Randall's voice became more serious. "Kate, Frank Peltier blackmailed me into paying for a whole table at the Beaux Arts Ball. Since you're acquainted with the architectural world, I'd like you to come with me."

A tidal wave of disappointment almost swamped her.

"Thank you, but I'm already going. With Oliver

165

Russell. He's one of David's partners at C/R/G," she felt compelled to add, quickly. How absurd to have two men invite her to the same event!

"Save a dance for me." Randall knew exactly who Oliver Russell was.

"Of course." She was appalled at how much she wanted to go to the ball with Randall. "What sort of mask are you wearing?"

"I don't wear masks."

"Now why doesn't that surprise me? Come on, Randall, you have to get into the spirit of the thing! Let's see. I don't think that Old Yeller would be quite right for you. Nor Balto – too goodie-goodie." Kate was sure she heard Randall snort again, so she went on. "How about the Werewolf of London!" This time he definitely was holding back a laugh. "No, I have it: the Hound of the Baskervilles!' she said triumphantly.

"Feel free to amuse yourself at my expense."

"Actually, I think something feline fits you far better."

"An alley cat, I suppose."

"That's tempting, but I was thinking of a much bigger cat. More like a panther." Kate could picture his hypnotic eyes focused through the slits of a snarling panther mask. In a tuxedo, he would look devastating.

"I'll see if I can arrange a change of theme. What about your mask?"

"I'm going as Gretchen, of course."

"Gretchen's a nice dog, but she doesn't fit you. I'd choose an Irish Setter. It would match your hair and you'd have a nice long nose to look down."

"Touché!" Kate acknowledged with a laugh.

"I'm sorry you can't come with me. It would make the evening interesting. Good-bye, Kate."

"Good-bye. And thank you for the invitation." Kate wasn't sure that he had heard the last. The man ended conversations as abruptly as he began them.

She frowned as the exhilaration of verbally fencing with Randall Johnson crashed against the sense of dread over his and Oliver's meeting. She firmly pushed that problem to the back of her mind. She wanted to savor the pleasure of knowing that Randall had invited her to the ball. "Just like Cinderella," Kate told herself, humming a waltz as she went upstairs to help Clay with his math.

Randall was not humming when he dropped the phone on his desk.

"Son of a bitch. There's an insider in this deal." He tossed the invitation to the Beaux Arts Ball into the trash can.

Fourteen

"KATE, WOULD YOU come to the conference room, please?"

She had been lost in blueprints and was startled at the buzz of the intercom. Now she quickly straightened her collar and rolled down her sleeves before heading down the hall. She couldn't interpret her boss's tone, so she wasn't sure what to expect when she walked through the conference room door.

Bruce Adler was holding an unopened bottle of champagne.

Susan Chen, Jim Mertens, her project partner, and several other senior staff members were milling around in front of a big oval table covered with catering platters and plastic champagne glasses.

"Kate!" Bruce said, waving her over. "Come join the celebration."

"I'll be happy to. But what are we celebrating?" she asked as she walked over to her employer.

"Just a minute and everyone will know," Bruce said. "Stand right here." He raised his voice above the conversations. "Ladies and gentlemen, I have an announcement to make."

Everyone fell silent and turned to listen.

"I just received a telephone call from the lieutenant governor of the fair state of Connecticut. He has unofficially informed me that we have won the contract to design and supervise the construction of State Highway Bridge Number 3309."

Kate gasped and the crowd erupted into cheers and applause. The D.O.T. had moved incredibly quickly. They hadn't expected to hear the results of their bid for at least three weeks!

"The lieutenant governor said that they were bowled over by the brilliance of our design, the thoroughness of our proposal, and our sterling reputation."

More applause greeted Bruce's speech. He held up a hand for quiet.

"I would like to thank Susan for heading the project up; our newest employee, Kate Chilton, for her innovative design work; and Jim Mertens for pulling together the proposal so quickly."

Kate smiled and blushed as once again the group applauded.

"And now, let's celebrate," Bruce said as he popped the cork from the champagne. More pops followed as the glasses were filled and refilled. Staff members introduced themselves and congratulated Kate warmly.

Susan Chen drew Kate out of the crowd. "The lieutenant governor told Bruce – off the record, of course – that we were the only firm to come up with a viable idea for keeping traffic flowing. That's why they made the decision so fast."

Bruce walked over and refilled Kate's glass from the bottle he carried. "You do good work, Kate. Susan will

169

continue to lead the project, but I expect you to be the on-site supervisor. We want this bridge built fast and well."

"I'll be breathing down the construction crew's neck, day and night," Kate promised.

"Try to avoid nights – overtime is expensive," Bruce joked. "Here's to on-time, under-budget, and still standing in a hundred years."

Kate laughed and touched her glass to the one he raised in a toast. "And to the commuters never noticing that they have a new bridge."

"Hear, hear!" Bruce agreed.

Kate floated back to her desk on a cloud of champagne and success. She was going to build a bridge! Pylons would be sunk into the riverbed, steel girders would be bolted and welded together, massive bulldozers, backhoes and dump trucks would roar and strain, all to turn her drawing into solid reality. She and the construction foreman would stand shoulder-to-shoulder, creating a structure that would serve hundreds of thousands of people for decades to come. "You'd think that I was building the George Washington Bridge itself," she laughed as she settled down to work.

"Guess what, guys. We got the job! We're building Bridge Number 3309!"

She was putting a thawed tray of lasagna she had made over the weekend into the oven as they walked through the door.

"Way to go, Mom!" Patrick shouted.

Clay gave her a high five. "I knew you'd get the job. Your design was so cool! When do you start construction?"

"Well, Connecticut has to hire a construction firm first, so I'm madly developing drawings for them to put out to bid. But they're in a big rush, so I'm hoping that it will go in a month or two."

"That's really great," Patrick said, doing a victory dance.

"I have to warn you both; it means more hours for me at work. I'll try to bring as much home as I can, but I'll have to be on-site a lot. I miss you, you know."

"We miss you, too," Clay said. "But we know this is important for a lot of reasons."

"How'd you get so smart?" Kate asked, rumpling his hair.

"He's related to me," Patrick said.

"Why do we have to be uncomfortable to be beautiful?" Kate asked her reflection.

She was dressing for the Beaux Arts Ball, struggling with the row of hooks on the strapless corset bra she had to wear with her gold dress. She smoothed on sheer stockings and pulled on dyed-to-match sandals.

"At least I had the sense to keep the heels low on these."

She dropped the dress over her head and then zipped it up easily over the tight undergarment. The satin bodice began at a low square neckline and fit tightly down to the waist. Three-quarter length sleeves of silky velvet outlined her shoulders and arms. The full taffeta skirt was gathered slightly in back to give the illusion of a bustle. The only decoration was a subtle sparkle of gold beading around the neckline.

She had to admit that it was a spectacular dress. David had picked it out for her. He said the shadow of cleavage the neckline revealed gave him something interesting to think about. Kate grimaced as she wondered when her cleavage had ceased being exciting to him.

She left her neck bare, adding only a pair of Victorian earrings made of gold and set with garnets. She brushed her hair up into a soft twist at the back of her head, leaving tendrils wisping around her neck and face.

Then she tied on the mask and looked in the mirror.

The black mask contrasted dramatically with the gold dress, while the jewels caught the same light as the beads on the gown's neckline. Even her eyes seemed to glitter through the slits of the mask. Oliver really had an extraordinary eye. She untied the mask and walked carefully downstairs, enveloped in a rustle of taffeta against carpeting.

Brigid saw her first. "'Tis a vision you are. You look like a princess."

"Thank you," Kate said, twirling around to show the boys her dress. "How about with this?" she said, raising the mask to her face.

"What do you think, Gretch?" Clay asked, scratching the dog's head as he gestured toward his mother. "Maybe you need some diamonds on your collar."

When Oliver rang the back doorbell, Clay and Patrick greeted him with compliments on his workmanship. Oliver thanked them before raising his head to greet Kate. For a moment, he was still. Then he came forward to kiss her on the cheek. "You look stunning, literally. I've never seen you more beautiful."

"Thank you, kind sir. You look very handsome yourself," Kate said lightly, as she moved toward the boys. "But you don't get the full effect without the final touch of your incredible mask." She took it from Clay and held it up again. "The colors complement this dress so perfectly that I'd think you had a picture of it to work with."

"In a way, I did. It was in my mind," Oliver said,

tapping his forehead. "I remember exactly how you looked at that dinner four years ago."

The direction of the conversation was making Kate uncomfortable, so she turned to pick up her black velvet jacket and her satin purse. "You two listen to Brigid," she said, dropping kisses on Clay and Patrick's heads.

"Och, they're always the best of boys," Brigid said. "And I've missed them! You've done a fine job of mothering these two."

Kate watched Oliver trade a joke with Clay. Her sons were so at ease with him; why couldn't she find some passion for him in her own heart?

Randall Johnson's sardonically smiling face rose in answer to that question. She shook her head to chase it away. For the past hour, she had been pushing aside the knowledge that she had carefully arranged the wisps of her hair and added extra coats of mascara to her lashes knowing that he would be there tonight. She wanted to dazzle him with her style and beauty.

She turned her attention instead to Oliver. She had to admit that he looked very distinguished in his tuxedo. The waves of his hair glinted with golden highlights in contrast to his dark jacket. His tortoiseshell glasses gave him an air that was both intellectual and artistic. *Any woman would be proud to enter a ball on Oliver's arm,* she told herself. She smiled at him when he caught her gaze.

"Shall we go?" he asked, smiling back and taking her jacket to drape over her shoulders.

They talked about the Tower Design offer as they drove into the city. As they crested a hill, Kate drank in the skyline of Manhattan strung across the darkening horizon like a brilliantly jeweled necklace.

173

Oliver read her thoughts. "That view takes my breath away every time I see it."

"It's truly electrifying."

Oliver reached over to brush his fingertips across Kate's cheek. "That's how I feel about you."

Kate sighed. Accepting this invitation really was a mistake. She would have to stop seeing him. Which was a shame. The boys would miss him so much. There was a small, practical voice in her mind that kept asking her why she couldn't just make life easy and marry Oliver. He would probably make a perfectly fine husband if she gave him time.

Kate glanced at him. He was waiting for her response.

"I'm still sorting through my feelings about David's infidelity, and I'm not in a very receptive mood right now."

"I just want to be able to treat you as the woman I love."

Kate looked down at her hands, clenched around her purse. She straightened her fingers. "I want to keep your friendship, but if you force this issue, I may not be able to." She waited as the silence lengthened.

Finally, Oliver spoke. "I see. I'll be patient as long as I can."

"I'm glad that you understand –"

He interrupted her. "I don't understand, but I've learned to wait."

Kate swallowed. After a few moments, she changed the subject, asking him who was likely to be at the Beaux Arts Ball. Oliver answered her with ease, and the conversation remained friendly for the rest of the trip.

As they walked through the ballroom's double doors, Kate laughed in delight. Some years the Ball's decorators strove for aesthetic impact, but this time they had given their sense of humor free rein.

The columns that supported the balcony running around three sides of the room had been turned into enormous fire hydrants. The centerpieces on the tables sprouted from dog bowls and had bones scattered among the flowers. The band was seated in the entrance of a giant doghouse. Huge, sparkling tennis balls hung from the ceiling and painted paw prints tracked back and forth across the mostly-empty dance floor. "Gretchen would love this," Kate joked.

Oliver was chuckling too. "Let's see what the silent auction has – that's always entertaining."

The Beaux Arts Ball raised a substantial sum for charity, not just by charging for places at the dinner tables, but by auctioning donated items that were bid on by the guests. Kate and Oliver admired the elaborate, handmade dog dishes and doghouses designed and built by various architectural firms. One could have a portrait of one's pet painted by a prominent artist or purchase a "Day of Beauty" for Rover at a fancy grooming parlor. When they came to a diamond "dog collar"-style necklace, Kate laughed. "I hope that that's meant for a human."

"I'm not sure," Oliver said. "People can be quite crazy about their dogs."

"Gretchen would look overdressed in that."

"But you would look quite *fetching*."

Kate groaned. "What an awful pun."

Oliver laughed and guided her toward the table where the place cards were lined up in alphabetical order. While Oliver searched for theirs, Kate scanned the array, noting that "Randall Johnson and Guest" were seated at Table 3 and had presumably not arrived yet, since their card was still waiting for them.

She found herself torn between envy and curiosity about the "guest."

"We're at Table Fifteen," Oliver said, tucking the card into his breast pocket. "Ted and Gina should be there, too. And I'm hoping that Paul Desmond and his wife were able to come."

The ballroom began to fill up. Kate and Oliver danced and talked and danced again. To her surprise, Kate was enjoying catching up with David's former business associates. After he died, she hadn't had the time or opportunity to socialize with the architectural crowd.

As they circulated, Kate could not keep herself from surreptitiously checking on Table Three. She even scanned new arrivals and was disappointed when Randall was not in their midst. The fizz of excitement began to go flat.

They sat down for dinner and discovered that Paul Desmond had indeed made it to the ball. Kate had a long conversation with him, and was reassured that he would continue in C/R/G's tradition of dealing well and fairly with clients.

The diners were picking at the remains of dessert and coffee when Frank Peltier appeared beside Oliver's chair. After Frank had described his new office in minute architectural detail, and expressed his personal condolences on David's death, he asked Kate to dance.

Surprised, she rose and moved to the dance floor with him. As they chatted, she sensed that he was moving her in a specific direction. "I was under orders to bring you back to my table," he explained as he stopped dancing and led her between the diners.

As they approached Table Three, a tall, sandy-haired man rose and offered her his hand. "Kate Chilton, a pleasure it is to meet you. I'm Tom Rogan. I work with

Randall Johnson at RJ Enterprises."

She did a fast scan of the table, but Randall had not arrived while she was on the dance floor. As she shook hands with Tom, she caught his look of assessment. Without speaking, Kate raised a quizzical eyebrow.

"A friend of Randall's is a friend of mine," he said with a disarming grin. "And I wanted to meet the woman with the impressive resumé."

"Resumé?" Kate repeated, frowning.

"Phil Gabelli sent it along to RJ Enterprises. But alas, someone had beaten us to you."

If Tom Rogan had read her resumé, Randall must have seen it too. Now he knew more about her than she was comfortable with.

Her discomfort became acute when an unmistakable voice sliced through the babble of conversation around them.

"Frank, how many mules did you have to ride to get here? Tom, you look like a waiter in that tux."

Tom responded, "You look like a cardsharp with all those diamonds flashing. I thought that you weren't coming because you couldn't get a date."

"My date just came with the wrong man." Randall knew that Kate had heard him because he saw her spine stiffen. His eyes gleamed with satisfaction. "I had to beat Prince Charming to the glass slipper."

In fact, he had not intended to come. A little over an hour ago, he had been sitting in his office at Eagle's Nest. When he realized that he was reading the same contract for the third time, he threw it across the room. He felt better so he picked up the next file and hurled it across the room, too. He swiveled around and stared out the window at the lights of Manhattan and then abruptly got up and strode into his bedroom.

Stripping out of his casual clothes, he ripped his tuxedo out of the closet. As he was stabbing diamond studs through the starched pleats of his formal shirt, he looked at himself in the mirror and said in disgust, "You're a damned fool."

He had muttered another curse when he arrived and saw Kate standing beside Frank Peltier. He trusted Frank's discretion, but he knew that Kate could get you to talk about things you wouldn't ordinarily. He hoped that she would not make any connection between Frank and Tower Design.

Kate turned to him and pointedly held out her hand. "Hello, Randall. I'm glad that you didn't miss the ball completely. The decorations alone are worth the price of admission."

Randall took her hand and held it as he let his eyes rove over her.

She had the Gretchen mask perched on top of her hair and yet she still managed to look like a duchess. The mask somehow emphasized the regal tilt of her head and the slender line of her neck. His gaze moved to the shadow between her breasts and he enjoyed the way her suddenly indrawn breath made the shadow deepen. When she pulled her hand away abruptly, he raised his eyes slowly to her face and let a smile tug at the corners of his mouth. He wanted to drag her into a private corner, slide his hands up under those billowing skirts...

Kate watched in fascination as Randall's smile changed into a look of pure lust. The people standing around them faded into a blur of color as she caught her breath. She knew what he was thinking. She was thinking the same thing...

"There you are, Kate. I thought that you might need a guide back to our table."

Oliver's voice was tight with annoyance, but Kate was grateful to him for breaking the pull of Randall's gaze. He held out his hand to Randall. "I don't believe that we've met. I'm Oliver Russell."

"Randall Johnson."

The two men shook hands so briefly it seemed more like the quick salute of two fencers. Oliver slid his arm conspicuously around Kate's waist. "I think that we've done some work for one of your subsidiaries, Pharmatech."

Randall nodded. "Did you work on the new lab?"

"We weren't the original architects. We got called in to do some exterior adjustments because the neighbors weren't happy."

"I just visited there a couple of weeks ago. You did a fine job."

Kate listened with growing incredulity. Oliver had never mentioned that he had worked on one of Randall's buildings. And Randall had never mentioned that he had seen C/R/G's work. She did not for a minute believe that he hadn't known exactly who the architects were at Pharmatech.

"I'm always amazed at what a small world it is," she said with a distinct edge in her voice. "You two have done business together, and none of us realized it."

Oliver had the grace to look slightly guilty. "I just put the two together myself, Kate. We did the job several months ago."

Randall quirked an eyebrow. Kate responded by lifting her chin in a gesture of disdain. She remembered his crack about the way she looked down her nose and added a glare before she turned to Frank Peltier. "I wish you the best of luck with your new location."

"Come visit me, and bring your sons," Frank said, kissing her on the cheek in farewell.

"That would be a long mule ride," Randall put in.

"Most people fly there," Frank smiled.

"Not Kate," Randall said. "She likes to keep her feet firmly on the ground."

Kate could feel Oliver stiffen as he caught the intimate tone of Randall's teasing. His arm tightened around her as he said, "Excuse us. A few members of our table are leaving and wanted to say good-bye to Kate."

"I'll come find you for the next waltz," Randall said.

"I believe that my dance card is filled up."

Randall leaned down so that only she could hear him. "I didn't come all this way to talk. We *will* dance."

"Hmm," Kate said vaguely as Oliver practically yanked her away.

As soon as the crowd allowed, Kate pulled away from Oliver. "Are you trying to crush my ribs?" she asked, shaking out her flattened skirt.

"I'm trying to get you away from a man who's looking at you as if you were a prostitute," Oliver said between clenched teeth. "Did he send Frank Peltier over to pimp for him?"

Kate gasped. "Really, Oliver, that's offensive."

"Is it? I found the way Randall Johnson looked at you more offensive." Oliver took her arm in a firm grasp. "Let's get back to our table. The Gershons and the Desmonds want to leave."

They made the trip back to Table Fifteen in silence. Kate was chatting with a builder and his wife when she sensed a presence behind her. Just as she was about to glance around, Randall took her wrist and said, "I hope that you folks will excuse us. Ms. Chilton promised me this waltz."

Before Kate could think he had propelled her onto the dance floor and pulled her into his arms. "I once heard that dancing is a vertical expression of a horizontal desire," he drawled. "Of course, I'm not that particular about the position, I'm just interested in the desire."

"Just be quiet and let me enjoy this," Kate said.

His eyebrows lifted in surprise but he obeyed her request. Kate was free to concentrate on the warmth of his palm against hers, and the strength of his arm around her waist. She, Randall, and the lilting music seemed to meld into a single glorious pulse as they spun across the dance floor. Kate tilted her head back and let herself luxuriate in the dark fire that burned in his eyes. When he tightened his arm around her, she welcomed the thrust of his thigh between hers.

The two dancers were happily oblivious to the interest of several watchers. Oliver stood rigid as he followed Kate and Randall's progress around the floor. When he saw Kate's gaze lock with her partner's, his nostrils flared white with fury.

Tom's date gestured towards the dancers. "Did you know that your boss waltzes like a dream?"

"I don't think I've ever noticed him waltzing before tonight," Tom said.

"Who is that woman? Randall's like a hawk watching a field mouse."

"Kate Chilton. She's the widowed mother of two small boys. Her husband was an architect, that's why she's here."

"Your boss and a woman with children? I can't believe it."

"The strangest part is that the lady seems to be the

181

reluctant player in this game."

"She doesn't look at all reluctant right now."

Tom watched the couple for a moment. "She's either playing a very deep game or she really wants him to leave her alone. He invited her to this ball and was in a foul mood when she turned him down."

"I would have said that Randall Johnson was virtually irresistible, particularly when he wants something."

"Then I hope he never sets his sights on you."

The waltz was rising to its triumphant finale, and Kate now knew with certainty that she could never marry Oliver. She couldn't marry any man unless every thought in her mind, every nerve in her body, and every pulse of her heart were as attuned to him as she felt to Randall Johnson at this moment. She reveled in the glorious feeling and despaired at the impossibility of holding on to it. Her mood shattered completely as she finally acknowledged that the attraction she had tried to shrug off had evolved into something much deeper. She felt like sobbing. *How could I have been so stupid as to fall in love with this impossible man?*

The music swelled and stopped. Randall ceased moving but kept his hold on her. "Come home with me."

"No. I came with Oliver. I have to leave with Oliver."

He shifted impatiently. "Call me when you get home. I'll come pick you up."

"No."

The music started again, this time a slow, Latin beat. Randall pulled her closer and started dancing. "What are you wearing – armor?" he asked, as he slid his hand up and down the velvet of her bodice.

"A corset. Like Scarlett O'Hara, but with the dubious modern improvement of elastic and hooks."

"I want to take it off of you."

"I'm sure you do, but I'm going to do it all by myself."

"Don't play with me. You want to make love as much as I do."

She sighed. "What I want and what I know I should do are two different things. I'm not playing, Randall. I have two other people depending on me, and no one, not even you, can make me forget that."

"So you're going to marry Oliver Russell and be a good little wife and mother."

"I don't care for the sarcastic tone."

Randall leaned down and ran the tip of his tongue around her ear.

"Stop that," she gasped as the warmth and wet sent a shock of sensation blazing through her. She pulled herself out of his arms and fled from the dance floor.

She managed to stumble into the Ladies' Lounge where she collapsed on a stool and buried her face in her hands.

Fifteen

"RANDALL CAN BE quite a handful, can't he?" a female voice said.

Kate raised her head to find a tall blonde in a form-fitting white sheath applying lipstick at the mirror beside her.

"I saw you dancing with him before I came in, so I assume he's what led to your need for sanctuary."

The woman examined her reflection for a moment and was apparently satisfied because she tucked her lipstick back into her purse and then swiveled on her stool to face Kate. "I dated Randall a few years ago. He's a wonderful lover, in case you don't know that yet. And while he's interested, he's very interested, but he always moves on."

"I appreciate your information, but I'm not quite sure why you're telling me this."

The blonde shrugged gracefully. "You seem like the easily bruised type. I just thought that I should warn you." She held out her hand. "By the way, I'm Sylvia Dupont."

Kate had automatically started to put her hand out but stopped abruptly.

"Sylvia Dupont? From Washington?"

Sylvia looked pleased. "I see that my reputation has reached even New York."

Kate choked back a snort. "My life has gone from soap opera to farce," she said under her breath. She laughed without humor. "This is rich. *Sylvia Dupont* is giving *me* advice."

Sylvia Dupont clearly was not accustomed to provoking laughter. She stood up. "You're drunk."

"No, don't leave yet. I want to take a good look at you," Kate said.

"Why?"

"Because I want to get a good look at the woman my husband had an affair with."

Sylvia's arrogant poise slipped for a moment. Her mouth opened and closed a few times but no sound came out. When she found her voice, it was a whisper.

"You're David's wife."

"I'm David's widow." Kate leaned back on her stool with her arms crossed and let her eyes scan Sylvia up and down.

"But you didn't know."

"Obviously, I did."

"How? We were so careful that you wouldn't find out until after the divorce."

Kate used every ounce of self-control she had to remain stone-faced at Sylvia's statement. "You thought that he was going to divorce me and marry you? You're kidding."

"He was going to marry me. We even stopped seeing each other so that he could ask for the divorce without complications."

Kate was dying inside but she held her contemptuous pose, merely lifting an eyebrow. "He had no intention of

185

divorcing me. He wouldn't leave the boys, and he wouldn't damage his reputation for a little piece of fun."

"You're wrong," Sylvia said but she had turned almost as pale as her dress.

Kate shrugged. "Am I? Married men always claim they're going to leave their wives. It's part of the game. And you weren't his only girlfriend. Didn't you know that?"

She turned to the mirror casually, with the pretense of tucking up loose strands of hair. She hoped Sylvia didn't notice that her hands were shaking.

Sylvia said, "I don't believe you," but she practically ran out the door.

Kate sat staring unseeingly into the mirror. *David had planned to divorce me.* She had thought his affair was the worst thing she would have to handle. *Wrong again.* She waited for her carefully rebuilt confidence to come crashing down. To her relief, her foundation was holding firm.

Suppose Sylvia really loved David? *Well, now she feels as betrayed as I did.* Kate wondered why she hadn't learned her lesson about revenge by now. Should she feel guilty about the lies she had just made up? The urge to give back a little pain had been irresistible.

"Plus, she knew that he was married," Kate pointed out to the mirror, "so she was in the wrong from the start." Her head was pounding. "This is getting much too complicated for me," she said, dropping her forehead to her hand. "I need to go home."

Now she had to make her way to Oliver, who was already angry, while avoiding Sylvia and Randall. She suspected that Sylvia would be just as interested in avoiding her, but Randall was probably ticked off, and he would want to let her know about it.

Kate sighed as she arose. If only she could walk across

a bed of hot coals instead.

Randall stood alone on the dance floor for a few moments, watching Kate's back disappear into the crowd. Then he stalked over to the RJ Enterprises table and asked Tom's date to dance. As soon as the music ended, he escorted her back to the table and said curt farewells to Tom and the other guests.

Tom watched Randall cut straight through the crowd to the exit. "I'd give my year's bonus to have heard the conversation that led up to that little scene."

His companion gave an exaggerated shudder. "I'd hate to have been on Kate Chilton's side of it."

Tom was smiling wickedly. "I think I'm going to enjoy the Monday morning meeting. I just have to think a bit about how best to bring up the subject."

"You're crazy. Leave it alone."

Kate stayed on the opposite side of the room as she looked for Oliver. Fortunately, she found him quickly, talking with a couple she didn't know. She greeted them politely and then said in a low voice, "I have a splitting headache. Would you mind if we went home?"

"We should have a last dance before we leave," he said.

"I'd rather not. I really don't feel well," she said with complete honesty.

"I'm sure that a dance will chase that headache away," Oliver said as he led her firmly toward the dance floor.

Kate was astonished by his insistence and looked up at his face. He appeared perfectly calm until she noticed an odd glint in his eyes and a tightness around his mouth. As he swung her into his arms, she summoned up every remaining ounce of her poise so that she could smile up at him and say, "You're right, I feel better already."

Oliver did not relax. He spun her away from him and brought her back against him hard and close. Kate stumbled slightly but his grasp was so tight that she had no room to fall. She tried to open some space between them but Oliver seemed oblivious to her attempts at loosening his hold. Kate decided that she didn't want to provoke him any further, so she followed his lead until the music ended.

"I think it's time to leave," Oliver said.

She nodded. All she had to do was get through the drive home – which was admittedly a daunting prospect – and then she could collapse.

Oliver behaved like a perfect gentleman as they made their way to the door, guiding Kate through the crowd with a light touch and stopping to exchange a word with the acquaintances they encountered.

Outside, he fell silent as they walked to the parking garage and got in the car for the trip home. As the BMW glided through the night, Kate was caught up in the mental kaleidoscope of Sylvia and David.

"I ran into Sylvia Dupont in the Ladies' Lounge," she said.

He started. "I'm sorry; I didn't know she was there. I wouldn't have had that happen for the world. How did you know who she was?"

"She introduced herself."

Oliver winced. "She's a cool customer, but I wouldn't have expected that."

"Oh, she had no idea who I was when she did it," Kate said with a brittle laugh. "We were just having a casual in-front-of-the-mirror chat."

Oliver did not respond immediately, so Kate decided to take the plunge. Somehow the words and the tears she had been stifling for the last hour got entangled in her throat so that it came out on a sob. "Sylvia claimed that David was planning to divorce me."

Oliver made an angry sound. "He had stopped seeing her months before he died."

The tears escaped down Kate's cheeks. "They did that to keep Sylvia out of the divorce, to keep it simple." Another sob forced its way out of her throat.

Oliver swore. "Sylvia was just trying to upset you."

"Maybe David didn't mean it, but Sylvia thought he did. Did he talk with you about it?"

"Of course not. I'm sure that he said it just to keep Sylvia happy."

Kate's tears subsided as she peered at Oliver in the flickering light of street lamps and oncoming headlights. She found that she couldn't read his face at all and turned away in frustration. "This isn't the exit for my house! Where are we going?"

"To *my* house. I want to talk with you where we won't be interrupted."

Amazed at his insensitivity, Kate put her hand to her aching head. "Could we please postpone this until a better time?"

"I don't think that's a good idea," he said, guiding the car steadily through the streets of Hoboken and into the garage of his brownstone.

Kate considered refusing to get out of the car, but Oliver leaned across her to open the door, making her feel claustrophobic. She got out as fast as her voluminous skirts would allow.

The first floor of Oliver's home was an excellent advertisement for his design abilities. He had gutted the interior and created an open space made interesting by exquisite architectural details and beautiful antiques. Usually Kate spent her first few minutes there lost in admiration at the perfection of the proportions, but tonight she was in no mood to appreciate anything other than a quick exit. She dropped her purse on a table by the door and stopped a few feet into the room.

Oliver flicked on the lights that were carefully placed to illuminate the best features of the rooms. "Sit down, Kate," he said, gesturing to a Biedermeier settee.

Kate hesitated a moment. Oliver simply stood and waited, his gaze locked on her unwaveringly. With a resigned shrug, Kate took the seat he indicated and Oliver sat down across from her.

"You've been through a terrible ordeal, and I blame myself. I didn't expect Sylvia to be at the ball; she's never come before."

Kate made a gesture of dismissal. "You aren't responsible for Sylvia Dupont's social engagements. In a way, I'm glad to have met her. It makes the pain easier to deal with because I have a flesh-and-blood human being to focus on, rather than some nebulous image of the perfect mistress."

"I've always admired your strength," Oliver said, coming around the table to sit beside her.

Kate inched away from him. He wasn't as physically imposing as Randall, but he was tall, and she had felt his strength on the dance floor.

Oliver turned to her. "Now it's my turn to be strong. Kate, I want to share your life: to be a father to Clay and Patrick, to support you so that you can stay home again. I'll protect you from people like Sylvia Dupont and Randall Johnson. I want to marry you and cherish you as you deserve to be cherished." He took both her hands in his. "I love you. And I will never be unfaithful to you."

When Kate sat silent, Oliver let go of her hands and got up to pace across the room. He turned abruptly and said, "I talked David out of asking you for a divorce."

Kate leaned back as though he had slapped her. "So it was true."

Oliver made a gesture of impatience. "David didn't know what he wanted. Sylvia had money and a position in society that he found immensely tempting; she was a shiny new toy for him."

In two strides Oliver was leaning over her, his hands braced behind her on the back of the couch. "Let me keep all that ugliness away from you for the rest of your life."

Oliver's declaration sounded stifling, and Kate desperately wanted to escape from the prison that he had created with his arms. "Stop. I've worked hard to make myself a new life. I've already told you I *need time to think*," she hissed.

Oliver's eyes picked up a hard glint.

"You didn't think with Randall Johnson. I saw the way you looked at him, and now you're going to look at me the same way," he said, grabbing her hair and pulling her head back to kiss her hard on the mouth. Kate pushed against his shoulders, but she had no leverage. When she tried to slide down out of his grasp, he tightened his grip on her hair and knelt over her on the sofa, trapping her in the fabric of her skirts. He released her mouth to slide his lips down her arched throat to the swell of her breast. His free hand moved down to circle her nipple through the velvet. "I've wanted to touch you for so long."

"Don't do this. Don't destroy all our years of friendship —"

"We'll be lovers instead."

191

Now he was pushing her sideways so that she was lying against the sofa's arm and he was crouched over her. "I know that you can love me, Kate. You're so beautiful..."

She tried to twist away from him but he was too heavy. Finally, she just lay still and sobbed, unable to fight this man whom she had known and trusted for so long.

"You're crying." Oliver touched a tear running down her face in surprise. He shifted his weight off of her and gently pulled her to a sitting position. Putting his arm around her shoulders, he said, "I'm sorry. I was angry, and I love you so much."

Kate watched him warily as she moved out of his embrace and slowly stood up. "I think I'll call a taxi."

"I'll take you home. It's the least I can do." He took her hand between his. "Forgive me, Kate."

She slid her hand away. "Please call a taxi."

He stood up, and Kate instantly moved away from him. Oliver's expression became bleak. "All right, I'll get a taxi."

They waited in silence for the cab.

As it pulled away from the curb, Kate saw Oliver standing on the sidewalk with his hand raised in farewell. She turned away without waving. She wondered what she was going to tell Clay and Patrick about Oliver's sudden disappearance from their lives. She knew she never wanted to face him again.

Her hands were still shaking when she tried to pay the driver. He waved her away, saying that the gentleman had taken care of it. Kate stood on the front porch for a few minutes to collect herself before walking into the house. Brigid was reading in the family room.

"Och, you look tired from dancing the night away," the Irishwoman said, closing her book. "Can I make you some tea before I go?"

"No, thank you. I think I just need some sleep."

"Oh, I almost forgot. That gentleman with the accent called and left you a message. He asked you to call him back, no matter what time you got home. I put his number on the kitchen counter."

"Thank you, but he'll have to wait until morning."

"He's a good-looking devil, that one. Good night and sleep deep." Kate walked into the kitchen and picked up the piece of paper with Randall's number on it.

For a moment, she considered calling him. She wanted to talk with someone – anyone – who could wake her out of the nightmare she had just lived through. Instead she went upstairs and checked on her sons, softly straightening their blankets and breathing in the comforting scent of their youth.

Then she stripped off her Cinderella ball gown and left it in a crumpled heap on the floor.

Randall was sitting on his terrace with a bottle of brandy and a snifter beside him. His bow tie lay on the stone floor and his cell phone lay in his lap, stubbornly silent. His sock-clad feet rested on the place where he had first made love to the woman who was making him crazy.

He had driven home in a rage at being left on the dance floor looking like a fool. But he knew he had brought it on himself. In fact, he grudgingly respected Kate for refusing to leave with him.

Now he stared at the night sky and tried to decide what he wanted to do about Ms. Kate Chilton. The most immediate answer, of course, was that he wanted to haul her up here, rip off all that taffeta and armor and make love to her until he was limp. He hadn't felt this sexually frustrated since he was about fourteen.

He tilted some brandy down his throat. But that wasn't enough of an answer. She had made it clear that her priorities were different from his. Actually, he respected her for that too. Thousands of people depended on him for paychecks, it was true, but unlike Kate, he did not have to live his life as an example to them. Having children held you to a whole different level of moral standards and responsibilities. Or it should, Randall thought, acknowledging his own childhood with a grimace of bitterness. He envied Clay and Patrick Chilton.

"Damn, I'm really losing it," he said, putting down his brandy glass. He stood up and his cell phone fell with a clatter. He kicked it across the terrace and then sat on the wall with his back to the view.

He knew what had induced all this soul-searching. It was the look on Kate's face as she had waltzed with him. He had felt a pull in a place where he didn't think that he could feel anything at all. And it scared the hell out of him.

An electronic tone sounded, and Randall was across the terrace in four swift strides.

"Yes?" he drawled.

But it wasn't Kate.

An officer of an English subsidiary was momentarily rendered speechless at reaching a live Randall Johnson in the middle of the night. He soon wished he hadn't because Mr. Johnson was in a very disagreeable mood. The Englishman got off the phone as quickly as possible.

Randall punched the end button and hurled his phone into the treetops.

Sixteen

SHE AWOKE TO the smell of scorched waffles.

Her half-open eyes fell on the crumpled heap of gold velvet and taffeta on the floor. She didn't want to get out of bed. She hadn't felt this awful since she first found Sylvia's letter. Dragging on her bathrobe, she washed quickly and walked down the steps to see who was burning breakfast.

"Hey, Mom," Clay said, looking up from scraping black bits off the waffle iron. "Would you like a waffle?"

"That sounds great," Kate said, even as her stomach flipped in protest. She loved it when her sons offered to cook for her. She shuffled into the family room to greet Patrick, blocking his view of the television as she leaned down to kiss him, and he shifted slightly to keep his eyes on the set.

"Mom, your waffle's ready!" Clay called.

She walked back into the kitchen and sat down. As she began to take her first tentative bite, Clay asked, "Is Oliver coming over today?"

She choked.

"Are you okay?" Clay asked, thumping her on the back.

195

She took a gulp of juice and croaked, "I just swallowed wrong." She took another swallow and said in a clearer voice, "No, Oliver's not coming today."

His face fell. "Oh. I'm working on a new sculpture, and I wanted to get his input on the welding."

Kate's heart twisted. "You know engineers are not totally without aesthetic judgment," she said. "Maybe I could take a look at your welding question."

"Thanks, Mom." He actually gave her a quick hug. "I know you have great taste. I just thought I'd let you rest today. Was the party fun?"

Fun was definitely not an adjective she would apply to her evening.

"The decorations were fantastic." She described the room and the auction items, and they were laughing over the idea of Gretchen at a dog beauty salon when the phone rang.

"Kate, it's Bruce Adler. Sorry to bother you on a Sunday, but I just got a call from the lieutenant governor's assistant. They want to do a press conference tomorrow on site, complete with blueprints, model, and especially the brilliant engineer who came up with the design. They're trying to fend off all the complaints that they've been getting about construction projects disrupting traffic for months at a time. I don't have to tell you what great publicity this is for us."

Kate smiled. "Especially since the project is still right on time."

Bruce laughed. "Let's hope they want to have another press conference at the end of it."

She spent the rest of the day enjoying the company of her children. They whiled away a couple of hours at the welding bench in the garage, experimenting with Clay's new project. Then they ran soccer plays and went out for ice cream. They rented a movie, and after dinner, the three of them sat together on the couch and watched it, totally immersed.

Not until Clay and Patrick were in bed, and Kate was tucked under her own covers, did she allow Oliver or Randall to emerge into her conscious thoughts. In spite of her flannel pajamas, she shivered at the memory of Oliver's hands on her. She couldn't bring herself to fight him because he was her friend. Yet he had been oblivious to the fact that she was unwilling. If she hadn't cried, what would Oliver have done?

She pressed her hands to her stomach as the pain of Sylvia's revelation lanced through her again. David had wanted a divorce. Oliver had confirmed that. She drew in a shaky breath. Her world would have disintegrated around her even if David had lived.

Suddenly, she understood.

Oliver had known all of this, but he hadn't talked David out of leaving her. He had planned to step right into David's shoes after the divorce. David's death had changed nothing in his mind. She threw off her quilt and paced across the room. "Why me?" she asked herself quietly. "Why would he obsess about me?" The question was unanswerable.

To complete the disaster that was her life, she had fallen in love with Randall Johnson.

"You are an idiot," she addressed herself in her dresser mirror. He wanted sex. She wouldn't kid herself that it went any further than that.

And that was her own damned fault.

What she needed to do was find a kind, loving man who would be a father for Clay and Patrick. Randall's voice floated through her mind: "I'm not a nice man, Kate. You don't want to mess with me." She punched a pillow. *How could she love him?*

It was the second unanswerable question of the night.

She decided to wear a pale gray tailored pants suit with a white silk blouse for the press conference. That way she could clamber around the site if necessary without worrying about immodest flashes of thigh. She and Bruce spent the morning reviewing the plans from every angle, trying to think of any questions that the reporters might ask them.

After lunch, they loaded the model into Bruce's car and drove up to the bridge.

Kate was trying to figure out where the cameras would be set up when the official entourage arrived.

Car doors flew open and men and women began to set up tables and unfurl flags. A small knot of people moved toward Bruce and Kate. At its center was a tall blond man in a beautifully cut navy blue suit.

"I'm Lidden Hartley, the lieutenant governor," he said, smiling and holding out his hand to Bruce. "You must be Bruce Adler." He shifted toward Kate. "And you're Kate Chilton. It's a pleasure to meet the people responsible for this innovative design. You've solved a big problem for Connecticut, and we appreciate it. My staff will help you position your visual aids. Thanks so much for coming."

With another warm smile, he swept away to greet the reporters emerging from the third set of vehicles.

"Wow," Kate said. "He's a smooth act. He even knew our names."

"His staff briefed him in the car on the way over. I told them exactly whom to expect," Bruce said, as they carried the blueprints and the model to the tables.

"But he bothered to remember."

"He's a politician. They're good at that or they don't get reelected."

Kate raised her brows. "You're very cynical."

"Not cynical, realistic."

The press secretary bustled up to them. She was a dark-haired woman with wire-rimmed glasses and a brisk air. "I'm Joan. What do you have here?" She looked over the model and the blueprints with an expert eye before more staff members whisked them away. Then she turned to Kate. "We'll want you to do at least some of the talking because you're a woman, and we want to encourage our female constituents."

Kate suppressed a smile at the PC-speak and listened carefully to Joan's outline of the press conference. Lidden Hartley would obviously get the lion's share of the attention but they wanted Kate front and center. "Sorry, Bruce," she said when Joan had moved away. "I didn't know that I would be encouraging female constituents."

Bruce rolled his eyes in mock disgust. "Upstaged by the token female."

Kate was amazed at the speed with which everything went forward. No one wanted to waste time hanging around the edge of a busy highway. Another surprise was the familiarity between the government officials and the reporters; Lidden Hartley traded jokes with the reporters as his hair was groomed.

Suddenly, the red lights glowed on all of the cameras, and Kate tried to look pleasantly professional as she faced the battery of lenses. The lieutenant governor gave a short speech about the ongoing improvements to the highway system. Bruce did his part by playing up Connecticut's emphasis on not disrupting traffic. Kate got to show off the model as she gave a simple explanation of how the construction would work. The reporters asked a few questions, most of which Lidden Hartley and Bruce fielded. One design question was directed to her. Then it was over, and the press vanished even faster than they had appeared.

Joan helped them carry the model back to the car. "This should appear on the ten o'clock news if you want to watch. Mr. Hartley is planning to run for governor next year, so the press is following him pretty closely. And they like to get their digs in about road construction, so this will give them an opportunity to make snide remarks."

Bruce was just slamming down the trunk when the lieutenant governor himself strode over. "An excellent presentation! We can use some good press on this highway construction, as I'm sure you know." Kate admired the smile that drew listeners into his charmed circle. "Bruce, thanks for making the trek up here and making us look so good. Kate, I can see why Randall Johnson is so impressed with you. That's a brilliant solution to our problem."

'Thank you, sir," Kate said, even as she was absorbing what he had just said. Randall had discussed her project with Lidden Hartley? And without bothering to mention it to her? Her blood was boiling as she shook hands once again with the lieutenant governor.

Bruce looked at her quizzically once they were alone. "I didn't know you had friends in such high places. It goes a long way toward explaining how we got the job so quickly."

"I hope that we won the job on the merits of our proposal," Kate said stiffly.

Bruce laughed. "I'm not downplaying the importance of

the work that went into our proposal. Hell, we probably would have been chosen without any intervention. According to my sources, we had the best solution. But for an unfamiliar firm to be approved so fast...well, Susan and I were amazed. It just proves the old adage. It's not what you know, it's who you know."

Kate's jaw clenched. Maneuvering her into his swimming pool or even into his bed was one thing. His manipulation of her livelihood went beyond the pale. Despite her determination never to see him again, she now longed to tell Randall exactly what she thought of his interference.

"You don't have to answer this but I'm curious: how do you know Randall Johnson?" Bruce asked.

"We have mutual friends," Kate said, watering down the truth considerably.

Bruce raised his eyebrows. "There's nothing wrong with using connections, Kate. The business and political worlds run on the 'old boy network.' It's naive to think otherwise."

A cell phone beeped as they got into Bruce's car. They both reached into their pockets. "It's mine," Kate said. "Hello, Kate Chilton."

"Kate, it's Denise. I'm at the hospital with Clay and Patrick."

Kate's heart froze. "What's wrong?"

"Patrick is fine. Clay got his hand tangled up in a dog fight. They've done everything they can here, and the doctor wants to talk with you."

"Denise, is he all right?"

"He's fine but his hand is pretty chewed up. Here's Dr. Mattern."

"Hello, Mrs. Chilton? I'm Andrea Mattern, the emergency room doctor. Your son is in no danger. We've stopped the bleeding and bandaged his hand. However, there is a fair amount of damage to the muscles and ligaments, and I would recommend that you take him to an orthopedic surgeon as soon as possible. Time can make a big difference in reattaching tissues."

"How bad is it?" Kate asked in a small voice.

"It's his left hand and I understand that he's right-handed, so his writing won't be affected. But he could lose a noticeable amount of mobility and strength. It's hard to tell so soon and I'm not a specialist. I could send him to the doctor we have on staff, but frankly I would recommend an orthopedic surgeon at Long Island Jewish Hospital. He's one of the best at treating hand injuries."

"Can you refer us to him?"

Dr. Mattern hesitated. "Yes, but I don't have much pull. To be frank, this man mostly works on athletes and celebrities."

"Give me his name and number and I'll do whatever I need to." Kate wrote down the information, then asked to speak with Clay.

"Hey, Mom. Sorry to be such trouble," came his shaken voice.

"Sweetheart, don't apologize. How are you?"

"Well, my hand hurts a lot, but other than that I'm fine. A little foggy because they gave me some painkillers, I think."

"I'll be there as fast as I can. I'm going to try to arrange for you to go to a fancy Long Island doctor while I'm on my way. I love you, Clay. Relax and don't worry about anything."

"Thanks, Mom. Here's Mrs. Costanza."

"Denise, I can't thank you enough for being there with

Clay. Will they let him leave soon?"

Denise consulted with the doctor. "Dr. Mattern says I can take him home now as long as he stays quiet. I think the painkillers will knock him out anyway. I'll take him to my house. You can come pick him up whenever you get home."

"I'm on my way now. I'll be there as soon as I can."

Kate ended the call and noticed that Bruce was already on the highway toward New Jersey rather than back to the city. She closed her eyes to gather her scattered wits and to keep herself from crying. "Thanks, Bruce," she whispered. "I know this is way out of your way."

"I gather it's a medical emergency?"

"My son got his hand mangled by a dog. The local ER did the best they could, but they want him to see an orthopedic surgeon as soon as possible." Kate glanced down at the name and phone number in her hand. "You don't know any doctors on Long Island, do you?"

Bruce shook his head. "I stay away from doctors as much as possible."

The moment Kate had heard the words "athletes and celebrities" she had known what she would have to do. A man who knew lieutenant governors would be able to get Clay in to see a mere orthopedic surgeon. She punched in the number for directory assistance. Bruce ought to enjoy listening to this phone call, she thought as she said, "May I have the number for RJ Enterprises in New York City?" She pushed the auto-dial button. Her pride was going to take a beating, but that was a small price to pay for Clay's health.

"Randall Johnson's office, please. This is Kate Chilton."

Kate had to take a deep breath as she waited. He had

every reason to ignore her call. He was probably still fuming over her behavior on the dance floor. Maybe he would think that she was calling to apologize. She felt her throat tighten.

"Hello, Kate."

Even at a time like this, his voice made her nerve endings leap. Kate tried to gauge his tone, but it was unreadable. "Hello, Randall. I have a favor to ask for Clay."

"A favor?" His tone was distinctly unfriendly now.

"Yes. Clay's hand was mangled by a dog and the local doctor strongly advises that he see an orthopedic surgeon on Long Island as quickly as possible. She gave me the doctor's name, but said that he's not accessible to the average patient. I wondered if you might be able to help."

There was dead silence, and Kate squirmed. She longed to say more but she was very aware of Bruce Adler's unavoidable eavesdropping. "My boss is driving me home from a meeting in Connecticut as we speak," she offered in oblique explanation.

"I see. Give me the doctor's name and number."

Kate let out her breath in a whoosh and read off the information.

"Who's the doctor who saw him? And at what hospital?"

Kate told him.

"Give me your cell phone number. I'll call you back."

Kate reeled it off and then softened her voice. "Thank you so much. I am very, very grateful for your help."

"Don't thank me until I see if I can do anything," he said abruptly and hung up.

Kate pushed the end button and let her head fall back against the seat in relief. She had complete faith in

Randall's ability to overcome any obstacles. The thought of how indebted she would be to him was galling, but her concern for Clay's well-being overwhelmed all other considerations.

"You're a quick learner," Bruce commented.

Randall had cleared his office of three senior staff members when Kate's call came through. He was looking forward to raking her over the coals without an audience. Her plea for help had dissipated all his anger and replaced it with an odd feeling of gratification.

He should have known that she wouldn't call him at work for a social conversation. In fact, he gave her a mental salute for what it must have cost her to make that phone call. Then he smiled smugly at the thought of how obligated she would feel to him for his help. The situation had some interesting possibilities.

But right now, he needed to help out a boy with a serious injury.

"Gail, tell Joe that I need the car in ten minutes and that he's driving for a change. I'll be working on the road."

As he picked up his cell phone and his Palm Pilot, Randall thought of Clay's extraordinary sculptures and the delicate welding that was required to create them. He grabbed his laptop and then strode out of the office.

It took four calls, but Randall got the surgeon to agree to an immediate evaluation. Two more phone calls got clearance for Janine to take the helicopter into the Long Island hospital's helipad. He glanced at his watch as he dialed Kate's cell phone: forty-two minutes had passed since she called. *Not bad.*

"Hello, Kate. I've got the surgeon lined up as soon as

you can get to Long Island Jewish Hospital."

"I can't begin to thank you adequately," she began.

"You may not thank me when you hear the rest. The surgeon wants Clay in ASAP so I've arranged for you to go in via the company helicopter. You just have to drive to the Fairfield Airport. My pilot, Janine Tanner, will take you from there. I know you hate to fly, but this will avoid traffic, and I thought that the circumstances warranted speed."

He heard Kate swallow, but her voice was strong. "That's really above and beyond the call of duty. I hate to put you to all this trouble, but I'll accept your offer for Clay's sake."

"Good girl. Janine will be waiting for you in the airport lounge."

"Thank you so much," she managed to gasp just before he hung up.

She let the phone drop in her lap as Bruce turned into Denise's driveway. "Everything's arranged. Thanks so much for driving me here."

"No problem. Don't worry about coming into the office. Just keep us posted on your son's progress."

Kate picked up her briefcase and pocketbook, gave Bruce a distracted wave, and raced into Denise's house.

"Denise, I'm here. Where's Clay?"

Denise took Kate's briefcase out of her hand. "He's upstairs sleeping in Robert's room."

Kate took the steps two at a time and then tiptoed into the bedroom. Clay lay sleeping on his back, with his injured hand lying beside him swathed in gauze and strapped to a board. He looked pale but peaceful. Kate watched him for a minute and then brushed a feather-light kiss over his forehead before turning to leave. She would wake him up after she talked with Denise.

When she came downstairs, Patrick had appeared from the basement playroom. He dashed into her arms. "Mom, it was so scary. This strange dog came over and attacked Thunder for no reason. Clay tried to grab their collars. The dog bit his hand and wouldn't let go until the lady came out of her house and threw water on him. I didn't know what to do, so I asked the lady to call Mrs. Costanza since I knew that you were at the bridge. It wasn't Thunder's fault. He was just walking along on his leash, and this other dog was loose and jumped on him."

"It's okay, Patrick. You did absolutely the best thing to get Mrs. Costanza," Kate said, kneeling so that she could hold him and see his face. "Clay will be fine. I'm going to take him to a doctor on Long Island now. He'll fix up his hand like new."

Patrick's tearstained face relaxed. "His hand looked horrible. You could see the bones."

Kate winced. Still holding Patrick, she stood up and turned to Denise. "You are a true friend to go through all this for me."

Denise waved a dismissive hand. "I know that you would do the same for my children. I'll keep Patrick here while you take Clay in unless you want me to drive you there."

"Mom, I want to go with you and Clay," Patrick protested.

"I'd love to have you, sweetheart, but we might be at the hospital for a long time. You'll be much more comfortable here. Why don't you go back downstairs while I organize things with Mrs. Costanza."

Patrick reluctantly left the adults. "He's going to be even more upset when he finds out that we're flying to the hospital in a helicopter."

Denise whistled. "How'd you manage that?"

Kate flushed. "Do you remember Randall Johnson?"

"He's pretty unforgettable."

"He pulled some strings for me."

"I see." Denise restrained her curiosity with obvious effort. "You owe me a long conversation when this is all over."

"I owe you a lot more than a long conversation," Kate said. "But right now, let's get Clay up and into your car. I need to borrow it, so I can drive to the Fairfield Airport."

The relief on Clay's face when he woke up to see his mother beside him made Kate's heart twist. "Hello, sweetheart. How are you feeling?"

"Really tired. And my hand hurts."

"I'm so sorry, love," she said, brushing his hair out of his eyes. "I'm taking you to Long Island to get you all fixed up. You'll even get to ride in Mr. Johnson's helicopter after all."

Clay looked confused as Kate helped him sit up. "Why am I riding in Mr. Johnson's helicopter?"

"Because the doctor wants to see you as fast as possible, and a helicopter is the fastest way to get there."

"Oh. Okay." Clay staggered slightly as he stood up, and Kate wrapped her arm around his waist. "I'm all right, Mom. Just groggy."

"I'll just stick by you until we get down the stairs."

A look of longing crossed Patrick's face when Kate told him where they were going, but he said only, "That's really nice of Mr. Johnson to lend you his helicopter." Then he took Clay's other hand and squeezed it, saying, "Good luck. I'll walk the dogs while you're gone."

Patrick hugged Kate more fiercely than usual and then walked back to the house with a backward wave. Kate suspected that he was fighting tears so she let him go.

At the airport they were greeted by a striking young blond woman who shook Kate's hand.

"Mrs. Chilton? I'm Janine Tanner. There's a wheelchair over here for Clay."

"I don't need a wheelchair," Clay protested in embarrassment. "I can walk fine, really. But thanks."

Janine smiled. "Okay, no wheelchair. We've got clearance to go anytime."

As they walked across the tarmac to a gleaming silver helicopter with *RJ Enterprises* painted in blue on the side, Janine spoke. "I understand that you're not a fan of flying, Mrs. Chilton, so I'll take it easy."

"I appreciate your concern, but I want to get Clay to the hospital as quickly as possible. Do whatever's necessary to make the trip short. And please, call me Kate."

"Okay, Kate, we'll do the Rambo Run," Janine said, opening the passenger door for them. "There are headphones on the seats if you want to communicate with me or listen to my communications. I'll keep you up-to-date on our progress."

Clay's eyes lit up and Kate gulped. They climbed into the leather seats, buckled their seat belts and fitted the headphones on. Kate arranged a pillow under Clay's injured hand and strapped it down with another seat belt. The rotors began to turn, and Kate closed her eyes and took three deep breaths. Janine's voice crackled through the headphones, informing the tower that they were ready for takeoff. The vibrations increased and suddenly they were airborne, moving upward and sideways at the same time.

Kate took several more deep breaths. Clay winced as he shifted to look through the window, and Kate fought down her terror to readjust the pillow.

"This is so cool, Mom," Clay said. "I wish Patrick were here."

"Who's Patrick?" Janine's voice came through again.

"My brother. He loves anything that flies."

"We'll have to get him up here then. I love anything that flies, too."

Kate was pleased to see Clay grin as she rolled her eyes heavenward. Janine gave Clay a rundown on the helicopter and their route. Kate listened with one ear as she surveyed the interior. The eight seats were silvery gray and very comfortable. Each was equipped with a folding table – for keeping up with paperwork, Kate imagined. The walls and floor were carpeted in a deep blue. Janine described the location of a built-in cooler stocked with drinks if they got thirsty and a compact cupboard that held snacks.

"It should be a nice smooth ride all the way out. How are you doing, Kate?"

"If I could forget the fact that I'm a couple of thousand feet above ground, it would be downright pleasant."

Janine chuckled. "Only the best for guests of Mr. Johnson's."

Kate flinched inwardly at the reminder of whom she had to thank for this ride. She tried to convince herself that having people flown around in helicopters was nothing out of the ordinary for Randall Johnson. Nor was making a few well-placed telephone calls. But she felt almost crushed by her sense of obligation; it seemed completely beyond her means to repay him. She couldn't even think of words that would adequately express her gratitude.

The timbre of the vibrations changed, and just as Kate

started to clutch the arms of her seat in a panic, Janine announced that they were making their descent to the hospital's helipad. Clay was glued to the window as the helicopter side-slipped and hovered over the white *H* painted on the building's roof. They touched down so gently that Kate wasn't sure they had landed.

"We're here," Janine said as the door flew open. Several scrub-clad hospital personnel swarmed around them, putting Clay in a wheelchair, firing questions at him and at Kate, and rushing them toward the elevator door.

Kate ducked low under the gently-turning rotors and waved her thanks to Janine in the cockpit. Janine gave her a thumbs-up and waved to Clay. Then she looked past Kate and saluted. The rotors picked up momentum and the helicopter lifted off as efficiently as it had landed.

Kate turned to see Randall Johnson, his suit jacket whipping in the wind, his hand lifted in farewell to Janine. A wave of relief and gratitude surged through her. He looked so familiar and solid, Kate had to quell the impulse to fly into his arms. Instead she smiled at him with her heart in her eyes.

Randall's arm seemed to freeze halfway down and an odd expression flitted across his face.

Kate raised her voice over the receding noise of the helicopter. "Thank you so much for everything, but especially for coming here. I dreaded facing the illustrious Dr. Lane alone."

Randall lowered his arm to his side and walked over to her. He looked at her a moment before speaking. "How did Clay do on the trip?"

"Clay did fine; the fascination of the ride took his mind off the pain."

"How did you do?"

211

"Janine made it very smooth."

Randall caught up with Clay's wheelchair as they entered the elevator. "Well, young man, you went to a lot of trouble to get a helicopter ride. You and I are going to catch heck from your mother about this later."

"Hi, Mr. Johnson." Clay smiled at him shyly. "Thanks for the trip. Mom was cool; she told Ms. Tanner to burn rubber, or whatever you call going fast in a chopper."

Randall smiled and patted him on the shoulder. "How's that hand feeling?"

Clay made a face. "Sore."

"They'll take care of you here."

The elevator doors opened and the group proceeded down the hall to an examining room.

Dr. Lane strode in with his attendants. A compact man with iron gray hair and rimless glasses, the hand surgeon wore his white coat with authority. After several quick questions to Kate and Clay, he suggested that she and Randall leave while he examined Clay's hand. "It won't be a pretty sight, so why don't you wait outside?"

Kate was about to object when Randall put a hand firmly in the small of her back and escorted her out the door. "Dr. Lane will report to us as soon as he's done," Randall said loudly enough for the doctor to hear and understand. "Let him do his job."

They walked down the hall to the lounge area. Kate sank down into one of the pale green vinyl chairs and stared straight ahead. Randall walked restlessly around the room until he saw the coffeemaker. He poured two foam cups full, and asked Kate what she took in hers.

"Cream and sugar, please," she said absently.

When he put the cup in her hand, she smiled briefly and

said, "Thank you."

He went back to his pacing. When he looked at Kate again, she was sitting ramrod straight with the untouched coffee still in her hand. He went over and sat in the chair across from her, his elbows on his knees.

"After Dr. Lane spoke with Dr. Mattern at the ER, he told me that he's very optimistic about being able to restore full function to Clay's hand."

"Really?" Kate's expression lightened slightly. "That's good news. Dr. Mattern thinks he's the best hand surgeon in the country. I just hate to think of Clay being limited in any way when using his hands."

"I know. Those sculptures of his require a lot of manual dexterity. But he's a smart kid, and even if there should be a problem, he'll learn to compensate for it."

"Yes, but I don't want him to have to compensate for it. He's too young to have to deal with limitations."

Randall stared down at the coffee cup he was fidgeting with. Kate was struck by how his hands enveloped the cup. She shook her head slightly to clear it. She kept fixating on odd details: Randall's huge hands, the splash of blue in the abstract print hanging on the wall, the hum of the coffeemaker. Around it all swirled worry and, of course, guilt that her son was injured when she was away.

"Stop beating yourself up, Kate."

Randall's clairvoyance startled her into looking at his face.

"I can't help it. I wasn't there when my child needed me. He had to depend on a friend to take him to the hospital. If I hadn't decided to go back to work..."

Randall looked down and turned his coffee cup in his hands several times before he responded. "Guilt is not a useful emotion. You can't protect your children from every

213

bad thing the world throws at them. You've done something better: you've given them the tools and the confidence to deal with adversity." He raised his head. "Clay and Patrick are two lucky kids."

Kate could barely trust her voice. "Thanks," she whispered. She managed a shaky smile through the tears spilling down her cheeks. "Not only do you get stuck in a hospital waiting room, but you have to comfort a guilt-ridden mother."

Randall's smile was solid. "It's not a role I have much experience with."

"You're doing an excellent job." Kate suddenly looked away and put her coffee cup down on the table by her chair. "You've done a wonderful job of everything. I don't know how I will ever be able to repay…"

"You don't owe me anything," Randall interrupted as his smile vanished.

"Then why…" Kate started to ask in genuine puzzlement when Dr. Lane's voice stopped her. Kate stood up.

"Mrs. Chilton, it looks promising. All the pieces are still there and still in good shape, and there doesn't seem to be any nerve damage. We can reattach the ligaments and sew up the muscles; and with physical therapy, Clay's hand should be as good as new."

"Thank goodness," Kate breathed.

"If you have no objection, I'd like to call in a plastic surgeon to work on the skin. I can handle the mechanics but Alice Reiffel is terrific on the aesthetics. When she finishes a job, there's barely a scar."

Kate quailed inwardly at the thought of the expense; she was sure her health insurance didn't run to plastic surgery. But she wasn't about to turn down anything that would aid in Clay's full recovery.

"Of course. I appreciate your concern with the outside, too." She hesitated a moment. "Dr. Lane, my son wants to be a sculptor, so he needs strength and mobility even in his left hand. I just wanted to tell you how much your help means to us."

The surgeon actually smiled. "So I gather. I told him that after all the physical therapy, his hand may actually be stronger than before."

"Thank you. When will you operate?"

Dr. Lane looked surprised. "Right now. The sooner the better."

"Oh," Kate said. "I didn't realize that you could arrange it so quickly."

The doctor glanced at Randall Johnson, standing just behind Kate. His expression took on a slightly sardonic cast. "We're always happy to accommodate a friend of Mr. Johnson."

Kate looked back to see Randall's lips tighten in irritation but all he said was, "Take good care of the boy."

Dr. Lane raised an eyebrow. "I always take care of my patients. By the way, Mrs. Chilton, you have a very brave son. He didn't even groan during the examination. I wanted to make sure to tell you that."

"Do you have children, Doctor Lane?"

"Five," he said with a proud grin.

"I'll tell Clay what you said." Kate smiled back. "May I see him before you operate?"

"Go on in. We're prepping the operating room, so you have about ten minutes. After that, I'd recommend that you give the reception nurse your cell phone number and then go out and eat. It will be several hours before you can see Clay again."

Kate turned to Randall. He said, "You go see him and then meet me back here. I'll find a place for us to eat."

She didn't waste time telling him that she would probably throw up if she put anything in her stomach. She started down the hall to see Clay, then stopped and turned. "Why don't you join me in five minutes? I know Clay would like to see you."

Randall looked surprised, but he nodded.

As she raced down the hall, Kate thought that, no matter how powerful and self-assured he seemed, Randall Johnson was not without his own vulnerabilities.

Seventeen

"HELLO, SWEETHEART. HOW are you doing?" Kate asked as she kissed Clay's pale forehead. She sat down very gently on the edge of the examining table.

"The exam wasn't fun," Clay said with macho understatement.

Kate brushed damp hair away from his face. "Dr. Lane was very impressed with how well you handled the pain. And I don't think he impresses easily."

"He's cool. He says my hand might actually be stronger when he's finished. Do you think that's true?" Suddenly Clay looked heartbreakingly young and scared.

"I don't think Dr. Lane makes promises that he doesn't expect to keep. He's one of the best hand surgeons in the country, so he's had lots of experience. I wouldn't worry at all."

Clay's expression relaxed so completely that Kate almost sobbed. Her son's trust in her was gut-wrenching.

"Dr. Lane says he's a sculptor, too, only with living tissues," he said, and smiled shyly. "He asked me what I enjoyed doing, and I told him about my sculptures."

Kate liked Dr. Lewis Lane more and more.

Clay's face tightened again. "He said the operation will take several hours. Will you be here when I wake up?"

"Of course I will."

"Don't you have to go home for Patrick?"

"He's fine with the Costanzas. Don't you worry about anything but getting your hand fixed. We have lots of good friends who will help us, and I'll be here until you're ready to go home."

"Hello, tough guy," Randall Johnson's voice came from behind Kate, and she jumped slightly.

"Mr. Johnson!" Clay's face lit up. Kate smiled ruefully and wondered if she should be jealous that her entrance hadn't evoked the same enthusiasm.

"The doctor says you'll have a hand like the Terminator when he's done with you. He might even build in an acetylene torch while he's in there," Randall said.

Clay chuckled. "I'd rather have a stainless steel clamp."

"That can be arranged." Randall dropped one hand gently onto Kate's shoulder. "Speaking of which, I've made arrangements for your mother to sleep here, but you'll have to share a room with her."

Kate looked up in surprise. "Th-that's great," she managed to stammer.

The door opened and a nurse bustled in, carrying a hospital gown.

"It's time to suit up the patient. You can pick up a beeper at the reception desk. We'll beep you when you can see this young man again."

Kate leaned forward and hugged Clay gently. "Everything will be fine. I love you." She kissed him again.

"He's in good hands with Dr. Lane, pun intended," the nurse said as she ushered them out the door.

Kate wondered how she would get through the next hours.

"The nurse is right," Randall said. "Dr. Lane will do the job."

"I know. I just wish that he were operating on me, not my child."

Randall put his arm around her shoulders and turned her gently toward the reception desk. "Let's pick up that beeper and leave the cell phone number."

"I can't leave," Kate said, taking guilty pleasure in being close to Randall as he steered her down the hall.

"There's a cafeteria here in the hospital."

"I can't eat, either."

"I understand your doubts about hospital food, but Ms. Morgan here assures me that the cafeteria serves a good meal," Randall said, as he handed the nurse his business card and accepted a beeper from her.

Kate caught the smile on the nurse's face and remembered she wasn't the only woman susceptible to Randall's charm. The pile of papers on the nurse's desk suddenly reminded her that she hadn't filled out or signed a single piece of paperwork. She frowned.

"Don't I need to fill out some forms for my son? You don't even have a copy of his insurance card."

Nurse Morgan shook her head. "Mr. Johnson has taken care of everything. You just worry about helping that boy of yours get better."

"Thank you," Kate said with a strained smile. She turned to Randall. "We need to discuss a few things."

"When we get to the cafeteria," he said, taking her by the elbow and moving her firmly toward the elevator.

The doors opened and Randall guided her out of the

219

Nancy Herkness

elevator with his hand at the small of her back. Once again, she savored his touch while feeling she shouldn't. Especially now that she was furious with him. And grateful. But furious, too. The warmth of his hand seemed to spread deep into her body. She felt chilled when he moved it away to pick up a tray and hand it to her.

Kate slid her tray along the metal shelf, randomly picking up plates of food. She decided not to argue when Randall paid for everything. She had a bigger battle to fight.

"I truly appreciate everything you've done," she began after they had settled at a table in a quiet corner.

"If you thank me one more time, I'm going to sit at another table," Randall said, cutting into a slice of meat loaf.

"Don't tempt me," Kate said before she could stop herself.

Randall's smile flashed. "I know you've been dying to read me the riot act for being an arrogant, high-handed pain in the ass. Go right ahead. I prefer that to being smothered in gratitude."

"Then stop being arrogant and high-handed and rearranging my life," Kate exploded.

The smile disappeared. "That's an overreaction to filling out a few forms."

"Oh, I'll deal with the forms in a minute." She had just remembered something else that Clay's accident had pushed right out of her mind.

"I met Lidden Hartley today, and I understand that he's a good friend of yours. It's funny that you mentioned me to him, but didn't mention him to me." With great satisfaction, Kate watched a tiny shadow of discomfort flit across Randall's face. It was gone almost instantly.

"All I did was speed up the inevitable. Yours was the

only design that they were seriously considering. Lidden just needed to be comfortable with a newcomer to the business. That's the way the world works." He jabbed his fork into a tomato so hard that it squirted seeds halfway across the table.

"So everyone keeps telling me. I'm just naive enough to want to get a job on my own merits."

"It's not naiveté, it's pride. One of the seven deadly sins, sweetheart."

"And one with which you are intimately acquainted."

"Oh, I'm pretty well acquainted with most of the deadly seven. It makes life interesting." Randall's drawl was suddenly in evidence.

"Is that why you're doing all this? For lust?" Kate snapped. Randall's fork stopped in midair. She braced herself as he slowly set down his fork and sat back in his chair.

"Don't flatter yourself, darlin'. I don't need to pull strings to get lucky."

"No, you don't." Kate's anger had turned to guilt. He had actually looked hurt when she accused him of base motives. But she was still confused. "So why? Why did you talk to Lidden Hartley?"

Randall looked away. "It came up in conversation." He picked up his roll and began systematically tearing it to pieces.

Kate watched him for a moment. "Did the helicopter just come up in conversation? And how about all the paperwork?"

He tossed the roll back onto the plate. "That's what I do. I solve problems. I handle crises. Isn't that why you called me?"

Kate derived an ignoble pleasure from knowing that she

was making Randall squirm. She just wished that she knew why he was squirming. "You've arranged everything perfectly, yet you're still here, eating hospital food and waiting."

He looked toward the cafeteria door. "I'm beginning to wonder about that myself," he said sardonically.

They both started as a beeper went off. Randall shook his head. "It's not ours." He leaned forward. "I'm making allowances for you because I know you're worried about Clay. But my patience is limited. Go back to the gratitude."

He picked up his fork and impaled a piece of meat loaf.

"Okay, but we still have to discuss the paperwork. I assume that you put everything on your bill. I need to have it on my bill."

"Do you have any idea how much this surgery will cost?"

"No, but that's what health insurance is for."

"Does yours cover plastic surgery?"

"I'm sure it does." She knew she didn't sound convincing.

Randall slammed his hand down on the table. "God damn it, Kate, do you know how much money I have?"

Kate was taken aback. "Not exactly, but I can guess the order of magnitude."

"I doubt it. I have a whole foundation set up just so I can give it away faster. Paying for this operation won't mean anything to me, and I know you can't afford it."

"And how do you know that?" Kate asked in icy tones.

He ran both hands through his hair in exasperation. "Because you're back at *work*. You wouldn't be there if you didn't need to be."

"After what David did to me, I need to restore my self-esteem."

"Don't give me that touchy-feely crap. Your husband left you without enough money, and you had to go back to work."

"So you view me as a charity case for your foundation to take care of."

"You have an offensive tendency to find the worst interpretation for everything I do."

"I'm sorry." Kate bit her lip. "I don't mean to sound that way." She drew in a long breath. "I know that you mean to be helpful. But after everything that's happened, I really do need to stand on my own. I can't let you just sweep down from your mountaintop and solve my problems whenever the mood strikes you."

"We're back to that, are we? I'm supposed to do exactly what you ask me to do and no more."

"Yes," Kate said as tears filled her eyes. "I have nothing to offer you that can make up for all you've done."

"I think that if we found a nice empty hospital bed, I could demonstrate a few of the things that you have to offer."

The tears spilled over, but she ignored them. "You always do that."

"Do what?" Randall asked, taking a sip of coffee.

"Stop the conversation with some crude comment."

He smiled unpleasantly. "I believe you brought the topic up first."

"I'm going back to the waiting room," Kate said, standing up and walking away before his coffee cup could hit the table.

Randall watched her go. He needed to think. When a cafeteria worker asked him if he was finished with his dinner, he gave a single nod of assent and continued to brood.

The distinctive double ring of his private cell phone number roused him. Gail was screening all his calls so this was either an emergency or a friend.

"Randall, Tom here. Are you still at the hospital?"

"Yes."

"How's the patient?"

"Lane is confident that he can repair the damage. The boy will need some physical therapy, but he should be fine."

"That's good news. How's his mother holding up?"

"As well as can be expected. She's worried, she's guilty. She's pissed off at me."

"What?"

"She doesn't want the easy stuff, Tom."

"The *easy stuff*?" Tom's confusion came clearly through the line.

"Things like helicopter rides and hand surgeons standing by. Money. Influence. The easy stuff."

"I see," Tom said with both understanding and amusement in his voice. "What *does* she want?"

"That's the million dollar question, isn't it?"

Tom was silent. Then he said seriously, "What do *you* want, Randall?"

Randall was silent for a long minute. "That's the *two* million dollar question."

Kate quickly swiped tear marks away as she hurried back to the waiting room feeling like an over-wound spring. She was worried about Clay. She was hungry and had a headache. She had just antagonized the man whom she should be down on her knees thanking.

Randall Johnson. When she fought with him, she was

really battling with her own weaknesses. She could admit that to herself. Her new world was still being rebuilt. If she tried to make him a part of it...well, he would become a wrecking ball. She couldn't control him and even worse, she couldn't control her own response to him. Yet she kept inviting him in. Again and again.

What should she do? She sighed. An apology was certainly in order. Then she needed to somehow discharge her debt to him without becoming further involved. She grimaced at the impossibility of that.

Well, she had gotten herself into this position, and she would just have to find a way to get herself out. Once Clay was on the road to recovery.

Slow footsteps sounded behind her, and she turned around.

Randall stopped, and stood with his hands clasped behind his back, looking down.

Kate drew in a deep breath to begin her apology.

"I owe you an apology," Randall said. He looked at her from under lowered black brows. "It's just that every time I see you, I want to drag you into the nearest broom closet and make love to you until we're both limp."

Kate laughed, torn between embarrassment and relief. "I can't picture you limp."

Randall smiled back, bringing out the deepest creases beside his mouth. "I'll take that as a compliment. Truce?" he said, holding out his hand.

His hand swallowed hers as she slid her palm into his grasp. "Truce. It was unforgivable of me to be so rude when you've been nothing but generous and helpful."

"Don't overdo it. I've been wrong, too," he reminded her. He let go of her hand. "If you'll give me your insurance card, I'll make sure that it's on Clay's admittance forms."

"A concession," Kate said as she dug into her pocketbook for the card. "This really is a truce! Now what do I have to concede?"

"Use your imagination, darlin'," Randall drawled, taking the card and walking away.

Kate checked her watch, paced around the waiting area, and wondered how she was going to get through another two hours. She was examining a painting on the wall when Randall returned and gave her back her insurance card. "All taken care of."

She smiled at him. "Doing what you do best."

Randall's answering smile was brief. He walked over to the coffeemaker, fiddled with a foam cup, then said abruptly, "You want to know what I want from you?"

"Ye-e-es..."

"I want you to look at me like you did on the roof today."

"How did I look at you?" she asked, startled.

"Like you were glad to see me."

Kate blinked hard against tears that welled up again. "You have no idea how glad I was to see you," she whispered.

His eyes locked with hers, and they both went completely still.

"Tell me."

"Mr. Johnson, your delivery is here," the reception nurse called out.

Randall gave Kate an unreadable look as he strode past her.

A man dressed in a chef's white side-buttoned coat stood at the desk with two coolers. Randall greeted him and handed one cooler to the nurse, saying, "I figured that you might be ready for some dessert."

"From the Four Seasons? I'd have settled for some dinner rolls!" the nurse joked.

Randall picked up the second cooler and brought it back into the waiting room. Pulling over a low table, he started setting containers of food out on it. Kate watched him with her arms crossed, and her eyebrows raised. Randall finally straightened and met her eyes.

"I couldn't blame you for not eating the dreck in the cafeteria, so I ordered something edible."

"From the Four Seasons?"

He shrugged. "Julian and I are old friends. And I owed you dinner there anyway," he added with a flash of a smile.

"I thought you were going to stop being arrogant and high-handed." Kate made an effort to keep the corners of her mouth from twitching upward.

"I have to ease into it slowly."

"If I weren't so hungry, I'd throw this shrimp cocktail at you," she said as she sat down and pulled the covers off the dishes. "Mmm, corn chowder with crabmeat. What heaven!"

She was halfway through the meal when she realized that Randall was just watching her. "Aren't you going to eat?"

He shook his head. "I had a plate of meat loaf in the cafeteria. And I'm enjoying the sight of a lady who likes her food."

"You're going to make me slurp my soup or something equally gauche if you just sit there staring at me."

"I can't stay much longer anyway. I have to be in Texas tomorrow on business, and I have a plane to catch tonight. But I had to make sure that you ate something."

"Sometimes you are the nicest man," Kate said, as her heart sank at the thought of his absence. "And other times you are the most annoying one."

"Keep 'em guessing, that's my motto," he said grinning at her. "Finish your dinner. I'll have some of those mussels to keep you company."

They ate in companionable silence. After the dishes were stowed back in the cooler, Randall checked his watch and stood up.

"Call my private number when you hear anything and leave a message. I'll call you back as soon as I can."

Kate stood up, too. "I don't have your private number."

Randall looked at her. "It's the same one I've given you already. Twice, in fact."

"I've thrown it away already. Twice, in fact."

He pulled out a business card to write on. "Don't throw this one away."

"I won't."

"Call Gail if you need anything quickly. And don't worry, Clay will be fine."

Then he leaned down and kissed her. It began gently, but when Kate tilted her head to give him a better angle, he pulled her against him with arms that felt like steel bands across her back. Kate ran her fingers up into his hair and held on, releasing all her pent-up guilt and worry and gratitude into the kiss.

When she opened her eyes, he was looking at her with some of the arousal she expected, but something else that she couldn't quite decipher was in his eyes as well. He took a ragged breath. "Where's that broom closet when you need it?"

Kate disengaged herself from his arms. Unsure of how to react, she pulled out the crutch of correct social behavior. "Have a good trip."

He made no attempt to hold on to her. Yet he continued

to stare at her with that enigmatic expression on his face.

"We'll finish this when I get back," he finally said.

Then he literally turned on his heel and walked out.

"Good-bye," Kate called.

She sat down slowly, aware of an aching sense of abandonment. It was ridiculous; she couldn't expect someone as busy as Randall Johnson to sit with her for hours in a hospital waiting room. He had already done far more than she had any right to hope. But when he kissed her like that, she wanted the moon and the stars from him.

"Mrs. Chilton?"

Kate stopped pacing and turned to find Dr. Lane smiling at her.

She smiled tentatively in response. "You look pleased. Did it go well?"

"Extremely well. Sit down for a minute," he said, seating himself beside her. "Clay was lucky; the ER doctor did a good job of preserving the tissues. I was able to reattach all the muscles and ligaments without any loss of length. The nerves look good, too. If he works hard at his physical therapy, he'll never know he got bitten."

"Oh thank God!" Kate breathed. "And thank *you* so very much."

"Some people accuse me of thinking I *am* God," the surgeon joked.

His jubilant mood reassured Kate even more than his words did. "When can I see my son?"

"He's in the recovery room now, and he'll stay there until the anesthesia wears off. If you'd like to be with him when he wakes up, you may sit with him."

Kate stood instantly. As they walked down the hall, she asked, "How long do you want to keep him here?"

"I'd like him to stay through tomorrow. If all goes well, he can go home Wednesday. But I'll want to see him every week until I'm satisfied that he's healing properly."

"Of course," Kate said. *Clay will think it a great comedown to have to drive to the hospital*, she thought wryly.

"And I'm going to refer you to a doctor in New Jersey who will change his bandages regularly." Dr. Lane pushed open a door for her. "He may be slightly disoriented when he first opens his eyes. Don't be concerned."

"I won't," Kate said, turning to shake his hand. "Dr. Lane, I can't begin to thank you adequately..."

"Just invite me to his first art show in New York City," the doctor said. "That's all the thanks I need."

"You'll be at the top of the list," Kate promised.

She turned to Clay. His hand was bound to an elaborate arrangement of splints and swathed in gauze. He seemed to be sleeping peacefully. She straightened the already pristine sheets and gently touched his face. Then she settled down to wait for the first flicker of returning consciousness.

Eighteen

RANDALL CHECKED HIS voice mail for the third time and was rewarded. There was a brief, whispered message from Kate, saying that Dr. Lane was very optimistic and Clay was still sleeping.

He smiled as he punched the "end" button. Glancing down at the papers spread out on the table in front of him, he knew that he should be concentrating on them – or sleeping himself. He had about four hours before the chartered Learjet touched down in San Antonio, and he came face-to-face with his past. He shook his head. He was finally in the driver's seat, and all he wanted was to be back in a hospital waiting room on Long Island.

He shoved the contracts to the far side of the table and leaned back in his seat to get his thinking in order.

He had known he was in trouble the night of the charity ball. The worst part was that he didn't feel like he was in trouble. In fact, he felt better than he had in a long while. Ever since the ball, when he woke up in the morning, he looked forward to the day. For the first time in years, his future seemed more compelling than his past.

How did Kate Chilton do that? He couldn't figure it out.

She wasn't drop-dead gorgeous – yet he wanted to undress her every time he saw her.

She generally assumed the worst where his motives were concerned – and she had no hesitation about telling him so.

Actually, he liked that about her.

She could go from ripping him to shreds to thanking him with utter sincerity in two seconds flat. He had fun when he was with her. Hell, he had fun with her two boys. The Chiltons knew about his wealth and position, but they didn't let that change their behavior; they treated him as a fellow human being.

The image of Kate's face, first at the ball and then on the roof of the hospital, rose up to keep him honest. He knew that look; she thought of him as more than just a fellow human being. If he'd seen it on any other woman's face, he would have sent the lady a diamond bracelet and deleted her name from his Rolodex. When Kate looked at him like that, something inside him that he thought had been killed years ago in Mason County, Texas, stirred back to life.

Randall refused to name the stirring.

He admitted that she made him want to slay dragons, and if her dragons were hand surgeons and lieutenant governors, so be it. He found that he enjoyed using all of his accumulated connections and money for something other than business.

But the more he did for her, the more Kate pushed him away. She was cussedly independent, which was another thing he liked about her. She made it clear that her children were her first priority in life. He admired that. He got a kick out of making her polished good manners disintegrate. And he loved making her laugh when she wanted to be pissed at him...

Randall cursed. His attempt at analysis was deteriorating into a besotted daydream.

All right, he'd established that Kate made him feel good, that he liked a lot of things about her, and that he wanted her naked. He allowed himself a few more moments to dwell on that image. He could handle all of that, especially the last.

What he kept backing away from was the softening in his gut when he thought of her. There was no place for that in his life. He'd worked for years to be where and what he was, and he wasn't prepared to deviate from his plan at this point.

He refocused on the contract in front of him. As he read each ironclad clause, he heard the satisfying slam of a door and the turn of a key in his mind's ear. Mason County Bank was going to be completely at his mercy. President "Gill" Gillespie was too blind to realize what was about to hit him. He planned to let Gill stay president just long enough to watch Mason County Bank get taken apart and sold off piece by piece. Then he would fire him.

It was finally Gill Gillespie's turn to find out what it felt like to have your future wiped out.

Before he left the plane, Randall walked forward to see the pilot. "Thanks for a good flight. I'll be back here by six o'clock this evening."

"Good luck with your business, Mr. Johnson."

Randall walked down the steps carrying nothing more than his briefcase. A limousine was waiting on the tarmac. The driver raced forward to greet him.

"Welcome back to Texas, Mr. Johnson. Mr. Gillespie thought you'd like to have lunch at his home before the business meeting."

Randall checked his stride for just a moment, then slowly smiled. "That's very hospitable of Mr. Gillespie."

The car swept around a circular driveway to a stop. The white columns of the Gillespie mansion gleamed in the Texas sun. For a moment, Randall was a seventeen-year-old kid with an alcoholic mother and a bad reputation, wanting everything that Golden Gill Gillespie had: money, influence, family, and a house with more bathrooms than people. The feeling passed as he remembered the contract resting in his briefcase. He started to walk up the shallow steps to the front door when it swung wide open.

"Randall Johnson, you son of a gun! It's good to have you back in the great state of Texas." Gill Gillespie came forward with his hand extended.

Randall looked at the man he had come to ruin. Gill still had all of his blond hair, although it had some silver shot through it. His waist had thickened since his high school days, but he looked like he made some effort to stay in shape. His eyes retained their clear startling blue despite the red veins in his nose that indicated a heavy drinker.

Randall finally shook the bank president's hand. "Gill. You haven't changed much."

Gill laughed heartily. "Still got all my hair. But you do too. Although I see you finally lost the ponytail. I guess those Wall Street sharks you swim with bit it off a long time ago."

"Actually, I'm thinking of growing it back."

"Midlife crisis, eh? We all go through those. If the worst you do is grow your hair, you're doing okay." Gill's jovial tone disappeared. "You know, I was surprised when your offer for the bank came through. You haven't kept in touch with anyone here in Mason County, so I thought there might be some hard feelings left."

Randall smiled. "I feel I should do something for the folks here, for starting me out in life."

Gill was still giving him a hard stare.

Randall continued to smile. "It was time for some pay-back," he continued. "I might never have left Texas if I hadn't gotten kicked off the football team. I owe you and your daddy for broadening my horizons."

Gill hesitated before relaxing into a smile. "It's good to know you're thinking positively about the past. This partnership will benefit the whole area. But let's not talk business until after lunch. Come on in. Lucinda can't wait to see you again." A uniformed maid relieved Randall of his briefcase. "You two dated for a while back in high school, didn't you? Before Lucy and I got together?"

Randall examined the house critically as Gill led him through a marble-floored entrance hall, past a curved double staircase, to an informal sitting room at the back of the house. The public spaces were typical Texas oil baron, deliberately ostentatious and expensive. The sitting room was far more tasteful. Sunlight filtered through gauzy curtains to gently illuminate the comfortable furniture upholstered in soft pastels. Randall guessed that Lucinda had decorated this room; her family had been as poor as his, but Lucy had always been able to make her home look welcoming.

As though she had stepped out of his thoughts, a tall blond woman came toward him, both hands outstretched. "Randall Johnson, what a pleasure to see you again. It's been – what? – twenty years since you've been here."

Randall took her hands but did not kiss the cheek she offered him. "Twenty-three. You look good, Lucinda."

She gave him a searching look before she disengaged

her hands. "You do, too. Success agrees with you."

Randall raised an eyebrow. "And marriage agrees with you."

The pretty girl whom he had loved so many years ago had become a beautiful woman. Her silver-gilt hair was styled smoothly around the classic oval of her face. She stood tall and slim in her peach-colored suit and heavy gold jewelry, the perfect lady-who-lunches. But the green eyes had shadows under them, and the set of her jaw betrayed a long-standing tension. He had an unexpected urge to reach out and run his palm down her cheek to relax it. He quelled it without difficulty.

Gill walked over to an oil portrait hanging above the fireplace. He beamed as he pointed to the three girls in the painting, "And these are my beautiful daughters: Lucy Junior, who's in law school; Danielle, our Texas A&M scholar; and Rose, who's still in high school. Lucky for them, they all take after their mother, although Rosie has my blue eyes. I'm sorry you can't meet them in person."

Randall strolled over and examined the picture silently, relishing the tension emanating from Lucinda. She jumped when he spoke. "You're lucky to be surrounded by beautiful women, Gill."

"Damn straight I am," Gill laughed. The maid rustled in and spoke quietly to him. He turned to Randall. "I'm sorry. I'm going to have to excuse myself for a few minutes. There's a phone call I have to make to the bank before lunch. I'm sure you and Lucinda will enjoy reminiscing about the good old days."

Lucinda half-rose as though to follow him, but then sank back down on the chair and forced a smile. "Of course, dear."

Gill dropped a kiss on her cheek. "I won't be long."

As he left, Randall sat down, leaning back to rest his elbows on the padded arms, steepling his fingers just under his chin. Lucinda perched on the edge of the couch with her knees and ankles pressed tightly together.

"Does Gill really think that all we did was date a few times?" Randall asked quietly.

Lucinda looked away. "I didn't think it was necessary to tell him every detail of my life. It would just have made things more complicated."

Randall's eyebrows rose. "You considered the fact that Lucy might be my daughter a detail?"

Now Lucinda looked straight at him. "She's not your daughter."

"You weren't so sure twenty-three years ago. Have you had her DNA tested in the interim to put your mind at ease?"

"I deserved that. But no, there was never any doubt in my mind."

"Never any doubt!" Randall snapped. "I was prepared to marry you because you told me she was mine! I didn't know how the hell I would support you and a child, but I was damned well going to do the right thing." The room was deadly silent for a long moment. "You played me for a sucker."

Lucinda flinched. "I'm not proud of my behavior, but I did what I thought was best for my child."

"You did what you thought was best for you." Randall swept a look around the room. "This is a real nice little house, but you could have had a penthouse in Manhattan, a villa in Tuscany, and a chateau in France if you hadn't decided to trap Gill instead of me."

"I didn't trap Gill. I made a stupid mistake." Lucinda hesitated a moment and then softened her voice.

"Remember Joe Foster's big pool party? I wanted to go so badly, and you wouldn't take me because you were studying for finals."

"Because Gill and his daddy got me thrown off the football team so that Gill could be the quarterback. That lost me my scholarship to Texas University. I was desperate to get an academic scholarship."

Lucinda stood up and faced Randall. "That was all Gill's father's idea. He was the one who wanted the glory for his son. Gill knew that he wasn't as good as you. But there was no stopping Victor Gillespie once he got an idea in his head."

"And Gill lost the championship for us. I enjoyed watching from the bleachers," Randall said.

"He suffered for that. He still hears about it."

Randall said nothing.

Lucinda went back to her story. "You were studying, so I went to the party without you. Gill asked me if I wanted a ride home, and I thought that just once it would be nice to see what it was like to be part of the rich crowd. So I took the ride. When he pulled into the parking lot behind Streeter's Pharmacy to neck, I went along. And then the necking got heavier and I let that happen, too. I didn't realize that he hadn't used protection until too late. I was used to you being so careful." Lucinda took a deep breath. "I was so angry with you—I felt that school was more important to you than I was."

"I was trying to provide for both of our futures."

"Well, I didn't know that, did I?" Lucinda snapped. "You hadn't shared your bad news with me."

"I hadn't accepted it myself," Randall said, turning away.

A look of longing crossed Lucinda's face. "I was crazy

about you, Randall, but you scared me."

Randall stood up. "Scared you? I never lifted a hand to you. Gill was the one with the nasty temper."

Lucinda shook her head. "Not scared that way. What scared me was that you were so focused, so driven to get out of Mason County, and I wasn't sure I could keep up with you."

"Christ, Lucy, you hated this place as much as I did."

"No, I hated being poor as much as you did."

"I see."

"I doubt it. I don't expect you to believe this, but I loved you enough not to want to ruin your life. I was even afraid that you might come to hate me for it. So I went to see Gill. First he told me he'd pay for an abortion. I refused and walked out. That's why I told you –"

"What made him change his mind?"

There were tears in Lucinda's eyes. "Gill's a decent person. He thought about it and accepted his responsibility. He even took me out to dinner and proposed. Then I did the hardest thing I had ever done in my life before or since: I told you that I was marrying Gill Gillespie."

Randall's face darkened. "And left me hanging for twenty-three years, not knowing if I had a daughter or not."

"You never showed any interest in finding out if she was really yours."

"How would I have done that without, as you put it, making things more complicated?"

Lucinda shrugged and then said in a tiny voice, "You just left. I never saw you after the day you graduated. I wanted to say good-bye, good luck, something. Maybe even to tell you the truth."

"I was already packed when I put on that cap and gown. I took the diploma and walked to the bus stop." Randall paced around the room.

Lucinda followed him with her eyes. "Why did you come back now?" she almost whispered.

"To buy Mason Bank. And to destroy it."

Her cheeks lost all their color. "Why?"

"You and Gill destroyed my future. When I left here, all that kept me going was the thought of being able to do the same for you."

"Maybe you should be grateful to us."

Randall laughed unpleasantly. "You're good, Lucy. Gill should have put you on the bank board."

"Randall, please don't do this. It's not worthy of you."

He gave her a hard stare and strolled over to a group of silver-framed photos arranged on the baby grand piano. "You're a prosperous-looking family," he said, as he picked up photos and inspected them. "Fine horses, nice vacations, pretty clothes – Christ, what's this?" His gaze was riveted on a photo of the three daughters, a few years younger, wearing soccer uniforms and holding trophies. "Who the hell in Texas plays soccer?"

"Besides you, you mean?"

Randall glanced sideways at her. "Victor Gillespie threatened to horsewhip me if he ever saw me near a football again. I stole my first soccer ball from Gill's backyard."

Lucinda moved to stand beside him and look at the picture. "They were in a tournament and all three of their teams won their divisions. They were more proud of each other than of themselves. It was one of those wonderful moments of being a parent when you feel that you've actually done it right."

Randall's face suddenly looked bleak. He put the photo down abruptly. "That's a pleasure I haven't had." He fell silent, staring at the array of pictures.

After a long pause, Lucinda put her hand very tentatively on his arm. "I'm sorry, Randall."

He looked down at her hand until she removed it.

"The deal's off."

"What?"

"Gill has his bank back."

Lucinda was thrown off balance. "I don't know what to say. What should I tell him?"

"Tell him that he's lucky his daughters played soccer. Have a nice life, Lucy."

The driver was leaning against the car and leapt to attention when Randall came down the front steps. He opened the car door but kept looking back at the front of the house. Finally he had the courage to ask, "Will Mr. Gillespie be accompanying you, Mr. Johnson?"

"No. And I'd like to get moving now."

"Yes, sir!" The driver slammed the door before he practically sprinted around to the driver's seat. He had the car in motion before he remembered to ask, "Are we going to the bank, sir?"

"No."

"Then where would you like me to take you, sir?"

Randall was silent for a long minute. "Do you know where the town of Doss is?"

"More or less, sir."

"That's where I'm going."

"To Doss? It's a fair drive."

"I know that. There's a bar there I want to visit...if it's still in business. What's your name, young man?"

"John, sir."

"John, drop the sir."

"Yes, si-...Mr. Johnson."

"Randall."

"Um, right. How long do you expect to be in Doss?"

"A long time."

John had no response to that. He silently turned the car in a smooth arc and headed northwest. From sheer habit, Randall took out his cell phone to check his voice mail. He had pushed the first button when he said, "Screw this," and turned the power off. He hefted it in his hand a couple of times, then opened the window and hurled it into a clump of bushes. He spent the rest of the drive staring out the window as the suburbs of San Antonio fell away, and they entered the hill country of eastern Texas.

Dobie's looked even worse than he remembered. A neon sign, lit even in midday, was the only new addition to the big clapboard rectangle with no windows. The paint had long ago flaked off, and the wood had weathered to a dark gray. The parking lot surrounding it on all sides was half-full of pickup trucks and motorcycles, making the couple of old Cadillacs stand out. Randall opened the car door before the driver could and got out to stand with his hands thrust in his pockets as he surveyed the bar's unprepossessing facade.

"I think I should wait, sir," the young man said as he watched two customers stare at the limo.

"Go home, son; I'm going to get drunk, and I don't need an audience." He pulled out his wallet and flicked a hundred dollar bill to John. "This is to help you forget that you were ever here."

"But how will you get back to San Antonio? I don't think taxis come out here."

"I'll hitch a ride," Randall said as he walked toward the door.

"Your briefcase, sir." The driver called to him.

Randall swung around to smile at him. "Put a red ribbon on it and give it to Mrs. Gillespie with my compliments."

Then he was swallowed up in the smoky depths of his past.

Nineteen

KATE OPENED HER eyes in the dimly lit room, wondering where she was and why she was awake. The second question was answered as a telephone shrilled near her ear. She reached in the general direction of the noise and almost pulled the phone off the small table before she realized that she was in Clay's hospital room, and that the receiver had a cord attached to it.

"Hello?" she rasped as she pushed herself up on her elbow.

"Kate Chilton?" a vaguely familiar male voice asked.

"Yes, this is Kate."

"This is Tom Rogan. I'm sorry to bother you at this time of night, and in the hospital, but I wondered if Randall had been in touch with you today?"

Kate sat bolt upright. "No, he hasn't. He said he was going to Texas on business."

"He did go to Texas, but his Learjet is still waiting to give him a ride home."

"Don't the people he went to see know where he is?"

Tom hesitated a moment, then said, "The bank

president won't even get on the phone with me. Something happened down there, and I'm worried as hell about Randall. He's not checking his voice mail or answering his cell phone. He told the pilot that he'd be on board no later than six o'clock, and now it's midnight in San Antonio and he's a no-show."

Kate tried to gather her sleep-scattered thoughts. "Didn't he grow up near there? Maybe he ran into an old friend?"

Tom's voice was worried and impatient. "He wouldn't ignore his phone because of that, and the bank president wouldn't be refusing my calls. Something's wrong."

"Is there anything I can do to help?"

"Leave him a voice mail asking him to call you. And let me know if he does."

"I will if you'll promise to do the same."

"I might wake you up again."

"I'd rather that you did." Kate paused. "You know, Randall seems pretty capable of taking care of himself. You probably don't need to worry."

"I'll keep that in mind. Good night."

Kate threw off the covers and started toward her pocket-book when a sleepy voice came from the cot in the corner. "Mom, who was that?"

"Just someone looking for Mr. Johnson, Patrick. Go back to sleep. I have to go make a phone call, and I'll be back."

Kate heard the rustle of sheets as Patrick subsided. She had dashed home that afternoon to bring her younger son to see his brother. Clay was so much more cheerful with Patrick there, playing cards, that Kate had arranged to have Patrick spend the night. If Dr. Lane gave the okay, they could all go home together tomorrow.

Kate quickly checked on Clay, but the painkillers were keeping him knocked out. Then she grabbed a sweatshirt to pull on over her pajamas and took her handbag out into the hall. It seemed utterly ludicrous to be so worried about a grown man being late for a plane, especially if Randall Johnson was the man you were worried about. Yet she believed Tom Rogan when he said that Randall wouldn't stay out-of-touch for so long unless there was a problem. She suspected that his telephone was never more than two feet away from him even when he slept.

As Kate tried to formulate a message to leave him, her mind conjured up possible explanations for his absence. CEOs did get kidnapped occasionally, although mostly in Third World countries, she thought. It seemed more likely that Randall had decided to revisit his past in some way. She knew it had been problematic. But then there was the odd behavior of the bank president, who she assumed had been involved in the business that Randall had flown down to transact. She shook her head in defeat and punched in Randall's private phone number, wryly noting that she had committed it to memory, so throwing away scraps of paper would now be meaningless.

His terse recorded request to leave a message came on. She wished it were longer and had more of that Texas drawl in it. Then she could just dial in when she needed a quick thrill. The beep sounded, and she said in a deliberately light tone, "Randall, it's Kate Chilton. Poor Tom Rogan is so worried about you that he broke down and phoned me. Now I'm worried, too. As soon as you get this message, call me at the hospital or call Tom wherever you usually call him. I hope everything is all right. Clay's doing fine. I'll talk with you soon." She hesitated a moment, wanting to say something more personal but unable to come up with anything appropriate. "Take care," she finished lamely and disconnected.

She suspected that Randall would get her message and be furious with both her and Tom Rogan. After all, he should be able to take some time away from his responsibilities when he wanted to without checking in with anyone. Obviously, Randall's wealth and power came with strings attached – *including widowed mothers calling for medical favors,* she thought with a grimace. She had always considered him a rather solitary figure, perched on his mountain-top beyond the reach of the daily hubbub. Tom Rogan's frantic phone call had dispelled that illusion; it seemed that Randall Johnson had less freedom than she thought.

She tiptoed back into the hospital room. After silently laying her cell phone on the bedside table with its power light still flashing, she confounded her own expectations and fell immediately asleep.

When the telephone rang again, Kate opened her eyes to pale morning light. Sounds of the hospital stirring to life came through the door as she seized the receiver.

"Hello?"

She was disappointed when Tom Rogan answered, but relieved when he said, "Randall's on the plane."

"Oh, thank goodness! Where had he been? What did he say?"

"I haven't spoken with him. The pilot called me." Once again, Kate heard Tom's hesitation, then he went on. "He arrived at the airport in a pickup truck with two, well, the pilot's exact word was 'rednecks.' He was dead drunk and had to be carried onto the plane."

"Drunk? I've never seen Randall drunk. I thought that

247

because of his mother..." Kate trailed off, not sure how much Tom knew of Randall's past.

"Exactly." Tom sounded grim. "You know, after we spoke, I thought about your idea of Randall meeting an old friend, and it reminded me of a comment he made about this deal. He said that he was going to 'repave memory lane.' That was when I expressed doubts about the soundness of his decision to buy this bank. Something blew up."

"When do you expect him to land?"

"In about four hours. I'm going to meet the plane myself. Right now, the pilot says Randall's passed out on the fold-out bed."

Kate was struck by a sudden worry. "I hope the pilots are discreet. Randall would hate having this become public knowledge."

Tom gave a short laugh. "These guys see much worse than passed-out drunks and never discuss it. Their jobs depend as much on their discretion as on their skill as pilots."

He cleared his throat. "Kate, I'm not sure exactly what your relationship with Randall is – and it's none of my business – but I think he will need his friends when he gets back, whether he'll admit it or not. My sense is that you're someone who cares about him. May I call you if I think you can help?"

"I'd be hurt if you didn't."

After hanging up, Kate dropped her head back on her pillow for a moment as she considered the fact that Tom Rogan knew she cared deeply about Randall Johnson. She couldn't help wondering what Randall had said to Tom about her. A tiny flicker of happiness warmed her at the thought that Randall's right-hand man saw her as his boss's friend.

She threw off the covers and padded into the bathroom to shower while the boys slept. When she emerged, dressed and wide awake, breakfast was on the rolling table. Clay and Patrick were joking about how awful everything was even as they devoured it.

"Rubber eggs."

"Plastic bacon."

"Unidentified gelatinous substance," Clay said, poking at what Kate assumed was oatmeal.

Patrick cracked up, then sobered. "Mom, who was looking for Mr. Johnson last night?"

"Um, a business associate of his," Kate said as she tasted the eggs. "Definitely rubber," she agreed with Clay.

"In the middle of the night? That's kind of weird."

Clay looked up. "Is Mr. Johnson okay?"

"He's fine. He's on a Learjet flying back right now." Kate threw in the jet to distract them.

"Cool," Patrick said. "I wonder what model."

Clay wasn't so easily redirected. "Why was his business associate so worried about him?"

"Oh, he didn't arrive at the airport when he said he was going to. And his associate said that was unusual for Mr. Johnson."

"But he's a grown-up," Patrick said.

Kate laughed. "Grown-ups worry about each other too, you know."

"Mom, I like Mr. Johnson," Clay said quietly. "And not just because he got the surgeon to operate on my hand. Or because he has a helicopter."

"So do I, sweetheart. He's a good man." Kate sighed.

Clay gave her a sharp look, but said nothing further. After that, they were swept into the hurry-up-and-wait routine of leaving the hospital. They dressed, packed, signed forms, called Denise, and then spent an hour and a half playing poker for pennies while they waited for Dr. Lane to release Clay.

Kate lost her stake unusually quickly because her attention kept circling around the twin worries of Clay and Randall. She was hugely relieved when Dr. Lane strode in, followed by his entourage of interns.

After a barrage of technical comments aimed at his students, the surgeon addressed Clay and Kate in plain English. "I'm very pleased with my work on this. It's a textbook case. Young man, you'll have full use of this hand *if and only if* you do all the physical therapy I'm going to recommend."

"Yes, sir," Clay responded with a brilliant smile.

Dr. Lane smiled back. "When your hand's healed more, you're going to get this really cool gizmo that will make you look like something out of the *Terminator*."

"Lucky dog," Patrick said.

"Let's not mention the word *dog* in this context," Kate joked.

The doctor slid her an amused glance. "That's the spirit. Good luck, Clay. I'll see you next week."

Kate shook his hand warmly. "I can't tell you how much we appreciate your miraculous work."

"Maybe you can talk Mr. Johnson into naming the new wing after me," Dr. Lane threw over his shoulder as he exited.

The three Chiltons looked at each other. Finally, Kate said, "He must have been kidding."

As they walked in the front door, Clay looked around and said, "I feel like I've been away for weeks instead of a couple of days."

"Anesthesia does that to you," Kate said as she dropped the duffel bags at the foot of the steps. "Would you like to go upstairs and sleep or would you rather lie down on the couch in the family room and watch a movie?"

"The family room," Clay said, heading that way.

"Are you hungry?" Kate asked as she arranged pillows for his back and hand.

"Definitely. Especially after the unidentified gelatinous substance," he said, setting himself and his brother off into a fit of laughter.

Kate smiled as she walked into the kitchen. If Clay was cracking jokes, he was feeling all right. Her smile widened when she heard Patrick politely ask Clay which movie he wanted to watch and accept his choice without argument. He was obviously still worried about his brother. She wondered how long that would last.

As she took out sandwich fixings, Kate punched the answering machine's play button. There were a couple of messages from Clay's friends, asking how he was doing. Then Tom Rogan's voice sounded from the speaker. "Kate, Tom Rogan. I missed you at the hospital. I met Randall at the airport. He informed me that he didn't need a nursemaid, jumped into his car and spun out of the parking lot. If you hear from him, please let me know. He looked like hell."

Kate glanced at her watch as the date and time sounded; the message had been recorded an hour ago. She stopped the playback. What in the world had happened in Texas? Should she try Randall again? She shook her head. Her message was on his voice mail already. Repeating it wouldn't help.

She pushed play once more. "Hello, Kate? This is Barbara Handley. I'm so very sorry about what happened to

251

Clay's hand. I do hope that he's all right. If I had known that Thunder would be a problem, I would never have accepted your boys' kind offer to walk him. I just can't believe that he would attack another dog. Please tell Clay I called to wish him well."

Kate frowned as she listened. Thunder was not well-disciplined, but he had never shown any sign of viciousness. And didn't Clay say it had been another dog's fault? She would have to ask him the details again. Several more messages from well-wishers spooled past as Kate fixed sandwiches. None were from Randall. She again debated calling him. But first she decided to talk with Barbara Handley.

"Mrs. Handley called to see how you're doing," Kate said to Clay as she carried lunch into the family room. "Would you tell me again exactly what happened when you got bitten?"

"Sure, Mom," Clay said, and gave Kate a more detailed description of the dog fight than she was comfortable hearing.

"I just want to make sure I know a couple of facts," Kate said when he had finished. "Thunder was definitely on the sidewalk and not in the lady's yard?"

"Definitely," Clay said. "We know that some yards have electric fences for their dogs so we keep our clients out of people's yards."

"Your clients?" Kate laughed. "I like that. And this other dog was definitely loose? No electric fence?"

Clay shook his head. "No fence. He came right down onto the sidewalk."

"Do you agree, Patrick?"

Patrick nodded solemnly.

"Thanks, boys. I'm going to call Mrs. Handley and reassure her that Thunder was not the attacker."

"Thunder and I were both victims," Clay said wryly. "I bet there's not a mark on that other dog."

Kate went back to the kitchen and called Barbara Handley's number.

"Oh, Kate, I'm so glad to hear from you. I've been so worried about Clay. He's the nicest boy. And so's Patrick," Barbara said. "How is Clay's hand?"

Not wanting to worry the elderly woman, Kate said, "It's going to be fine. He had to have a little surgery, and he's all bandaged up now. How's Thunder doing?"

Barbara's voice wavered. "He's got some bandages, too. The vet gave him some shots, just in case, and said that he would recover. But he seems depressed. And Mrs. Lattuca – that's Pal's owner – claims that he's vicious and should be put to sleep. I don't understand it; he's never attacked another dog before."

"Well, according to Clay and Patrick, he didn't attack," Kate said firmly. "Clay doubts that Thunder even bit Pal in self-defense. And he says that Pal came onto the sidewalk to get at Thunder."

"Oh, that's such good news! I mean, not that Pal attacked Clay and Thunder, but that it wasn't Thunder's fault. That's such a weight off my mind," Barbara Handley said, still sounding as though she was near tears. "I was afraid I'd have to put Thunder to sleep."

"Don't even think about it," Kate said, reassuringly. "Would you like me to call Mrs. Lattuca?"

"Would you? That would be so nice of you. I'll give you her number."

Kate was about to say good-bye when the older lady said, "Kate, I should warn you that Mrs. Lattuca is not a very nice person. She used rather strong language with me.

And she seemed very sure it was Thunder's fault."

"We'll see about that." After hanging up, Kate looked at the phone number as she considered the best way to approach the not-so-nice Mrs. Lattuca. She decided that as always, being pleasant and polite was a good way to begin.

"Mrs. Lattuca? This is Kate Chilton. I'm the mother of the boy who had a problem with your dog Pal."

"Pal isn't the problem. That German shepherd is the problem. He attacked my Pal for no reason in his own yard. Your boy couldn't control him so I had to intervene. If your child got bitten, it's his own fault."

Kate's temper began to simmer. Pleasant and polite was clearly not going to do it. "I'm afraid that I have to disagree. Both of my children have confirmed that your dog came onto the sidewalk to attack Thunder and that Thunder did not even bite back. Clay tried to get hold of Pal's collar to separate the dogs, and Pal bit his hand. I am acquainted with Thunder, as are many people in this neighborhood, and we all know that he is not a vicious dog."

"Your boys are lying to try to stay out of trouble. That German shepherd should be put to sleep. Pal has bite marks all over his face and neck."

"Would your veterinarian be willing to confirm that?"

"I didn't take him to the vet."

"He has bite marks all over his face and neck, and yet you didn't take him to the vet?"

"I haven't had time," Mrs. Lattuca said, sounding slightly defensive for the first time. She went back on the offensive immediately. "But I'm going to call Town Hall and file a complaint against that German shepherd. He should be put to sleep before he attacks anyone else. And your children should not be walking dogs they can't control."

Kate's blood was at full boil but her tone was icy. "Mrs. Lattuca, I made this telephone call with the intention of straightening out a misunderstanding between neighbors. However, your attitude and accusations have changed my intention drastically. I am now considering suing you for my son's medical expenses and his pain and suffering. Your dog was loose in a town with leash laws. Your dog attacked another dog – who was leashed – without provocation on public property. Your dog did serious injury to a child who tried to protect the leashed dog. You will be hearing from my lawyer, Georgia Jenson, from Cravath, Swaine, and Moore."

Kate hoped that Mrs. Lattuca didn't know that Cravath wasn't in the business of prosecuting dog bite cases.

"You can't sue me," the other woman blustered.

"Try me," Kate said. "This conversation is over."

"Wait!" Mrs. Lattuca hesitated a moment, then said grudgingly, "I won't file a complaint about the other dog."

Kate waited.

"What else do you want?"

"An apology."

"For what?"

"For accusing my children of lying."

"I'm sorry. They didn't lie."

"And now the truth, please," Kate said implacably.

Mrs. Lattuca made a sound of disgust. "Pal got loose from his stake in the backyard. I keep him tied up because we don't have a fence."

"Has he ever attacked anyone else?"

"No. Well, once. But it was a long time ago."

Kate controlled her desire to scream at the woman. Instead she said with ice dripping from every syllable, "Mrs. Lattuca, I do not believe in destroying dogs because they

255

have bad owners. However, if I ever see or hear of Pal being loose again, I will not only report him to Town Hall, but I will slap a lawsuit on you so fast that you won't know what hit you. So I suggest that you invest in a good fence."

Kate was about to hang up when she had another thought. "I also expect you to call Barbara Handley to apologize to her and assure her that Thunder is safe."

"You snotty bitch!" Mrs. Lattuca shrieked. "You can't make me call anyone!"

"If you don't, my next call will be to Cravath, Swaine. And you had better be very polite to Barbara. Good-bye, Mrs. Lattuca."

Kate could hear the woman swearing as she hung up.

Six months ago, she would never have threatened a lawsuit or forced someone to apologize to someone else, even if she knew that she was right. Georgia would be proud of her. Even better, she was proud of herself.

Barbara Handley called five minutes later to describe the miraculous turnaround in attitude of the previously nasty Mrs. Lattuca. Kate smiled as she listened, the feeling that she could take care of her own flowing like wine through her veins.

Twenty

KATE HAD DOZED off while sitting in the den with Clay and Patrick watching *Star Wars*. The peal of the doorbell startled her awake. "Mom, the door," Patrick said without taking his eyes off the television screen.

She stretched quickly and went to the front door. Randall Johnson stood on the porch. Kate gasped at his appearance.

"Randall, what happened? You look awful."

He ran a hand over the stubble on his chin. "I haven't gotten around to shaving today."

His beard was the least of his problems. "Come in," she said, making a waving motion for him to enter. His face was battered, and his clothes were a mess. "Would you like some coffee?"

Randall winced. "No more coffee. My stomach feels like hell." He limped into the living room and dropped onto the couch, letting his head fall back as he closed his eyes.

Kate looked him over to decide what he needed most. He had a black eye and a cut on his cheek. The knuckles of his hands had cuts and bruises scattered across them. His suit jacket was ripped in several places, and his once-white shirt was grimy and bloodstained. His whole posture indicated exhaustion and something worse that she couldn't quite put a name to. *Defeat? Despair?* Not words she generally associated with him.

Tending bodily wounds was easier than dealing with emotional ones, so Kate collected ointment, Band-Aids, a washcloth and a towel. She stuck her head into the den and told the boys that Mr. Johnson was here, and not feeling well, so they should continue to watch their movie. Clay and Patrick looked at each other and then at her. She hurried back to the living room. Randall grunted when she sat down beside him. "Did I hurt you?" Kate asked.

"I'm just sore all over."

"I'm going to clean up your cuts and put some antibiotic ointment on them. It may hurt a little."

He started to object, then said, "Oh, all right."

She smiled at his grumpiness. Holding his left hand on her thigh, she gently cleaned away dried blood and spread ointment on the cuts, bandaging the worst ones. She moved to his other side and did the same for the right one. He smelled of smoke, alcohol and sweat.

She folded the washcloth to a clean side and began working on his face. A bruise stretched across one cheekbone and the other bore a deep cut. Thank goodness his nose seemed undamaged. As Kate gently soaked the dried blood from his whiskers, she tried not to remember how his lips had felt on various parts of her body. But her pulse quickened just the same. She finished her ministrations, then hesitated a moment. Deciding that his condition warranted it, she gently smoothed his hair back from his forehead and dropped a feather-light kiss there.

Randall smiled without opening his eyes. "I saw you do

that to Clay in the hospital. I must look worse than I thought."

"I guess you haven't been near a mirror today," she answered. "Would you like to tell me what happened?"

The smile vanished instantly, and the bleak expression returned. "Not yet. Just sit here with me." He reached out and found her hand. "How's Clay doing?"

Tears welled up when he wrapped his hand around hers. She very gently laid her free hand on top of his. "Just fine. He really wants to thank you in person for introducing us to Dr. Lane." She thought it would help if she just kept on talking. "Patrick's planning to pester you for a helicopter ride so he can keep up with Clay."

"That can be arranged if his mother agrees."

"I suppose that I can't stand in the way of balancing the scales of sibling rivalry. Even if it means another flight for me.

"You don't have to go."

"Yes, I do. I couldn't bear to be alive if my children crashed."

"Tom Rogan always says that mothers are saints, but it sounds more like martyrdom to me."

Kate was relieved to hear the sardonic edge return to Randall's tone; it temporarily dispelled the bleakness.

"Actually, Janine is such a terrific pilot that I really didn't mind flying too much. The next time, maybe I can even admire the view."

"I knew from the beginning you had guts." He shifted and flinched, opening his eyes to stare at the ceiling.

It wrenched at her heart to see his strength flattened like this. He didn't seem to want to talk, so she suggested one of her favorite forms of comfort. "Would you like to soak in a nice hot bath? It might take away some of your aches."

"Do I stink?"

"You smell like a really cheap bar," Kate admitted, making an educated guess.

"Bingo." He grimaced. "If I smell like Dobie's, I definitely stink." With another brief flash of his usual self, he turned his head toward her and said in a low voice, "Will you scrub my back?"

Kate laughed. "You're in no condition to think about me scrubbing your back."

Instead of throwing back a joke, his gaze focused intently on her face. "The only good idea I've had in the last twenty-four hours is having you scrub my back." He turned away and gingerly lifted himself off the couch. "But I guess that would be pushing your hospitality too far. I should go home and bathe myself."

"No, you shouldn't!" Kate was on her feet instantly blocking his way out. "I'll run the bath. I'll scrub your back or wash your hair or do whatever else you need, but you're not leaving until I say you can."

Randall looked down at her from his superior height. "How are you going to stop me?"

"By any means necessary. I can call on reinforcements if I need to," she reminded him, nodding toward the den. She took his hand again, to gently pull him toward the stairs. "Come on. To the bathtub with you."

He stood like a rock for a moment, then gave in and went with her. "I don't want anyone to get hurt. I won't hold you to your offers, except running the bath."

"You see, you are a nice man," Kate said teasingly. She wanted to coax another smile from him.

But her remark had the opposite effect. His face hardened to granite. "So I've got you fooled."

Kate didn't hear him; she had suddenly realized that to

get to the bathtub she would have to take him through her bedroom; the boys' bath had only a shower. She shrugged inwardly; Randall's need for comfort was greater than her need for privacy. She took him to her bedroom, saying, "Let me turn on the water, and I'll get you some towels."

The bathroom retained its original Victorian tile in a black and white pattern, as well as an enormous claw-footed bathtub. Kate turned on the brass taps and adjusted the water to a just-bearable temperature that generated lots of steam. She piled up two big bath sheets and a washcloth beside the tub. When she returned to the bedroom, Randall was standing at the window with his back to her.

"Your bath is..."

Her voice died as Randall turned around. His shirt was unbuttoned and open over his chest. He was in the process of pulling his belt out through the belt loops.

She wanted to lay her hands on the warm skin his shirt exposed and feel the texture of the dark hair sprinkled over it. She wanted to pull off her own shirt so that she could press her skin against that solid wall of muscle. She wanted those big hands...

Randall's voice was like sandpaper. "If you look at me like that, you'll be joining me in the bathtub."

She forced her gaze to drop as she smoothed an imaginary wrinkle in the quilt on the bed. Her voice was as rough as his. "I wasn't expecting to see your...to see you undressing."

Suddenly, his hands were covering hers, and he leaned forward across the bed so that his face was inches away from hers. "Don't apologize. It makes me feel..." He stopped and frowned. "Human."

She tried to slide her hands out from under his, but his weight held her trapped. She didn't want to tell him what he made her feel. "I think I should turn off the water before it overflows," she said instead.

He released her by straightening. As she retreated into the bathroom, she called, "Leave your clothes on the bed, and I'll see if I can clean them up."

There was a pause, and then Randall said, "Burn them. There's an overnight bag in the trunk of my car that I keep packed for emergencies."

Kate walked back into the bedroom. "Give me your keys, and I'll bring it up."

He considered her offer for a moment, and then fished the keys out of his trouser pocket. As she took them, he reached up and brushed the back of his fingers against her cheek. "Thank you, Kate."

She summoned up a shaky smile. "You're welcome," she managed before she turned and exited hastily. She stopped at the top of the stairs, hefting the keys in her hand and trying to collect her composure before facing her curious sons.

As she walked through the den, Clay asked quietly, "What's going on with Mr. Johnson? Is he all right?"

"I'm not sure," she answered honestly. "He has a black eye and looks like he may have been in a fight. He's tired and doesn't want to talk about it."

"Why'd he come here?" Patrick wanted to know.

"Because we're his friends," Kate said, although she wondered the same thing. "And right now he needs friends."

"Wow, Mr. Johnson needs us," Patrick said. "That's weird."

Privately, Kate agreed, but aloud she said, "He's a person just like you and me. He has his own problems that we don't know about." She heard water run briefly. "I have to get something from Mr. Johnson's car. I'll be right back."

She dashed out to the Jaguar parked by the curb and grabbed the black leather bag from the trunk. Carrying it upstairs, she knocked softly on the bedroom door. Hearing only splashing, she ventured a few steps in. Noting with relief that the bathroom door was closed, she set the suitcase on the bed. She debated whether to unpack it for him, deciding that handling his clothes was more intimacy than she could deal with. She dropped the keys beside it and left.

Remembering that Tom Rogan had asked her to call him, Kate went back to the kitchen and dialed RJ Enterprises.

"Tom, this is Kate Chilton. Randall's here, and I think that he's all right. I cleaned up his cuts, and he's taking a bath."

"Thank God." Tom's voice held noticeable relief. "I kept wondering when I would hear about a smash-up involving a Jaguar."

"I'll try to keep him off the road, although he seems sober." Kate hesitated a moment. "Has he ever mentioned a bar called Dobie's to you?"

"Dobie's?" Tom was silent as he thought. "Yes, I think he used to go there to drink when he was underage."

"That's where he was in Texas. He said he smelled like it."

"Why would he go to some dive in Nowhere, Texas?"

"Maybe he wanted a drink," Kate said. "He won't talk about anything yet, but I'll keep trying. He seems... depressed."

"I can't figure this out. I finally got hold of one of the Mason Bank VPs, and he says that Randall backed out of the acquisition. No explanation, no negotiation. He left without even going to the bank. He's been watching this bank for years, waiting for the right time." Tom sounded upset and frustrated.

"I'll take care of him, Tom."

As she hung up, she puzzled over the business deal. She remembered Randall's story about the wrong oil wells that he had bought anyway. Something very serious had to have happened if he had cancelled a long-standing deal.

Kate heard the floor creaking as Randall shifted in the tub. Then his footsteps traveled back and forth between the bedroom and bathroom several times. By the time she heard the door open, Clay and Patrick were debating the relative merits of different combinations of toppings on the brick oven pizzas they had voted on for dinner.

Randall walked into the family room looking vastly improved. Nothing could hide the black eye, but he had shaved and his damp hair was brushed neatly away from his face. He was wearing charcoal gray slacks and a white button-down shirt with a thin maroon stripe that he had left open at the neck. He dropped his overnight bag in the corner. "Good evening, Patrick, Clay. How's the hand doing?"

"It's going to be great, thanks to you and Dr. Lane," Clay said. "I'm really grateful..."

Randall held up his hand. "Your mother has already thanked me so often that it's not necessary to say another word. I'm glad you're on the road to recovery." He moved to a chair with a return of his usual fluidity and sank into it. "Did I hear the word pizza being bandied around?"

"I'll be happy to grill you a steak," Kate said quickly.

"I'm in the mood for pizza," Randall said. "What toppings do they have?"

Patrick took the menu over to him and then stood waiting as he examined Randall's battered face. "Were you in a fight, sir?" he asked politely.

"Patrick!" Kate and Clay spoke simultaneously.

Randall gave a half smile as he gingerly touched his cheek. "Your mother wants to know the same thing." He paused, then sighed. "I was in a place where I had no business being anymore, and yes, I got in a fight. But I didn't start it, and I doubt that I could have ended it," he said, ruefully inspecting the marks on his hands. "Some people with more brains than I have persuaded me to leave before I really got hurt."

"What was the fight about?" Patrick persisted.

"I have absolutely no idea. And I'm sure that there's a moral in there somewhere, but I'm too beaten up to figure it out."

"Don't get between two fighting dogs or two fighting men," Clay offered wryly.

Randall gave a short laugh. "We are a pair."

Patrick had opened his mouth to say something else, but Kate quelled him with a stern look. "I'm going to go order the pizza," she said.

"Good, I'm starved," Clay said.

After pizza, the boys decided to play poker, so Kate set up the card table. Randall was stretched out in a chair with his feet on an ottoman, but when Patrick shuffled the cards, he stirred. "Don't get up," Kate said quickly.

He ignored her and rose stiffly. "Poker's my game."

Poker might usually be his game, Kate thought, *but his heart wasn't in it tonight.* He only won when he was the dealer, so ordinarily she would have suspected him of cheating. Tonight, though, she concluded that he simply wasn't focused on the game except when he had to be. In fact, she often caught him watching her with an odd expression on his face.

"Last hand," Kate announced after glancing at the clock. "You have school tomorrow, Patrick, and Clay needs some rest."

Randall pushed what was left of his poker chips into the center of the table and shuffled the cards several times.

"Let's try a game of real skill: high card, winner takes all," he called. Everyone laughed and shoved their chips into the pile. Randall fanned the cards on the table. "Patrick, you have the draw. Now Clay. Kate. And myself." He chose a card and laid it facedown. "Ladies and gentlemen, display your cards," he said in his thickest Texas drawl.

Patrick turned up a king and cheered. Clay had a ten and Kate a three. With a flourish, Randall flipped over the Ace of Spades. He then proceeded to draw from the spread deck the Ace of Clubs, the Ace of Diamonds and finally the Ace of Hearts.

"Wow." Clay breathed. "How did you do that?"

"I stacked the deck. I'm good at that," Randall said with an edge in his voice. "Good night, young men. Thank you for your company."

Kate stood up. "Patrick, upstairs and get ready for bed. Clay, I'm going to give you one of those painkillers to make sure you get a good night's sleep."

"Aw, Mom, I don't need one."

"I know, sweetheart, you're very tough, but I don't want to stay up all night worrying about whether you're sleeping or not, so take it for me."

Clay muttered but he swallowed the pill and trudged up the stairs.

"I'll be right up to give you a hand with your hand," Kate joked. Then she turned to Randall. "Let me get them settled, and then I'll be back down."

Randall was slotting poker chips into their stand. "Don't worry about me."

"I just don't want you to disappear while I'm upstairs."

He looked up at her. "You've been talking to Tom. He thinks I've gone off the deep end."

"He's concerned," Kate corrected. "You're lucky to have such a good friend."

Randall snorted and went back to sorting poker chips.

Twenty One

KATE GOT THE boys in bed and walked back to her bedroom to pick up a sweater. She started as she saw Randall standing beside the bed, putting on his watch. He looked up. "I remembered that I left my wallet and watch on the bedside table."

"But not your phone?" Kate teased.

"I got rid of that in San Antonio."

"I hope you get free replacements from that telephone company you own."

Randall didn't smile.

Kate closed the door softly behind her. "Would you like to tell me what happened down there?" she said, walking to the chaise longue by the window. She perched on the foot and looked up at Randall expectantly. "I'll never repeat anything you tell me to anyone – not even Tom," she said with a slight smile.

"I know that," Randall said sharply. He adjusted his watch with great precision, then sat down on the edge of the bed. He leaned his elbows on his knees and clasped his hands. Keeping his gaze on his hands, he said, "I went to

Texas to destroy a man."

Kate let the silence go on for a while before she decided that he needed help. "The man at Mason Bank?"

Randall glanced up at her. "Tom told you that?"

"Just the name of the bank."

Randall stared out the window. "Tom knew the deal stank from day one. He didn't understand that I had no intention of making a profit from the bank; I intended to take it apart piece by piece and wipe it off the face of the earth."

"Why?" Kate whispered. She was shocked by the hatred in his voice.

Randall's laugh was as unpleasant as his expression. "I wanted to take everything away from Gill Gillespie because he took everything away from me. Mason Bank was more than his job; it was his heritage. His granddaddy started it, his daddy made it solid, and Gill grew it. I couldn't just fire him; I had to ruin the bank, too."

"I don't understand. You have so much. What did he do to you?"

"He got me thrown off the football team."

Kate almost laughed, thinking that he was joking. But Randall was staring straight ahead with no sign of amusement on his face.

"I guess you really loved football," she said lamely.

That made Randall look at her. "Yeah, I loved football, but I loved the scholarship it got me to Texas University more. I had to lead Mason County High on to another championship if I wanted to go to college. Gill and his father made that impossible. Gill didn't need a scholarship; he just wanted to play quarterback his senior year. And for that, he destroyed my future."

Randall got up and walked to the window before

turning to face Kate. "I worked my ass off to get that scholarship. It was my ticket out of the dirt and the squalor and the shame of a mother who everyone knew was an alcoholic. My brothers and sisters left as soon as they could lie about their ages and get a paying job. And I was right behind them. But I was going to do it better; I was going to get a college education."

"But you did get a college education. You went to Princeton."

Randall swung back to the window. "That's another long story. It took me six years of struggling to get through Princeton. I wouldn't care to repeat the experience."

"But you did it. And look where you are now."

"I'm looking," Randall said with a mean edge to his voice. The edge was gone when he continued. "The scholarship wasn't the only thing Gill took from me. He also took Lucy, the only good thing in my life from age twelve on." He stared out into the night. "And for twenty-three years, I thought that he took my daughter, too."

Kate's eyes widened. "You have a daughter?"

"Evidently not. But I thought I might."

His voice was so bleak she longed to put her arms around him for comfort. His stance was so rigid she was afraid he wouldn't welcome being touched.

"Tell me about Lucy," she urged softly.

"It's a sordid story."

Kate lifted an eyebrow. "I've been through sordid myself. I can handle it."

Randall gave her a humorless smile in acknowledgment, then sat back down on the bed. "It starts further back than twenty-three years. Lucinda Nelson was a year younger than I was and just as poor. But her parents didn't drink. Some weeks, I spent more time at her house

270

than at mine.

"She was a pretty girl: blond, tall and slender, green eyes. She had a real talent for making her house pretty, too. We made all the usual plans young lovers do. I'd go to college and then come back and marry her. We'd move to San Antonio and have a family and a house. That was what kept me going, in spite of my mother and the teachers who thought I was nothing but trouble. My idea of heaven was to have a house in San Antonio with Lucy in it to make it pretty and to be the mother of my children. She had a sweetness that I knew would make her a good mother – and a good wife." His expression hardened. "But Gill got it all instead."

Once again, Randall stood up, this time to pace around the room.

"It was the summer before my senior year. Lucy came to my house crying because she was pregnant." Randall stopped in the middle of the room. "I can still feel the kick in the gut that gave me. I hadn't told her that I had lost the only hope I had of getting both of us out of Mason County." His lips twisted in self-mockery. "I thought she was counting on me, and I was trying to be the big man and find another way.

"I told her that we'd get married right away, and I told her about losing the scholarship. But we loved each other and everything would work out."

Randall started pacing again. "Three days later, she told me that I was off the hook. She was going to marry Gill Gillespie."

Kate gasped.

Randall sent her a sardonic look. "Exactly. It was an ugly scene. I told her that I didn't want someone else raising my child. She told me that it wasn't mine, but I didn't believe her. I figured that since my future looked dim, she was going for the sure thing with the banker's son. When she pointed out that Gill was in a better position to support a wife and child than I was, I stopped arguing."

He sat down again. "On graduation day, I collected my diploma and got on a bus out of there. I swore not to come back until I could make Gill pay for what he had taken from me."

"So you left and made your fortune and then went back to exact retribution," Kate prompted.

"I made my fortune in order to exact retribution," Randall corrected her.

"You created RJ Enterprises just so that you could take revenge on the man who got you thrown off your high school football team and married your pregnant girlfriend twenty-some years ago?"

"Yes."

"I don't believe that for a minute," Kate said, standing up and facing him.

Randall stood up, too, and ground out his words. "I've been watching Mason Bank since the day I left, waiting for the perfect moment to pick it off. Not a day has gone by that I haven't looked at some piece of information about that bank."

"You just got into a bad habit."

His laugh was short as he turned away. "Why am I arguing with you? For the last twenty-four hours I've been trying to convince myself that I haven't wasted most of my life."

"Why would you think that?"

"Because I spent twenty-three years planning my payback, and I threw it away!"

Kate sat down again. "How did you throw it away?"

"I cancelled the deal. I left Gill with his bank and his house and his wife and his daughters."

"In other words, you did the right thing," Kate said.

"Yeah, I did the right thing," Randall said with contempt in his voice. He spun on his heel and came back to her. "Because of you."

"Because of *me*?" Kate's voice went up an octave in astonishment.

"Gill invited me to his house. I saw Lucinda there, and she filled me in on some of the details. Like the fact that she knew all along that her baby wasn't mine." He seemed to notice that Kate was leaning back in order to look up at him and he took a step away. "Lucinda and I were finishing our enlightening conversation when I took a stroll around the room and saw a photo. It was a picture of her three daughters in soccer uniforms with their arms around each other, holding trophies and grinning at the camera."

Randall took a deep breath. "The soccer uniforms and the grins reminded me of Clay and Patrick. I realized that I wouldn't be destroying a man; I'd be destroying a family. And I couldn't do that after knowing you and your boys. I just couldn't God damn do that. So I went out and got drunk."

He walked slowly back to the bed and sank down onto it. "So now what do I do, Kate?"

She got up and went over to him, kneeling in front of him to cup his face with her hands. "You had your dream before Gill Gillespie intervened: You were going to get out of Mason County and go to San Antonio. Revenge had nothing to do with that. Lucinda and Gill just nudged you along the track. And you've gone so far beyond that first dream."

She dropped her hands and sat back on her heels.

"You're an extraordinary person, Randall. Remember, I watched you run straight toward a burning gas tank to rescue two men because they worked for you, and you felt responsible for them. You put all your resources at the disposal of a twelve-year-old who got bitten by a dog."

He made a sound of protest, but Kate continued.

"You just sacrificed what you believed was your moment of triumph, the ultimate goal of your life, for three girls who played soccer." She stood up. "You're not a destroyer; you're a builder."

Randall dropped his face into his hands, threading his fingers up into his hair. Kate rose and sat down beside him.

"It may take some time to get used to the idea that you aren't some sort of an avenging angel, but I know you'll find another project to focus on." She moved her hand up to massage his neck. "You could spend more time on that charitable foundation of yours. Or join Habitat for Humanity." Kate was warming to her theme. "Run for president!"

"Win the Nobel Peace Prize," Randall's voice emerged from the depths of his hands. "End world hunger."

"That's the spirit," Kate approved.

When he lifted his head, he was smiling. He turned slightly so that he could take Kate's face between his hands, and he kissed her on the forehead. Then his gaze dropped to her lips. He shifted toward her ever so slowly, giving her all the time in the world to pull away.

But she met him halfway. He had trusted her with the story of his past. He had come to her for help and she loved him all the more for it. She wanted to touch him as much as he needed to touch her.

He began the kiss like a desperate man, pressing his mouth hard against hers, his tongue forcing entrance. Kate had to grab his shoulders to brace herself against the on-slaught.

Then suddenly the attack ended. He gently brushed her lips with his and traced her mouth lightly with his tongue. Kate moaned as she released his shoulders and slid her hands up into his hair.

He pulled her hard against him for a long minute. Then he gently lowered her onto the bed and stretched out beside her. Propping himself on one elbow, he looked at her with a half-smile. "We're going to go slowly for a change." Then his expression clouded. "I don't want you to make love to me out of pity."

"Don't be an idiot," she said affectionately, as she reached up and unbuttoned his shirt.

Randall's eyebrow quirked upward, and then he laughed and buried his face in the crook of her neck. "Oh God, I love you, Kate."

She went still for a split second, then drew in a steadying breath. She realized he hadn't meant it as a declaration; it was the sort of statement he would make to a friend who made him laugh at a difficult moment.

All such thoughts scattered when Randall lifted his head and began to unbutton her blouse. As he released each button, he ran his fingers lightly over the new area of skin that was revealed. "I want to see every inch of you this time," he said.

Kate arched her back as he slid his hands under her to unfasten her bra. When he pushed it up and began teasing her nipples with his tongue, she arched even higher. Then he closed his lips on one nipple and ran his thumb around the other one. Kate gasped and grabbed handfuls of the bedspread. The longing to have Randall fill the hollow between her legs had just multiplied tenfold.

"Oh... my... goodness," Kate whispered as Randall blew a warm breath across the nipple he had just released. She couldn't stand the torture any longer. She reached up and finished unbuttoning his shirt, yanking it out of the waistband of his slacks and down his arms. She stopped briefly to run her hands across the springy dark hair on his chest and to circle his nipples in retaliation. When his head fell back in pleasure, she ran her tongue up the line of his throat.

Then they were both unbuckling, unbuttoning and unzipping madly.

The second the last piece of clothing hit the floor, Randall was on top of her. Kate closed her eyes and opened her legs, waiting for the thrust that would begin to assuage the demanding ache.

It didn't come. Instead, Randall's voice growled, "Do I need a condom?"

Kate looked up at him and shook her head. "Not because of me. I won't get pregnant, and you won't catch anything. Do you need a condom for any other reason?"

A grin of pure lust curled Randall's lips. "No reason at all." And then the thrust came.

Kate had to swallow her shout of satisfaction. Randall was not so quiet. Kate tilted her hips and wrapped her legs around his waist so that each stroke slid along her most sensitive spot. Randall came first, his orgasm pulsing in and against her. He reached down and with one touch sent Kate convulsing over the edge. Her climax seemed to go on forever, and when she finally collapsed in satiation, tiny after-tremors ran through her inner muscles.

Randall did not withdraw but rolled so that Kate lay draped limply on top of him. She sucked in a deep breath and let it out in a long contented sigh.

"I agree completely," his voice rumbled against her ear.

Kate's eyelids drifted closed. She thought how unique the feeling of skin against skin was; two living fabrics stretched over flexing muscles and pulsing veins. Each part felt a little different. There was the focused pleasure of her breasts' softness crushed against the wall of Randall's chest, the provocative tangle and slide of thigh between thigh, and, as she laced her fingers with his, the warm affection of two palms touching. The steady stroke of his hand on her hair made her scalp tingle with tiny vibrations of bliss. She sighed again.

"The road to hell is paved with good intentions."

Kate's eyes flew open. "I beg your pardon," she said indignantly.

A deep chuckle vibrated against her cheek. "I said that we were going to go slowly, but slow doesn't seem to be in our vocabulary when it comes to this."

She let her eyes close again. "Maybe next time," she murmured.

As their breathing slowed and their blood began to cool, Randall pulled up the down quilt that Kate neatly folded at the foot of the bed each morning. He nestled Kate comfortably but firmly at his side and then wrapped the quilt around them.

Kate knew that she should go check on Clay, but she couldn't deny herself the indulgence of lying in the arms of the man she loved, completely naked and totally satiated. The knowledge that Randall wanted her close against him even after making love warmed her heart. She didn't pretend to herself that he had come to her for anything other than solace in a moment of crisis. For now, that was enough.

Randall lay with his eyes open, staring at the ceiling

277

and savoring the feel of Kate's warm, bare body snuggled against his. The thought of returning to his empty mountaintop sent a chill into the center of his bones, and he involuntarily tightened his grip on her. Kate responded by melting closer to him, and he smiled.

With Kate's presence to anchor him, he let his mind drift back to the moment when he had been awakened on the plane by the co-pilot gently shaking his shoulder. The man's look of concern had resurrected with shattering ferocity the memory of how he had gotten there. Randall had wanted nothing more than to close his eyes and fall back into the oblivion he had found in his drunken sleep. But he had dragged himself off the plane with what dignity he could muster.

Only to be confronted by Tom in his role of guardian angel. Randall winced when he remembered his harsh dismissal of his oldest friend. He knew that he owed Tom the truth, but he hadn't been prepared to give it to him. So he had gotten rid of him as fast and efficiently as he could. Now he owed Tom the truth and an apology.

After treating Tom disgracefully, he had gotten in his car and driven for hours. When he noticed that he was in Pennsylvania, he had turned around, the one thought in his head being that he needed sanctuary and that Kate Chilton was it.

Randall dropped a whisper of a kiss on her hair, being careful not to disturb her. He had been right to come here. He believed Kate when he couldn't believe himself. Now he could see that he had lost his passion for revenge years ago, but that he was accustomed to the focus that it gave his life.

And now what? His life was hollow at the core. He felt aimless, adrift.

Kate said that he needed a new project, but he felt burned out and cold. Except here and now. He had made himself invulnerable for so long that it felt good to be seen as human again. Kate admired him for reasons that had nothing to do with his wealth or position. In fact, those things formed a barrier in her mind.

He smiled again as he thought of how much he enjoyed ruffling her calm, polite control and fanning the flame of temper beneath it. He never feared being burned; she was the warm glow of the hearth, not a raging bonfire. Although when he thought of how they came together physically, he remembered that chimney fires could burn down houses.

His thoughts refocused on the here-and-now, and he ran his hand along Kate's hip and thigh, admiring the curve and flow of her body. He regretted his action, though, when she stirred and said, "I have to go check on Clay," shifting her warmth away from him as she scooted to the edge of the bed and sat up. He enjoyed the view as she walked across the bedroom to open the closet door and slip on a deep green silk robe.

When she finally looked at him, he was delighted to see that she was blushing slightly. He quirked a brow at her. She smiled, saying, "I haven't walked across a room naked in front of a man in quite a while."

"It must be like riding a bicycle because you did a fine job of it."

Her color heightened. "Thank you," she said and then padded noiselessly out of the room.

Randall pushed himself up and stacked the pillows so that he could lean comfortably against the big Victorian headboard. He gazed across the room into the empty fireplace and did some hard thinking.

He had reached a very satisfactory decision when the

door reopened, and Kate slipped back into the room. Her gleaming auburn hair had caught the mood of their love-making and was curling wildly around her face. The silk of the robe flowed like liquid over the swell of her breasts and the glorious roundness of her hips and thighs. He was grateful for the puffy down comforter that covered his immediate arousal. She closed the door softly and gave him a sweet, slow smile. He answered her with a smile of his own and said, "Marry me, Kate."

A riot of emotions exploded through her. Having performed her motherly duties, she had walked back to her room, thinking how extraordinary it was to know that Randall Johnson lay in her bed waiting for her to return. She had opened the door with a mixture of shyness and anticipation. The sight of him naked to the waist, lounging on her pillows, had made her temperature rise several degrees. He looked magnificently male and at ease, with his shoulders spanning half the headboard's width and the dusting of dark hair highlighting the muscles of his chest and arms. She had wanted to hurl herself on him, but instead she had smiled her thoughts and started to untie the belt of her robe.

Then he spoke and she froze.

She had expected a sexy come-on, and instead, he had casually proposed marriage!

Her surge of pleasure was swamped by a tidal wave of hurt and anger. He was no better than Oliver, trying to find himself a ready-made family.

"I don't believe that my name appeared on the list of projects for you to pursue," she said coldly, pulling her belt into a knot.

"I screwed that up, didn't I? I would have gotten down on my knees, but in my present state," he said, glancing down at his lap, "you would have suspected me of ulterior motives."

Refusing to let his humor disarm her, Kate walked to the foot of the bed. "I'm not Lucinda," she said.

His brows snapped down, and his smile vanished. "Hell, I know that. You don't resemble Lucy in any way."

She tried not to be insulted as she recalled the glowing terms with which he had described his childhood sweetheart. "I meant that I'm not a substitute for your dream of having a wife and a family."

Randall's scowl deepened. He was furious with himself. He was usually the most controlled of negotiators, carefully laying the groundwork so that the other party was drawn inexorably and inevitably to the conclusion he wanted. He had completely fouled up this deal.

"That's not why I proposed, but now I withdraw the offer."

Kate gaped at him. "Two seconds ago you wanted to marry me and now you don't?"

"I didn't say I didn't want to marry you. I *temporarily* rescinded my proposal."

He got out of bed and stalked across the room, six-feet-three and naked. Kate backed up. He caught her in two strides and slid his arms around her and cupped her buttocks, pulling her hips against him. The thin silk of her robe offered no barrier to the warmth of his hands or the friction of his arousal against her.

"I have a different proposition in mind now," he whispered against her neck.

Kate had crossed her arms when he approached, but that was proving no defense against his assault on her better judgment. The fact that she had walked into the room wanting him didn't help. She was confused and furious and utterly without willpower when one of his hands slid up into her hair and he ran his lips along her jawline and onto her mouth. Then he stooped and swept his arm behind her knees, lifting her and carrying her to the bed.

He set her down gently and began slowly peeling back her robe, letting his hands drag slowly across the skin he bared. When he had exposed her completely, he stood looking down at her with an expression that made her nipples harden. Instead of coming down on top of her, he rolled her onto her side and fitted his body along her back with his erection against her bottom. He adjusted his arm so that her head was pillowed on his biceps. Then he covered her breast with his free hand.

"Watch me touch you, Kate," he commanded in her ear.

She looked down involuntarily. The tan of his big hand against the paleness of her breast was startling, and she couldn't tear her eyes away. He slowly trailed his hand down the other breast, stopping to tease her nipple, then moving lower until his fingers disappeared between her legs. Kate caught her breath at the sight and the sensation. There was little that she could do to respond in this position, so she reached behind her and held on to his hip as he played and stroked and drove her mad. Finally she gave in and begged, "Please, Randall, now."

Again he surprised her. He bent her top leg by pushing his knee against the back of hers. "I learned that trick from an engineer friend," he drawled.

Then he slid down her back and drove himself into her from behind and below. She was so wet that he slid in effortlessly, and she cried out at the almost instant sense of fullness. The lack of friction made the lovemaking go on and on. He never halted his rhythm but his hands roved freely up to her breasts and down her stomach. He explored the whorls of her ear with his tongue, whispering how good this felt and how wet she was and how he wanted to stay inside her for hours.

Kate was incapable of speech. She answered him with moans and the clamp of her hand on his hip. Finally, his strokes quickened, and he slid his hands down to hold her hips at the angle he wanted.

Kate forgot that her children were in the house. She forgot that this man was an arch-manipulator. She forgot that she was three days behind at work and that the mortgage was due. All she knew was that her body and Randall's joined with an intensity that wiped away all other considerations. She came with an explosion of sound and motion that made Randall's hold almost bruise her. And he joined her, her convulsion triggering his own roar of release, muffled by his mouth against her hair.

She lay limp, wondering if she had wakened Clay or Patrick, and knowing that she couldn't move even if the door opened and they both barged in. She also knew that she shouldn't have let Randall make love to her again since he now undoubtedly thought that she would change her mind about marrying him.

For a moment she contemplated the thought. Oliver's voice rang in her head: "He won't marry you, you know." Even Georgia replayed: "He isn't interested in relationships." Well, it seemed like little old Kate Chilton had brought Randall Johnson to his knees figuratively, if not literally. She had proved both of them wrong and enjoyed the ignoble spurt of triumph she felt at that.

It was a tempting offer in many ways. The sex alone would sway a lesser soul, something she was sure that Randall was counting on.

But she could imagine nothing worse than marrying a

man who didn't love her heart and soul as well as body. What happened when he got bored with sex with her, when it became comfortable rather than explosive? She would always wonder whether he was seeking that combustion elsewhere.

More important, what sort of father would he be for Clay and Patrick? He was great at handing out treats like helicopter rides and indoor swimming, but how would he handle throwing up and undone homework assignments? Kate pushed aside memories of Randall coaching the soccer team to victory and showing up at the hospital to smooth the way for Clay. She didn't trust him to continue in that vein when the novelty wore off.

When it came right down to it, other than the physical attraction, she had no sense of how he felt about her at all. He teased her, he bullied her, he seduced her, and he came to her for comfort. What did all of that mean? Could she trust him with her own life and that of her children?

Randall interrupted her thoughts by saying hoarsely, "That gets better every time."

She laughed at the contrast in their thoughts.

"After an orgasm like that, you laugh at me?" he asked in mock horror, as he propped himself up on his elbow to look down at her face.

Kate rolled onto her back. "After an orgasm like that, I'm lucky that I can draw enough breath to laugh."

"That's better." He stroked her cheek with his thumb. He hesitated a moment before saying, "May I sleep here tonight? I'll leave early, before the boys wake up."

Her throat tightened around the tears she wouldn't allow in her eyes. How could she say no to the plea in his normally confident voice? "Of course you can sleep here. I'll set the alarm."

"That's not necessary. I've been getting up early all my life. I'll be gone long before anyone stirs."

"Let's get under the covers this time," Kate said, pulling back the blanket and sheets. After they had arranged their pillows and snuggled in against each other, she felt compelled to confess, "I haven't slept beside a man since David died. I'm glad you wanted to stay."

The man she was sleeping beside pulled her closer. "I want to stay forever, darlin', at least till death do us part. But we won't talk about that now. Go to sleep."

Twenty Two

KATE WAS IN the midst of a strange dream that involved Randall Johnson kneeling in front of her on the dirty floor of a run-down bar while a fight raged in the background. She was trying to grab him and pull him outside, but other people kept getting in the way. Then someone caught her hand in a clasp too solid and warm to be a dream, and Kate slowly pried her eyes open.

Looking better than any vision, even with his black eye, Randall was sitting on the side of the bed holding her hand. His damp hair was neatly combed back and his white shirt looked crisply pressed. The memory of the previous night came rushing vividly back into her brain and she started to sit up.

Then she realized that she was completely naked under the covers.

"Go right ahead and get up." Randall kissed the back of her hand with a wicked smile. "I've been resisting the temptation to peel those covers off of you ever since I woke up."

"I didn't know you ever resisted temptation." Kate adjusted the covers a bit higher.

"Darlin', if you didn't have two impressionable boys in the house, I'd keep you naked and tied to the bedposts all day long."

She held the sheet firmly across her chest as she scooted upright. It was a severe enough disadvantage to be nude when he was clothed. At least, she could be vertical instead of sprawled flat on her back.

"Well, I'm glad Clay and Patrick are here," she managed to say.

"Are you really?" he asked as he kissed the spot where her neck flowed into her shoulder.

Hanging on to the sheet for dear life, she used her other hand to push him away. He moved back, but only a few inches. His eyes held her.

"Are you really glad, Kate?" he repeated as his hand trailed down her shoulder and over the swell of her breast. His thumb brushed her nipple, and she jumped. He smiled smugly and stood up.

"You're being deliberately provocative," she accused him.

"No, lady, that's you. You're sitting in a bed that smells like sex. Your hair looks like a man ran his hands through it over and over again."

She started to sputter but he kept going.

"Then there's the fact that you're wearing absolutely nothing over that gorgeous body but a blanket. And your eyes go wide every time I touch you. That's being provocative. And if I don't get out of here soon, those impressionable boys are going to get an education."

The corners of Kate's mouth twitched. "I don't know whether to be flattered or outraged."

"Maybe you should be both." Randall glanced at the clock. "I'm going to indulge in a little blackmail now. I won't leave until you promise you'll have dinner with me this Saturday. And I want a solemn promise, no crossed fingers, no conditions."

Kate shook her head. "I don't want to leave Clay that soon."

Randall stretched out on the chaise longue, crossed his long legs at the ankles and pillowed his head on his hands. He looked very comfortable.

"You wouldn't really stay if I didn't agree," Kate said.

"Try me."

She made a sound of frustration. She desperately wanted to get out of bed so that she could confront him, but her robe was somewhere on the floor where she couldn't see it. And her closet was across the room. She checked the clock. It was 6:00 a.m. The boys wouldn't wake up for another hour. Still... She decided to beg.

"Please, Randall, for Clay and Patrick's sake."

"Sorry, that won't work."

"I guess that appealing to your better nature would be useless, as you don't have one," she said in a haughty tone.

Randall closed his eyes.

"Oh all right! But I'm doing this under protest. You're forcing me to be a bad mother."

His only movement was to open his eyes. "I want your promise because I know you won't break it."

"Yes, yes, I promise."

Immediately, he was off the chair and standing at the door. "I have to get to the office but I'll call you later." His voice dropped. "Thank you, darlin', for everything."

The door clicked closed behind him.

Kate slid back down into the bed and listened to the front door open and shut, and the sound of his car purring down the street. She lay with her eyes open, trying to make sense of last night's roller-coaster ride. All she could conclude with certainty was that he was a terrific lover and that he seemed like his old self again this morning. In fact, it was difficult to reconcile this morning's Randall with yesterday's Randall. She almost regretted his return to steely CEO. She had liked the glimpse of the person inside.

As for his now-withdrawn proposal of marriage, she couldn't begin to comprehend that in the light of dawn. He had clearly been temporarily overwhelmed with loneliness and then had come to his senses.

Kate threw back the covers. She needed to shower and straighten up the bed before anyone else stirred. Routine was a good thing. It had gotten her through David's death, and it would get her through whatever Randall decided to throw at her.

Randall strode into RJ Enterprises as though he hadn't pulled a disappearing act for the last two days. "Good morning, Gail."

"Good morning, sir. I'm glad that you're back safely," she said. He turned, and her eyebrows shot up at the sight of his black eye, but she refrained from commenting.

He acknowledged her forbearance with a half-smile. "I need to talk with Julian Howard at Tower Design. And find out who the best real estate agency would be for selling my house."

"Eagle's Nest?" Gail gasped.

"That's the one. It's time to come down off the mountaintop," Randall said, heading for his office.

"Have you seen the *Wall Street Journal* today?" she called after him.

Randall stopped and turned. "No."

"I didn't think so. I put it on your desk, just in case.

There's an article on the front page that you're not going to like," she warned him.

He went over to his desk and dropped into his chair. Picking up the newspaper, he found the article Gail had referred to. As he read, his eyebrows lowered until they almost met.

"Well, you're front page news."

Randall looked up to see Tom Rogan lounging against the door frame. "Why do they print this crap, Tom?" he asked.

"Maybe because you won't tell people the truth." Tom looked at him for a long moment.

Randall looked back in silence.

When Randall didn't speak, Tom strolled the rest of the way into the office and sat down. He read out loud from the copy of the paper he had carried in with him. "Let's see…. Your word can't be trusted…you backed out of a deal with Mason Bank for no reason –"

"I did the man a favor. He's too stupid to figure it out."

"The companies you own have terrible safety records." He looked up at his boss. "They must mean the fire at Tex-Oil." He continued, "And your judgment has become questionable as demonstrated by grossly overpaying for a share in a small architectural firm."

Randall shrugged. "I've decided to become a patron of the arts."

"Well, according to Gill Gillespie, president of Mason Bank, you're losing it. And frankly, I'm not sure I disagree with him."

For a moment the two men's gazes locked and held. Then Randall shifted in his chair. "I deserved that. And you deserve an apology."

"You're damned right I do – and an explanation," Tom

said.

"I don't think I can do both."

"All right, you stiff-necked pain in the ass," Tom laughed. "I'll take the explanation."

"It's all ancient history." Randall leaned back in his chair. "I slept with Gill Gillespie's wife."

Tom sat bolt upright. "No wonder he's pissed."

Randall leveled a hard look at his second-in-command. "Before she was his wife. And he doesn't know that. At least, he didn't when I left his house."

"Well, it sounds as though he knows it now," Tom said, leaning back again. "And?"

Randall took a deep breath and launched into a flatly factual version of the story of Lucinda and Gill. Tom knew him well enough to fill in the emotional blanks. When he stopped talking, Tom let out a long whistle.

"You do such a fine job of holding a grudge that I may have to make you an honorary Irishman. That explains all those times when you took risks that boggled my mind. I used to wonder what devil was driving you." He smiled reminiscently. "It made for one wild ride."

Randall gave a short laugh. "I scared the hell out of myself sometimes."

"I'm thinking that maybe you need to take some of those risks in your life right now," Tom said. "Maybe you need to work on a different deal."

"And which deal would that be?" Randall asked in a dangerous voice.

"You're a smart man. You figure it out." Tom waited for the explosion.

He almost got it as Randall half-rose out of his chair. Then the anger drained from his face, and all that was left was bleakness as he sat down and turned his gaze back to the window.

"Yeah, I'm real smart." He stared out at the panorama spread before him for a minute, then turned wearily back to Tom. "I need to get out of this Tower Design deal gracefully. Do you have any good ideas?"

Tom hadn't expected the change of topic. "I'll see what I can come up with," he promised, wishing that Randall had asked him to do almost anything else.

Patrick was at school, and Clay was settled with several videotaped episodes of *Star Trek,* so Kate was free to check in with the office and catch up on emails and voice mails. Almost all of the construction companies bidding on the bridge had questions about building one structure over another. Some were too complicated to email an answer, so she spent an hour on the phone with various skeptical men. After checking on Clay, she played her personal voice mails.

"Kate, a promise made under duress isn't binding. So you can say no. But I'm asking you to have dinner with me Saturday because it's very important to me. I hope you'll come."

She smiled as he almost choked on the last sentence.

Randall wasn't used to requesting rather than commanding. She considered turning him down, but given what he had just been through, she couldn't do it. And he had *asked* this time. Of course, she also wanted to see him. Desperately, foolishly, and passionately. So after checking with Clay and Brigid, she called him back, only to be told that he was in a meeting. She left a brief message accepting and went on to her emails.

Friday she took Clay to the local doctor recommended

by Dr. Lane. He changed the bandage and said that the hand was healing beautifully. Clay was given permission to return to school on Monday if he wasn't in pain and that elicited a whoop of gratitude. Even *Star Trek* began to pall when one was an active, healthy boy with merely a hand injury. Kate took him out for a celebratory lunch at their favorite diner. They had just returned to the house when the telephone rang.

"Hello, Kate. It's Oliver."

Kate felt every muscle in her body tense. "Hello, Oliver," she said in a neutral tone. "How are you?"

"I know that you don't want to talk with me," he said, brushing aside her polite question, "but I'm very concerned about a business matter."

"Really?" Kate said.

"I want to fax you a document. When you get it, will you please call me back?"

"Can't you just tell me what this is about?"

"After you have the fax."

"All right," she agreed reluctantly. She was relieved to hang up, even temporarily. Oliver's voice brought back unpleasant memories.

The fax machine rang and beeped upstairs in the office, and she headed up to read it. As far as she could tell, it was nothing more than a copy of an electronic transfer of funds, from a company called Avanta Capital Corporation to Tower Design Corporation. It was dated about three weeks before, and the amount was several hundred thousand dollars.

Kate dialed Oliver at C/R/G. "I have the fax."

"I noticed the name under 'Instructions.' Kate, what does this mean to C/R/G? Are we going to be sold off or become a subsidiary? What are your plans?"

She was no longer listening. In tiny print under "Instructions," she read "cc: T. Rogan."

She sat down suddenly, her mind racing to put together the chronology of her relationship with Randall. She couldn't remember what she had told him when.

"Kate?"

"What? I'm sorry; my mind was elsewhere:"

Oliver's voice was suddenly gentle. "Why didn't you come to me if you were so worried about money? I would have helped. I wanted to help in any way that I could. You didn't have to sleep with Randall Johnson to solve your financial problems."

"You think that I got involved with Randall for money?"

"I don't know what to think anymore." Oliver sounded genuinely distressed and bewildered.

Kate felt her fury draining away. "I know less about this deal than you do." She sighed. "Although I certainly intend to find out more." She thought for a moment. "What would it mean to C/R/G if the deal got cancelled?"

"We'd have less working capital; and you would get less cash from the company. There might be some speculation in the architectural community as to why Tower Design pulled out, but with Paul Desmond coming on board, we'd be fine."

"Good," Kate said. "Because this deal is about to become a really bad idea for the dealmaker."

"I know that I have no right to say this, but I'm very, very glad that you didn't know about it," Oliver said. "I'm sorry I jumped to the wrong conclusion."

Kate slumped back into her desk chair and closed her eyes. "I'd appreciate it if people would ask me before making assumptions about what I want or need."

Oliver was silent.

Rubbing her hand over her face, Kate sat up. "I think you should go forward with Paul's buyout at the original number."

"Umm, I think the number will be somewhat higher in view of Tower's figures. We may have slightly undervalued your share," Oliver said, sounding uncomfortable.

"You tried to lowball me, didn't you, Oliver?" She blurted it out, but once the words were spoken, she knew in her gut they were true. "Your figures always seemed too low."

Oliver said nothing.

Kate broke the silence. "This is unbelievable."

"I didn't think it would matter to you because we would be married, and it would all blend together anyway. I wanted to do what was best for you and the business," Oliver defended himself.

"I don't want to talk about this anymore. Good-bye."

In truth, she didn't even want to think about it, but she knew she had to. More than ever, she understood that money was power for these men. They might convince themselves that they were trying to help her, but in fact they used money as a tool to manipulate her into doing what they wanted. "That's why men don't want us to earn equal wages," Kate said to Gretchen, who had followed her upstairs at the sound of the fax machine. She picked up the phone again to call Randall, but didn't dial. "No, I'm going to throw this in his face in person. He wants to get together tomorrow, fine, we'll get together. And he can eat his money for dinner."

She went downstairs to give Clay a hug. "Try to stay as sweet as you are, even when you're grown up," she told him.

He looked up at her with a quizzical smile. "Having man problems, Mom?"

"What would you know about *man problems*?"

"Well, I am one. So if you need any advice, feel free to ask."

Twenty Three

SHE DECIDED TO wear what she remembered as a rather severe black velvet evening suit. The jacket had long straight
sleeves; the skirt was slim and had a modest slit at the side
for ease of movement. However, the deep plunge where the
jacket closed across her chest spoiled the conservative effect. She rooted around in her drawers until she found a
dull gold chiffon scarf that she could tuck into the neckline.
She started to tame her hair into a neat page boy, then
decided that leaving it in waves crackling with static
electricity suited her mood better.

"Wow, Mom, you look pretty but kind of scary,"
Patrick said as she came downstairs. "Like a school
principal or a judge."

She kissed the top of his head. "You just said exactly
the right thing."

"Mom's having man problems," Clay said to his
brother.

"Och, don't we all?" Brigid said.

Patrick clearly had questions to ask but the doorbell
rang. Kate walked calmly out of the kitchen, then stopped

for a moment to square her shoulders and lift her chin. She relished a flood of cold anger as she pulled open the front door.

Randall stood squarely in front of her, smiling. "Hello, darlin'," he said as he moved forward.

She backed up to let him in. As he scanned her from head to feet, his smile faded. She gave him full credit for interpreting visual messages.

"Hello, Randall," she said coolly.

He eyed her speculatively, clearly trying to assess her mood. "May I say hello to the boys?"

"Of course. They're in the kitchen," she said smoothly, leading the way.

"Hi, Mr. Johnson!" Patrick said, bouncing out of his seat to shake hands.

"Good evening, young man," Randall said. "Are you taking good care of your brother?"

"I've let him watch any movie that he wanted," Patrick said.

"Well done." Randall greeted Brigid and then turned to Clay. "How's the hand feeling?"

"Much better, thank you, sir," Clay responded.

Kate saw him glance back and forth between Randall and herself and crossed her fingers that he wouldn't hint about any "problems" she might be having. "The doctor here is very pleased with the way Clay's hand is healing," she said quickly.

"I'm glad to hear that. But don't rush things, Clay. Proper healing takes time."

"I won't push it, but I'm glad to be going back to school on Monday."

Randall smiled. "I don't blame you. It's good to get

back in the saddle. Good night, boys," he said, reaching for Kate's elbow.

"Good night, sir," they chorused.

"Have a nice dinner, Mom," Clay said.

Kate kissed them both, and then let Randall steer her out of the house and into his car.

After he had closed her door, he came around to the driver's side and slid in himself. Instead of starting the engine, he leaned back against his door and looked at her. "You're mad as hell about something, and I'd like to know what it is."

She took a deep breath and turned her head to look him in the eye.

"I just found out that Tower Design didn't have a sudden desire to overpay for a share in C/R/G. They had a little help from a company called Avanta Capital, which wanted to make sure that Tom Rogan knew that the deal was in the works."

Randall sighed and ran his hand over his face. "How did you find that out?"

"What difference does it make?"

He shrugged. "I'd just like to know where we fouled up."

"Is that all you care about?" Kate shifted in her seat so that her whole body was facing him. "Where you fouled up? It doesn't matter to you that you – and Oliver – are treating me like some puppet whose strings you can pull? He tried to bankrupt me into marrying him and you've tried to *buy* me!"

"Wait a minute. Give me some credit. I was trying to help, and I had to do it in a roundabout way because I knew you wouldn't just take money from me."

"You're damn right I wouldn't! I'm not Lucinda, you

know. I don't need to be rescued from a life of poverty. Did it ever occur to you that I might want to make it on my own? That maybe I needed to know that I could support myself and my family?" Randall started to speak but Kate interrupted him. "No, of course not. Because you see me as some image of what you want, some adjunct to your vision of your own life. But I'm a person in my own right, and I'm tired of having that ignored!" Kate reached for the door handle. "So take your Tower Design deal and shove it."

"Wait a minute! You can't shout at me and then leave," Randall said, pushing a button which locked the car's doors.

"Unlock the door."

"Not until you've heard me out."

Kate straightened in her seat and stared out the windshield.

Randall took her chin in his hand and turned her face toward him. "You're looking down your nose again, darlin'."

She didn't move. He dropped his hand and sat back. "You won't believe me, but I'm already in the process of canceling the Tower Design deal."

Kate snorted.

"All right, Kate. You said yourself that I'd gotten into bad habits. One of them is knowing everything that I can about anyone I do business with. So when I met you, I did my homework. And when I realized that you were having financial difficulties, I used the information. But my intentions were purely honorable. I didn't want you to know, and I didn't expect anything from you."

"And what about your little chat with Lidden Hartley?"

"More of the same. It cost me nothing to help you out."

"Do you know why I liked you? Because I thought you were honest. After my experience with David, that was very appealing." Kate shook her head. "How can I love a man who hides things from me, important things that change my life?"

That made Randall straighten up abruptly but his tone remained casual. "The same way I can love a woman who looks down her nose at me."

Kate glanced over and saw the look in his eye. She put her hands out to keep him away. "Don't touch me. You are not going to distract me with sex."

Randall took both her hands in his, raising them to his lips. His voice dropped into the deep velvet register. "Distracting you with sex is the only way that I can get past that prickly facade of yours to the heat underneath. I don't want to rescue you or buy you; I want to marry you. Is that a crime?"

Kate felt his words as warmth and vibration against her skin, piercing her armor so that her strength of will began to bleed away. She pulled her hand out of his grasp. "Why would you want to marry someone you don't believe in? You don't trust me enough to let me handle my own problems. How could you trust me to handle both of our problems?"

"For Christ's sake, how can you say that I don't trust you?" Randall said, flipping on the engine and ramming the car into gear. He twisted toward her as he backed too fast down the driveway. "I came here and spilled my guts to you. I told you things I've never told another person!"

"Yes, and I've done things with you that I've never done with another person," Kate said sharply. "But that doesn't mean I should marry you! Maybe just the opposite. Randall, what I'm trying to say is that you don't know me. You don't know what made me what I am."

He kept driving. "I can find that out, but it doesn't make

a damned bit of difference. I want the woman that you are right now, this minute."

"And what about the woman I might become? Will you want her?" Kate asked, then waved her hand to dismiss her questions. "Never mind. No one can answer that."

"Is that what you're worried about? That I'll lose interest and cheat on you like David?" The Jaguar's speed increased with the volume of Randall's voice. "I never break a promise. Never."

"I'm not worried about you breaking a promise. There are other things that can be broken," Kate said, thinking of her heart the day she found David's letter. She took a deep breath. "I think I've said about all I want to say about this right now. If you really insist on the charade of taking me to dinner, perhaps we could agree to drop this subject for the evening."

Randall nodded. "A cooling-off period might be a good idea."

There was dead silence in the car.

Finally, Randall broke it. "What's the status of your bridge?"

Kate did a quick change of mental gears. They spent the rest of the drive into New York City carefully discussing professional topics.

At the curb in front of the Four Seasons restaurant, a uniformed doorman rushed to open the car door for Kate. Randall handed the keys to a valet and took her hand to lead her through the doors and up the stairs to the *maitre d'*s station. Despite all of her best intentions, Kate enjoyed the feel of his warm fingers laced with hers. Even worse, she felt proud to walk up the steps beside him with his hand clearly claiming her as his chosen companion.

She really needed to get a grip on herself.

Julian greeted them warmly. "Mr. Johnson, what a pleasure to see you again. We have your usual table ready."

"Thanks. I'd like you to meet Kate Chilton. Kate, this is Julian Niccolini, an old friend and brilliant restaurateur."

"I am delighted to meet you," Julian said, raising Kate's hand to his lips.

"Well, well, well," a heavily-accented voice boomed from the Grill Room to their right. "Look who's here. I remember when you couldn't afford to buy a beer at Dobie's, much less dinner at the Four Seasons."

Kate felt Randall stiffen as he turned slowly to face the tall blond man sauntering toward them. "Gill. I didn't know you were in New York."

Kate almost gasped as she recognized the name of the man Randall hated enough to try to destroy. He was followed by an elegant blond woman who was clearly trying to prevent a confrontation.

Randall nodded to her. "Hello, Lucy. Kate, I'd like you to meet Lucinda and Gill Gillespie. Lucy and Gill, Kate Chilton."

Kate murmured polite greetings as she shook hands with Lucinda. Gill did not offer his hand as his focus was entirely on Randall. Kate tried to decide if he had been drinking too much, or if he was just so angry that he didn't care who heard him.

"All that money hasn't made you a man of honor, has it? You're still just poor white trash dressed up in an expensive suit." Gill Gillespie's Texas accent made the insults sound even worse, somehow. "I did business with you for old times' sake and look where it got me: holding a contract that wasn't worth the paper it was printed on."

Randall appeared utterly impassive but his grip on

Kate's hand had tightened to the point where she couldn't feel her fingertips.

Lucinda tried to intervene. "Gill, let's go back to our hotel."

"When I'm finished with this SOB," he snapped. He lowered his voice but it vibrated with hatred. "I know about you and Lucy. She told me all about it after you left. If I'd known that you'd laid a finger on her, I would have had you horsewhipped then."

Kate opened her mouth to leap to Randall's defense, but she saw his gaze shift to Lucy, who looked back at him with a plea in her eyes. Kate closed her mouth as Randall's grip on her hand relaxed. "I don't believe this is the time or place to discuss your wife's past," he said. "Whatever pain I may have caused her I regret, and she knows that."

"You bastard. I ought to..." Gill took a step toward Randall. He shook Lucinda's grip off his arm. Kate watched in horror as he drew back his fist.

With skill gained from years of dealing with the public, Julian stepped between the two men, saying, "Claire, Mr. Johnson's table is ready. Won't you escort him to it? And Mr. Gillespie, allow me to offer you and your lovely wife each a glass of this marvelous Merlot I found in France when I was there last week." A hostess came over, and Gill stood rigid for a moment. Then he relaxed and smiled in a way that made Kate shiver. "Hell, you'll get what's comin' to you without me having to dirty my hands. Enjoy your evenin', Ms. Chilton."

"Good night, Lucy," Randall said, his voice softening.

Lucinda's main concern was getting her husband away from Randall, but as she urged him toward the bar, she looked back over her shoulder and mouthed, "I'm sorry."

Kate discovered that she was shaking as she followed

Claire to their table. She did register that they were seated in the Pool Room, right by the rectangular pool of water that was the room's centerpiece, a coveted position. But she was so perturbed by the scene that had just taken place that she noticed nothing else about the famous design of Philip Johnson and Mies van der Rohe.

As soon as the hostess had presented them with their menus and left, Kate leaned forward and said in a low voice, "Gill Gillespie is seriously unbalanced. I think that he really might be planning to hurt you in some way."

Randall reached across the table to cover her hand with his. "I apologize for that ugly scene. Gill's just blustering. He's mad about the deal, and he's mad about whatever Lucinda told him, but he's already mouthed off to the press. I'm not concerned."

Kate noted how thick Randall's Texas accent had become. Evidently, Gill's presence took him back to his roots. She turned her palm up to meet his. "I know that you're a big, strong man who can take care of himself," she teased gently, "but that man hates you too much to be thinking straight. Please be careful for a while."

His brilliant smile dissolved all her tension. "I like having you worry about me. And I'll watch my back." He squeezed her hand and then picked up the wine list. "I think I could use a good stiff glass of red wine."

Kate laughed and looked around as Randall concentrated on his selection.

The white marble pool was punctuated at each corner by a fifteen-foot tree, decorated now with the foliage of fall. The wait staff's cummerbunds and jackets matched the trees' color scheme. As her eyes swept the perimeters of the high-ceilinged room, she was delighted by the ripple and shimmer of thousands of strands of silvery beads hanging over the windows, creating the illusion of rain or a waterfall cascading down. The room was spare and minimally decorated, deriving its beauty from its lines and proportions. Even the silver was architectural; David would have loved this.

Randall had ordered the wine, and he handed Kate her menu, saying, "The food ought to taste better here than at the hospital."

"Nothing tastes good in a hospital, although you certainly did your best."

The wine arrived and Randall went through the ritual tasting with brisk efficiency. Once Kate's glass was filled, he lifted his in a toast. "Here's to the powers of persuasion of a good meal and a fine wine."

"I'm not sure I should drink to that," Kate objected, swirling the wine in her glass as she inhaled its fragrant bouquet.

"I never drink alone," Randall said, pausing with his glass just before his lips and locking his gaze on hers. "Bottoms up."

Kate took a cautious sip and then closed her eyes in ecstasy. "Umm, this is delicious."

Randall's lips curved in a smug smile that Kate just caught. She raised an eyebrow at him. "Don't smirk. It counteracts the effect of the wine."

He chuckled. The waiter arrived to take their order, and Kate had a grand time choosing delicacies whose mere descriptions made her mouth water.

Once they were alone, she said carefully, "Lucinda is very beautiful. It's hard to believe she came from poverty. Of course, it's hard to believe that of you, too."

Randall's smile evaporated. She saw him tense and then relax with a visible effort. "Lucy's like the wine, better with age."

"As strange as it may sound, I'm glad to have met Gill and Lucinda. Putting faces to the names makes your past seem more real to me."

"Is that a good thing?"

Kate smiled wryly. "It depends on your point of view. I feel more included in your life somehow."

"Then I'll fly you down to Texas tomorrow and show you the house where I grew up, if it's still standing, and the dirt road where I learned to drive a twenty-year-old pickup truck. Hell, maybe I can even find the truck again. Then we'll visit my old dorm rooms and track down a few college buddies." Randall took a drink of wine.

Kate laughed. "I want to see the oil wells you bought by mistake. That makes you seem almost human."

"I'm about as human as they come."

The appetizers interrupted them. By tacit agreement, they kept the remainder of the conversation on less emotional topics, and Kate found herself sliding under the spell of his charm. He listened to every word she said, and his thoughtful responses made her feel that she was in fact worthy of his undivided attention. Her spirits lifted, then soared, and she sparkled in his company. Too soon the last mouthful of chocolate soufflé melted on her tongue.

When Randall rose, Kate was struck again by the power of his physical presence. Sitting across from her, his eyes were level with hers and she felt his equal. Standing, he dominated her view completely, and she experienced a quick grab of panic at the thought of how he might dominate her life. Only if I let him, she told herself as she preceded him out of the Pool Room with her head held high.

This time she noticed both covert glances and overt

stares from other diners as Randall passed their tables. One man nodded and smiled a brief greeting. Julian gave the sign that all was clear in the Grill Room and walked over to wish them a warm good-night.

"I feel like royalty," Kate said as they walked down the stairs.

Randall took her hand and raised it to his lips. "Then the dinner was a success."

"Well, it all depends on your point of view."

Randall arched an eyebrow and stepped back to let her through the door being held for them. The Jaguar was pulled up directly in front of the restaurant's entrance and the moment he saw them, the valet leapt to open the passenger door. "Have a nice evening," he said, closing the door ever so gently after Kate had settled into her seat.

She wondered if Randall even noticed how everyone jumped to open doors for him and, of course, for his chosen consort. The thought made her giggle.

He gave her a questioning look, but she only smiled and shook her head. Some jokes were impossible to share.

Twenty Four

THEY RODE IN companionable silence until Randall braked for a red light. "There's something that's been bothering me all evening," he said seriously.

"Really?" Kate braced herself. "What is it?"

Hooking a finger into the chiffon scarf where it curved around her neck, he said, "This."

Kate grabbed for it as she felt the silky fabric slide out from under her collar, but Randall was too quick. He whipped it out and tossed it onto the backseat, leaving her clasping her hands over nothing but bare skin.

"Now the view's much better. You have a beautiful neck," he said, running the back of his fingers along her jawline and down to the skin he had just uncovered.

"You're trying to cloud my thinking again," Kate said, as she attempted to ignore the treacherous shiver of anticipation that streaked through her body.

"Does it ever occur to you that maybe *you* cloud *my*

thinking?" he complained. "There I am, trying to review a contract at the office, and instead, I'm thinking about the best way to get you back in bed with me. That's not doing me any good, so I move on to trying to figure out how to pay for Clay's surgery without getting lacerated by your very sharp pride. On top of that, I've canceled two deals this week because of you."

She knew she looked like the cat who swallowed the canary but she couldn't keep her smile under control. It thrilled her that he actually thought about her at work.

"Serves you right. They were bad deals to begin with."

"Now who's smirking?" Randall said, swinging the car onto the FDR Drive.

She sighed with delight. "I love this route home. It's got a whole symphony of bridges along it."

"*A symphony of bridges*!"

Kate stuck by her metaphor. "Yes. There are the big brassy bridges like the Queensborough that we just went under and, up farther, the Triborough. Then the string section intersperses itself with bridges like the Willis Avenue. The little footbridges are the woodwinds, I guess. And it all crescendos to the big guy, the George Washington Bridge. That's my favorite."

"I've never known anyone who had a favorite bridge."

"You don't know many engineers then." She chuckled. "One of our best Sunday afternoon outings with the boys was walking across the George Washington Bridge. David loved the simple, functional lines of it. The boys loved being two hundred odd feet in the air. I loved everything about it, but especially the fact that mankind could conceive of and create such a grand structure for such a practical purpose."

"I see that I'll have to reexamine my view of bridges.

Maybe I could join one of those Sunday afternoon outings."

The vision of strolling along the high, windswept walk-way with Randall's big hand wrapped around hers and the boys racing ahead was so vivid and so glorious that Kate felt tears start in her eyes. She swallowed hard.

"I'm sorry, I don't mean to intrude on a happy memory," Randall said in a bleak voice.

"No, no, it's not that at all." She shook her head decisively. She looked straight ahead and said with dangerous honesty, "I hesitated because I realized that I want to walk the bridge with you much too much for my peace of mind."

His smile gleamed in the dimness of the car. "Good."

The lighthouse at the end of Roosevelt Island flashed by, and Kate noticed that Randall was weaving in and out of traffic with uncharacteristic aggressiveness. She glanced over at him to see his eyes narrow as he looked in the rearview mirror.

"What is it?" she asked.

"You may have made me paranoid, but I think we're being followed. Fasten your seat belt, I'm going to do some dodging and weaving just to check."

"I'm strapped in," she said, double-checking the security of the buckle as they accelerated around a taxi. After several more quick ins and outs, she ventured to say, "You're good at this."

"I took an evasive driving course a few years ago at the request of my insurance company," he said, checking the rearview mirror as he sped past a line of cars and cut in front of them to move all the way over to the right lane. Slowing down to a normal pace, he looked back again. Kate saw his lips tighten. "We're definitely being followed," he said.

"Do you think it's Gill?" she asked nervously, turning to see a dark sedan pull in one car behind them.

"Gill himself? I doubt it, but it might be someone he hired. It's more likely to be some freelance photographer looking for a picture."

"You get followed around by photographers?"

"Not generally. But occasionally they'll latch on. I don't know who would buy a picture of me, but I guess they have some market for it. I'm going to call security," he said, turning on his car phone. "Maybe they can scare them off."

The private security company answered on the second ring, and Randall explained the situation and their location. "We're notifying the police now," the dispatcher assured him. "We recommend that you remain on the FDR and in motion."

"No problem," Randall said.

"Do you have one of those radio transponders you told the boys about in this car?" Kate asked.

"Yes, and I think it's about time to use it," he said, reaching down to flip the switch. "Now we'll get serious about losing them."

Kate took a firm hold of the hand grip above her door as Randall raced the Jaguar through three lanes of traffic, accelerating and braking through openings that appeared too small for a Volkswagen Beetle.

She glanced over at him as the bridge to Randall's Island whipped past. His eyes were focused on the road but a distinctly feral smile played over his lips. She realized that incredibly, Randall was enjoying this mad dash through the night. His voice startled her.

"Do we take the brassy Triborough or the big guy?" he asked as the Jaguar practically flew over a rise in the highway.

"The George Washington," Kate said, refusing to allow him to joke about the situation. "The security company told us to stay in motion. You'll get stopped at the Triborough."

"All right but let's make 'em think we're taking the Triborough," Randall said, speeding into the far left lane of the two which exited to the Triborough Bridge. He flicked a look in the rearview mirror. "Good, they're moving with us."

The lanes began to separate from the main highway and Kate gasped as Randall suddenly swerved right across one lane of traffic, a dividing berm, and into the left lane of the Harlem River Drive exit. She twisted around as she heard horns blaring and brakes squealing. The pursuing car had forced its way through behind them and was now rocking wildly right on their rear bumper.

"That shook them up," Randall said with satisfaction. Then he barked, "They're pulling up on your side. Keep your head low, but see if you can see how many people are in the car."

Kate scooted down in her seat and looked right. The driver had his window down and was clearly shouting at them although she couldn't hear his words.

"There's a driver and another person beside him," Kate said. She was trying to peer into the backseat when the passenger suddenly leaned forward and pointed a gun at her. "Duck, he has a gun!" she yelled, dropping her head onto her knees. Randall crouched down over the wheel and hit the gas harder.

"Where are the God damned police?" he shouted, looking into the rearview mirror.

Kate shifted in her seat. "Keep down," he barked, putting his hand on her head and holding her face against her knees. "I don't want you to get shot. Call security," he commanded the car phone.

A different male voice answered instantly. "Mr. Johnson, we're trying to..."

"They're pointing a gun at us," Randall snarled. "Get the police here now."

"Mr. Johnson," the voice tried again. "You're moving so fast that we're having difficulty tracking you. The police are on their way."

"Light a fire under them. We're on the Harlem River Drive headed for the George Washington Bridge. Tell them to meet us there."

"Roger, Mr. Johnson," the voice confirmed.

"I guess we made the bad guys mad," Kate said, trying to sound normal from her doubled-over position.

"I'm sorry. You shouldn't be involved in this."

He had stopped cutting in and out of traffic and was simply staying ahead of their pursuers' car. Kate took that as a sign that it was safe to raise her head.

"As long as we're in it together, I'm fine," she said and realized that it was the absolute truth.

As they rounded a corner, Yankee Stadium lit up the sky on their right like a Christmas tree. Kate thought longingly of all the policemen who were stationed around the stadium. But it was too far away to help them.

"The Yanks are home tonight," Randall commented in what struck Kate as an absurdly conversational tone. "If the Series goes to seven games, I'll take the boys."

His attempt to ease the tension made her want to seem brave.

"I'll buy the hot dogs," she managed to choke out.

A sign with a simple graphic picture of the George Washington Bridge caught their headlights and she had a sudden inspiration.

"We can lose them on the bridge! The towers have all sorts of cross-girders and dark corners to hide in!" She closed her eyes to concentrate. She knew the GWB better than anyone. How could they best utilize her knowledge?

"Last time I looked, it was hard to park a car in four lanes of traffic," Randall said, weaving between two cars.

"Then you didn't look very hard. There's space on the upper level just before you get to where the cable meets the roadway." She pulled up the picture in her mind. "Right after we go under the apartment building built over the access road, the right lane has to merge left and two lanes come in from the right. If you can get across the two right lanes, there's a pull off for maintenance vehicles." She could tell he was listening intently. "We go over the pedestrian railing onto the walkway and make a run for the tower. The only flaw is that we'll be running in the same direction as traffic." She tried to gauge how far they'd have to run and decided that it was possible. Especially with fear-induced adrenaline. "Thank goodness we're both wearing dark colors." Kate looked down at her pumps. "These won't do though."

"Wait a minute, Kate," Randall said, as she slipped out of her shoes. "What happens when we get to the tower?"

She closed her eyes again, conjuring up both blueprints and memories of family walks on the bridge. "We get onto the stairs and go down toward the lower level. There are catwalks there that will take us onto the supports for the upper roadway."

"What's stopping our friends from doing the same thing?"

"Surprise for one thing; they won't expect us to stop on the bridge. Also there's the slight problem that the stairs are behind solid steel gates with locks so you have to know how to get on them. It can be done though."

"All right, how?"

She could tell from his tone that he was now seriously considering her plan.

"You have to climb over a four foot railing onto an extension of the security fence. Then you reach across to a brace girder on the tower, and from there the stairs are just an easy climb over another railing." She deliberately omitted the fact that below the security fence extension there was nothing but two hundred feet of thin air over solid bedrock, and that the wind whipping up the Hudson River was going to be powerful and cold.

She underestimated Randall's analytical skills. "I don't suppose there's a safety net."

"Umm, no," she admitted.

"And hitting water from two hundred feet up is not a good idea."

"Actually, the New York tower is on the shore. There's a nice park around the base." And a fence topped with razor wire, she mentally added. But that didn't really matter except to one's imagination.

Randall actually chuckled. "Well, that's much better. All right, we'll do it."

Kate took a deep breath. She briefly considered the fact that Randall was trusting her with his life. Then she dismissed the thought as too disquieting and concentrated instead on envisioning every step of their route.

Randall spoke again. "When I pull over, you get out and start running immediately. I'll catch up with you."

"Got it," she said, bracing herself.

"Hang on. Here we go," Randall said.

Kate glimpsed the awesome tangle of highways, bridges and access ramps which all converged on the

George Washington Bridge. Then they were charging up and around the exit ramp, and a quick glance behind revealed that their enemies were in hot pursuit. The next few seconds were a confused blur of taillights, overpasses, and merges left and right. Randall rocketed unerringly toward the upper roadway of the bridge. They blazed through the weird pinkish light of the apartment building underpass and past the blinking electronic merge sign.

He put his hand on the horn and yanked the car right.

Mass pandemonium among the cars in the right hand merge was the immediate result. But then the Jaguar's brakes were squealing and they slammed to a halt at the pullover. Kate unclipped her seat belt, jumped out of the car and ran between the rails of the fence.

The noise of the wind and traffic assaulted her ears as she raced along the concrete sidewalk. Despite her exertions, she was freezing in a few seconds and her feet were throbbing from the pounding and the cold. She drew comfort from the dark shape that almost immediately came up running beside her.

As they raced past the fence protecting the two massive cables that carried half the load of the bridge, Kate prayed that the sidewalk access gate was open. It was easy to get around, but it would cost them precious seconds to do so. Luckily the barred metal gates stood wide open. From there the sidewalk ran straight to the tower. Randall reached for her hand and picked up his pace, sharing his strength with her. The evenly spaced sets of vertical support cables on either side of the walkway seemed to mark their progress as they sprinted past.

They were almost at the tower when a sudden squeal of brakes and honking of horns made them both redouble their efforts. Their pursuers had stopped. "Stay low," Randall yelled as a tractor-trailer roared past.

As they approached the soaring steel structure, what looked airy and graceful from a distance became a complex puzzle of giant girders, trusses and plates. The sidewalk turned to the right and Kate led Randall past the caged passageway through the tower to the corner where guardrail and security fence met. Just as they reached it, two men ran out of the pedestrian throughway to their left. Randall pushed Kate against the fence and flattened himself over her. Kate literally held her breath and thanked her lucky stars that the Port Authority's budget didn't allow for illuminating the tower except on holidays.

She couldn't see or hear the men because Randall's coat was covering her face. She was grateful for the warmth of his body counteracting the achingly cold metal bars of the fence she was crushed against. Suddenly the warmth was gone.

"They're headed toward our car. Let's go," Randall said.

Kate closed her eyes for a split second and uttered a brief prayer. Randall helped her over the railing. She resolutely kept her eyes up but she could practically feel the thinness of the two hundred feet of air beneath her. She gulped and released her right hand to grasp the fence extension. She slotted her right foot between two of the fence's vertical bars and found the horizontal crossbar. Then she shifted her left foot and left hand onto the fence. Now she had to maneuver around the end of the fence so that she could reach for the girder slanting up on the other side.

Without thinking, she looked down to see where to place her feet. Panic struck, freezing her in place. Suddenly the gusts of wind and the vibration of the traffic seemed to conspire to shake her loose from the fence and she locked her fingers around the bars in a death grip.

"Kate, are you all right?" Randall's voice cut through the fog of terror.

"N-n-no," Kate quavered.

"Hang on. I'll be right there."

Kate felt rather than saw him come over the guardrail and onto the fence. Then he caught her wrist in a grip that was reassuringly firm. "Let go now and turn your hand to hold my wrist," he instructed.

Unhesitatingly, Kate obeyed.

"Good girl. I'll hold you while you move your feet to the end of the fence. That's it. Now wait a minute while I catch up to you."

Kate felt his suit jacket flapping against her side. The panic subsided as quickly as it had flared. With Randall holding her, she would never fall. She swung gracefully around the end of the fence and moved far enough down for Randall to join her. She saw his eyes narrow as he gauged the gap between their perch and the girder.

"I make it about four feet," he shouted over the wind. "I'll keep hold of your wrist while you swing across. Then I'll follow."

Kate freed her right foot. "I'm going on three," she yelled back to Randall. He nodded.

"One. Two. Three," Kate counted and released her grip. Randall's hand was clamped on her wrist like a steel vise, and Kate had a brief sensation of soaring across the space. Then both her right hand and foot hit solid metal cross-trusses and held. For a moment she hung spread-eagled in the gap. "I've got it," she yelled.

Randall released his grip, and Kate swung her left limbs onto the girder. "I'm going on to the stair platform now," she called to Randall, as she climbed down perfectly spaced cross-braces.

"I'm right behind you."

By the time Kate had climbed over the railing around the landing for the maintenance stairs, Randall was climbing down the girder. He swung onto the platform and yanked her into his arms. "Don't ever do that again," he whispered in her ear. "Where to now?" he asked, as he released her.

She scooted down the steps to the lower roadway of the bridge. As she jogged along a catwalk, she thought she heard a gunshot and flinched.

"I think they just shot the lock on the gate to the stairs," Randall said. "Let's move."

She cut left and then they were in the underbelly of the upper level. She stepped off the catwalk and onto a girder leading out over traffic. She had walked girders before on construction sites, but it was a different experience in a skirt and bare feet. She wished heartily for her rubber-soled running shoes. Her pantyhose were in shreds across the bottoms of her feet, and it took all her willpower to keep stepping onto the frigid, filthy beams.

"Don't move," Randall's voice hissed behind her. "They're coming down the steps."

Kate froze as dark shapes pounded down the steps behind them. As they kept going down to the lower roadway, she dropped to a crouch and headed for the center of the bridge where it would be hard for their pursuers to follow.

Suddenly, Randall grabbed her wrist. She stopped and looked back at him questioningly. Silently, he pointed toward the middle of the span. Kate squinted to see what he was gesturing toward. Just beyond the tower, a corrugated sheet metal ceiling had been hung below the girders for

320

some construction project. If they could get to it, they would be invisible to anyone below.

Kate turned onto a perpendicular girder and threaded her way through the system of support beams. Fortunately, the lights hung below the superstructure and pointed downward so their progress was largely in shadow. The vibration of the speeding cars made the steel seem almost alive under her feet and suddenly a wave of exhilaration swept over her. She knew why Randall had been smiling as he piloted his car at high speed with an unknown enemy in pursuit. It had been his turn then, but now she was pitting her skill against that same enemy and winning. She almost laughed aloud.

A few more careful steps, and they would be in the protection of the construction ceiling. A loud bang made her teeter. "They've found us," Randall said, steadying her with his hands on her waist. "Go!"

Kate no longer cared what she was stepping on as she raced for their hiding place. Another shot rang out. And then the ceiling was between them and their attackers. It was much darker and Kate had to slow down to give her eyes time to become accustomed to the change in light. The traffic noise was deafening as it echoed off the sheet metal below their feet.

"Head for the eastbound lanes," Randall yelled. "And take a few detours."

Kate simply nodded and took off on a diagonal beam, then another, then picked up a straight one for a few yards, zigging and zagging, but always working them over to the other side of the bridge.

"Damn it!" she heard Randall yell behind her. He pulled her close to say in her ear, "They've come up a ladder. We need to get behind something bulletproof."

They both scanned the dim, thunderous interior. He found what they were looking for and tapped her shoulder, signaling her to follow him. Kate gave him full marks for nerve and balance: he jogged along the girders as though they were sidewalks. She glanced back to see if they were being followed.

The two men had split up, and with guns held ready, were systematically working their way across the westbound lanes, checking every shadowy niche as they went. Kate almost collided with Randall when he stopped abruptly.

He had tensed in a crouching position for a moment and then suddenly leapt up and slightly forward to swing onto an overhead beam. He straddled it and reached a hand down to her. With his steely grip on her wrist, she leapt as hard as she could, catching the beam with her hand and leg, and coming up in front of him.

He gestured toward a heavy steel plate that was bolted flat where two beams came together. Kate crawled over and rolled onto its welcome protection. Randall joined her and then inched forward to try to see their followers. "I can't spot them," he said, sliding back. "Check over on the other side."

Kate pulled herself to the other edge, scraping along grit which she had a horrible feeling was pigeon droppings and cautiously peered into the confusion of steel below. "I see one west of us about five cross-beams. I can't find the other one."

"Neither can I," Randall murmured back, his voice a low rumble in her ear. "I'm going to look behind us. Don't move."

Kate lay still as he used his elbows to pull himself around. She tensed and held her breath when she felt his hand grip her ankle in a warning. After what seemed an eternity, his grip relaxed. Then he moved back to her side again.

"Where'd he go?"

"I don't know but I'm not worried."

"Why not?" Kate demanded. "We're crawling around the underside of the GWB with two gun-toting maniacs after us!"

"Listen."

She closed her eyes to concentrate. Very faintly at first but gaining in volume, she heard a siren and then another one and then a third. "Oh, thank heavens!"

Their pursuers heard the sirens too. They exchanged shouts in a language Kate couldn't quite understand. Feeling safe, they looked over the edge of their plate to see the two men converge on the ladder and disappear from sight.

"Were they speaking Spanish?" Kate asked.

"With a Mexican accent."

"Could you understand them?"

"Leaving out the expletives, the gist of it was that the cops were coming, and they should leave."

"Should we try to stop them?" Kate offered tentatively.

"Hell, no. I don't want to get shot," Randall said.

Muscles that Kate didn't even know she possessed re-laxed as the knowledge that they were safe surged through her. The filthy, rusty metal plate on which they lay suddenly felt like a feather bed. Randall's arm slid under her and then he rolled her on top of him. "It's time to celebrate," he said, pulling her mouth down to his.

When their lips touched, all the terror, all the tension, and all the exhilaration of the last hour poured forth in a kiss so mind-bending that Kate couldn't stop even when she heard the police calling Randall's name on the bullhorn.

"Mr. Johnson, we're the police! Are you here? Randall Johnson, it's the N.Y.P.D. You're safe! Are you here?"

Randall muttered a curse against Kate's lips so she lifted her head.

"Damned police," he complained as he helped her to her feet. "They take forever to get here and then they have to talk to you immediately."

He took a firm grip on her hand before he raised his voice. "We're here and we're fine. We're in the girders under the upper roadway and we're coming over to the steps."

Randall helped Kate down from their elevated roost. She was surprised to find that it seemed like the merest stroll back to the nearest catwalk.

Men in uniforms were pouring down the tower stairs. "Did you see anyone?" one yelled.

"Yeah, but they ran when they heard your sirens. I don't know which way they went," Randall shouted back. Policemen ran east and west on the narrow walkway by the lower roadway. Several officers greeted them as they approached the stairway.

"Are you all right, ma'am? Sir?" voices asked.

Randall tucked Kate securely in at his side and answered all inquiries about their well-being in the affirmative. Someone handed him a blanket that he shook open and wrapped tightly around her shoulders.

As they climbed slowly up the steps with their police escort, another voice sounded. "We have their car. Bring Mr. Johnson over to take a look."

The strobe lights of the police cruisers temporarily blinded Kate as they stepped onto the walkway. Then she gaped in wonder at the four empty lanes of the George

Washington Bridge's westbound upper level. Police cruisers were parked at all angles and a line of stationary headlights stretched away behind them to the east. The New York-bound lanes were practically at a standstill as drivers tried to catch a glimpse of whatever disaster had brought forth such a collection of official vehicles. She couldn't help pitying the poor souls caught in the traffic jam.

"Randall, they've got half the highway stopped for us."

He surveyed the scene. "So they do. Let's go take a look at their car."

The soles of Kate's feet were beginning to throb painfully, but she was not about to lose the comfort of Randall's arm around her shoulders, so she bit her lip and matched his stride.

Men in uniforms and suits were swarming around a sedan pulled up against the railing farther along the bridge. "Don't touch anything please, sir. But take a look in the back. Does that mean anything to you?" an officer asked.

Randall drew Kate down with him as he bent to peer into the shadows of the car's interior. There on the backseat, coiled like a rattlesnake about to strike, lay a bullwhip. Kate instantly remembered Gill Gillespie's earlier comment. She had a sudden horrifying vision of Randall's back bleeding under the lash of it. It was with amazement that she heard him say, "No, I have no idea why they'd have a whip in the car."

She opened her mouth to protest, but she felt his arm tighten around her shoulders in a silent command. So she changed the subject by saying to the policeman, "May I please sit down? My feet are sore from climbing around on the bridge."

Instantly, she was swept up into Randall's arms. "I'm so

325

sorry, darlin'. I forgot about your bare feet. Let's get you into a warm car."

"I can walk," Kate said without much conviction.

Randall ignored her and strode over to the Jaguar. It seemed to crouch against the barrier. Depositing her gently in the front seat, he said, "Turn on the heat and stay here while I talk to the police. I'll get us out of here as soon as possible."

"Wait, Randall. Gill must have sent those men with the whip. Why didn't you tell them that?"

"I'll deal with Gill privately. And I promise you that he will never bother us again."

Randall's expression left no doubt in her mind that she would never again encounter Gill Gillespie in this lifetime. Having chosen not to destroy the man once, she supposed that he was again protecting Lucinda and her family from public disgrace. However, she found it much harder to be sympathetic after her experience tonight.

As the heat blasted and her shivering subsided, Kate watched Randall walk over to the man who appeared to be directing the operation. After a brief exchange, the man nodded and waved a uniformed policeman over to escort Randall back to his car. "Are you sure that you don't want someone to drive you home, sir?" the officer asked as Randall slid into the driver's side.

"Thanks, but I'll be fine. I'll see you all in the morning," he said, shifting into gear.

"Go slowly," Kate said as Randall pulled onto the roadway.

He looked questioningly at her.

"I've never been the only car on the bridge," she explained. "I want to enjoy the view."

He started to laugh. "You are a strange woman, Kate

Chilton. After what you've just been through, you want to look at a bridge."

"It took care of us, didn't it?"

"I guess it did." He looked around himself. "Look at the size of those cables."

As the Jaguar rolled majestically down the middle of the empty lanes, Kate silently gave her own thanks to the great span of concrete and steel. It had not only protected her, but it also had given her the answer to an important question.

They enjoyed the view in silence until they passed the tollbooths spread across the eastbound lanes. Then Kate spoke. "I'm sorry I lost it on the fence."

Randall reached for her hand. "You saved my life, darlin', or at least my back. You don't have anything to apologize for."

Kate turned her hand into his and held on. "Do you think they meant to kill us?"

"I don't know, but I'm sure as hell glad not to have found out."

"Me, too."

They cruised along the highway at what seemed a snail's pace after their earlier headlong flight. Kate looked down at their clasped hands. Despite the fact that Randall's hand dwarfed hers, she felt no threat from his strength. Instead she drew comfort from it as she had on the bridge. She shifted her gaze to the road unfurling before them. "Randall? You know that proposal that you made and withdrew earlier in the week?"

"Yes."

Kate glanced toward him out of the corner of her eyes. He was grinning.

327

"Would you be willing to, um, put it on the table again?"

"Consider it reissued."

"You're not making this easy," she complained, then grabbed for the door handle as the Jaguar swerved off the road and came to a sudden halt on the shoulder.

Randall put the parking brake on and leaned back against his door with his arms crossed. "I think we have some negotiating to do, but I'm willing to make an agreement in principle."

"What does that mean?" Kate asked, crossing her arms in turn.

"Will you marry me?"

"Yes."

"That's an agreement in principle. In a business deal, we'd shake hands and let the lawyers work out the details," he said, reaching for her and somehow dragging her around the gearshift and onto his lap. "In this deal, there will be no lawyers, and I can do a hell of a lot better than a handshake."

Kate snuggled happily against his chest as he enfolded her in his arms. "I love you, darlin'," he said into her hair. "I keep forgetting to say that at the critical moment."

Kate raised her head, knowing that her feelings were plain in her eyes. "I love you, too. I knew that, but it wasn't until tonight that I trusted you."

His half-smile vanished. Kate felt the heat of his focused gaze as he said, "I promise I will never give you cause to regret your decision."

"I'm not worried," she said with a soft smile, "because I know this is a good deal."

She had no time to see if Randall smiled back, because his mouth came down on hers and all she could do was *feel*.

Passing cars regularly rocked the Jaguar with the wind they created, but it was a long time before the sleek car purred back onto the highway.

A Year Later...

"I'M HOME," KATE said, dropping onto the mudroom bench to unlace her work boots.

Clay and Patrick thundered down the stairs. "Hey, Mom! Is everything ready for tonight?" Patrick asked.

"It looks like it," Kate said as she wiggled her freed toes. "We just have to cross our fingers that the precast roadbed arrives. I've checked with the shipper about four times today, and they swear it's on schedule."

"Are we really going to be on television?" Patrick said, dancing with excitement.

"Stick with me, kid, and you'll be on camera," Kate promised. "Hi, Georgia," she greeted her friend who had followed the boys at a more leisurely pace. "Thanks so much for coming."

"I wouldn't have missed this for the world. It's not every day that you get to christen a brand new bridge. And I want to be on television too," she said, ruffling Patrick's hair.

He bore it with an embarrassed grin. "I'll bet that Randall's helicopter will be on TV. He says he's flying in from the airport just in time to see the ribbon-cutting."

Kate reached down to put her boots under the bench so

she missed the significant glances exchanged among Georgia, Clay and Patrick. "Let's hope his plane from Tokyo gets in on time," she said, as she straightened.

"You have your choice of pizza or lasagna for dinner," Georgia said, opening the oven in which two dishes were warming.

"Pizza," Kate said. "I don't have the energy to cut the lasagna."

"You eat and then go right upstairs to get dressed. I'll clean up and make sure these two young hooligans look respectable," Georgia said.

Kate followed her advice. When she sat down on the bed to pull off her socks, she allowed herself the luxury of flopping backward to close her eyes for a few minutes.

What a year it had been! Her bridge was going to be completed tonight amid much fanfare from the press and the politicians. The politicians loved it because the project was on time and on budget. Not a single commuter had been inconvenienced as the traffic flowed uninterrupted under the new construction. In fact, the old bridge would still be carrying cars up until nine o'clock this evening. Then the barricades would go up and the detour signs would be uncovered for just twelve hours. Any late drivers would be rerouted through a nearby town as the cranes and pavers worked through the night. By Sunday morning, traffic would once again cruise straight along the highway and over her creation, the old bridge beneath already forgotten. If she hadn't been so bone weary, she would have been leaping around the room with joy.

She desperately hoped that Randall would be there. He had assured her that his trip to Japan was unavoidable, but she had missed him this week. She hadn't had time to visit the big rambling Victorian he had bought to replace Eagle's

Nest, and she wondered how the kitchen renovation was progressing. She blushed as she remembered how the general contractor had almost caught them as they made love on the new window seat. Randall liked to try out all the home improvements in his own way.

Once the bridge and the house were finished, they had a wedding to plan. A small one, but Randall wanted it done right. She smiled as she thought about her hard-nosed CEO wanting a romantic ceremony. While he sometimes surprised her with his sentiment, he still drove a hard bargain.

She remembered their argument about her engagement ring. Randall had wanted to get her a major diamond. Kate had preferred a more modest ring that she wouldn't feel ostentatious wearing. So they had agreed "in principle" on the smaller ring and then Randall had bought her a matching pin and earrings. When the saleswoman tried to show him a bracelet, he said, "I don't give diamond bracelets anymore."

Kate laughed and sat up. She had to shower and change. Her mood of taking stock stayed with her as she worked her shampoo into a lather. This time Oliver came to mind. She had not seen him for months after the Beaux Arts Ball. He had even absented himself from the final signing of the partnership sale papers. Then one day he had called to say that C/R/G was opening a branch office in Boston, and he was moving there. Even as her throat tightened with regret, she had breathed a sigh of relief. Now she could begin to remember him as a friend. She rinsed away her sad thoughts along with her soap bubbles and stepped out of the shower.

When she slipped on the jacket of her wonderful new russet-colored suit, she once again felt on top of the world. She had decided that she owed herself a great outfit to wear in her great moment and this was it. The wool was so fine that it felt almost like silk. The double-breasted jacket fit her like a glove, emphasizing all the right curves without being blatant about it. A cream silk blouse draped softly in the vee of the jacket. She had to wear low-heeled shoes since she would have to walk around the construction site after the press conference, but she had splurged on new flats in a rich brown. She fastened a heavy gold circle pin on her lapel and added gold twisted knots to her ears.

"Dynamite!" Georgia said when Kate came back down the stairs. "You'll be the best-looking engineer there."

Kate laughed. Then she whistled in appreciation as Clay and Patrick appeared in the kitchen. They were wearing navy blue blazers over khaki slacks. Clay's yellow paisley tie looked elegant against his light blue shirt. Patrick wore a pink shirt paired with a tie sporting an eye-popping pattern of electric blue and purple.

"You guys look so handsome. Did Randall take you shopping?"

"Yeah, he didn't really like my tie," Patrick said, "but he had promised we could pick out our own. I think it's cool."

"As long as you wear sunglasses," Clay said.

Patrick punched him halfheartedly in the shoulder.

Kate slung her pocketbook over her shoulder and grabbed her car keys. "Let's go, gang."

"I think you should look out the front window," Georgia said.

Kate threw her a questioning glance and walked into the living room. She pulled aside the lace curtain to see a long black limousine parked across her driveway. Kate rolled her eyes in a mixture of amusement and exasperation. "Sometimes Randall gets a little ridiculous. I'm perfectly capable of driving to the bridge myself."

"He knows that, but he thought it was a special occasion," Georgia said.

"So you knew about this, and you didn't warn me?"

Georgia smiled mysteriously. "I know lots of things."

"I should tell the driver to go home and take the minivan anyway," Kate muttered but she knew she wouldn't do it.

The boys spent the beginning of the trip pushing every button in the limousine to see how the roof opened, the lights flashed, the television worked, and what the bar had in it. Kate refused to let them make a call from the car's built-in telephone.

When they had finished their explorations, Patrick poured himself a Coca-Cola, and after taking a sip, leaned back and said, "So Mom, you and Randall are going to get married now that the bridge is done, right?"

"That's the plan," Kate said.

"And we'll move into the new house?"

"As soon as the workmen are out."

"Should we start calling Randall 'Dad'?"

Kate was taken aback. She glanced at Georgia who just raised her eyebrows and smiled. Kate and Randall had held long discussions about his relationship with the boys. He planned to adopt them but he didn't want to force anything on them that they weren't prepared to accept. So they had told Clay and Patrick to call him by his first name.

"Would you like to call him 'Dad'?" Kate asked carefully.

Patrick looked at his older brother. "Well, we don't want to upset you, and we weren't sure how Randall would feel about it; but if he's married to you, we think that he should be 'Dad,'" Clay said.

Tears pricked Kate's eyes. "He'd be honored if you

would call him that."

"Cool," Patrick said. "My dad owns a helicopter," he tried out.

"Don't be a dork," Clay said.

"You know," Kate said, "it would be really nice if you would tell Randall what you just said to me."

"No problem," Clay said.

As they rolled onto the temporary parking area at the bridge site, Kate felt that her day could not possibly get any better. She could see the silver and blue RJ Enterprises helicopter sitting squarely in the middle of the southbound lanes of the new bridge. Randall was here. She opened the limousine's door before the driver could do it for her and jumped out to look for her fiancé.

"Hello, darlin'," he said, magically appearing at her side.

Kate threw herself into his arms and kissed him. "I'm so glad you made it on time. I missed you so much. How was your trip?"

His arms locked around her and he kissed her back for a long time. Randall used her hair to mask a quick nip on her neck. "This is torture for a man who's been away from you for a week." He released her and Kate got a chance to survey the scene.

The arrays of construction floodlights bathed the bridge in a brilliant white glow so the crew could see to work. Kate checked that the giant cranes were in position to lift and deposit the last eight pieces of the roadbed in place. The slip form pavers stood ready to smooth the connection between the old highway and the new bridge. A police cruiser sat ready to coordinate the closing of the road.

Beyond that she saw Lieutenant Governor Lidden Hartley's entourage clustered around a table laden with drinks and sandwiches. The construction crew lounged by the bulldozers. Kate waved to the foreman who had become a good friend during the project.

Her brow creased when she saw Denise Costanza and her three boys standing next to Janine Tanner, the helicopter pilot, who was chatting with Brigid. Tom Rogan emerged from the driver's seat of a car at the same time that a man who appeared to be a priest got out of the passenger side. Tom nodded to her with a grin and then escorted the priest onto the bridge. Halfway across the structure, rows of white folding chairs were neatly arrayed between huge baskets of flowers.

Kate turned back to Randall. "What's going on? What's Tom doing here?"

"He's my best man," Randall said.

"What?" Kate squeaked.

"He's my best man," Randall repeated patiently.

Kate glared at him.

"Having second thoughts about marrying me?" Randall asked.

"Only at times like this," she said.

"This is your last chance to have them, darlin'. Once you say 'I do,' you're stuck with me for life."

Kate softened instantly. "I'm counting on it."

Randall smiled in a way that made her want to laugh and cry at the same time. He strode around the limousine's trunk and came back to hand her a bouquet of yellow and peach roses.

"I love you," Kate said.

"I'm counting on it," Randall said, offering the bride his arm. The entire assemblage of people – the lieutenant governor, construction crew and all – moved to the folding chairs and waited.

As Randall and Kate stepped onto the bridge, bagpipes skirled to life behind them. Randall looked down at her with an expression so filled with love that Kate could hardly breathe.

"You've built your bridge, darlin'. Now we're going to cross it together."

The End

Proof

Made in the USA
Charleston, SC
17 October 2011